Saladin and the Assassins

Novels of Islamic History in Translation Series

Written by Jurji Zaidan and published by the Zaidan Foundation.
(in historical chronological order)

The Conquest of Andalusia
translated with an Afterword and Study Guide by Roger Allen

The Battle of Poitiers
Charles Martel and 'Abd al-Rahman
translated with a Study Guide by William Granara

The Caliph's Sister
Harun al-Rashid and the Fall of the Persians
translated by Isaa J. Boullata with a Study Guide

The Caliph's Heirs
Brothers at War: The Fall of Baghdad
translated with an Afterword and Study Guide by Michael Cooperson

Saladin and the Assassins
translated by Paul Starkey with a Study Guide

Saladin and the Assassins

A historical novel narrating the transition of Egypt from the
Shi'ite rule of the Fatimids to the Sunni rule of the Ayyubites at the
hands of Sultan Saladin with a description of the Isma'ili sect known as
the Assassins

Jurji Zaidan

translated from the Arabic by
Paul Starkey

With an Introduction by the Zaidan Foundation
and a Study Guide

The Zaidan Foundation
For Intercultural Understanding, Inc.

7007 Longwood Drive
Bethesda, MD 20817
Email: george@zaidanfoundation.org
Website: www.zaidanfoundation.org
Tel: (301) 469-8131
Fax: (301) 469-8132

Table of Contents

Saladin and the Assassins

Introduction

About the Novel[1]

Saladin and the Assassins is a historical romantic novel set at the time of the
famous Salah al Din al Ayyubi, simply known in the west as Saladin, the
great religious reformer of Kurdish origin, mythical leader, and legendary
unifier of an Islamic world in disarray by political and social contradictions
at the beginning of the twelfth century. Enemies are lurking everywhere
and the crusaders are solidly implanted in the region, having taken
possession of the tomb of Jesus Christ in 1099 AD (492 AH).

The events of the novel unfold in the closing years of the reign
of al-'Adid, the last of the Fatimid caliphs in Egypt, and the first years
after Saladin's assumption of power. He officially assumes power in Egypt
after the death of the last Fatimid caliph, al-'Adid, thus bringing to
an end the Fatimid Shi'ite dynasty and restoring the official status of
Sunni Islam and the formal authority of the 'Abbasid caliphate in Egypt.
When Egypt had fallen under Fatimid control in 969 AD (358 AH),
the political situation changed and it became a completely independent
state, referring no matter to any outside authority and acknowledging no
sovereignty other than that of the Fatimid caliph residing in Cairo. This
was the first time that Egypt had become a fully independent sovereign
state since the coming of Islam.

There were eleven Fatimid caliphs who ruled Egypt in succession,
for just over two hundred years 969-1172 AD (358–567 AH). During
that period, the 'Abbasid caliphate in Baghdad continued as it had always
been, while the Spanish Umayyad caliphate had been instituted under the
Marwanids. The Islamic Empire therefore became an object of contention
for three caliphs, each of whom claimed the right to the true caliphate

---

1 First published in 1913 in Arabic as *Salah al-Din al-Ayyubi*.

for himself and denied it to the other two. The struggle was at its most intense between the caliph in Baghdad and the caliph in Cairo. There was also a religious difference between them, for the 'Abbasid caliphate was Sunni, while the Fatimids were Shi'i. It was essentially a political struggle into which religion was introduced to aid their respective causes.

The position of the Shi'a had weakened considerably in Persia and Iraq during the closing years of the Fatimid's dynasty, and this deteriorating situation was reflected in Egypt, where Sultan Nur-al-Din (Nuradin), the Seljuk commander who ruled Syria, had become the effective authority. The Seljuks put their mamluks² and commanders known as the Atabegs in control of the provinces, and each one ruled his province independently -- among them was Nuradin Zanki in Syria. Among Nuradin's commanders were a group of courageous Kurds, including Najm al-Din Ayyub (Najmudin), Saladin's father, and his brother Asad al-Din Shirkawih (Asadin), Saladin's uncle. Both had attained a high status in Nuradin's eyes. In 1161 AD (556 AH), the caliphate in Egypt had passed to al-'Adid li-Din Allah ibn Yusuf, who was weak-willed. His ministers competed with each other for a monopoly of influence and gained control of the state, and over time they destroyed the country, while the caliph became impotent. Among the rivals for power was a vizier called Shawar, who had lost influence. So he asked Nuradin Zanki for assistance against his rival for the ministry. Nuradin took that opportunity to seize control of Egypt. He sent him Asadin with an army of mamluks, who restored the ministry to Shawar. The crusader wars had erupted during this period, and Nuradin and his deputy in Egypt, Shirkawih, had begun to intervene more in Egypt's affairs, together with Shirkawih's nephew, Saladin. Shirkawih died in Egypt two months later and was succeeded by Saladin in the office of deputy, with the title of vizier. He was an ambitious man whose aim was to rule Egypt as an independent state. How he used his position to become the ruler of an independent Egypt is the subject of this novel.

---

2 Mamluks were soldiers of slave origin most often of Turkish ancestry. Over time, mamluks became a powerful military caste in various Muslim societies. Most notably, mamluk factions seized the sultanate for themselves in Egypt and Syria in a period known as the Mamluk Sultanate (1250–1517 AD). The Mamluk Sultanate famously beat back the Mongols and fought the Crusaders.

Romance and intrigue, woven in the context of the broader picture of important historical events, are a distinctive feature of all of Zaidan's novels, and *Saladin and the Assassins* is no exception. Princess Sittalmulk, the "Lady of the Realm" and sister to the Caliph al-'Adid, has many suitors. Saladin has been persuaded that his political ambitions would be enhanced by a union with the caliph's sister. Hasan is also a man with political ambitions who wants to become caliph. He claims Fatimid ancestry and is trusted by the people. He too believes that a union with the caliph's sister would enhance his claim to the caliphate after al-'Adid's death. A conspirator with few scruples, he arranges to abduct the caliph's sister after she rejects his overtures and conspires to get rid of Saladin by every means -- first by exploiting the rising tension between Saladin and Nuradin and then by using the Assassins, a religious sect, first to threaten and then to do away with him. One morning Saladin wakes up with a dagger firmly planted over his head with a threatening letter signed by the "old man of the mountains," the imam of the famous Assassins ready to sacrifice their lives in the service of their cause... But lurking in the background was 'Imadin, a loyal and courageous commoner who was admitted to be a member of Saladin's inner circle and who is determined to come to his master's rescue by personally confronting the Assassins. Princess Sittalmulk, for her part, is a strong-willed woman who knows her mind and falls madly in love with 'Imadin after he saves her life and honor. But he embarks on a faraway and dangerous mission that takes him to the headquarters of the Assassins in Syria to save his master from all the dangers he is facing. Meanwhile, Hasan is intent on having his way with her, even though the caliph would like his sister to marry Saladin, who had come to her rescue.

The stage is thus set for a contest for the Princess's heart, interlaced with the battle for the caliphate to succeed al-'Adid. Who will prevail and how? The fast-paced action is full of twists and turns and of unexpected surprises and suspense, keeping us guessing to the very end.

Jurji Zaidan—The Historical Novelist

Jurji Zaidan (1861-1914) was a prolific writer who at the dawn of the twentieth century sought to inform and educate his Arab contemporaries about the modern world and the heritage of the Arabs. He is considered one of the most prominent intellectual leaders who laid the foundation for a pan-Arab secular national identity. Pioneering new forms of literature and style in Arabic, he founded in 1892 one of the first and most successful monthly journals, *Al-Hilal*, a magazine that is still popular today in its 120th year. The *Dar al-Hilal* publishing house in Cairo is one of the largest publishing houses for periodicals in the Arab world. It is a fitting tribute to Zaidan's legacy that new studies reassessing his contributions, and translations of many of his novels—this one among them—are being published one hundred years after his death.

Zaidan was one of the pioneers in the composition of historical novels within the modern Arabic literary tradition and in their serialization in magazines. New editions of the entire series of the novels are still being published almost every decade and are widely distributed throughout the Arab world – a testament to their lasting popularity. Zaidan's novels were not just for entertainment; national education was his primary goal. The twenty-two historical novels he wrote cover an extensive period of Arab history, from the rise of Islam in the seventh century until the decline of the Ottoman Empire in the nineteenth. The stories depicted in these novels are grounded in the major historical events of various epochs. The particular manners, lifestyles, beliefs, and social mores of those periods, as well as political events, provided the context into which Zaidan weaved adventure and romance, deception and excitement. They were, therefore, as much "historical" as "novels" reminiscent of the historical novels of Alexandre Dumas in France and Sir Walter Scott in Britain, though Jurji Zaidan's novels more closely reflect actual historical events and developments.

Over the last hundred years, Zaidan's historical novels have been translated into many languages; every novel has been translated at least once, many into four or more languages. To our knowledge there are about one hundred translations of individual novels into more than ten different languages -- most in Persian, Turkish/Ottoman, Javanese, and Uighur (in China), Azeri, and Urdu, but several also in French, Spanish, German, and Russian. What is noticeable, however, is that not a single one has been translated into English until the present time with the publication of the first novel in this series, *The Conquest of Andalusia*.

The Zaidan Foundation has so far commissioned the translation into English of five of Jurji Zaidan's historical novels, and more are being planned. The present novel, *Salah al-Din al-Ayyubi*, was first published in 1913 and takes place at the time of the Crusades. Since then there have been eight translations of this novel – four in Persian, two in Kurdish, one in Ottoman, and one in French. The Foundation has also commissioned the translation of four other novels. Two are set in Spain – *The Conquest of Andalusia* (*Fath-al Andalus*, 1903), published in November 2011, as well as *The Battle of Poitiers – Charles Martel and 'Abd al-Rahman*, (*Sharl wa 'Abd al-Rahman*, 1904). Another two novels are set during the 'Abbasid period. *The Caliph's Sister – Harun al-Rashid and the Fall of the Persians* was first published in 1906 and set during the reign of Harun al Rashid, perhaps best known to the Western world as the caliph whose court is described in the *Arabian Nights;* and *The Caliph's Heirs – Brothers at War: The Fall of Baghdad* (*al-Amin wa'l-Ma'mun*, 1907), whose events occur in the period immediately following the reign of Harun al-Rashid.

The Zaidan Foundation[3]

The Zaidan Foundation, Inc. was established in 2009. Its mission is to enhance understanding between cultures. To this end, the Foundation's principal objective is the international dissemination of the secular and progressive view of the Arab and Islamic heritage. Its first program is the study and translation of the works of Jurji Zaidan. Our audience is the broader English-speaking world: the United States, England, and Canada to be sure, but also English-speaking Muslim populations with little or no knowledge of Arabic such as in Bangladesh, India, and Pakistan. To achieve its objectives, the Foundation supports directly or through educational or other institutions, the translation and publication of historical, literary, and other works, research, scholarships, conferences, seminars, student exchanges, documentaries, films, and other activities.

Acknowledgments and Thanks

The Zaidan Foundation was fortunate to have Professor Paul Starkey, a noted scholar and translator of Arabic works, translate this novel. He is the head of the Arabic Department at Durham University, England and was co-author of the *Encyclopedia of Arabic Literature*, London: Routledge, 1998. He is the author of several books on Arabic literature,

---

3 More information about the Zaidan Foundation and its activities can be found on the Foundation's website at www.zaidanfoundation.org.

most notably *Modern Arabic Literature* (Edinburgh, Edinburgh University Press, 2006), and has translated many Arab literary works, most recently some of Jurji Zaidan's selected writings for the forthcoming volume by Thomas Philipp on *Jurji Zaidan's Secular Analysis of History and Language as Foundations of Arab Nationalism.*

Many people have generously contributed their time and energy to the Zaidan Foundation, helping to craft our mission and goals, designing and advising on the implementation of our programs, and reviewing studies and translations. Foremost among these are Ambassador Hussein A. Hassouna, ambassador of the Arab League to the United States, Ambassador Clovis F. Maksoud, professor of International Relations and director of the Center of the Global South at American University, as well as Edmond Asfour and Bassem Abdallah – all members of the Foundation's Advisory Council. Professor Thomas Philipp was instrumental in helping launch the Jurji Zaidan project following our fortuitous meeting after several decades. Thanks are also due to Said Hitti, who read several manuscripts of the translated novels. Last but not least, my greatest debt is to my wife, Hada Zaidan, and our son George S. Zaidan for their support of all aspects of this project. The original idea of the Jurji Zaidan program came from Hada, who had more than a marital interest in this project as her grandfather, Jabr Dumit, was one of Jurji Zaidan's closest friends. In addition to their general and unstinting support, both she and George Jr. helped design the program and made detailed reviews and many suggestions on the products sponsored by the Foundation.

George C. Zaidan
President
The Zaidan Foundation

Washington DC
March 2012

Dramatis Personae

THE CALIPH AL-'ADID   the last of the Fatimid caliphs in Egypt

PRINCESS SITTALMULK   sister of Caliph al-'Adid
(Sitt al-Mulk)

YAQUTA   the princess' maid and confidante

SULTAN SALADIN   Yusuf Salah al-Din al-Ayyubi

NAJMUDIN   Saladin's father
(Najm al-Din)

BAHADIN   Saladin's minister (vizier)
(Baha' al-Din Qaraqosh)

'IMADIN   one of Saladin's inner circle
('Imad al-Din)

'ABD AL-RAHIM   'Imadin's friend

'ISA AL-HIKARI   jurist and close counselor to Saladin

HASAN   a conspirator aspiring to the caliphate
(Abu al-Hasan)

SULTAN NURADIN   the Seljuk commander, ruler of Syria
(Nur al-Din Zanki)

RASHIDIN   leader of the Isma'ilis (the Assassins)
(Rashid al-Din Sinan)

ASADIN   Saladin's uncle
(Asad al-Din Shirkawih)

Chapter 1

The Historical Context

Egypt was brought under Fatimid control in 358 AH (969 AD) by the commander Jawhar. As a result, the Ikhshidid state came to an end, and Egypt ceased to be under the control of the 'Abbasid state. Although the Tulunid and Ikhshidid dynasties had ruled autonomously, Egypt remained under the patronage of the 'Abbasid caliph in Baghdad, who had confirmed their independent authority and sent them a ceremonial robe and a letter of appointment[4] just as the Ottoman sultan did with the emirs of Egypt centuries later. The internal affairs of the government were administered by the Tulunid or Ikhshidid sultans independently, without reference to Baghdad. It was a situation like that described by contemporary writers as administrative independence, though the degree of that independence varied.

When Egypt fell under Fatimid control, the political situation changed, and it became a completely independent state, referring no matter to any outside authority and acknowledging no sovereignty other than that of the Fatimid caliph residing in Cairo.

This was the first time that Egypt had become a fully independent sovereign state since the coming of Islam. The 'Abbasid caliphate in Baghdad continued as it had always been, while the Spanish Umayyad caliphate had been instituted under the Marwanids. The Islamic Empire therefore became an object of contention for three caliphs, each of whom claimed the right to the true caliphate for himself and denied it to the other two. The struggle was at its most intense between the caliph in Baghdad and the caliph in Cairo. There was also a religious difference between them, for the 'Abbasid caliphate was Sunni, while the Fatimids

4 Known as *firman*. *Editor's Note.*

1

were Shi'i. It was essentially a political struggle into which religion was introduced to aid their respective causes.

The Fatimid state was the first Shi'i state to call its rulers caliphs. There was another contemporary Shi'i state, that of the Buwayhids, in Iraq (Basra and Kufa) and Persia, but their rulers did not call themselves caliphs and did not claim ancestry from Quraysh[5] to justify their claim to the caliphate. On the contrary, they maintained their allegiance to the 'Abbasid caliphate, despite believing that the 'Abbasids had usurped it from those who were entitled to it. And they used the authority of the 'Abbasids to rule the common people. After the foundation of the Fatimid state, some people suggested to the Buwayhid ruler, Mu'izz al-Dawla, that he should transfer his allegiance to the Fatimid caliph or to another 'Alawite,[6] but one of his inner circle raised an objection to this, saying: "This would not be sensible. At the moment, you have a caliph whom you and your colleagues believe is not legitimate, so if you ordered him to be killed, they would kill him and think it quite permissible to shed his blood. But if you were to install an 'Alawite as caliph, you and your colleagues would be saddled with someone you considered a legitimate caliph, so if *he* ordered them to kill *you*, they would do so!" So Mu'izz al-Dawla abandoned his intent to do so.

The Fatimid caliphate became established in Egypt, with the 'Abbasid caliphs in Baghdad. The 'Abbasids' Sunni followers all over the world denied the truth of the Fatimids' claim to be related to Fatima[7] herself, but they took no notice. Their concern was to reinforce their rule by duplicity and the sword, particularly in the first years following the establishment of their state. When Jawhar built the city of Cairo for Caliph al-Mu'izz li-Din Allah, the people came out to meet him. Among them were some descendants of the Prophet, including the well-known 'Abd Allah ibn Tabataba, who approached the caliph al-Mu'izz and asked him, "To whom does our master trace his ancestry?" "We will hold a

---

5 The Qurayshi tribe was the Prophet's tribe from Mecca. After the introduction of Islam, the Qurayshis gained supremacy and produced the three dynasties of the Ummayads, 'Abbasids, and Fatimides, who ruled as caliphs. *Editor's Note*

6 'Alawites are folllowers of 'Ali and are an offshoot of the Shi'ites. *Editor's Note*

7 Fatima Zohra, the Prophet's daughter. *Editor's Note*

meeting," he replied, "in which we will gather all of you and explain to you our ancestry." When al-Mu'izz moved into the palace, he gathered the people together in a general assembly, sat before them, and said, "Are any of your leaders left?" They replied, "There is no one of account." So he drew his sword and said to them, "This is my ancestry." Then he scattered a lot of gold in front of them and said, "And this is my noble descent." They all said, "We hear and we obey!"

There were eleven Fatimid caliphs who ruled Egypt in succession, for just over two hundred years, 358–567 AH (969-1172 AD). The first of them was al-Mu'izz li-Din Allah, and the last was al-'Adid li-Din Allah. The state passed through three phases during this time: at first, it relied on the Arabs and Berbers[8] who had conquered Egypt with Jawhar, and influence was shared between the two groups. Then it came under Berber control, and finally passed to the Turks, just as influence in the 'Abbasid state passed from the Arabs and Persians to the Turks.

The reason there were so many Turks in Egypt was that when the caliph al-Hakim bi-Amr Allah died and was succeeded by his son al-Zahir li-'Izaz Din Allah in AH 411 (1020 AD), he indulged in amusements and sport, and he favored the Turks and other Easterners so much so that the Berbers' importance declined—indeed, their numbers continued to shrink so much that they almost disappeared. When al-Mustansir succeeded to the throne in 427 AH (1036 AD) after al-Zahir, his mother, who was a black slave girl, brought in a large number of her fellow countrymen among his soldiers until there were a thousand black slaves among them. At the same time, her son enlisted a large number of Turks, so the army came to consist of two large groups who competed with each other for a monopoly of power. This competition led to a war that exhausted Egypt, and the caliph was forced to seek the help of the ruler of Syria. The commander of the armies, Badr al-Jamali (an Armenian by origin), came from Syria and put to death the head of state, setting up in Egypt an army that was mostly composed of Armenians and Turks. As they dominated the military, the influence of the Berbers diminished further; they became just another subject

---

8 Jurji Zaidan uses the Arabic term barbari to describe the indigenous peoples of North Africa. We have thus translated it as Berber. More recently, however, that term has come to be regarded with disfavor by the people whom it describes, the preferred term being the one by which they describe themselves: Amazigh (plural Imazighen). *Editor's Note*

people, of no particular importance in the state, despite having once provided its most prominent personalities and occupied the senior positions.

Meanwhile, the Seljuks[9] had conquered Iraq and Persia. The Buwayhid dynasty disappeared, and the influence of the Shi'ites there diminished. The Seljuks put their mamluks[10] and commanders known as the Atabegs in control of the provinces, and each one ruled his province independently. Among them was Nur al-Din (Nuradin) in Syria. Among Nuradin's commanders were a group of courageous Kurds, including Najm al-Din Ayyub (Najmudin) and his brother Asad al-Din Shirkawih (Asadin), who had both attained a high esteem in Nuradin's eyes. In 556 AH (1161 AD), the caliphate in Egypt had passed to al-'Adid li-Din Allah ibn Yusuf (al-'Adid), who was weak-willed. His ministers competed with each other for a monopoly of influence and gained control of the state and over time they destroyed the country, while the caliph became impotent.

Among the rivals for power in Egypt was a vizier called Shawir, who had lost influence. So he went to Nuradin in Syria, asking for his assistance against his rival for the ministry. Nuradin took that opportunity to seize control of Egypt. He sent him Asadin Shirkawih with an army of mamluks, who restored the ministry to Shawar. The latter subsequently paid one-third of the land tax collected in Egypt to Nuradin.

The Crusader wars had erupted during this period, and Nuradin and his deputy in Egypt, Shirkawih, had begun to intervene more in Egypt's affairs, together with Shirkawih's nephew, Yusuf ibn Najmudin, who is no other than Saladin.

---

9 The Seljuks were a Turkish tribe from Central Asia. In the eleventh century, they established an enlightened, tolerant government in Central Anatolia. They conquered Persia in 1037 AD and established their first powerful state, the Empire of the Great Seljuks. They captured Baghdad in 1055 AD. *Editor's Note*

10 A mamluk was a soldier of slave origin. They constituted a specific warrior class, that was of great political importance and was extraordinarily long-lived, lasting from the ninth to the nineteenth century. Over time, mamluks became a powerful military caste in various Muslim societies, particularly in Egypt, but also in the Levant and Iraq. *Editor's Note*

Shirkawih died in Egypt in 556 AH (1161 AD) and was succeeded by Saladin in the office of deputy, with the title of vizier. Saladin used this position to become the ruler of an independent Egypt. How he did so is the subject of this novel.

Chapter 2

The Caliph al-'Adid's Procession

"Come on, brother!" shouted Hussein[11] to 'Omar al-Makari. "Haven't you slept enough? Cairo is in turmoil and everyone is rushing about. Get up, and rescue your donkey!"

"To go where? And why?" replied 'Omar. "Have they set fire to Cairo, as they did to Fustat? Or have they imposed some new tax on us? I left Cairo and brought my donkey to this spot outside Bab al-Futuh to escape their attacks, and the tyranny of these Turks and Kurds, and ..."

"Be quiet, 'Omar!" replied Hussein. "These Kurds are goodness itself. Have you forgotten the torments we suffered before them? It was so bad that none of us could move without a tax being imposed on us. Who dared mention the hallowed names of the caliphs Abu Bakr or 'Omar[12] may God's blessings be upon them?"

"You are right," said 'Omar. "My parents regretted giving me this name. But what's happened now, Hussein? Can we move? Here you are telling me to get up and rescue my donkey!"

"I'm saying that because the caliph al-'Adid li-Din Allah is leaving his palace in a procession and will be followed by a group of Turks and others. And one of them might attack your donkey and mount it or might take it for himself."

---

11 Name changed from Hasan in the original to distinguish this character from Abu al-Hasan, a major character in the novel whose name was abbreviated to Hasan (see Dramatis Personae). *Editor's Note*

12 Abu Bakr and 'Omar ibn al-Khattab were two of the four Righteous Caliphs. *Editor's Note*

"The caliph is leaving his palace?" asked 'Omar. "And what have we got to do with his palace? We're outside Cairo."

"He is coming this way and will pass through this gate, Bab al-Futuh."

"Through this gate? Where's he going?"

"He's leaving Cairo to meet Najmudin Ayyub."

"The caliph is leaving Cairo to meet Najmudin? And who is this Najmudin?" asked 'Omar.

"He's the father of the vizier Yusuf Saladin. He's come from Syria to visit his son!"

"My God!" exclaimed 'Omar. "What is the world coming to? The caliph and commander of the faithful, descendant of the Prophet's daughter, and the shadow of God on earth, is leaving his palace and going out of Cairo to meet the father of his vizier? Whenever did the Fatimid caliphs do this, Hussein?"

"Things have changed, my friend," replied Hussein. "The caliph is caliph only in name. Influence has passed to this Kurd. Poor al-'Adid!"

"Poor, why poor?" replied 'Omar. "No, we are the poor ones, and this Kurd may be better than he is."

"The Kurd better than the caliph?" asked Hussein. "No!"

"But what do we get from these rulers?" asked 'Omar. "They fight each other to tyrannize us, but what does it matter to me whether my ruler is an Arab or a Kurd, or an Indian? I'm only concerned that he shouldn't treat me unfairly, isn't that so?"

"Be quiet, they're coming!" said Hussein. "Can't you hear the trumpets and cymbals? Rescue your donkey! Hide him somewhere then come here!"

"I'll go and come back quickly to see the caliph's procession," said 'Omar. "That's been a source of regret in my heart ever since I was born. I've often heard about this procession with its numerous horsemen riding on all sides of the caliph fully adorned with jewels and silk, and..."

"I'll wait for you," said Hussein. "Hurry, 'Omar!"

"No, no, it's better that you follow me, so that we can put the donkey in this building, then climb up ourselves onto the roof. That way, we'll have a better view and be out of danger."

"Very well. Let's go!" said Hussein.

"Now we're on the roof and can watch the procession!" said 'Omar.

"They're coming from the palace," said Hussein. "They'll reach Bab al-Futuh in a moment. Can't you hear the clanking noise of the bridles?"

"Yes, I can hear them," replied 'Omar. "And I'm afraid we may be in danger."

"No, there's no danger. I think you're imagining it!" replied Hussein.

"Don't criticize me, brother Hussein! It's a case of once bitten, twice shy, as they say! Every time these soldiers have come out like this, they've attacked us and taken our animals."

"The procession has arrived!" said Hussein. "Take a good look at it in the streets of the city before it moves out."

"I can see the flags waving," said 'Omar, "the horses neighing, the spears glinting, and the swords shining. The street is surging with people just like the Nile in flood! God preserve us! Thank you, dear Hussein, for this sight. Tell me, now that they've started moving through Bab al-Futuh, which one is the caliph? Is it the man riding on the grey horse wearing the clothes with gold and silver brocade?"

"It seems you've never seen high officials in your life before," replied Hussein. "There are a lot of people walking in the caliph's procession. Do you think that the caliph would wear brocade? That's what some of his servants wear. Those people you can see at the head of the procession are the emirs and their children, and a variety of soldiers, and others in splendid dress. Then you can see two eminent gentlemen, who are the highest men in the state. Look at their stunning clothes, which dazzle the eye, at the saddles of their horses covered in silver, and at the Turks and other servants in their train. But all this is nothing compared with the caliph's procession. Look, look, there is the caliph's procession by that canopy!"

"The shade of the canopy is obscuring him, so I can't see him very well!" said 'Omar. "I can only see his horse, and the flags surrounding it, with the riders by his side. Who are they?"

"You don't need to be in such a hurry to ask questions!" said Hussein. "The procession is advancing slowly, so I'll explain everything to you. Can you see the caliph's horse? Look at it carefully! Its saddle is of red silk brocade embellished with gold and coated with enamel. If you look at the front part of the saddle, you will see precious stones on it. There are gold necklaces around the horse's neck, and if you look at the horse's legs, you will see golden anklets around them. They reckon that each horse with its trappings is worth a thousand dinars.[13] The viziers' and emirs' horses are also fitted out in the same way. They were originally a gift from the caliph, who gives them to his emirs on national celebrations."

"Congratulations, Hussein," said 'Omar. "You must have ridden these horses when you were a servant in the sumptuous palace."

"I was privy to so many things, my lad, and saw jewels that dazzle the mind," replied Hussein. "I almost forget them now. As for the caliph's clothes, look at this canopy: it is shaped like one of the pyramids and is made of sky-blue brocade. The caliph's clothes beneath it are of the same color. If it had been red, his clothes would have been red, too. Look at the golden crescents hanging from the sides of the canopy, and how the legs and rods of the canopy are covered with gold. Then at the top is a big golden pommel, with a smaller gold pommel on top of it inlaid with jewels. Look how it sparkles: it takes one's breath away!"

"That's true," said 'Omar, "but I can't see the person carrying the canopy. And how can he carry it when it is so heavy?"

"The person carrying it is riding a horse alongside the caliph's horse," replied Hussein. "The canopy has a shaft that the horseman sticks in his horse's saddlebow. His job while he rides is to watch the caliph's position in relation to the sun, so that the rays do not fall on him."

"And what would happen if the sun's rays fell on him?" asked 'Omar. "Now I can see the caliph's head, for the man holding the canopy has turned away from him. Goodness, what on earth is that on his head?"

13 A coin, usually minted from gold, used in ancient times in various parts of the Islamic world. The weight of the dinar is one mithkal (about 4.25 grams). *Editor's Note*

Chapter 3
Al-'Adid and Saladin

"Slow down, so that I can finish what I am saying," said Hussein. "Look at the turban on the caliph's head. It's white and elliptical, and on top of it, over his forehead, there is an ornament in the shape of a crescent made of red rubies, like no other in the world. And in the middle of the crescent there is a large, famous jewel, said to be unique and priceless. Its weight is said to be seven dirhams,[14] and the weight of the whole crescent eleven mithkals.[15] And in the circle of the main jewel is a stick of emeralds, of great value."

"God protect us!" said 'Omar. "Does this man deserve to possess such valuable jewels, when people in his kingdom are dying of hunger, and he takes their wealth from them unjustly? Brother Hussein, my heart is pained at this sight."

"Be quiet, my friend!" said Hussein. "God gives His blessings to whom he will. Perhaps if you knew what was in the heart of this caliph, you would not begrudge him these jewels. But for now all this is none of our concern. Listen, do you see the horseman to the caliph's left with a white handkerchief in his hand?"

"Yes, I can see him," replied 'Omar. "What is in the handkerchief?"

"In this handkerchief there is the precious inkwell that is the wonder of the age," said Hussein. "It is made of gold, adorned with pearls. Look on the other side of the caliph and you will see another horseman carrying

---

14 The dirham was a unit of weight in North Africa, the Middle East, and Persia, with varying values slightly above three grams. (It was also a coin minted from silver and less valuable than a dinar). *Editor's Note*

15 A mithkal is also a unit of weight equivalent to about 4.25 grams. *Editor's Note*

a sword decorated with gold, inlaid with jewels, sheathed so that only the top of it is showing. The man carrying it is called 'The Swordbearer' and he holds a very high rank. Then look at those around the caliph's horse, and you will find dozens of youths, with flags showing their rank, with swords around their waists, their waists tied with cloths, and unsheathed spears in their hands. They are on both sides of the caliph, like wings, and between the two wings, there is an empty space in front of the horse's head. Near the horse's neck are two Sicilians holding fly whisks, raised aloft like palm trees to ward off birds or anything else that might fall from above."

"I can see a magnificent horseman coming and going to the left of the procession, giving out orders and issuing prohibitions," said 'Omar. "Who is he?"

"That is the governor of Cairo," said Hussein. "He ensures order in the procession so that it can proceed smoothly, and he prevents crowds from assembling and obstructing the procession. Look at those behind the caliph's mount. There is a group of youths called the 'stirrup youths,' who are carrying polished, gilded daggers instead of curved swords. They have red and black pins in their hands, with rounded heads. Some of them are carrying iron poles, and in their hands is the caliph's personal standard. Around it are twenty-one flags, each one with a silk inscription in a different color on which is written, 'All help comes from God and victory is near.' Can't you read it?"

'Omar laughed and said, "How could I do that? My family did not send me to the Azhar[16] because the instruction there follows the Shi'i rite, and my family are Sunnis."

Hussein interrupted him and said, "You can study there now, because Saladin has required the instruction there to include the laws that apply to different Islamic sects…"

"It's too late for me to enjoy this blessing," said 'Omar. "Can one study after the age of forty? Let's leave that to our children. But who is this man I see? His entourage is every bit as large as the caliph's, and I can see he is wearing even finer clothes."

---

16 The reference is to al-Azhar University, the leading religious university. *Editor's Note*

"This is the vizier, Saladin, and the robe that he is wearing is the sultan's robe of honor, which this caliph himself bestowed on him three years ago. As you can see, there is a finely woven white turban with edges decorated with gold; under it is a brocaded robe, embroidered with gold. The cloak that he is wearing is also decorated with gold, and over it he has a gilded shawl. Then look at his neck; can you see the necklace? It is made of jewels worth ten thousand dinars.[17] And besides that, he has a sword with ornaments worth five thousand dinars. He is riding a horse worth eight thousand dinars, with a gilded saddle on it, and two hundred jewels on its head. Look at its feet: there are four chaplets of jewels around them, and on its head is a pure white golden cane. That is Saladin, whose appearance inspires even more awe than the caliph's. Look how his demeanor and the expression on his face project courage! No one could look at him and fail to respect or fear him. It is now common knowlege that power is in his hands, and he is the one who gives orders and issues prohibitions, as I told you earlier. Look at the men surrounding him. They include a group who are called the 'Youths of Mail;' they are strong soldiers, whom he chooses for himself—several hundred of them, walking on either side of him, leaving an empty space in front of him just like the caliph. Behind him there are drums, cymbals, and whistles. Can't you hear the noise they are making? The whole land is reverberating with it. Then behind the vizier's entourage comes the Bearer of the Spear. Look at it: it is a fine spear in a holder strung with pearls and a short head decorated with gold. With it is a shield decorated with leather that they say is the shield of Hamza ibn 'Abd al-Muttalib, may God's blessings be upon him."

'Omar the muleteer listened to the words of his friend Hussein in astonishment. When he heard him mention Hamza's shield, he was caught unawares and asked, "Hamza ibn 'Abd al-Muttalib, the uncle of the Prophet?"

"Yes," replied Hussein. "So they say. But let me not go into details now, because the procession will continue for a long time. Look at what is behind the vizier's entourage, and you will see groups of soldiers of different kinds, one troop after another—a vast number of them, more

---

17 A coin minted usually from gold.

than four thousand. Then come the flag bearers, and behind them more bands of soldiers of different races: Turks, Kurds, and others."

"Stop for a moment," said 'Omar, "and tell me about the horseman I can see riding beside Saladin, wearing splendid clothes."

"He's one of his close confidants," said Hussein. "He's a horseman that Saladin likes very much. In fact, he cannot bear to be without him. His name is 'Imadin."

'Omar the muleteer was surprised by that and asked, "How is it that all these men have names related to religion, ending in *din*?[18] There are three people whose names you have already told me—Nuradin, Saladin, and Najmudin—and now we have 'Imadin."

"That is their usual practice when giving people names," said Hussein. "But now that the procession has ended and I've told you all about it, forgive me if I leave."

"Goodbye," replied 'Omar. "May God multiply the likes of you!" And they departed.

Such was the procession of the caliph al-'Adid—described succinctly so as not to bore the reader, though it would be possible to describe it in much greater length.

The procession moved on in this fashion after passing through the Bab al-Futuh Gate. It was followed by people walking or riding, while others stood on the roofs of their houses to watch it. Dust had surged in the air, hiding the sky and dropping on people's heads and shoulders. There was not a young man or young girl who did not go out into the street or climb up to the rooftops. The common people were amazed that the caliph had come out to welcome the Kurd, while those in the know found nothing strange about it, so weak had the caliphate become.

---

18 *Din* in Arabic means religion. Salah al-Din, abbreviated to Saladin, literally translated means "the true or correct religion" and so on for other names. Najm al-Din, abbreviated to Najmudin, literally means "the star of religion." Nur al-Din, abbreviated to Nuradin, literally translated means "the light of religion." *Editor's Note*

Chapter 4

The Golden Hall

The procession continued in this fashion until it reached the Golden Mosque, at the end of al-Husayniyya. News came that Najmudin was near, and they met him there. As they assembled, Najmudin dismounted out of respect for the caliph, as did the men who were with him. Saladin dismounted and kissed the hands of his father, and his father kissed him back. When he saw the procession and the robe of honor on his son, he could not help crying with joy, thanking God for his blessings. Najmudin was an intelligent and wise man, so he threw himself before the caliph, kissing his hand to show his gratitude for such an honor. The caliph responded politely but did not leave his horse.

After the exchange of greetings and respects, the procession returned solemnly to al-Qasrayn, Najmudin riding alongside his son. Beside them both was the brave young 'Imadin. They spoke together for a long time in Kurdish, a language that al-'Adid's men could not understand. Most of the conversation was about Nuradin, the ruler of Syria, and about al-'Adid, ruler of Egypt.

As for the caliph al-'Adid, if you had been able to see his eyes under the canopy, you would have seen them glistening with tears, and if you could have fathomed what was in his heart, you would have heard it thumping with sorrow and grief because he had been forced to lead this procession to honor a man from whom he feared for his position and his life. But he realized he had no choice, so he suppressed his anger and went out to greet Najmudin. That was a greater burden for him to bear than being hungry or destitute. Perhaps he would have preferred to be one of the common people and not to have to endure such humiliation.

The procession reached Cairo's Great Eastern Palace before sunset. This consisted of a collection of palaces possibly numbering more than a dozen, among them the Emerald Palace, the al-Muzaffar Palace, the Iqbal Palace, the Sea Palace, the Harem Palace, the Thorn Palace, the Minister's Residence, the Guesthouse, the Mint, the Contract's House, the Great Library, and others. All of them collectively were known as the Great Eastern Palace, just as the palaces of 'Abd al-Hamid in Istanbul were later called the Yildiz Palace, though they were in fact a group of palaces.

The Great Eastern Palace today is situated to the east of Old Cairo. It extends over the area between al-Azhar and Bab al-Futuh, including Khan al-Khalili, the Judge's House, al-Jamaliyya, and al-Nahhasiyyin. This palace is called the Eastern Palace to distinguish it from another, smaller, palace to the west called the Western Palace. Between the two is a square known as Bayn al-Qasrayn,[19] while behind the Western Palace going further west is a large garden known as the Kafuri Garden, bounded by the Cairo Canal, on which the parks of the Fatimid caliphs used to be situated.

Among the complex of buildings that formed the Great Eastern Palace was a building called the Golden Palace, in which the caliph used to receive people on Mondays and Thursdays of each week. There the procession ended.

The caliph dismounted and entered the hall that had been readied to receive him, called the Golden Hall. To enter it, one has to go through a gate called the Golden Gate, where stood the Hospital of al-Mansour in al-Nahhasiyyin. The caliph sat on a throne of gold inside the hall—a throne that, it was said, weighed thousands of pounds. Around it was a curtain embellished with gold, inlaid with jewels of different colors, five hundred and sixty in all. Above the throne was a golden chandelier weighing thirty pounds. Most of the walls of the room were covered with decorated brocade curtains. Anyone looking at these surroundings would think he was in a dream, especially if he looked at the jewels glittering on al-'Adid's turban.

After the caliph sat down on his throne, the vizier Saladin entered and sat on a mattress reserved for him. No local officials were allowed to enter that day, as the session was reserved for Najmudin's welcome. The caliph ordered the doorman to receive and admit him, and Najmudin

---

19 In Arabic this literally means "between the two palaces." *Editor's Note*

came in, with a smiling face. He had an extremely distinguished air and made a great impression on al-'Adid, who greeted him and motioned for him to take a seat, which Najmudin did respectfully. It was the custom that when the vizier entered the presence of the Fatimid caliph, he would kiss the caliph's hand and foot. But Saladin did not do so, nor did he let his father do so, and the caliph did not feel offended.

Among those present in the hall was an elderly, stocky, finely muscled man with a pale complexion. He was sitting among those close to the caliph and looked as if he wanted to conceal himself from view. But Saladin noticed him. From the way he sat, he was sure that he was an emir,[20] but he had never seen him before.

When everyone had settled down, al-'Adid started to speak. At that time he was a young man of no more than twenty-one, although he had assumed the caliphate ten years ago in 556 AH (1161 AD), being eleven when he had received the pledge of allegiance. Anyone looking at him now, however, would think he was in his forties, so many were the worries and trials he had endured. He never set eyes on Saladin without regretting having asked Nuradin, the ruler of Syria, to come to his rescue.

---

20 A prince, chieftain, or governor. *Editor's Note*

Chapter 5

Hypocrisy

When everyone had sat down, the caliph addressed Najmudin. "I hope that Commander Najmudin is not tired from his journey," he said.

"No, sire," replied Najmudin. "My journey was extremely restful, especially as I was expecting to have the honor to meet the caliph, may God exalt him..."

The caliph gave a forced smile and said, "Greetings, you are most welcome here! I have ordered the palace head to prepare the Pearl Guesthouse for your stay. It is the most beautiful of our palaces; indeed, it is one of the wonders of the world..."

Najmudin sat politely, showing respect and showering praise on the caliph.

"The action of Your Majesty in going out to meet my father is a blessing that I shall not forget," said Saladin. "Wherever we may be, we will always pray for long life for the caliph."

The caliph scratched his nose with his finger and took the caliph's scepter from the cushion beside him. It was a short stick, covered with gold. He busied himself staring at it for an instant. Then he coughed and turned to Najmudin. "How was our friend, the Atabeg[21] Nuradin, when you left him?" he asked.

"He was well when I left him," he replied, in a polite and friendly tone. "He asked me to convey his profuse greetings and affection to our caliph, al-'Adid, may God protect him. He prays for his long life and continued good health."

---

21 Seljuk commander; see footnote 9 above. *Editor's Note*

"I appreciate his friendship and also wish him a long life," replied the caliph.

"That is a great honor for him. He has entrusted me with conveying to Your Majesty, may God exalt him, that he and his men are at your service, in support of the truth!"

These were painful words for al-'Adid to hear because they reminded him of the source of his troubles. They had started with his calling on Nuradin for assistance. But he steeled himself and did not betray any emotion as he turned to Najmudin and said, "He helped us more than once, may God reward him with goodness! We now have in the presence of your son, the victorious leader, unlimited resources we can draw upon," as he pointed to Saladin.

"My son is only one of your vassals, sire," said Najmudin. "He will spare no effort to serve you and stand by you."

In response, al-'Adid took off a string of jewels that adorned his neck, similar to jewels that were on Saladin's neck. He handed them to Najmudin, smiling. "This is a gift from us," he said, "by which to remember this visit. You deserve to be referred to as the primary leader! Gifts and presents will be bestowed on you in the Pearl Palace, and we shall entrust you with the revenues from splendid estates. And you deserve even more than all this..."

Najmudin stood up and took the necklace as he kissed the caliph's hand. Then he kissed the necklace and put it on his neck, saying, "You have showered me with blessings that I do not deserve, Your Majesty. The title you have bestowed on me is more than I am worthy of..."

The caliph interrupted him, saying, "No, you are 'the primary leader,' just as your son is 'the victorious leader.'" Najmudin repeated his thanks and sat down politely.

Silence reigned in the the great audience hall for a few moments. Saladin's attention was drawn toward an older, frail man he had noticed earlier because he had appeared so anxious and engrossed in his thoughts.

The caliph became aware of this. Wanting to distract attention from his gifts, he addressed Saladin, pointing with his hand at that other person sitting there, his eyes blazing, almost on fire from concentration, "I don't think you know the honorable Hasan. He is one of our cousins.

He was traveling and has just arrived." Then he turned to Hasan and said, "I don't think you need any introduction to Saladin, our valiant vizier."

Hasan signaled with his head, eyes, and shoulders that he was grateful for this introduction. He bent slightly forward as though preparing to get up. Saladin then said, "I am honored to make the acquaintance of this noble man. It suffices that he is directly related to the caliph."

Meanwhile, Najmudin was watching Hasan very closely. He did not like the cunning and craftiness that he could detect in his eyes and on his face. But for now he gave his full attention to the caliph, expressing his gratitude for this introduction.

After that, al-'Adid laid down the caliph's scepter he was holding in his hand onto the cushion, and people understood this was a signal that they should leave. Najmudin asked permission to do so and bade the caliph farewell. Then Saladin came forward to take his leave. He showed his readiness to kiss the caliph's hand, but the latter gently withdrew it.

Najmudin and his son left the caliph's audience room. Their men were waiting for them outside the palace with their horses and weapons. Among them was the young 'Imadin, who had been riding alongside Saladin in the procession. He was a young man in the prime of life and seldom left Saladin's entourage except for some important purpose. Everyone who knew him liked and respected him for his handsome appearance and his valor, as well as his intelligence and eloquence. Saladin had the utmost trust in him. As soon as he emerged from the audience with the caliph, he shouted, "Where is 'Imadin?"

The young man came forward, his eyes speaking volumes without saying a word. He was wearing the uniform of Saladin's guards: short trousers with a leather belt around his waist that had a gilded fastening, and above it a loose jacket decorated with gold and silver threads. On his head he wore a small turban like a skull cap, embellished with gold and silver; a short sword as well as a dagger were attached to his belt. "Come on, let's go to the Pearl Guesthouse," Saladin said, as 'Imadin stood in front of him. "The caliph has ordered my father to stay there, and I will stay there with him."

'Imadin carefully guided the entourage in the right direction, and they all rode together to the guesthouse, which was on the Cairo canal.

They crossed the square between the palaces, passed beside the Western Palace to the Kafur Garden, one of Cairo's recreation areas, and finally came to the guesthouse on the right bank of the canal. It looked over the canal from the west, while beyond the canal further west was a pool called the Cow's Belly. Beyond that were the al-Tabbala area and the Maqsa Garden[22] and, even further, the Ezbekiyya Pond, leading to the Nile River.

---

22 This subsequently became al-Fajjala and the Shi'riyya Gate. *Author's Note*

Chapter 6

The Pearl GuestHouse

This guesthouse was one of the most beautiful recreation areas in Cairo, with a garden extending straight to the canal, full of all kinds of luxurious and aromatic trees, plants, and flowers. There were halls and palaces with the most expensive and beautiful furnishings, typical of those that caliphs had in their palaces: curtains of silk brocade decorated with gold, carpets woven in gold, vessels of ivory and sandalwood, and couches and cushions. In the garden, hundreds of tame multicolored birds of the rarest species were chirping with their distinctive tunes and flew freely, while others were in cages. On the bank of the canal were carpeted balconies adorned with decorated seats, over which hung wooden canopies covered with plants. Everything in the guesthouse was precious, dazzling, and eye catching—not surprising since it was the main recreation area of the Fatimid caliphs during their reign.

Najmudin and his son arrived with their entourage to be met by the guesthouse staff and servants with incense and perfumes. They went into a large hall to rest, with some of their close associates. They sat for a while, making general conversation about travel and the hardships travelers encounter on their journeys. Naturally, from time to time the conversation was interspersed with mention of the European Crusaders, who at that time held sway over parts of Syria, Palestine, and many of the cities therein.

Low in the sky, the sun approached the horizon as it was about to set. The supper table had been set, and a group of their favorite associates had supper with them. When they finished their meal, they all retired in the guesthouse, leaving Najmudin and his son on their own, for they knew that Najmudin had come to Egypt for one important reason alone, which he wanted to convey to Saladin.

Najmudin withdrew with his son to a room lit with enormous candles, each one weighing several ratls.[23] Najmudin could see in the palaces of Cairo a level of luxury and ostentatiousness that he had never seen in Damascus. As soon as he was alone with Saladin, he leaned on a cushion and motioned to his son to sit down in front of him. Both were in light night attire. Najmudin held in his hand a pipe that he had been clutching since changing his clothes.

When they were both seated, Najmudin said to his son, "Yusuf, I was pleased to see that you enjoy a good reputation in the eyes of this man, but I noticed that you do not respect him much and that he regards himself as caliph and ultimate ruler."

Saladin laughed. "Father," he said, "does it matter to you that he should see himself in that way, when we know that he is our slave and our creature?"

Najmudin interrupted him. "Let us not get ahead of ourselves, my son. We haven't finished with him yet," he said. "There is no harm in flattery and observing the usual conventions. On the other hand, I can see that you are wary of his men's and supporters' anger. But our major problem concerns the oath of allegiance in favor of the 'Abbasid caliph that Nuradin is asking for so insistently and is intent on getting quickly."

"How so, father?" asked Saladin.

"We wrote you a year ago, asking that you issue an order to proclaim the sovereignty of the 'Abbasid caliph from the pulpits of Cairo. So why did you delay in doing so?"

Saladin was silent for a moment. His face registered concern. Then he looked up at his father and said, "You are asking me to humor and flatter the caliph, then you blame me for the delay in issuing the order. And this order implies nothing less than the proclamation of the sovereignty of the 'Abbasids over Egypt and the end of the Fatimid dynasty! You will not be unaware of how heartbroken and depressed our poor caliph will become— and he is already so frail. Why should we be concerned about Egypt, beyond

---

23 A unit of weight used in Islamic countries, varying in value, but usually equivalent to about five pounds. *Editor's Note*

having the decisive word, an audible voice, and the necessary profit? Let us leave this young caliph to enjoy the caliphs' usual titles and flatteries until we see what fate will bring. The proclamation of our sovereignty over Egypt will be easy to accomplish whenever we choose. And from my experience of you, I know that you like to proceed with caution!"

"Yes, my son," said Najmudin. "But Nuradin is insisting on it. He promised the 'Abbasid caliph al-Mustanid bi-Allah that he would be proclaimed as caliph from the pulpits of Cairo. When this did not happen for some time, however, the caliph asked for an explanation, and Nuradin wrote a letter to you urging you on and sent me to deliver the letter. This is his letter!" he continued, thrusting it toward him.

Saladin took it and read it, paying the most careful attention to its contents, especially with respect to the announcement of the proclamation: "You must hasten to take this noble initiative—it is a rare privelege that is offered to us before death makes its assault and oblivion catches up with you—the more so as the caliph and imam of our times is wholeheartedly expecting it and it is one of his most fervent wishes."

Saladin pondered this letter for a long time, as his father watched the change in his expression. He had realized what was on his mind. "What is the matter, Yusuf?" he asked. "How do you feel about this?"

"You know very well what my heart tells me," replied Saladin.

"The 'Abbasid dynasty must be proclaimed," said Najmudin. "Is that so difficult for you?"

"No," replied Saladin, "but I think you ignore something else that is on my mind."

"I understand what you mean," said Najmudin. "If the proclamation of allegiance to the 'Abbasids is made in the mosques, you must be thinking whether Egypt will become subservient to Syria and to Nuradin, or...?"

Saladin's features lit up and his eyes shone as he finished his father's sentence, saying, "...or just to Saladin alone?"

His father smiled and said, "Let us not hasten matters but keep our cool. This question needs some careful thought. For now what concerns us is the proclamation. We absolutely must support the 'Abbasid caliph."

"So far as the proclamation is concerned, we shall have to wait," said Saladin. "But you haven't given me your view on the other aspect of it."

"And what is that?" asked Najmudin.

"You know very well," said Saladin, "but you want to hear me say it, so let me tell you. I have taken care of the victory and arranged everything, using my sword and counsel as I used my uncle's sword before me. Nuradin is sitting in his palace in Damascus; his kingdom is vast and his mamluks are many. Would it be right for him to have control of Egypt as well, and for us to remain his servants or commanders? How is Nuradin different from us? Has he used his wealth to buy us? We are not his mamluks. We are commanders no different than him. And he cannot take control of Egypt without me. I will only swear allegiance to the 'Abbasid caliph on condition that I am master of Egypt, and not Nuradin."

No sooner had he finished speaking than he raised his brow, and his face showed both concern and irritation. He looked carefully into his father's face to see if he could decipher his reaction to what he had said. Najmudin smiled and said, "You are seeking power, Yusuf, may you be blessed. And you are certainly worthy of it. But every goal is governed by fate."

"I would like to know your opinion," said Saladin. "Don't you think I am right in what I am seeking?"

Najmudin laughed dismissively, playing with his beard, which he combed with his fingers, then said, "Might is right, my son. That is the principle of every politician. Otherwise, we would be obliged to leave this land and leave it to its people, because its ruler has sought the help of the Atabeg Nuradin against one of his closest associates, who had rebelled against him. He supported him through your uncle Asadin, and you were with him, but the two of you should have left Egypt after completing this mission and receiving your due reward. It will be terrible for you to remain here, whether in the name of Nuradin or in your own name. But you can count it as right if you are able to achieve it, for might is right, my son; that is the law of those who conquer."

Najmudin's argument was so strong that Saladin had no response. He was protective of his prerogatives in this country, and he was prepared to use any means to prevail. He got up, adjusting his small turban, then started to twirl his moustache, gazing at one of the walls and inspecting some colored pictures that he had not noticed before. Beside every picture there was a fine gilded shelf. Under each picture he could see the name of the person portrayed. They were poets of the Fatimid era, who had flocked to their caliphs in the days of their glory. He recalled a story he had heard about the Fatimid caliph al-Amir bi-Ahkam Allah. When he built the Ram's Pool Palace, he had portrayed each poet and his village on the walls, and each poet had that day composed a poem in his honor to be inscribed on the picture beside that poet's head. And beside each portrait was a gilded shelf. When al-Amir entered and read the poems, he ordered that a sealed bag should be placed on each shelf containing fifty dinars and that each poet should come in and take his bag with his own hand.

Saladin stood for a little while beside each picture, deep in thought. His father realized what was passing through his mind, so he said nothing, waiting for his reaction. He pretended he wanted to leave and that he was about to go to bed. But Saladin could not get himself to go to sleep without his father's approval. He turned to him and said, "Go easy, my father. This caliph has summoned us to help him against the Franks, and the people of Cairo themselves wrote to Nuradin giving him a third of Egypt as a fiefdom. They agreed that my uncle Asadin should also remain among them, so he and his men also deserve a fiefdom—it would not have been right for him to just complete his task and leave, as you say. Because his vizier Shawar failed to keep his promise, I killed him with my own hand, and the air was cleared for us. If I hadn't killed him, Nuradin would not have received the fiefdom, and..."

Najmudin interrupted him, stepping toward him as he did so. His tone was that of a venerable sage. "You are competing with Nuradin for a prize that is still in the hands of its owners. It is not right that the two of you should be squabbling over it before it has even left their hands. And that can only happen when allegiance is transferred from the Fatimids to the 'Abbasids, after which we will see what happens. That is enough for now..."

Najmudin's influence over his son was such that Saladin was mesmerized by what he had heard, accepted it, and moved away, saying, "I think you need some sleep, father!" He ordered the servants to prepare their beds, to which they both retired.

Chapter 7

Al-'Adid and Hasan

We left Caliph al-'Adid in the Golden Hall, alone with Hasan, after Najmudin and his son had departed. He was in need of rest after the two Kurds had left, so he ordered the chamberlain not to let anyone else enter, apart from his dresser to undress him and take off his jewels. The chamberlain came and busied himself, taking off his turban and the jewels that adorned it. He put each piece of jewelry in its allotted box. Then the slave girls came, carrying a change of clothes for the caliph to put on. His expression had changed, and he had begun to frown. His eyes had reddened and he felt so cold that his teeth and his knees were quivering—indeed his whole body was trembling so much that he could no longer stand. Hasan hurried over to him, supporting him with incredible gentleness. As soon as he felt his hand, however, he realized his temperature was high, and he knew that the caliph had a fever. But he tried to minimize the gravity of his condition so as not to heighten his anxiety.

When the caliph had finished changing his clothes, he lay down on a couch, feeling extremely weak. "How are you feeling, Your Majesty, Commander of the Faithful?" asked Hasan.

"I feel a tremor in my joints and cold spreading over my back," replied the caliph. "I think it's just a consequence of having to put up with injustice that exasperates and oppresses me. Oh, Hasan!"

He spoke in a strangled voice with tears glistening in his eyes. Hasan hurried to calm him, saying, "Every end is fated, Your Majesty! This crisis must come to an end!"

"I have felt this shaking ever since I was riding in the procession to meet this Kurd," he replied, gasping for air from the effects of the high fever. "How will I be strong enough to put up with them, when they have robbed me of my authority and wealth? And after all they have done to me, I have no choice but to be polite and courteous to them and welcome them…"

Hasan fingered his beard then took hold of it, muttering as though he were praying or making an invocation, pretending to be pious. "We have to be patient, Your Majesty. God will no doubt hear our supplications. I pray day and night, asking the Almighty to grant you justice and relief from these evildoers."

"How long do we have to be patient for, Hasan?" replied the caliph. "You seem not to be aware of what they have done to me. You have only heard them flattering me and talking to me deceitfully about my supremacy. But they have left me nothing of this authority except the name of caliph. This Yusuf Saladin has prevented the muezzins from using the ancestral customary call to prayer of the Fatimids, as was done when we were in control. He has sacked all the Shi'ite judges in Egypt that belonged to our denomination and appointed instead Shafi'i judges loyal to him, and he has taken control of the state apparatus with a hand of iron. And you ask me to be patient? How far can patience go?" He was swallowing hard as he spoke.

Hasan was a man with a morose temperament who did not speak much. He never showed any emotion, however much his heart might be affected. It may be that he had no real emotions. But that did not prevent him from feigning anger, joy, or sadness or other feelings as he chose. When he heard the words of the caliph, he cleared his throat, pretending to be affected, and said, "I still say to you, Your Majesty, be patient! You can rely on me, for I am devoting all my energy to pursuing this matter, which is of as much concern to me as it is to you. Isn't the state our state and the party our party? If it lives, do we not live? And if it dies, do we not die? God forbid! You can be confident that I will do whatever you would like me to. Indeed, if it weren't for my fear of increasing your stress, I would give you all the details that are in my mind. But now, sire, you seem to be in need of rest, so it would be best for you to retire to bed if you please. Should I give the information to the noble companion, who will convey it to Your Majesty?"

"Do as you see fit," the caliph replied restlessly, shaking from his temperature. "I am going to the women's quarters." He got up, helped by Hasan. Some eunuchs came and helped to carry him on a litter along a corridor leading to the women's quarters. Hasan bade him farewell and said, "I will go, by your command, to meet the noble companion and relay to him the information according to your wishes; then he will join you at the women's quarters."

The caliph signaled his agreement. The women's quarters comprised a palace standing on its own, but it was connected to the Golden Hall via a roofed corridor so that the caliph could go there whenever he wanted. The palace had a special door guarded by eunuchs. The head eunuch was known as the guarantor of the caliphate. A short time ago, the head eunuch had had the clumsiness to displease Saladin, who had him executed and appointed in his place Bahadin Qaraqosh, one of his most faithful men.

As soon as al-'Adid arrived in the women's quarters, the eunuchs lifted him down from the litter. He walked supported by some slaves, who thought he was asking to go to one of his wives' rooms. But instead he told them to take him to the room of his sister, Sittalmulk. She was a decisive and intelligent woman whose words gave comfort to al-'Adid and whose views he sought and trusted. And in the situation he found himself in, he felt the need to talk to her and seek her advice.

Chapter 8

Sittalmulk

The servants walked with him along a gallery leading to her room, which was set apart from the other rooms in the palace. When the lady heard that he was coming, she went out to receive him and greeted him. She helped him into her room, where he sat down. "What is wrong with my brother, the Commander of the Faithful?" she asked. "What is he complaining of? I'd give my life for him!"

"I'm complaining of a cold and trembling," replied al-'Adid. "Send the servants away; I'd like some peace and quiet, with no one except us in the room!"

Sittalmulk did so. She was pretty, tall of stature, with a smiling face, golden hair, and an attractive appearance. When you looked at her, you were conscious of a certain dignity that was apparent in her eyes and her demeanor. She was twenty-five years old, several years older than her brother, the caliph.

When she was alone with him, she sat down beside him on the bed and put her arm around his shoulder. "What is wrong with my brother?" she asked. "What is he complaining of? May God protect him from every harm. If the Commander of the Faithful is sick, everyone is sick!"

He rested his head on her shoulder and sighed, saying, "I appear to be complaining of a fever that gripped me. But the true sickness is here in my heart." He pointed to his chest but could not prevent his hand from dropping, so weak had he become as the fever became more intense. She felt his hand, which was very hot, and asked, "Shall I call a doctor for you?"

"No," said al-'Adid, "this fever will pass tonight. But if you know a doctor who will save me from those Kurds, then call him!"

She pretended to make fun of him and said, "If I knew a doctor in India and knew that he could cure you, I would go and fetch him myself, but…"

As he lifted his head from her shoulder to give her a chastening look, his turban fell down. He made a feeble attempt to catch it with his hand, but she seized it and put it back on his head. "You are pretending not to understand, Sittalmulk," he said. "You are smart enough to know very well what I am driving at."

She laughed and said, "Suppose I did understand what you are referring to. I still don't see that the problem requires so much attention. Be patient, for relief will surely come."

He sighed, resting his head again onto her shoulder, then turned his eyes toward her, and said, "I have found no one among my men to help me in this matter except my cousin Hasan, who is both pious and zealous. He assured me that he would make every effort in this regard."

When she heard the name of Hasan, she recoiled. The surprise would have been visible on her face had she not hurriedly composed herself. If al-'Adid, who was lying on her breast, had been more alert, he would have been aware that her heart raced whenever she heard that name. But he was too preoccupied with himself to notice. She braced herself and asked, "And how did he assure you of that?"

"He gave me his assurance today," replied al-'Adid, "and he will give the details to the noble companion, who will tell us about it when he comes shortly."

"Do you believe this man?" asked Sittalmulk, the irritation visible in her eyes.

"Why should I not believe him?" asked al-'Adid. "He is a loving, faithful man, and one of our relatives. And you know how protective he is in matters connected with our dynasty."

She shook her head and said nothing, as if to suggest she thought he was a hypocrite and a liar.

Al-'Adid straightened up. His fever had begun to abate, and his determination strengthened. He gripped his sister's hand, saying, "I can feel the fever loosening its grip on me, isn't that so? Sittalmulk, you have not thought well of this man ever since we have known him, without reason or evidence. He is a cousin. He is not a grandson of al-Hafiz li-din Allah, our grandfather, but a grandson of al-Amir bi-Ahkam Allah!"

"As you wish," said Sittalmulk, clearly unconvinced, as she played with the end of her golden plait, twisting it between her fingers, her anger apparent on her face.

"Why does mentioning him make you angry?" al-'Adid asked. "You hate him for no reason—he is not at all the man you think. I've always known him to speak well of you. He is desperate to please you!"

She gave him a sideways glance, as if to scold him, and said, "And what good does that do? As far as I am concerned, I ask nothing of him."

"We do not have to continue to reject him," said al-'Adid, "given that he is our cousin."

"Who can vouch for his allegiance to the caliph?" she interrupted skeptically. "There is no proof except for his own testimony. But let's forget about him; he doesn't deserve all this attention."

"You're doing him a gross injustice in judging him in this manner," said al-'Adid. He was about to finish, but a slave boy had come in and stood there. Sittalmulk realized he was there to convey some news and asked, "What do you want?"

"The noble companion is at the palace gate, requesting an audience with his Majesty, the Commander of the Faithful. But the eunuch Bahadin will not let him in…"

She turned to the caliph and asked him if he felt comfortable enough to sit with the noble companion. "I feel rested," he replied, "so let him come!"

She turned to the slave and said, "Tell the head eunuch that the Commander of the Faithful is here and wants to see the noble companion; therefore he must let him in!"

The slave boy left. Sittalmulk was conscious of her brother's anger at Bahadin's behavior, but she pretended not to notice. After a while the noble companion came in. He was an elderly sheikh who knew the caliph very well: he regularly kept him company, talking with him about all kinds of matters and often acting as the depository of his secrets.

When the caliph saw him, he smiled and ordered him to sit down. Sittalmulk did not need to conceal herself from him because he was a relative, and she had been accustomed to seeing him ever since she was a child. She merely covered her hair, wrapped herself in a silk fabric shawl over her clothes, and sat on a chair beside her brother's couch.

The caliph gave the companion an inquisitive look that asked him why he had come. The companion knew what he was after and said, "I have come to ask after Your Majesty's health. I heard from Hasan that you had a fever. May God protect you from any harm. We are your loyal servants."

The caliph smiled, appreciating the way in which the companion addressed him, and said, "Through your prayers and kind thoughts, all my illness has left me. Feel my hand...the fever has gone... But what else have you brought us?"

He felt his hand, pretending to look satisfied even though he could feel he still had a high temperature. "We praise God for that," he said.

"Tell me what you have brought us," said the caliph.

"I hope it is for the best," he said, his face indicating that he had things to say that he did not want to mention in front of Sittalmulk.

Realizing this, she got up and said, "If my presence is preventing the companion from speaking, I will leave."

Her brother grabbed her dress and said, "Sit down. You are not someone from whom things are to be hidden. Speak, my dear relative, and tell me what you have brought with you!"

"I've come on an important matter," he said. "Will you permit me to reveal everything?"

"Yes," said the caliph. "Do not be afraid. What has Hasan told you about the efforts he has been making in our cause?"

"You are right, Your Majesty, Hasan is very zealous in defense of the Commander of the Faithful's office, and he is striving to save it from this persistent enemy."

"I have heard him say that," said the caliph, "and he promised to explain it. Has he explained it to you in detail?"

"He gave me a full explanation. It was surprising, and I liked it very much," he replied.

"And what exactly was it?" asked the caliph, turning eagerly with anticipation to the companion.

Chapter 9
The Assassins

The companion spoke in a hushed voice, craning his neck as though he were trying to avoid being heard. "Your Majesty, Hasan believes that the obstacle that must be overcome is none other than this Yusuf Saladin. If he goes, we shall be rid of all these evils. And Hasan is trying to save us from him!"

"How is he proposing to do so?" asked al-'Adid.

The companion clutched his neck with the palm of his hand, meaning that he would kill him. The caliph looked very surprised. "Who will kill him?" he asked. "In the whole of Egypt there is no one who would dare lay a finger on him."

"That isn't his plan," replied the companion. "This man will be assassinated without the murderer being known."

"How would that be possible?" asked the caliph.

"Doesn't Your Majesty know about the secret community of the Isma'ilis or the Assassins?" asked the companion.

Al-'Adid was startled at the mention of these names and replied, "Yes, I know of them, and I heard that they are among our supporters."

"They are Shi'ites like we are," replied the companion, "but now their people are only obsessed with political assassinations."

The caliph interrupted him, "That's not just a recent obsession. I think you mentioned their deeds on several occasions. Didn't you tell me that they assassinated al-Malik al-Afdal, the army commander, and the minister al-Amir bi-Ahkam Allah? At that time their leader was called

Bahram. They also assassinated Nizam al-Malik, the Seljuk minister, and others."

"Yes, sire," replied the companion. "And they assassinated many others. This is their sole preoccupation."

"Who is their leader now?" asked al-'Adid. "And where are they?"

"They were originally followers of al-Hasan ibn al-Sabah, sire, in the time of your grandfather al-Hakim bi-Amr Allah—may God have mercy on him—that is, more than one hundred and fifty years ago. This Hasan was living in the Fortress of Alamut near to Qazvin.[24] He formed a group of freedom fighters who did not fear death. They were known as the Assassins, after the drug that they took called hashish.[25] They had several leaders in succession in Persia, Iraq, and Syria. Their leader now is called Rashidin Sinan, and he lives on the Masaq Mountain in the province of Aleppo. He hides himself in fortified castles there, and he has experienced, hardened men who will obey him to their death. If he orders the assassination of a caliph, emir, or sultan, he will be obeyed immediately. Hasan is a personal friend of this Sinan, by virtue of his noble lineage, and he has influence over him. He can prevail on him to have someone assassinated."

Al-'Adid's eyes registered a mixture of pleasure and surprise. "How can a man undertake such deeds here when he has to overcome so many barriers and hurdles, as you know?" he asked. "And how could a murderer escape after he completes his mission?"

"These freedom fighters usually disguise themselves in the clothes of riders or servants," replied the companion. "They mingle with the servants for a period of time in order to assess possibilities, then, when an opportunity presents itself, they move to assassinate their target. They have no concern for what may befall them after they fulfill their deed. They pay no attention to death, because they regard killing for the cause as preferable to living."

---

24 Qazvin was a city in Persia northeast of present day Teheran. *Editor's Note*

25 Arabic name for the cannabis drug. The origin of the English word assassins comes from the Arabic word Hashshashin (alternately spelled as Hashishin or Hashashiyyin) which refers to users of hashish. The Assassins were also known as the Batinis. *Editor's Note*

The caliph turned to his sister, hoping to have her partake in his surprise and admiration for what he had heard, but he found her downcast, deep in thought. "Don't you see how concerned this nobleman is for our interests?" he asked her. But she remained silent and pensive.

He turned to the companion and asked, "Did he tell you when he would be undertaking this deed?"

The companion was uncomfortable as he rubbed his nose, cleared his throat, and spluttered. His eyes betrayed confusion, so the caliph did not know what to make of these signs. But Sittalmulk was well aware of what those manifestations really meant. She glanced furtively at him and listened intently as he said, "Sire, he is placing a single condition on this deed."

"And what is that?" asked the caliph. "I suppose he means marriage to my sister!"

Sittalmulk recoiled when she heard this sudden declaration. But she quickly pulled herself together as she turned her face toward a curtain hanging on the wall, decorated with rich colors, with pictures of birds and trees to dazzle the eyes. She pretended to be examining one of the pictures.

"He didn't mention that to me," replied the companion. "But Your Majesty knows well that Hasan is of a noble and ancient lineage. And he is the eldest of your cousins who are eligible to assume the succession by the usual convention…"

Sittalmulk immediately understood what he was driving at. She interrupted him and sought to counteract her brother's words about Hasan marrying her. "I think that what he is doing is making it a condition to be next in line to the throne after the Commander of the Faithful!"

The companion responded immediately, as if apologizing for and minimizing the effect of Hasan's audacity. "This request of his is a sort of madness," he said. "It is meaningless, because Your Majesty the Commander of the Faithful—may God preserve him and hasten our deaths before he is afflicted with harm—is still a young man in the prime of life, while Hasan is middle-aged. He is putting this condition only to convince himself that he should take on that burden with all the danger that it entails. Who knows if he will survive a single day after carrying out his task?"

"He is making it a condition that he should be next in line to the caliphate after me?" asked the caliph.

"May God lengthen the life of the Commander of the Faithful," he replied. "The man is not expecting to seize power but would simply like to be next in line, so it appears."

The caliph, deep in thought, said nothing. The hesitation was clear in his eyes. Then he raised his head, looking at the companion, and asked, "And what is your view?"

The companion replied, "Your Majesty, if you will permit me, I think that you should grant him the succession, but as a condition of this agreement the succession after him should pass to your son, Prince Daoud, who is the true heir. If he can save us from this Kurd and restore power to our caliph, the Commander of the Faithful, he will have done something no one else was capable of. Being heir to the throne would only be a formal title that would reward him and provide him with psychic satisfaction but have no consequence beyond that."

Chapter 10

Freedom of Thought

Sittalmulk noticed that her brother was on the point of accepting. From what he was saying, she thought he was willing to give her away in marriage. She could not imagine becoming Hasan's wife. Indeed, she hated the idea for more than one reason, quite apart from her personal feelings. She thought him wicked and treacherous, and she was right. She did not consider that Saladin deserved death, because he had done nothing that justified that. It was simply unbridled ambition in the pursuit of power that led her suitors to concoct absurd arguments. She looked at her brother and said, "Do you want to have Saladin assassinated and replace him with Hasan?"

"I will not put him in Saladin's place," replied the caliph. "But if he can have him assassinated, I will name Hasan as heir to the throne."

"And what will you do with Daoud, your son?" asked Sittalmulk.

"He will be next in line after him," replied the caliph.

"What reason is there for such an action?" asked Sittalmulk. "Why would you want to get rid of Saladin? And what prompts you to commit such a despicable act? What has he done?"

"You ask me what he is guilty of as if you do not know," replied the caliph.

"I may know," replied Sittalmulk, "but I would like to hear it from the Commander of the Faithful himself."

"He has seized all power for himself," said the caliph, "and left me with no authority except in name."

Sittalmulk replied, "Did you exercise effective power before? Weren't your ministers those who wielded real authority and ran the state? And all of those were foreigners, Armenians or Turks, whereas this minister is a Kurd. So what is the difference?"

"But he has used his power to a much greater extent in a tyrannical way, making massive changes," replied the caliph.

She felt she had a winning argument. She did not let him finish what he was saying as she responded, "If he used his powers in a despotic way, it was to remove injustices that afflicted the people. The taxes were intolerable, so he removed or reduced them. Is it not for that reason that plots are being hatched against him and schemes being devised to kill him? Those who are trying to do that are those seeking power. They are envious of the man because of his position and are stirring up the anger of the Commander of the Faithful against him. If my brother wants to know the true worth of this Kurd, let him remember the way in which we sought the help of his sultan, Nuradin. Didn't you send some locks of our hair with a letter to Nuradin in which you said, 'These are locks of hair from my women, who seek your help to deliver them from the Crusaders'? The man answered your request and rescued you through Asadin and Yusuf Saladin. Could a leader use a more humiliating method of seeking help than that? My hair is still short because of that lock that I cut off!"

As she said that, she felt her hair as if to check that what she was saying was true. Then she continued, "In return, Nuradin asked for a third of our territory as a fiefdom, in addition to land for his men. After they came and rescued us from the Franks, we showed no gratitude. Shawar, your minister, began to resist them and put them off so they killed him. God is my witness that Saladin is more favorably disposed and more faithful to you than that Shawar. But we did not benefit from that event. The eunuch who guarded this palace before Bahadin was suspicious of Saladin's motives and encouraged us to challenge Saladin and his men. He connived with a group of Egyptians to form an alliance with the Crusaders in order to kill Saladin. Did he do so out of concern for you or the state? At all events, Saladin learned of the plot and had him killed. The palace eunuchs rebelled because they were blacks of the same race. Fifty thousand of them rallied to fight Saladin's men, and the two armies clashed in front of this palace while we were still in it. I will never forget the horror of that day. I will never forget the Commander of the Faithful, as he sat in the watchtower observing the fighting, routing for the eunuchs to prevail. Their resolve strengthened, and Saladin began to fear that the tide might turn against him and his men. So he ordered the oil throwers to hurl bottles of boiling oil over the watchtower and the palace, and…"

The caliph interrupted her, "But I encouraged Saladin's men and sent a spokesman for the caliphate to say, 'Take these dogs and slaves! Get them out of your country! And stop throwing the oil!'"

Sittalmulk continued, "But you only said that because you were afraid of what the fire would do to the watchtower."

She was speaking passionately, the movements of her whole body reinforcing her words. Her cheeks were flushed, and her eyes sparkled. But when she began to recall the fire, she turned pale and her expression changed by the sad memory of that event. Suddenly she stopped speaking. Her brother found this change odd and turned toward the companion, who was also looking at her.

She pulled herself together and started to speak again, "And it was not your words alone that stopped them."

"How so?" asked the caliph.

"Let's not discuss this topic now," replied Sittalmulk. "Talking about it will be painful for both of us, and you are greatly in need of rest and relaxation."

As she busied herself adjusting her veil on her head, al-'Adid felt his own hand and said, "I am fine; there is nothing wrong with me. The fever has abated, thank God! Tell me, what is the other reason?"

"Do you really want to know?" asked his sister.

"Yes," replied the caliph.

Chapter 11

The Lock of Hair

Sittalmulk put her hand to her pocket and took out a golden lock of hair, the color of her own hair, and handed it to him, saying, "Do you recognize this lock of hair?"

He could barely conceal his surprise and said, "It is your hair. This is the lock that I cut from your head and sent to the ruler of Damascus with the rest of the women's hair. Where did you get it? How did it reach you?"

"I got it the day the war flared up between our slaves and Saladin's men."

"How did this happen?" asked the caliph.

"You yourself mentioned just now that Saladin had stopped his men from throwing the bottles of oil before any damage was done to the palace," she answered. "That may be true, but I know that when we were in the palace, we were trembling with fear, as the arrows rained down on us from Saladin's men. I saw a bottle of burning oil fall onto the palace near my room here, but I didn't know where it came from. I was frightened and appealed to the servants to protect me from any danger, but none of them heard me because the men were busy shooting arrows some distance from where I was.

"Meanwhile, while everyone in the palace was preoccupied, I saw a man disguised in eunuch's clothes cover his face with a veil and leap out from inside the palace. I didn't know how he had entered the palace in the first place. I was frightened, but I thought he had hurried to help me. Almost immediately, I felt him grasp my hand and drag me toward him as if he wanted to pick me up and carry me off. There was no one in the room to see what was happening. I shouted and called for help, but no one heard me amid the noise that filled the whole place. Then another man came and both men dragged me away. They indicated that I should follow them at once, one of them threatening me with a dagger that he drew from his belt. The sight of it upset me, and I collapsed. I was shell-shocked; my veil had disappeared, and my hair was undone. While I was in this state, I saw a young man leap toward me. His clothes indicated that he was one of Saladin's men, so I was sure that he would help me escape from those two men. He shouted loudly at them, and with his dagger between his hands was about to kill both of them. When they saw this, they took flight, left me, and started to run away, while he himself stayed standing there like a lion. He looked at me gently and said, 'Who are those wretches?' 'I don't know,' I replied, 'and who are you? And what do you want from me?' 'Don't be afraid, my lady!' he said. 'I am one of Saladin's men who are besieging this palace. I saw those two men trying to abduct you. When I saw your golden hair, I knew that you were one of the caliph's women, so I rushed to help you. Thank God that I succeeded!' 'Are we in danger from the fire?' I asked. He assured me that they had not thrown any oil over the palace, but that thieves had thrown the oil from a different direction for their own purposes. Perhaps they wanted to distract people with the fire and abduct me…"

At that point Sittalmulk's expression changed. Her cheeks flushed and she swallowed hard, breathing heavily from emotion.

The caliph and his companion were listening to her words, watching the passion that was reflected all over her face. They noticed the change that had come over her when she mentioned the young man. They had not been aware of her feelings toward him. When she had finished, al-'Adid asked, "Who is this young man? And how did he know that you were one of the caliph's women? It is very strange. How is it that a strange young man should know who you are when you only go out veiled? And yet, this is one of Saladin's men… Tell the truth!"

Glancing at him sideways, she said, "You are accusing me, Commander of the Faithful! There is no room for doubt! I asked this young man how he knew me and he put his hand into his pocket and took out this lock of hair, which he thrust toward me, saying, 'Isn't this your hair?' Then he put it beside my own hair, and they were one and the same color..."

"He touched the hair on your head with his hand?" interrupted the caliph.

"He didn't touch me," replied Sittalmulk. "He just put the lock beside the hair on my head. He's an innocent youth, and I owe him my life and my honor. If it weren't for him, I would have become the victim of that traitor!" And she gritted her teeth.

"Do you know who that traitor is?" asked the caliph.

"Not for certain," replied Sittalmulk, "though I did have my suspicions."

"Who was he? Tell me!" said the caliph.

"I cannot," replied Sittalmulk, "because I am afraid that my suspicions may be wrong and that I may cause an innocent man harm. If it weren't for that, I would have told you about that incident at the time it happened. More than a year has gone by, and I haven't told you about it so as not to arouse your suspicions."

Al-'Adid was so angry that he had turned pale. "Why haven't you told me earlier?" he yelled. "Something like this happens, and you tell me nothing all this time? Who would dare do such a thing? Who do you think that man was? Tell me!"

"Don't be angry, oh brother," replied Sittalmulk. "I have not told anybody and will not do so now for fear of harming innocent people. I escaped, thank God! But I have been remiss regarding the valiant young man who saved me!"

As soon as she mentioned him, her eyes brightened. If her brother had looked carefully at her chest, he would have realized that her heart was racing, but he did not notice. "Don't you know the name of the person who saved you?" he asked. "Who was he?"

"I didn't ask him his name," she replied. "I was expecting him to come and see you the following day and tell you what had happened so that you could reward him, but it seems that didn't happen. After he had satisfied himself that I was out of danger, he gave me back my lock of hair, saying, 'Take this lock of your hair, my lady, to keep it from being touched by those who are not worthy of it! It was not right for the caliph to send it as a means of seeking help!' And with those words, he disappeared with the speed of lightning, and I never saw him again!"

Chapter 12

Who are you Accusing?

The caliph was so angry that his chest began to heave, and he forgot how weak he had become. Unable to restrain himself, he quickly rose, seized the lock of hair, and snatched it from Sittalmulk's hand. He started to examine it closely, comparing it with the rest of her hair. It was no different. Turning to his companion, he asked, "What do you think, my friend? How can strangers enter my palace with my women's hair? But no, I am the guilty one, having been too quick to plead for assistance by sending the hair of my women to the ruler of Damascus. But how did this young man get hold of this lock of hair, and how did he keep it until he recognized its owner? I don't know!"

The companion was watching and listening in utter surprise. When he saw how angry and incensed the caliph was, he said, "Calm down, sire! Everything has a reason. How the lock of hair reached that Kurd is not so important for us to know as the identity of the man in disguise who tried to abduct Sittalmulk. Who would dare do that?"

Al-'Adid turned to his sister and said, "Tell me, tell me... Who do you suspect? Who do you believe was that rascal who had the audacity to come into my palace and violate the privacy of my harem?" He was breathing very heavily as he said this, and his eyes had turned red. He gave the lock of hair back to her and went back to his seat, exhausted.

His sister came up to him and tried to calm him down by wiping his forehead gently. "Don't be so angry, my brother!" she said. "Allow me to say no more for the time being, for all I have now are suspicions, and I cannot accuse a man on the basis of suspicion. Doing so, however weak the accusation, would be enough to expose him to death, and it would be wrong for me to expose a soul to destruction!"

"No, you have to tell me who the traitor is," replied the caliph. "I promise you that I will not rush to exact any quick revenge but will act on the matter with deliberation and fairness."

She said nothing as she adjusted the veil on her head then started to fidget with the lock of hair between her fingers. Meanwhile, her brother looked at her, waiting for her response. "Why don't you say something?" he asked, when she failed to answer immediately.

"Please, don't press me." she replied. "I will respond later. Let me think for a while!"

The companion turned to al-'Adid and said, "Leave her for now, sire! Do not pressure her any more! She will tell us, but there is no need to hurry. Let us go back to what we were talking about earlier: how to free ourselves from these people! Would Your Majesty be able to give me his reaction to the proposals of Hasan?"

On hearing Hasan's name again, a shudder ran through Sittalmulk's body, but she pulled herself together, waiting to hear what her brother would say. He turned to his companion and said, "He is promising us to have the man assassinated and is demanding the succession as a reward, so we will promise it to him!"

"The Commander of the Faithful's promise is enough of a guarantee, and he is always true to his word, but Hasan will not believe me. Can you write him a letter?" asked the companion.

"No," replied the caliph. "It will be enough for us to tell him so orally!"

"So be it," replied the companion. "I will tell him…but there is…" He stopped speaking, stroking his beard as though he were reluctant to reveal anything more.

"But there is what? Tell me!" said al-'Adid.

"I am afraid that Sittalmulk may be irritated, because she…" replied the companion, and fell silent.

"What will irritate me?" asked Sittalmulk. "How do you know that this will be the case?"

He smiled and said, "I understood from the tenor of your conversation that you did not like Hasan…"

She interrupted him, "And why should I like him? Is that something he requires of me?"

"No," replied the companion, "but he is trying to ingratiate himself with the Commander of the Faithful and to have the honor of…"

"Of what?" interrupted Sittalmulk, raising her voice.

The companion turned to al-'Adid and asked, "Shall I say, sire?"

"Say what he wants to have the honor of?" asked al-'Adid. "I think I know his intentions, for he has often hinted at them in his conversations with me. And the truth should be told; it is only right for the man who seeks it."

He cleared his throat and turned his face toward Sittalmulk.

She understood perfectly well what he meant. He had mentioned to her once before Hasan's wish to marry her, and she had refused. When she heard him make another allusion to this, she feigned ignorance and said, "I don't understand. What do you mean?"

"I think you understand very well what I have in mind," replied al-'Adid. Then he turned to the companion and said, "What do you think about all this, my friend? I cannot see anyone more worthy of my sister than Hasan."

The companion straightened up and said, "There is no doubt that he is the best suited because of his noble ancestry, quite apart from his intelligence. And we have seen how devoted he is in protecting Your Majesty's interests and freeing him from these people. I believe we should agree to this request, which will make it easier for him not to press for the other condition. I mean, if Your Majesty's reply with respect to the hand of your sister is positive, then I do not think that he would press his demand to be next in line for the caliphate. He would be content with this, for he has great respect for Sittalmulk and would regard winning her as an enormous blessing. And so he would become our unconditional ally in fulfilling our aims."

Hearing this, Sittalmulk tried not to raise her voice as she asked, "He is asking to marry me, and you are approving? I need to know the views of my own brother, the Commander of the Faithful!"

Obsessed with the need to get rid of Saladin, al-'Adid thought for a moment that she might give in. So he said, "This is my view as well, as you already know from our previous conversations..."

"But it is most certainly *not* my own view," she replied emphatically and coldly, turning her face away from him.

"It seems you are persisting in your errors," said al-'Adid. "There is no one in the whole of our family who would make a better match for you than he would. Quite apart from his devotion to our service!"

"The question is not whether he is the better match or someone else is," replied the princess. "I told you earlier that I don't want to marry anyone. Let's change the subject now!"

"But my lady," the companion replied, "if you accept, you will be serving the cause of our caliph, the Commander of the Faithful, for Hasan is the best qualified man in the world to save him."

"Hasan is a duplicitous liar," she replied, looking at him with contempt. "He is quite incapable of doing anything of the sort!"

The companion laughed derisively and said, "My lady, you have judged him unfairly. I am certain of his devotion to the service of our cause, and he is sincere in his desire to protect the honor of the family of the Prophet, because he belongs to it himself!"

"He is lying about that, too!" replied the princess. "The Prophet's family is known for sincerity and devotion, but this man is a hypocrite, that's all!"

Al-'Adid was very displeased to hear her express her views so openly and strongly. He said, "You have no proof for what you say. I have known the man for several years, and I have only known him to be perfectly amiable and sincere. I do not know how you can accuse him of being a liar and a hypocrite."

"I know better," replied Sittalmulk, "and time will prove the truth of what I am saying. I think you are tired, my dear brother. I am sorry that we have talked so long. You are in a peculiar mood, so go to sleep, and tomorrow you will see that I am telling the truth!"

Al-'Adid was indeed tired. Her words had had a great effect on him. So he decided to take her advice and come back to this question on another occasion. He got up with his companion, and they both retired, the caliph being more in need of sleep than anyone else.

Chapter 13

The Guesthouse

The companion, however, was the least able to sleep, for he had failed in the task that Hasan had entrusted to him. The companion was an honest and somewhat naive man who had been misled by Hasan's cunning and promises, persuaded by his eloquent proofs that to transfer the succession to him would be best for the dynasty and for everyone else concerned. The companion had no doubt that Hasan would be able to save the dynasty from Saladin. When he had entrusted this task to him, he had striven with all his heart to make it happen, determined to make al-'Adid accept it for he believed that he would be thereby serving the caliph's interests.

When he failed, he was unsure how to communicate the result of his efforts to Hasan. He began to think of ways to do so in a soft and gentle manner so as not to anger or disappoint him.

Hasan was staying in the guesthouse a short distance from the Western Palace. It was a large house that had originally served as a palace for al-Muzaffar ibn Amir al-Juyush. He had stayed there until his death, and it had then been made a guesthouse for messengers sent by emirs and other rulers. It was in the charge of a deputy for the gatekeeper in receiving envoys arriving from a distance, putting them up in suitable houses, and arranging for them to be served.

The deputy was very attentive to Hasan when he saw how close he was to the caliph and the status that he enjoyed in his eyes. So he allocated him a private residence and ordered the slaves to attend to him. Hasan had charmed him by his appearance and the tales he had told of his might and exalted status. The dynasty in its last days was awash with fanciful gossip, and its masters held fast to fantasies rather than to facts and to appearances rather than to substance. They did so because of the decadence that had taken hold of the state, as its foundations began to crumble and it became exposed to conquest. The rulers lost their pride, and they all began to be concerned only with themselves, their main aim being to ensure their survival and that of their families as they awaited the end of the dynasty. When their survival could not be guaranteed and their hopes were dashed, they clung to the weakest excuses and the feeblest of promises. If a man is overtaken by despair about something, he will believe anything that is said to restore hope to him, even when it is not realistic. In this situation of fishing in murky waters, unscrupulous people will flourish, inventing rumors based on fantasy and expounding on deeds that have no basis in fact. And so appearances will flourish as they become the main thing most men will hold on to.

Hasan was one of those opportunists, being a man of both intelligence and cunning—a convincing charlatan, who had no qualms about saying and doing anything to achieve his goals, be they murder, lying, flattery, or currying favor. An intelligent rogue, when he does not follow his conscience or act with honorable intentions, will be able to achieve his aims, whatever these may be. Hasan coveted the caliphate, or at least the succession. And as will have been clear from the words of the noble companion, he used every means possible to achieve that goal—among which was his request to marry Sittalmulk, because he knew of her influence over her brother and because his relations with the 'Alawites would be strengthened by marrying her. He preferred to marry her first so that his marriage would smooth his path to everything else he wanted. But she did not love him, was not loyal to him, and did not believe that his lineage was authentic. Indeed, she thought her brother was not sincere when he said that he accepted the correctness of his supposed ancestry.

However, he saw fit to seek the help of the noble companion, because he knew of the status he enjoyed in the eyes of al-'Adid through his seniority. He had entrusted him with the task and persuaded him of his honorable intentions, so that he trusted and supported him. But the companion was unable to persuade Sittalmulk. He went back that evening regretting the failure of his mission and spent the night thinking about how he could help Hasan achieve his goals.

The following morning he hurried to Hasan in the guesthouse before the caliph could summon him. Hasan was waiting for him eagerly and leapt to welcome him when the servant boy announced his arrival. But as he greeted him, he pretended he had not been expecting him or to be so concerned about the outcome of his visit with the caliph. He first inquired about the caliph's health, and the companion replied, "I left him last night in the best of health."

"I hope the signs of fever have abated, with God's help," said Hasan, "now that the cause has disappeared."

The companion realized what he was alluding to and said, "I hope that the cause will disappear completely and that we can then ensure the disappearance of the original problem."

"The cause will disappear, by God's leave," replied Hasan. "Do you think that I am backtracking in this affair? I am acting in the interests of the Commander of the Faithful, whom I love and respect—not for any ulterior purpose of my own."

The companion felt admiration for his apparent integrity and high principles and became even more embarrassed to tell him what had happened the day before. But Hasan could tell the reason for his discomfort, for he had been expecting the caliph to refuse his request, knowing since his first proposal that Sittalmulk did not want to accept him. He pretended to ignore the companion's uneasiness and gave him a naïve, straightforward look. "I hope that His Majesty the Commander of the Faithful may be confident that from now on he will be free of all evil—that his mind may be at rest and that he may recover his health. Have you persuaded him of that?"

"I have assured him of your resolve, and he believes you are capable of it, but..." said the companion, as he hesitated, fiddling with his beard and unsure how to continue. He was trembling.

Hasan interrupted him, saying, "I would rather you had not spoken to him about the matter we were discussing yesterday—the succession, that is—so that he does not think I attach much importance to this condition. Indeed, I do not consider it a condition, and I do not want to make the restoration of the caliph's real authority dependent on its fulfillment. For me, there are no conditions for saving the Commander of the Faithful. Indeed, it is an honor for me to do so in all circumstances. But when I do so, I can only hope and expect that he would designate me as his successor of his own accord. I can assure you that if he does, I will hasten to refuse, because the responsibilities of the caliphate are so burdensome. I would prefer to be one of the advisers and confidants of the caliph…"

The companion did not wait for him to finish his words but interrupted him, saying, "God bless you. This is what I would have expected of your generous nature, but I did raise this matter with the caliph yesterday…"

"No doubt this was a difficult question for him," said Hasan quickly. "Naturally, because it was foreign to his way of thinking, I would not be surprised if he rejected it. I am a fair man and only speak the truth!"

"No, no, he didn't reject it," said the companion, "but…"

"Did all this take place in a secret session just between the two of you?" asked Hasan.

"No, this was not possible," the companion replied. "Circumstances dictated that we had this conversation while he was in the harem."

"In his sister's presence, I believe?" probed Hasan.

"Yes, that was the case," said the companion.

"She must have been more surprised than he was!" said Hasan. "I don't blame her for that. Nor do I blame her brother. Maybe you mentioned to them something other than the succession…"

As he said that, he stared into the companion's eyes with a probing look. The companion smiled and said, "Yes, I did… I spoke of a subject that my sincere regard for you required me to do." Then he swallowed hard and looked away.

Hasan immediately realized that she had not accepted him. But he decided to hide his failure under a mask of cunning. "I wish she had delayed her reply to this request as well," he said.

The companion was surprised by this wish and said, "Yes, she did hesitate a little… I think that she has delayed her final reply until this crisis has been resolved, or… I'm not sure."

"Tell me frankly, my friend," said Hasan, "She refused, and it may be that her heart is set on someone else. Whatever she wishes should be... I do not blame you, but I blame her brother, the caliph, for he is responsible for his sister's conduct and reputation."

The companion looked at him straight into his eyes as he said unequivocally, "I assure you that the Commander of the Faithful thinks well of you."

Hasan fiddled nervously with his beard as he said, "That's enough! I thought that she was as intelligent as they say, but it appears that she doesn't recognize her own interests. I cannot be blamed for this! I don't mean that I won't continue to serve the Commander of the Faithful loyally, but I see no reason for the refusal. Let me say what is bothering me—even if I speak without the caution normally required. Sittalmulk is not being sought in marriage by someone who is more worthy of her than I am. Unless, that is, her heart is preoccupied with another man—which would be another matter altogether!"

"No, she just said she did not want to get married at all!" revealed the companion.

Hasan laughed as he rose and said, "She doesn't want to get married. That's incredible. She'll find herself compelled to marry someone and regret she did not accept me!"

As Hasan rose, so did the companion, who waited to see what he wanted. "I think I have kept you from joining the Commander of the Faithful, who may need you," he said. "Please assure him of my total devotion to him as his faithful servant. But it is unnecessary to tell him anything about my feelings toward Sittalmulk, who has gone astray! May God forgive her and bring her back to the right path!"

The companion bade him farewell, full of respect and admiration for his high ideals, generous and forgiving nature, loyalty, and strength of resolve. He went back home to await the caliph's command.

Chapter 14

'Isa al-Hikari

As soon as Hasan was alone, he kicked the floor in anger. He was furious. He walked around the room with his hands clasped behind his back, deep in thought. For a time, he calmed himself down by coughing, clearing his throat, rubbing his chin, and adjusting his turban. But then his anger resurfaced. He stopped and started talking to himself, "Al-'Adid refused to make me his successor, but he will see me as caliph. As for his wretched sister, she is still refusing to marry me. Her refusal weighs on me more heavily than his denying me the succession, but she will change her mind when she sees how shrewd I can be, and she will come to me crying in submission. I think she must reckon that I am in love with her and want to marry her because I am intoxicated by her beauty. But I'm not a person with any time for these delusions. My heart has no love for anyone. Love for women is one of those fanciful delusions that distract men from high ideals. I am seeking to do something that her brother, the caliph, is incapable of. I shall arrange for Saladin to be killed but not out of respect for her or for her brother. I will do so to clear the ground for myself. I will kill him and al-'Adid, together with anyone who stands in the way of my path to the caliphate. It is my right, and they have taken it from me!"

He was in such an emotional state that his voice was almost audible, but when he became aware of it, he fell silent. He walked to an inner room and shut the door behind him. "As for that traitor, I will make her suffer the bitterest of torments!" he said, making a threatening gesture with his hand. "I will make her really regret it!" Then he busied himself changing his clothes, busily hatching a scheme in his mind that would anger Sittalmulk first and foremost. When he finished dressing, he ordered that his donkey be brought to him, mounted it, and rode it to where Saladin and his father were staying with his retinue. Among them was an extremely capable man called 'Isa al-Hikari, who was one of Saladin's emirs. Saladin relied on him for his advice and opinions. At first, he had occupied himself with Islamic jurisprudence in Aleppo but had then made contact with His Lordship Asadin, Saladin's uncle, and became his imam, leading him in the five daily prayers. When Asadin traveled to Egypt with Bahadin, they were accompanied by this 'Isa, who was loyal to Saladin. Then, when Asadin died, 'Isa and Bahadin joined forces to install Saladin as vizier, having devised a number of schemes to succeed in their aim. For this reason 'Isa became influential with Saladin and could speak to him about matters that few others could. He was also an 'Alawite by descent and friendly with Hasan. 'Isa treated Hasan gently, thinking that he would need his support to fulfill Saladin's objectives. He treated him with kindness and respect, without Saladin's knowledge, because Hasan scrupulously avoided any interaction with Saladin.

At that time, 'Isa al-Hikari was in the Pearl Guesthouse, involved in discussions with Saladin and advising his father, Najmudin, on ways to facilitate the mission that had brought him to Egypt.

Hasan rode over toward the Pearl Guesthouse. He had no intention of going in, but he knew that al-Hikari frequently visited the nearby House of Science around that time. He expected to come across him on the way and contrived to arrange what would appear to be a chance encounter. This would make it easier to draw him casually into conversation about his desired objective. The House of Science was an institution established by al-Hakim bi-Amr Allah. It had a library that had a rich collection of books, and it became a place for students to come to study or copy many of those books. There were pens, ink, and inkwells. A special budget had been allocated for its operation. Scholars would gather there to argue and debate, and during the time of al-Afdal ibn Amir al-Juyush, it had become a gathering place for contentious and dangerous theological discussions that sometimes bordered on the renunciation of one's faith. So al-Afdal prevented the general public from going there in order to avoid the corruption of orthodox doctrine with conflicting and confusing theories. But it continued to be the repository of a very large number of books on history and religious law. And if any learned person from the elite wanted to consult any of them, he would be given permission. Al-Hikari was one of those who frequented the place.

As Hasan approached the Pearl Guesthouse, he asked one of the servants about al-Hikari and was told that he had gone to the library. So he pointed the mule in that direction, pretending to be going for a different purpose than to meet him. When he reached the door, the doorman, who did not recognize him, stopped him. Rather than identifying himself, he said, "I want to consult some books then go back!"

"That's not permitted, sir," replied the doorman.

"How can it not be permitted?" asked Hasan. "I saw someone go into the building a moment ago!"

"That was the scholar 'Isa al-Hikari," replied the doorman.

"The scholar 'Isa al-Hikari is here?" he asked, feigning surprise.

"Yes," replied the doorman.

"He is my friend," said Hasan. "Please ask him for permission for me to go in to see him."

"Who shall I say you are?" asked the doorman.

"Tell him that Hasan is asking to see him!" replied Hasan.

The doorman went away and returned with 'Isa al-Hikari. When he saw Hasan, he hurried to greet him. Hasan abandoned his mule, and al-Hikari went in with him, apparently happy at this chance meeting. Al-Hikari was wearing a mixture of a soldier's uniform with a *faqih's*[26] turban. When the pair met, Hasan teased him, saying, "You're combining a soldier's uniform with the dress of a religious scholar! Are you a scholar or a soldier at the moment?"

"I am a scholar at my studies at the moment," replied 'Isa.

"I myself have said goodbye to *fiqh*,[27]" said Hasan. "I have come to consult some books for scientific purposes." With that, he walked forward, and 'Isa went in with him, saying, "Please come in! You are probably investigating a linguistic problem?"

"No," replied Hasan. "I don't think that would be helpful now. I am looking into a historical question. I want to study the history of the Seljuks, for they were a strong people with a glorious history!"

---

26 A faqih is a religious scholar. *Editor's Note*

27 Fiqh is religious doctrine. *Editor's Note*

'Isa turned to him and said, "I think you want to investigate the reason for the assassination of Nizam al-Mulk, poor fellow!"

"No," replied Hasan. "He was killed by a member of the Isma'ilis, the supporters of the Supreme Sheikh of the Mountain, wasn't he? But it's not for that that I've come. I want to research the basis of this dynasty!"

"Follow me to the history book archive," replied 'Isa al-Hikari.

Chapter 15

Tughrul Bey

Hasan followed him until he let him into a room full of shelves on which books were arranged according to subject and period. Al-Hikari helped him and collected for him several books on the Seljuk state and the basis for its authority. Hasan took them and began to peruse them, saying, "Help me look for a book with a biography of Tughrul Bey, the founder of the state and a really strong man!"

After searching, al-Hikari found a book with a biography of Tughrul Bey, which he passed to him. Hasan took it, saying, "I think I have distracted you from your own purpose in coming!"

"Not at all!" said al-Hikari. "On the contrary, I'm extremely pleased at this chance encounter because I would like to know the history of this man, the founder of the dynasty that conquered the whole world! Please, sit down!" And he pointed to a pillow on a seat beside him.

Hasan sat down, and al-Hikari sat in front of him. He took another book that Hasan passed on to him and began to turn over the pages, with his eyes fixed on the book that Hasan was reading. He saw him pause at a particular page, which he read and reread, nodding his head in amazement. Then he read the next page and then another, until he finished the book, put it down, and picked up another book. This aroused al-Hikari's curiosity, who was keen to look at the page that Hasan had looked at so intently. He picked up the book, believing he had done so without Hasan noticing. Opening the page, he found that it was a discussion of Tughrul Bey's engagement to the daughter of the 'Abbasid Caliph al-Qa'im bi-Amr Allah in 454 AH (1062 AD) and of how Sultan Tughrul Bey, who was a Turk, asked to marry the daughter of this caliph, which was something no one before him had dared to do. A judge had told the caliph that day that the sultan's aim in effecting such a union was for the caliph's daughter to give him a son with 'Abbasid blood in his veins, on which basis he would be appointed to the caliphate. The caliphate would then pass from the 'Abbasids. The caliph had been disturbed by this request, first finding all kinds of excuses to postpone his response and then imploring the sultan to absolve him from acceding to it. The sultan, however, had insisted on a response, and the caliph was forced to give him his daughter in marriage—though in fact Tughrul Bey died that year, without his wife having borne him any children.

Al-Hikari was reading this, with Hasan pretending to be reading another book while his eyes were stealing glances at al-Hikari. When he realized that he had finished reading that chapter, he raised his eyes to him and said, "Did you see how brave Tughrul Bey was and how he was able to found this dynasty through his wisdom and persistence? If it had not been for this dynasty, neither the ruler of Syria nor the ruler of Iraq, nor others…"

"Yes," replied 'Isa al-Hikari. "He was a man of singular ruthlessness! I am amazed at what I read on this page about his ambitions for the caliphate—something that no one who had not been a Qurayshi, I believe, had ever aspired to!"

Hasan turned to him attentively and said, "'Adid al-Dawla ibn Buwayhid had a similar ambition before. He wanted to give his daughter in marriage to the caliph al-Ta'i'lillah so that she could bear the caliph a son with his blood in his veins, and then he would inherit the caliphate. But he did not succeed. This man made a bigger mistake than that woman. He wanted to marry the caliph's daughter so that her son would inherit 'Abbasid blood. But do you know how the caliph escaped this danger and kept the caliphate for the 'Abbasids?"

"He escaped by chance!" replied al-Hikari.

"Do you think Tughrul Bey's death was an accident?" asked Hasan. "Could his death have been an accident in the wake of the contract obtained by coercion? I have no doubt that they gave him poison to drink. If he had behaved more sensibly, he would have looked after himself, escaped from danger, and his enterprise would not have been wasted."

"And how should he have looked after himself?" asked al-Hikari.

"By not exposing himself to the threat of murder through seeking the caliph's daughter in marriage," replied Hasan. "I mean, if he had sought to marry the caliph's sister or one of his cousins, for example, they would not have guessed his intentions; then, if she bore him a son, he would have had enough 'Abbasid blood in him for him to lay claim to the caliphate. But that Turk was shortsighted!"

Al-Hikari was so obsessed about Saladin's desire to consolidate his power that whenever he read of some historical incident or heard of some important political event, he would apply the lessons to Saladin's situation to see if he could extract from it lessons that could further his interests. When he heard Hasan's words, he realized that Saladin could marry al-'Adid's sister. He had heard of her beauty and devotion, and al-'Adid was surely too weak to deny Saladin's request. In this way, he would become the ruler of the state and found his own dynasty. His face lit up at this idea, and he resolved to speak to Saladin about it that very day. But he did not let on what went on through his mind. He started to busy himself reading other chapters. Meanwhile Hasan continued to appear to be speaking quite abstractly. He soon changed the subject and asked al-Hikari about Najmudin, and whether he was happy with his stay in the Pearl Guesthouse. Al-Hikari gave him a cursory response because he wanted Hasan to leave quickly so that he could pursue his new ideas with Saladin.

After a while, Hasan finally took his leave and bid his friend good-bye. He rushed to the guesthouse on his mule, muttering to himself as he rode back. In fact, he was almost talking to the mule, so happy was he that his plan was taking shape. He had no doubt that al-Hikari would be going at once to see Saladin and urge him to seek the hand of Sittalmulk. He knew for certain that this would fall like a thunderbolt both on her head and her brother's. Al-'Adid would not be able to find any way of refusing such a powerful suitor, unless they were to claim that his sister was already engaged to her cousin—that is, to Hasan himself—in which case he would have achieved his objective in the easiest possible way!

Chapter 16

Sittalmulk

Sittalmulk went to her room, where she was greeted by her personal maid, who helped her undress in preparation for bed. She didn't discuss any of the conversations she had had with her brother, although she would have liked very much to do so. Servants are prone to gossip, for they have nothing important to amuse or occupy them. Their knowledge of the secret events that go on in the houses of their masters, observing them like spectators, leads them to criticize one person one day and praise another the next without much logic or consistency. They love exchanging the latest gossip amongst themselves, each relating what he or she knows of the circumstances of their master. It is rare to find a servant who can keep his master's secrets and protect his reputation. But Yaquta, Sittalmulk's maid and confidante, fell into this rare category.

Yaquta had been brought up in the caliph's house when Sittalmulk was a girl, and she had a special relationship with and concern for her. Sittalmulk had grown up trusting and relying on her, until she made her the repository of her secrets. None of the emotions and feelings that dwelled in her heart were hidden from her maid. This was understandable in the circumstances of a veiled woman of those times, who did not mix with people or find anyone to converse with except for her maid. Yaquta had known, ever since the caliph arrived, that he suffered from an ailment, so she would hide behind a curtain to listen to various conversations, curious as anyone in her position to pick up gossip, as well as wanting to make use of what she learned for the benefit of her mistress. When Sittalmulk came to undress, she hoped to hear her news, but she immediately noticed how extremely anxious she appeared to be.

When Sittalmulk had finished changing her clothes, she sat on her bed, having let down her golden hair and making it flow in a single lock over her back. She gave a deep sigh and looked down, silently. Yaquta noticed what looked like tears glistening in her mistress' eyes, so she stretched herself out at her feet and started to kiss her knees, pretending to know nothing and asking, "What is wrong, my lady? Why are you crying? What is making you cry?"

Sittalmulk raised her eyes, in which tears could be seen. She sighed again and said, "Are you asking me why I am crying, Yaquta? Do you find my sadness strange? My sadness is not strange. What is strange is that I do not spend my whole day crying and lamenting." So saying, she swallowed hard.

Overwhelmed by the condition of her mistress, Yaquta also wanted to cry, but she steeled herself and said, "What has happened, my lady? Has something new happened?"

"Aren't there enough things that have happened that you already know about?" asked Sittalmulk. "You are intelligent, and nothing escapes your notice. Don't you know the situation we face with these Kurds and how they are playing havoc with our dynasty? My brother came to me today, feverish and extremely angry at the state of the caliphate. How can I help crying?"

"There is no harm in crying," replied Yaquta, "but it is useless. Patience and wisdom are more useful, so that God's will may prevail. All things come to an end, and this disaster will also end, by God's will. Only..."

"No, no," she interrupted. "This disaster will only end in death. Who will save us from these Kurds, who have laid their hands on everything, including this palace of ours, which is now guarded by one of their men?" She gulped and wiped away her tears, and then continued, "But all this is trivial, Yaquta, trivial and straightforward by comparison with something else that the noble companion brought to my attention today."

Yaquta craned her neck forward and asked, "And what is that, my lady?"

"He came to us with a mission that he says will save us from this distress, but if it is true, it will plunge us into even worse distress!"

"Could there be anything worse than the present situation?" asked Yaquta.

"Yes," replied Sittalmulk, "if that old and impudent man should be granted the succession after my brother, may God preserve him, things would indeed be worse!"

Yaquta indicated that she had not understood what she meant. Sittalmulk explained in detail the events that had occured and then said, "Let us suppose that that lying nobleman was able to have Saladin murdered. Transferring the succession to him instead of my nephew would in my view be far worse than remaining under the tutelage of Saladin!"

Yaquta showed great concern but said, "I don't share your view, my lady. On the contrary, I think that Hasan's efforts will lead to deliverance, because if he is unable to kill Saladin, nothing will come of it. And if he is succesful, then he will never become caliph, because our caliph, the Commander of the Faithful, is a young man in the prime of life—and may God grant him a long life! In any case, who knows what the future reserves for us?"

Sittalmulk no longer had the patience to listen to these views. She got up quickly, and Yaquta rose with her, waiting to hear her reaction. "But he also put another condition," she said, "and for me death would be far preferable than accepting it!"

Yaquta knew of Hasan's desire to marry her. She indicated that she had understood what she meant and said, "You hate this man very much for no reason. Be patient, my lady, and listen carefully to what I have to say. If we look closely at his demands and conditions, we will not find anything that is so very disturbing. He is a cousin of yours of noble lineage. He is proposing to kill our bitterest enemy and save this dynasty from a danger that no one other than he is able to overcome. If he is granted the succession, then I do not think that you could reject marriage to a man who has saved the dynasty from extinction, particularly with his heritage!" As she said that, she leaned over her and began to kiss her and embrace her in order to calm her down.

Sittalmulk moved away. She quickly turned her face toward a curtain decorated with Arab pictures that was hanging on the wall. She pretended to look at it, but could see nothing, so angry and upset was she. She continued to say nothing. Yaquta thought that she had convinced her and returned to the subject, wrapping her arm round her mistress' neck and saying, "Don't jump to conclusions, my lady! Think about the matter carefully! The whole survival of the dynasty may depend on what you choose to do. In addition, you will find that none of your cousins can do anything similar, so there is no reason to reject him!"

Sittalmulk turned toward her, cutting her off with anger blazing in her eyes. "You say, 'There is no reason to reject him!'"

"Yes," replied Yaquta, "I say that because I really can see no reason. If there is one, tell me! What reason could you have to reject him?"

"My reason is that I cannot bear to set eyes on this hypocrite," said Sittalmulk. "When I see him, my whole body trembles at the sight. May he perish! There is hell in his eyes! When he looks at me, I imagine that Satan is staring from his eyeballs, intent on seizing me! Leave me be, for I cannot bear to think about him!"

Yaquta shook her head and said, "How strange! You hate this man for no reason. I think you do him an injustice. I haven't seen anything that would prompt such a reaction!"

"Can't you see the evil in his face?" asked Sittalmulk. "It is so clear and tangible to me. Stop talking to me about him!"

Yaquta took her by the hand and steered her gently toward the bed, where she could relax.

"Sit down, my lady," said Yaquta, "and I will talk to you as a mother talks to her daughter, even though I may not deserve this honor."

Chapter 17

The Complaint

Sittalmulk sat down and looked into Yaquta's eyes. "You are a young lady in the prime of life," said Yaquta. "God has granted you beauty and intelligence, and you have to marry someone who is your equal and worthy of you. I can see no one more suited than Hasan, who is of impeccable 'Alawite lineage."

Sittalmulk leapt up from her bed. Suddenly she became livid with anger. "Marriage is not necessary for me," she said. "And if it is necessary, then it is not important that my husband should be an 'Alawite." As she said this, she sighed deeply, and her face turned pale. Then her cheeks became suddenly flushed. She averted her eyes from Yaquta in embarassment and buried her face in her hands. Yaquta was surprised by her reactions. She recognized these to be the actions of a girl whose heart was attached to a man she was too embarrassed to mention. She began to speak to her tenderly, clasped her to her breast, and kissed her between her eyes, saying, "Now I understand something that I did not know before. You are in love with another man."

Sittalmulk did not like this sort of plain speaking. She pulled herself away and continued to say nothing, holding her head down. Yaquta followed her, saying, "Perhaps I spoke too freely. Perhaps you found my words painful. Forgive me. But I beg you to trust me. Are my suspicions right? I am with you every hour of every day. I never leave you. Not a single man has access to us, except for your brother and some of his young cousins and your own cousins. So it would be difficult for you to form an attachment with anyone. But I still see the signs of love in your eyes!"

She became more embarrassed and blushed even more. She was on the point of replying but stopped.

"Speak, have no fear," said Yaquta. "Are you in love with someone? If so, let's discuss him!"

"Leave me alone, please," pleaded Sittalmulk. "Let's not discuss this now. It will bring nothing but more sorrow." So saying, she indicated that she wanted to sleep. Yaquta helped her lie down on the bed, spread the cover over her, and began to arrange the sheet and pillow around her, watching her carefully for any sign that she might want to talk. She could then resume the conversation or, alternately, let her sleep.

The conversation had stirred Sittalmulk's grief. She would have liked to share her heart's secrets with her maid, but she was too embarrassed. She thought that her maid would have insisted on continuing the discussion and reaching some conclusion. But now that she saw that she helped her go to bed and respected her desire to be left alone, she felt sorry and started looking for a pretext to resume the discussion. So she pretended to be uncomfortable with the cover, sighed, and turned to Yaquta in a way that touched the depths of her heart. She leaned over her, kneeling beside the bed, and said, "What is wrong, my lady, my dear one? Are you hesitant about confiding some things in me?"

"I am afraid that what you hear may amuse you or that you will make fun of me," she stammered.

"God forbid that I could ever do such a thing," she replied. "Why would I want to?"

"Because I am in love with a man you would never imagine!" she replied. "And if my brother found out about him, he would consider my feelings so incredible he would think I had gone mad! I myself don't..." With that, she fell silent, as she pretended to straighten her hair under her head and lifted up the cover to adjust her hair.

Yaquta became very confused. She didn't understand what she was driving at—or, perhaps, she did but pretended not to so her mistress would tell her more. "I don't understand what you mean, my lady!" she said. "Who is this man that has made such an impression on you? He must be the wonder of the age!"

"Do you really not know?" asked Sittalmulk. "No, you must know very well! You saw him in the palace, just as I did. And you yourself said that you knew no one with a nobler character or who was more valiant or generous. You saw him holding the lock of hair that my brother sent to the ruler of Damascus when he sought help for the women of his palace. My brother did something so humiliating that only this man could wipe it out, by returning my hair to me after saving me from death and redeeming my honor from disgrace."

"You must mean the young Kurd!" exclaimed Yaquta.

"Yes, that is who I mean!" she cried out eagerly. "I mean that noble hero!" And as she said that, she regained her energy and passion, and her eyes lit up.

Yaquta came up to her, smiling. She empathized with her feelings. "Now I understand what you mean," she said. "I know the young man well... I will never forget that day!"

"Do you know his name?" asked Sittalmulk. Her maid looked down and thought for a time, as if she were reaching back into her memory. Then she said, "Yes, I recall his name. But do you know who he is and what his relation is to Saladin, our bitterest enemy—of whose wickedness your brother, the Commander of the Faithful, is always complaining?"

"No, no, I don't know," said Sittalmulk.

"He is one of Saladin's inner circle," said Yaquta. "He does not take a step unless he is beside him."

"So he has been rewarded because of those lofty and valiant deeds," she replied, smiling. "And he has advanced in the eyes of his master. What is his name?" she asked, her eyes sparkling.

"His name is 'Imadin," replied Yaquta. "I have often seen him standing at the door of the Golden Hall, waiting for Saladin when he was with His Majesty, the Commander of the Faithful. Haven't you seen him from the window of your palace?"

"I haven't seen him there," replied Sittalmulk. "But I've seen him more than once standing at the door of this palace, speaking to the learned Bahadin. He never raised his eyes to the windows, and he never turned his head right or left. He seemed not to know anyone in the palace. I

often wished he would look up in the hope that our eyes might meet…
and I might read in his eyes something to show what his feelings were
toward me. All this only increased his attraction to me and the value of
his exploits. Oh, forgive me, forgive me, Yaquta, I have hidden this love
from you for so long, out of shyness and embarrassment, and I actually
found pleasure in keeping it hidden! But now I have revealed it, and that
is that!"

Chapter 18

Love Rules

"My lady, you are in love with 'Imadin, Saladin's guard?" said Yaquta. "How can this be? How did you fall in love after just a single glance? It is so unreal! There are dozens of young men more handsome than he is among your cousins and in your brother's palaces. You have been seeing them for years; they have all yearned for a glance from you, yet you paid no attention to any of them." And she shook her head in amazement.

"You are right, Yaquta," replied Sittalmulk. "I am even more surprised than you are at what has happened after just one glance. But it was really not just a glance. It was an hour that lasted longer than a lifetime. I found myself between life and death. I looked at that young man as I was about to meet face-to-face with God Almighty and be stained with shame. He stretched out his hand and delivered me from both evils at once, so that I imagined he was an angel coming down to me from heaven. And what a noble angel he was!" As she said this, her cheeks blushed with embarrassment, and she lowered her head again.

"So you are in love with 'Imadin!" said Yaquta.

Her eyes had been listless, glistening with tears, and reflecting dejection. But now they lit up, and she smiled. The grief that had become so visible on her face dissipated as she nodded her head to say "yes". Then she quickly raised the bedcover over her head to hide her embarrassment.

Her words surprised Yaquta, who gently pulled the bedcover from her face and said, "Yes, my lady, 'Imadin is an exceptional man, but he is not suitable for Sittalmulk, who is descended from al-Mu'izz li-Din Allah!"

She got up then sat down with her hair loose so that it covered her cheeks and shoulders. "Al-Mu'izz, may God have mercy on him!" she said, giving Yaquta a reproachful look. "Al-Mu'izz only achieved power through his valiant exploits and noble character, and his sons only inherited this vast state. 'Imadin's heroism is no less than his. You know how chivalrous this young man was the day of the slaves' battle— how he made every effort to save me and brought me the lock of hair, although he did not know me. You may have forgotten that, but I will always remember it. I will never forget the day when those two wretched creatures approached me, wanting to carry me off. This stranger saved me with no thought of reward or fear of punishment. He just did it, driven on by his lofty character. It was on account of his character that I fell in love with him, without regard for his origins or lineage." She paused for a moment to lift the hair from her eyes and said, "Don't you remember those two men who were intent on abducting me that day? If you were to learn that they were sons of kings or caliphs, would you be happy to see me marry one of them?"

"God forbid," replied Yaquta, "they have no honor!"

"You should know," replied Sittalmulk, "that I am almost certain one of them is Hasan, the nobleman who covets the caliphate and that you are trying to convince me I should marry. And the other is his servant whose help he sought to abduct me when he realized I did not want to follow him." No sooner had she finished than she regretted her revelation; it seemed to have escaped her almost against her will. She fell silent and cast her head down.

Yaquta was taken aback. "Are you certain of what you are saying, my lady?" she asked.

"I cannot say that I am absolutely certain," replied Sittalmulk. "But I think that I am more than likely to be correct. Be that as it may, what I am absolutely certain of is that ever since I witnessed 'Imadin's behavior, I have felt a very strong attraction to him. I expected to see him again— that he would come to my brother to demand a reward for his action, but he has not done so. This has only increased my admiration for him and the esteem in which I held him in my heart. This admiration and esteem have turned into an intense love." Then she sighed and said, "Do you suppose he has the same feelings toward me?" As she said that, she choked on her words and could no longer hold back her tears. Her maid could still not understand how such a strong attachment could result from a single glance. She started to soothe her, kissing her and saying, "Calm down, my lady! Be rational! Someone like you should not feel so intensely about a person they have only seen a few times, and before knowing whether their feelings are reciprocated. Be lucid, and return to your senses! Suppose you were to find out, while you are so infatuated, that 'Imadin was in love with someone else. How would you feel then? Just think for a moment!"

Sittalmulk pulled herself together and returned to her senses. She said nothing, as she reflected on what her maid had said. She thought that she must be right. But love is a powerful and irrational master; it does not submit to the truth and does not recognize what is right. It likes to act like a tyrant, without reason, and to destroy without being held accountable. Love is only appealing when it acts blindly. If it were subject to rational judgments, logical rules, or economic considerations, it would be a teacher, a religious scholar, or a merchant. But in fact, it is an absolute ruler, unconstrained by any constitution or fear of punishment, whose subjects are not subject to reason but are happy with its tyrannical behavior, accepting its injustices as justice and its harshness as mercy. That was how Sittalmulk felt at that moment. Her mind pointed to the dangers that her behavior could expose her to, but her heart did not want to see it. So she gave way to her emotions while giving Yaquta a look that seemed to acknowledge the wisdom of what she had said. She was confused as she said, "You are right, Yaquta, but I don't think he would do that. No, no, but anyhow, I cannot see any other way—but what do you think?"

Yaquta could not think of an answer. She thought that the conversation had gone on for too long. Surprise had followed surprise that evening in quick succession. She needed time to think on her own, and perhaps she would find a solution that would satisfy her mistress as well as her own conscience. She started to kiss the hands of her mistress, saying, "Calm down, my lady! I am your ever-faithful servant. Relax. You have exhausted yourself today, and it is time to sleep. Lie down in your bed. Let me think about the problem. We have time, and you know that. Your brother—may God preserve him—will not force on you anyone you do not love. I know the high esteem in which he holds you. But you need to devise a way to see 'Imadin. Lie down in your bed, and I will leave you. I will think of you a lot tonight, though I don't think you will think of me!" She laughed at her own comment then said, "Think of who you love!" Sittalmulk found her words comforting. Her dearest wish was that Yaquta should share her views and her heart's feelings with her. This calmed her down and made her feel better. So she cheered up and followed her maid's suggestion. She went to bed, and Yaquta, too, went off to sleep.

Chapter 19

The Jewel Store

Sittalmulk was so disturbed that she spent the rest of the night alternately sleeping and waking up in fits and starts. She awoke the following morning to the muezzin's call to prayer. She was not required to pray, but she could no longer sleep. She began to toss and turn in her bed, as her thoughts wandered. She remembered her brother and was eager to know how he had been after he had left her. Had he recovered? She got up, wrapped herself in a silken shawl to try to keep warm, then went out of her room into a hallway leading to a balcony overlooking the caliph's prayer room. She saw that her brother had gone to pray, and she felt reassured. When she returned to her room, Yaquta met her and asked her how she was. She started to talk to her, trying to amuse her, and went with her to her room, where she helped her dress. She sat with her, saying, "I can reassure you about the health of His Majesty, the Commander of the Faithful, who is well!"

"I deduced that from the fact that he went out to pray," said Sittalmulk, "and I thank God for that. But I would like to see him..."

"You will see him tonight after he returns from the Golden Palace and has discharged his duties with the affairs of state," replied Yaquta. "Let's go eat now!"

She walked across to the dining room. As she was eating, she expected that Yaquta would broach the subject of 'Imadin with her, but she didn't. She was too embarrassed to mention him herself, so she spent half the day occupying herself with different matters. After lunch, she felt an urge to sleep, still tired from her exertions the previous day. She lay down on the bed and slept deeply. When she awoke, her nerves had been soothed, and she felt much less tired. Nervous exhaustion makes a person feel troubled, often leading to depression and seeing only the dark side of things.

She got up, her face bright again, and her smile returned. She clapped her hands to summon her maid, who had been slow to appear. When she arrived, her face clearly showed that she had some news. Sittalmulk's heart beat faster, and she couldn't help asking what was the matter. Yaquta replied, "Nothing's wrong, my lady! Everything's fine! Come on!"

"Where are we going?" she asked, as she jumped up.

"To the jewel store," replied Yaquta.

She turned away, dismayed with what she was hearing, and said, "Where are the jewels? They haven't left me anything in the store!"

"They took a lot but left a lot," replied Yaquta. "But I'm not inviting you because of the jewels, my lady. I want you to go to the store to meet His Majesty, the Commander of the Faithful. He has sent a message asking you to appear before him in the treasury, for what reason I do not know."

"My brother is requesting me to go to meet him there?" she asked anxiously.

"Yes, my lady," replied Yaquta. "But there is no need to change your clothes, because you will reach the palace via a hall that leads to it in privacy where no one can see you. Come on!"

So saying, she signaled for her to move. She wrapped her head in a sky blue wrap and walked on, wondering what could be the motive for such a summons that day.

They left the women's palace and entered a hall that had been cleared by the servants and maids. Sittalmulk walked through it with no one in her path until she came to the jewel store. This was a set of rooms arranged with shelves and cupboards, and couches on velvet carpets. She had not been to these rooms for a long time, but she had heard that they contained valuable collections of precious jewels taken from the conquests of al-Mustansir billah Abi Tamim about a hundred years earlier. But she didn't expect to find there any jewels of any value.

She reached the door, where she was met by the chamberlain, who let her in, motioning to Yaquta that she should leave. As she did so, Sittalmulk went in, her eyes searching for her brother. She saw him sitting by himself on a chair in the middle of the central hall. He was dressed lightly and was wearing a small turban, with a rosary[28] in his hand, counting the beads and deep in thought. When the chamberlain told him that his sister had arrived, he looked up, smiled at her, and started to greet her. But she threw herself on him, asking about his health. "I am in the best of health, thank God!" he replied. "How are you?"

"So long as the Commander of the Faithful is fine, I am fine," she replied. So saying, she detected from his expression there were things he wanted to tell her. But she did not let on. As she sat on a cushion close to him she said, "I have not been in this palace for several years. The last time I came here, I was a child, and I don't recall being aware of what was here."

He interrupted her. "And what might you have been expected to know?" he asked. "It's enough that you have heard what was here before the time of our grandfather Imam al-Mustansir—may God have mercy on him. Look at this chest!"

She looked at it. It was perfectly constructed and decorated. She thought he was drawing her attention to the decorations, so she said, "It's beautiful!"

"No, no, I'm not referring to its outward appearance," replied al-'Adid, "I am referring to the precious stones that were in it. My father—may God have mercy on him!—told me that at the time our grandfather al-Mustansir was defeated, fourteen pounds of emeralds valued at 200,000 dinars per pound were pillaged, which people fought over and seized from one another."

"That is quite unbelievable," she replied, astonished.

"If I wanted to tell you the names of all the precious objects in this palace, just naming them would take several hours. But I will simply mention a jeweled necklace worth 80,000 dinars that was sold for 2,000 dinars on that day. Of the silver and gold rings alone, they took around 1,200 rings, including three square gold rings encrusted with all kinds

---

28 A string of beads often used in prayers by Muslims. *Editor's Note*

of precious stones—one with emeralds, the other with rubies, and the third with garnets. The last three rings were sold for 12,000 dinars. That is apart from other jewels and a multitude of small precious objects that were taken in batches. One batch of jewels originally bought for 700,000 dinars was sold for 20,000 dinars. There was also a golden peacock inlaid with jewels, with eyes of red rubies and feathers of enameled glass inlaid with gold the color of peacock's feathers. Last but not least were the treasures bequeathed to us from the caliphs or taken from the 'Abbasids or others, for example, chess pieces decorated with jewels, gold, silver, and ivory. All this, and hundreds of other things taken during the insurgency of al-Mustansir, of which there is no time to speak of now."

Sittalmulk was saddened on hearing all this. She said, "This disaster happened a long time ago, my brother. There is no point in recalling it now!" She said that, waiting for and suspecting the reason for being summoned by her brother.

"You are right," replied al-'Adid, "but fortunately those thieves did not take everything that was ours. Some of our faithful servants and close retinue were able to remove some of our most valuable treasures during those fateful times, and they have been hidden until this day." So saying, he got up and went over to a cupboard in the wall that would not normally attract attention. He opened it with a key he had in his pocket. He reached out with his hand for a small box containing a dazzling jeweled necklace, which he passed on to her. She stared at it and inspected it as she turned it around in her hands. "Take it, and try it on your neck!" he said. She hesitated and put it back in the box, but he retrieved it and placed it around her neck. "It is yours!" he said.

Once again, she wanted to put it back in its box, but he stopped her from doing so, saying, "Take it! It is not fit for anyone else!" From another box he took out a ring decorated with emeralds and rubies. He placed it on her finger. This sudden generosity jarred Sittalmulk. Her brother noticed her consternation and said, "Don't be surprised by all that you see. These cupboards contain other treasures that no one knows of except me. I will give you all of them, so that they shall not be wasted like the others."

She thought she could detect from his words what he was driving at. "What do you mean, my brother?" she asked. "God forbid that what you are hinting at should come to pass! These treasures shall be enjoyed by no other than yourself and your descendants!" She said that in a voice choking with emotion. As she summoned up all her willpower and tried to continue, she noticed tears glistening in her brother's eyes, as he gave her a pleading look. "So you don't want these treasures to remain ours?" he said.

Chapter 20

Between Two Suitors

Sittalmulk understood he was alluding to her refusal to accept Hasan as her husband, even though he had pledged to arrange Saladin's assassination. She felt a pang of conscience, affected by the way her brother had chosen to rebuke her. But she could not abide by his wishes and did not believe that Hasan could keep his promise. However, this was not the right time to be defensive. "You are rebuking me, my brother, for not doing something that is beyond my power to do," she said. "I promised myself that I would not marry. Let this man meet his commitment to us, then we will see what happens!"

He detected in her answer a possible conditional acceptance. So he pressed on, saying, "What is needed first and foremost is for you to show an acceptance of him so that he can proceed. Isn't that so? How could he embark on such a dangerous deed knowing that he had been rejected?" He was smiling broadly as he said that in his attempt to soften her. On her part, she was almost persuaded, her love for her brother almost convincing her to agree to his appeal. But then a picture of Hasan flashed through her mind, which made her shudder in disgust. She quickly rid herself of this image as she remembered 'Imadin. Her heart leaped with joy, and her cheeks flushed. Her brother took this to mean she wanted to comply with his request but that modesty prevented her from doing so. "How would it harm you to accept my request?" he asked. "This is the most suitable man for you, quite apart from the favors he has promised us. You will be happy with him as your suitor. But if you think that accepting him will be a misfortune, it can only be a very small misfortune." His eyes shone, as if he were finally conceding something he had only admitted to himself for a long time, as he busied himself counting the beads on his rosary.

Sittalmulk bowed her head as she keenly weighed her brother's words. She came to the conclusion that her suspicions might be right. "What do you mean by a very small misfortune, brother?" she asked. "Could there be any bigger misfortune?"

"A bigger misfortune, my sister, would be for a foreigner outside our family to seek your hand and make a proposal we could not refuse. Do you understand?"

"What do you mean?" asked Sittalmulk. "Who would dare make such a proposal?"

"The person who would make such a request," replied al-'Adid, "is the same man who dared appropriate our suzerainty for himself and usurp our power while we are still alive. The same man whose power we fear and whose movements we are so apprehensive about. Couldn't this man make such a proposal? And if he did, how could we deny him what he seeks?"

She was startled, refusing at first to accept what her brother had stated. But then she sought to find out explicitly to whom he was alluding. "Make what you are saying clear," she said. "Do you mean Saladin?"

"Yes, that is who I mean," al-'Adid replied. "What have you to say?"

She hesitated. Her knees were trembling, and her whole body shook. She felt weak and could not keep standing. She sat down on the chair, turning pale, as the blood almost froze in her veins. She said nothing.

Her brother sat beside her. He put his arm around her shoulders to soften the effect of what he had said, then continued, "I shocked you by telling you all this, but you put me in a difficult position. This matter has not yet been completely settled. He has not asked for your hand openly. But one of his confidants came to me this morning and alarmed me by raising the issue after leading up to it with a lot of expansive words. 'Sultan Saladin wants to be honored with such a union,' he said, 'and has chosen to make inquiries of you through me before making a formal proposal, in case there is some impediment.'"

"And what was your reply to him?" asked Sittalmulk.

"I almost told him you were engaged to Hasan, for I knew this to be a strong enough argument that would allow us to avert this calamity.

But I put him off until tomorrow, in order to ask you. And I chose this place to meet with you so we could do so in complete privacy. Now that I have explained everything to you as clearly as can be, what do you think? Is it not better to accept our cousin's proposal?" Al-'Adid was convinced she had no choice but to accept. But when she hesitated and said nothing, he repeated the question.

She herself was thinking of a way to escape from the dilemma she faced. She would have preferred marriage to Saladin to marriage with Hasan. But she preferred 'Imadin to either of them. She was tempted to reveal her inner thoughts, but she was afraid of the consequences. So when her brother repeated the question, she said, "You are right! Arguing that I am already engaged might deflect Saladin from his purpose. Tell him that I am engaged if you like, but do not say to whom!"

"But he won't believe it unless we tell him who the suitor is," replied al-'Adid. "He will think we are lying and will not give up his pursuit!"

She interrupted him. "No, don't tell him; that wouldn't settle the matter!" she said, raising her voice and shouting despite herself.

"Before this dilemma arose, I was polite and kind to you," he replied, the anger clearly visible on his face. "But I can see no sense in your refusal now that I have explained the reason to you. Yours are not the feelings of a sister who loves her brother. You know what Hasan promised us. Now that he knows that Saladin is his rival for your hand, he will pursue his objective with even greater zeal. Tell me you will accept him—otherwise my confidence in your good sense and sincere love for me will falter. You should also know that it is the Commander of the Faithful who is speaking to you and making this demand, and he is your guardian."

Al-'Adid spoke with emotion and, when he came to the last sentence, also with the authority of his position. The threat weighed heavily on her as she was overcome with anger and felt her heart racing in her breast, but her self-esteem would not allow her to accede to her brother's demands. She looked straight into his eyes as she said, "You are threatening me with the authority you have over me and the fact that you are my guardian. But this does not change my resolve in any way. If you want to use your formal authority, then do so, but I cannot accept that hypocritical swindler. I might prefer Saladin to him, if necessary. But really I do not want either of them."

When he heard his sister talk in this way, al-'Adid became furious and said, "Have you grown so bold as to speak to me with such impudence? I think I was wrong to consult you about this. As your guardian, I did not have to do so but have the authority to do whatever is in your best interest. You may think that you can just go out to the market and pick your husband from anyone wandering over there. But that is not the way for a caliph's daughter to behave. Divine providence has set you among the class of caliphs and has given you a distinguished noble heritage. So it is not right for you to marry someone unsuitable. Hasan, our cousin, is the most suitable man for you. But that's enough for now."

As he said that, he prepared to go, as if what he had just said could neither be denied nor brought to closure.

She remained standing but only barely so, feeling she was on the verge of fainting to the floor with emotion. She couldn't reveal her thoughts after hearing her brother's reactions to her preference for Saladin. What if he knew that she actually loved his guard? She thought it would be better to keep quiet in such circumstances, but she resolved to do as she pleased even if it was contrary to law and to custom. When she saw he was preparing to leave, she walked away quietly and calmly, without saying a word. He, on the other hand, believed that his authority had had its effect on her and that she had accepted. But he pretended to be angry and reproachful, concealing his happiness.

As he left, she saw Yaquta waiting for her in the hall. They both went to her room. The maid noticed a marked change in her expression and resolved to find out what had happened.

Sittalmulk, however, had resolved to do something that had not occurred to her maid or to anyone else. She thought it would be better to conceal it so that Yaquta could not prevent her from carrying it out. She had the idea of summoning 'Imadin and fleeing with him from her brother's palace to escape from captivity, but she needed Yaquta in order to look for him and summon him.

Yaquta was afraid of her mistress' anger and, despite the influence that she had over her, she didn't dare question her. She was eager, however, to find out what had happened and decided to do so by feigning ignorance. As soon as she entered the room, she said to her, "I can see that my lady is angry. What has made her angry? I can see a jeweled necklace around her neck and a ring of emeralds and hyacinths around her finger. If they were mine, all the cares of the world would disappear!"

Sittalmulk remembered the necklace and the ring, which she had almost forgotten, so upset was she. She tore the necklace from her neck and the ring from her finger and threw them to the ground. Then she sat down on her bed, sighing.

Yaquta picked up the necklace and the ring, saying, "What's the matter, my lady? What has made you so very angry? If it's this necklace that has upset you, give it to me..."

"Take it, yes, it's yours!" said Sittalmulk, seizing it from her hand and putting it in her pocket with the ring.

Yaquta gave her a teasing smile and said, "If you are angry with the Commander of the Faithful, what fault is it of mine, my lady? I am totally devoted to your service."

She pretended to be soothed by these words and hid her anger. "God bless you," she said. "Leave me now!"

"No, no," said Yaquta. "I won't leave you until you tell me what happened between you and our master, the Commander of the Faithful."

"He may be your master, but he is not mine," replied Sittalmulk.

"He is our master, by God's command, and may God prolong his life!" replied Yaquta.

"God prolong his life, but he..." said Sittalmulk, then stopped and burst into tears.

"Why has your behavior toward me changed?" asked Yaquta. "Why don't you share your concerns with me? I may be able to help you in some way. Weren't we due to look into this business of 'Imadin?"

When she heard the name of 'Imadin, she regained her composure, turned to Yaquta, and smiled, her eyes brimming with tears. The sight affected Yaquta, and she bent down kissing her mistress's hands and saying, "Please don't be angry, my lady! Don't treat me harshly. Tell me what is in your heart: I am your slave and will do anything for you! Tell me. Have no fear!"

She sighed, resigned herself, and said, "Yes, we were due to discuss the question of 'Imadin. What do you think? And what have you arranged?"

"I have no opinion," replied Yaquta. "It is your problem. I am at your service, and whatever you wish, I will do. Just tell me what you would like me to do, and I will fulfill your wish immediately!"

Sittalmulk gave her a look that went straight to the point and said, "I want 'Imadin to come here tonight!"

"Tonight? Why?" asked Yaquta, incredulous.

"Don't ask why!" replied Sittalmulk. "You say that you will fulfill my every wish. I want to see 'Imadin tonight!"

"I will take care of that for you," replied Yaquta. "Relax now, be sensible, and tell me what happened to you today with His Majesty, the Commander of the Faithful."

Now that she felt glad about summoning 'Imadin, she calmed down and sat on the bed. She ordered her maid to sit as well and told her what had happened with her brother from beginning to end. That somewhat affected Yaquta's view. She thought that her mistress had been wrong to resist the caliph, but she didn't dare tell her so directly, so she pretended to share her view, resolving to return to this matter later. She reassured her that she would do what she wanted, then changed the subject and distracted her attention with other things.

Chapter 21

'Imadin

Al-'Adid's conversation with his sister revealed that Saladin had sent an envoy to ask orally for Sittalmulk's hand. In fact, when 'Isa al-Hikari had left the library of the House of Science, he had hurried to meet Saladin alone in a secluded room. He had then turned the conversation straight to persuading Saladin to ask for the caliph's sister's hand using the political arguments already mentioned. Saladin agreed with his views but urged him to wait while he consulted his father; al-Hikari dissuaded him from doing so. He worried that he might try to placate the caliph, which he did not think wise. Al-Hikari reminded Saladin that he had tried to look after his interests ever since he had known him. Yet Saladin noted, "We hold the reins of the state, and we use them as we like. We can appoint and dismiss whom we choose. We have all the wealth and power we need, so why should we covet the caliphate? No one who was not an Arab ever claimed it before us. I am afraid that by asking for too much we may end up being the losers. "

"I am not used to seeing you so weak-willed, my lord," replied al-Hikari. "If a non-Arab has never sought the caliphate, why shouldn't you be the first? Or lay the groundwork for your children to do so through marriage with the caliph's sister? In addition, Sittalmulk is a very beautiful woman, not to speak of her intelligence and her shrewdness. As for the caliphate, if you seek it, and a Qurayshi lineage to the Prophet's tribe were needed, we could devise some noble connection with them. For many of the Qurayshi Companions[29] were dispersed as a result of the conquests, and some of them settled in Kurdish territory. So it may be that your grandfather could be descended from one of them." He said all

---

29 The reference is to the Prophet's companions. *Editor's Note*

this very seriously. Saladin grasped all this but was still nervous about venturing to ask for her hand. When he saw how insistent al-Hikari was, he said to him, "If I have to act on your recommendation, let it come from you by way of a tentative enquiry, without anything in writing from me."

"I will do this on my own initiative," said al-Hikari. "I will speak to the caliph about your wish and see what happens..."

"Very well," replied Saladin.

So, as we saw, al-Hikari went straight to al-'Adid to sound him out on the proposal and inviting him not to give a hasty answer...

After al-Hikari had left him, Saladin remained alone; he pondered over what had passed between them and felt he had been too hasty. He should have spoken frankly to his father before embarking on such an important step. But he put this off, waiting for al-Hikari to come back with an answer. He still felt he had the freedom to act as he saw fit in this matter. After a while, a servant arrived with an invitation to join his father for a meal on the other side of the Pearl Palace.

While they were eating, Najmudin addressed his son Saladin, "Yusuf, I haven't seen you being at all interested in the race tracks. You shouldn't leave your men with nothing to do for so long. Set up some tracks for them so that they can race horses. It will strengthen their bodies, keep them busy, and avoid their concocting any intrigues."

"You are right, father," replied Saladin. "Not a week goes by without our organizing a race, and we promote and reward the winners. Let me try and set up a race for you to see right now. I will choose my most skilled riders." He called 'Imadin, who came quickly; his happiness was apparent on his face, bravery shone in his eyes, and his energy came through in his upright stature and bulging muscles. When Najmudin's eyes fell on him, he felt sympathetic toward him. He scrutinized him for some time, as Saladin ordered him to prepare for a race with some others whom he named. 'Imadin signaled his obedience and left. Saladin turned to his father with a smile of admiration and said, "Father, what is your opinion of this young man?"

"I was about to ask you," replied Najmudin, "because he made a favorable impression on me. I can discern in him valor and loyalty, and I am sure that he will achieve an exalted position among your men."

"But what does it matter to you to see his skill in horse riding and test his praiseworthy character? It is enough that he should be totally devoted to my service. He loves me to excess. If I told him to throw himself in the fire, he would do so!"

"Look after him and promote him!" replied Najmudin.

"I do not let any opportunity to honor him go by," said Saladin. "He is now one of my guards. He deserves to be a high-ranking commander, but he is still young, and his time will come… I am happy that you have seen in him the same qualities as I have seen myself in dealing with him."

"Have you found him a wife?" asked Najmudin.

"I wanted to have him married to a pretty slave girl," replied Saladin, "but he showed little desire to marry."

Najmudin shook his head and said, "Those are the qualities of an ambitious man who seeks and devotes himself totally to achieving lofty goals." He repeated, "Take good care of this young man and promote him!"

While they were talking, they heard the sound of drums heralding the upcoming race. Saladin sat with his father on a couch with a canopy of colored silk over it, in front of the palace, overlooking the race track. The horsemen raced off. 'Imadin was riding a horse adorned in blue that easily stood out from the other horses. The spectators recognized him from a distance, and Najmudin immediately noticed that he was more nimble and skillful than the other horsemen. They played a number of games, raced each other, and had competitions to determine who was most skillful in the use of their spears—but in every game and race, 'Imadin proved superior.

They spent several hours in this way, Saladin sitting with his father under the canopy. Then the horsemen started to assemble to parade in front of the canopy to pay their respects. Saladin praised their skill and spoke to each of them as the occasion demanded, until 'Imadin arrived; Saladin ordered him to dismount and go to his father, and he stood respectfully in front of Najmudin. "I foresee a great future for you, 'Imadin," he said, "and I am pleased that you have secured the admiration of your sultan."

'Imadin bent over and kissed Najmudin's hands. "I am at the service of my lord, the sultan," he said. "I would give my life for him. If it is my destiny to achieve anything of importance, it will be through his beneficence, not because I deserve it."

Najmudin patted him on his back, then took a dagger from his belt and handed it to him, saying, "Keep this dagger as a memento from me."

'Imadin prized this honor from Saladin's father, for he knew that Saladin himself revered him. He bent down to kiss his hands while Saladin was addressing some of the riders. When he had finished, he turned to his father, who was speaking to 'Imadin. He was happy that he was so favorably impressed by that young man and said, "I am pleased that you think so highly of him."

"He is a worthy young man," replied Najmudin. "I think that you should promote him and make him one of your inner circle."

"He is one of my guards, as I told you," said Saladin.

"I would like him to always be with you, day and night," said Najmudin. "You should listen to him as a friend and grant him access to you without him having to ask permission."

Saladin turned to 'Imadin and said, "That is what my father has ordered. From this moment on, you shall not leave me wherever I go." Then he left to go with his father to the palace, with 'Imadin following them. Saladin ordered the palace chief to give 'Imadin a room near his own room. 'Imadin was so grateful that he could find no words to express what was in his heart, but he resolved to devote himself to the service of his master. And indeed, it is a common trait that those who are faithful in their affections and devoted in their actions are often inarticulate and that their feelings are reflected much more through their deeds rather than their words.

Chapter 22

A Strange Affair

They had no important tasks that day. After dinner, everyone went to his room. Najmudin spent several hours in Saladin's room discussing various matters connected with Egypt's relations with Nuradin before retiring to bed.

Saladin spent the night as usual, thinking about Egypt's situation and his own ambitions, until he was overcome by fatigue and fell asleep. The palace lights had been put out, and all the guards were loosening up, except for 'Imadin. Now that Saladin had brought him into his inner circle, he felt that he ought to be as watchful and solicitous as possible for his life. So he spent the night deep in thought, so unsettled that he dreamed that Saladin was calling him. Terrified, he woke up and listened carefully but could hear nothing. So he went back to bed. But he was on tenterhooks, no longer tired as he tossed and turned, sleeping intermittently and lightly. Suddenly he heard footsteps. He leaped up from his bed and listened carefully, but he could hear nothing more. He thought it most likely that he had been having a nightmare, then looked up at the sky and realized that dawn was near. He realized that he could no longer sleep, so he got dressed. At dawn, he went out to check Saladin's room. He saw that it was closed and that everything was quiet, with the guards at the door at usual. So he went back to his room.

A few moments later, he heard a startled Saladin call him loudly and distinctly. He rushed to his room and saw him sitting on his bed in his night clothes, looking badly shaken. Hurrying across, he greeted him. But Saladin, pointing to the pillow beside his head, was screaming, "What is this?" 'Imadin stepped forward and saw a drawn dagger with traces of old blood on it. It had been placed where Saladin's head would lie on the pillow. He jumped and shouted, "Who did this, my lord?"

"I don't know," replied Saladin, "but I woke up just now, and everything was just as you see it now." 'Imadin thought for a moment but then his eyes focused on something at the foot of the bed. It was the sheath belonging to the dagger. He picked it up and looked at it carefully, at a loss to identify its owner. But when he looked more carefully, he saw that there was a note inside it, which he took out and gave to his master. Saladin unfolded it and read it. His eyes registered utter astonishment. Then he passed it to 'Imadin and clapped his hands. A servant came in, and he ordered him to call at once his father, the emir Najmudin.

'Imadin himself read and reread the note then picked up the dagger and examined it several times. "How could anyone come into my room while I am asleep in the palace with the doors shut, without any of the guards noticing?" asked Saladin.

'Imadin felt that the criticism was being directed at him because he was the guard closest to him. This disturbed him so much he began to panic and was about to reply, when Najmudin came in. When he saw them in this state, he took the note and read it. Here is what it said:

From a follower of the Supreme Sheikh of the Isma'ilis to Yusuf Saladin:

You should know, Yusuf, that even if you lock your doors and surround yourself with guards you will not be able to escape punishment. I can see that you have been excessively insolent and have acted arbitrarily and unjustly, and have forgotten the Supreme Sheikh of the Mountain, the leader of the Isma'ilis. If I had wanted to kill you tonight, I would not have spared you. But instead I preferred to let you live and give you a warning to allow you to mend your ways. Do not try to find out who I am, for you will never succeed. I could be your own brother, or your most faithful servant, or your most ferocious guard. Or I could be a thread in your turban or a hair on your head, without your ever knowing it. I merely ask you to observe your limits. Farewell.

Everyone was silent for a moment. Then Najmudin told 'Imadin to close the door, so that they could be by themselves, with no intruders permitted. As he did so, 'Imadin's heart was boiling with anger. Above all, he was furious that this had happened on the first night since he assumed his responsibilities as personal guard. This incident was so painful to him that he became completely tongue-tied, not knowing what to say. Najmudin realized how disturbed he was. So he called him, smiled at him, and said, "Don't be upset and don't be afraid—though I don't think that either you or Yusuf know these people…"

"I do recall that I did learn something about them," replied Saladin. "But which Isma'ilis are these? And what sort of bravery is this? How can they intrude upon me in my bedroom with the guards around me? What they said was true—there was nothing stopping them from killing me!"

'Imadin could contain himself no longer. "Let them be chased away like dogs!" he exclaimed. "They can never do such a thing! They could not touch a single hair of my lord, the sultan! Their accursed leader will be killed!"

Najmudin sat down and ordered 'Imadin to do likewise. "Do you know who this leader is?" he asked.

"No, my Lord," replied 'Imadin. "And whoever he may be…"

Chapter 23

The Isma'ilis

Najmudin interrupted him and said, "Take it easy, young man! Listen to what I am going to tell Yusuf about this tyrant who calls himself the leader of the Isma'ilis, though in reality they are more properly called Assassins."

He turned to address Saladin and said, "What you should know, my son, is this. The Isma'ilis—also known as the Assassins[30]—are a group of Shi'is with a connection to the Fatimid dynasty at its inception that few people know about, which is why I am eager to explain it to you in detail. The Isma'ili creed and that of this dynasty were the same at the time of the conquest. The Fatimid dynasty promoted this ideology, especially the caliph al-Hakim bi-Amr Allah, who revived it and propagated it with the aid of a Persian called Hamza al-Darazi.

"During this period, a Persian by the name of Hasan ibn al-Sabah came to prominence. He had many disputes with Nizam al-Mulk and 'Omar al-Khayyam, which we have no time to discuss now. This Hasan brought together a group of freedom fighters and established his base in Mount Alamut near Qazvin[31] more than a hundred years ago. He used to incite his men to assassinate anyone of high rank that he pleased. Among the people they killed was the Seljuk vizier Nizam al-Mulk, as well as many rulers and military commanders. To fulfill their chief's command, they would murder without knowing who they were murdering—and if they found out, it did not matter to them."

---

30 *Op cit.* Footnote 25.

31 A Persian city located a little over 1,100 kilometers to the northwest of present day Teheran. *Editor's Note*

Saladin was listening attentively to what he heard. "I seem to have heard something of this sort, but I did not believe it," he said. "It is implausible that a man would expose himself to death in this way only to carry out his master's command."

'Imadin interrupted him with eyes blazing. His head seemed to be on fire as he spoke, "No, my lord, it is quite understandable that someone would risk his life for his master, if he loves him and respects him!"

Najmudin could see what he was referring to and said, "God bless you, my son, but people like you are few and far between. Most people would only do that if they wanted something in return for themselves. But these commandos do what they do purely to obey their master. People have differed on how to explain this devotion. Some have said that Hasan used magic to secure their obedience, or fed them hashish, which numbs the intelligence, and for this reason they were known as Assassins, or smokers of hashish. But whatever the reason, the existence of this band of men is a danger to every prominent individual.

"In the time of this Ibn al-Sabah, they were based in Qazvin, a long way away from here. But now they are based in Mount al-Summaq in the province of Aleppo, where they have strongholds and fortresses and propagandists in the region. The group had a long history before it moved to Syria. In short, the leadership passed to two other people after Ibn al-Sabah, and the fourth leader in Alamut, about fifty years ago, was also called Hasan. They glorify him by always adding to his name the phrase, 'May peace be on his memory.' His missionary zeal spread through Syria, after the Franks had conquered it. So the Franks formed an alliance with the Isma'ilis and sought their help against the Muslims in many places, sometimes openly, sometimes covertly. The Frankish king who controlled Aleppo gave them permission to reside in the mountains of al-Summaq not far from the summit of al-Nusayriyya. So they stayed in Banyas,[32] and their leader at that time was called Bahram. During his time, they were able to exterminate a group of kings and commanders in Egypt and Syria, among them the leader of the army in Egypt. It is said that they did so because they claimed he had usurped the authority of the Fatimid caliph al-'Amr. I also heard that subsequently al-'Amr got rid of Bahram and had him killed for some reason that I do not know. He may

32 A town located in present day Syria. *Editor's Note*

have been angered by the murder of the commander in chief, even though his assassination was in his interest. At all events, they paraded Bahram's head through the streets of Cairo. They also killed many Franks on various pretexts, among them Raymond, the master of Tripoli. To this day, they have several fortresses in the mounatins of al- Summaq, including Misyaf, Marqab, 'Aliqah, Rusafah, and others, where they can take refuge. I think that their present leader, Rashidin Sinan ibn Suleiman, originally from Basra, is the worst leader of all. He had served the leader of the Isma'ilis in Alamut and studied science and philosophy. Then he moved to Syria and took up residence in Aleppo. He is lame and was able to win over the common people by a great show of piety and religiosity. For nothing attracts ignorant people as much as religion. I have heard from some of our people there that this Sinan used to sit on a rock to meditate until his body became as rigid as a stone. As his missionaries multiplied, his message to them was that they should cooperate with each other. He succeeded in controlling their minds—whether by cunning or magic I do not know—to such an extent that he got them to merge all their possessions together and share wealth among themselves, including their women and daughters. And then he confiscated all their belongings for his benefit."

"News of all this reached the leader of the Isma'ilis, Muhammad, in the mountains of al-Summaq where he resided, and he summoned Rashidin Sinan. But nothing came of this because he died shortly thereafter, to be succeeded by Rashidin, who became the leader of the sect just a few years ago. I heard all this shortly before I traveled. He now enjoys unlimited authority and undivided power, having surrounded himself with thousands of commandos and propagandists who would give up their lives for him. When he orders one of his disciples to kill an emir or ruler, that man will disguise himself and enter into the service of that emir or ruler as a stableman or servant or guard. He will continuously look for opportunities until one arises, at which point he will plunge his dagger into his heart. Thank God that they did not do so this time, though the threat can be more painful than the actual killing..."

Chapter 24

Volunteering

Saladin was deep in thought as he listened to this account, while 'Imadin watched Najmudin's movements carefully, his ears registering his every word. His generous and impetuous spirit had been aroused and his fervor excited. When Najmudin had finished speaking, he looked at 'Imadin and saw the sparks almost flying from his eyes, though he pretended not to notice.

"We must do something to avoid the menace from this group," said Saladin. "We are not keeping a close enough eye on them."

"Keeping an eye on them will do no good at all," objected 'Imadin. His eyes betrayed his unshakable determination as he added, "We have to eliminate them."

"What do you mean?" asked Najmudin.

"If I am allowed to express a view, I can find a good remedy for this evil so that the leader of this band is killed and his followers dispersed."

"That is too difficult, impossible even," replied Najmudin. "The people are hidden away in their mountain fortresses, and they have spies everywhere. We know now that they even have men in this palace. So how could we possibly reach their leader and kill him?"

"As I said before, my lord, a man who loves his master will devote himself to his service. If this cursed Isma'ili can enter Sultan Saladin's room and do what he did, someone else can go into the Isma'ili leader's room and plunge a dagger into his chest. And even if he is killed as a result, he will have performed a noble duty in saving worthy souls from murder. The sole purpose of this wretched man is to murder prominent people, so devoting one's energies to murdering him is something any honorable man with a noble heart should seek to do."

Najmudin had the feeling that the young man was volunteering to accomplish this mission himself. He was determined to deter him, however, to spare his life, as he believed that such a mission would expose him to mortal danger. "Only a madman would embark on a mission like this," he said. "However, we should not rule out another stratagem: winning them over by promises of wealth. People will often carry out assassinations out of greed, and some men in authority can be persuaded to kill their enemies in exchange for a large sum of money..."

"You are right, my lord," replied 'Imadin. "But it's better to kill their leader and conquer evil at its root."

"No, this is not a realistic suggestion," replied Najmudin. "It would be very hard. And you will not find anyone willing to undertake it once he realizes the danger."

'Imadin pointed to his chest, and his eyes blazed with fervor. "Your servant 'Imadin puts himself forward to undertake this mission immediately," he said. "And I hope that you will not refuse my request."

"God bless you," replied Najmudin. "This is bravery of a sort that is seldom seen. But we need you here!"

"What is the use of my being here?" countered 'Imadin. The first night I was on guard duty, my lord the sultan was almost assassinated. I beg you, in the name of my lord, Sultan Saladin, to give me permission to depart and accomplish this mission, which will be the greatest possible honor for me! I hope that my offer is accepted without any reservations."

Saladin had remained deep in thought during this exchange, trying to fathom why the events he had encountered should have happened on that particular night. But when he heard his own name mentioned, he realized what 'Imadin was saying and answered, "This is a very dangerous mission indeed, and we have need of you here!"

'Imadin replied, "I swear by your life that I will go, so please grant me permission!"

Saladin turned to his father as if to consult him, but Najmudin addressed 'Imadin, "Obey me, and spare yourself this danger!"

"I am an obedient servant," replied 'Imadin. "But I swear on the head of my lord that I shall leave tomorrow morning. My departure must remain a secret to all except the two of you! We can no longer distinguish our friends from our enemies. So no one must know the purpose of my leaving."

"If there is no alternative, then go," said Saladin, "and may God grant you success in your mission. While we were talking about all this, I was thinking for reasons that might explain what happened tonight. I could not find one. But..." He recalled the proposal to Sittalmulk through al-Hikari and thought it possible that this might be the reason for the Isma'ili action. But he found this explanation implausible and said nothing.

His father noticed his hesitation and said, "What is the matter, Yusuf? Say what is going through your mind! You seem to shy away from speaking plainly. As for 'Imadin, who is offering his life for you..."

"No, father," replied Saladin. "But I have been thinking about possible reasons for what happened last night, but I could not find one that made sense—that is why I preferred to say nothing."

"Tell me what went through your mind," implored Najmudin.

"Father, I confess that I made a mistake yesterday morning. I was led to do so because I acted on the spur of the moment following the advice of a dear friend of mine without first consulting you—something I should have done. Now I am paying the penalty for my haste."

"What was that? Tell me," said Najmudin.

"Our friend 'Isa al-Hikari came to me," replied Saladin. "You know how strong is his affection for me and how often he has given me wise advice. He presented me with a proposal that he thought would benefit me greatly. So I paid heed to him. However, I did not commit this proposal to paper, letting matters be handled orally until I could consult with you."

Najmudin could not bear to wait any longer to learn what he was getting at. "What was this proposal?" he asked.

"He put it to me that he should speak to the caliph al-'Adid about his sister Sittalmulk and propose her as a wife for me."

Najmudin's face registered complete surprise. "And did you agree to that?" he asked anxiously.

"I hesitated a lot," replied Saladin, "but I was finally persuaded that he should put this proposal to the caliph verbally as coming from himself."

"You are still meddling in matters that are not the concern of sultans," replied Najmudin. "Why should we be concerned with this man and his relatives? Why should we expose ourselves to the risk of failure? Do you know the girl?"

"I have heard that she is stunningly beautiful," replied Saladin.

'Imadin was listening to this conversation in silence. He knew that they were talking about Sittalmulk. He had seen her on the day of the slaves' massacre, and had, as we know, returned to her the lock of hair. He had thought she was attractive but had not dreamt of winning her over for himself. So when he heard his master's proposal, he felt a mixture of satisfaction and jealousy. He felt pleased that that beautiful girl should belong to his master rather than anyone else, but at the same time he also felt jealous.

Najmudin noticed from the expression on his face that he was deep in thought and asked, "Do you know the girl, 'Imadin?"

"I had a chance to see her," 'Imadin replied, "when she was very agitated. It was the day of the slave massacre, the day when my lord first ordered the naphtha throwers to pour oil on the palace, before ordering them to stop. I was among the group of people that entered the palace. I saw the girl in a terrible situation, from which I rescued her, and I still remember her beautiful face and golden hair. She is certainly suitable for my lord Saladin. Could she expect to find anyone better than him?"

Najmudin, however, spoke with confidence as he asked, "Why should we have anything to do with her? I doubt that Yusuf only acceded to al-Hikari's suggestion because he did not want to embarrass his friend." Then he turned to address Saladin and asked, "And did al-Hikari bring you a reply from the caliph?"

"He spoke to the caliph, but the caliph asked to think the matter over for some time before giving a response," said Saladin. "And we don't know what may..."

Najmudin shook his head and said, "It will not be easy for him to give a positive reply because these wretched people are extremely attached to the last remnants of their authority. I mean, they are attached to their ancestors' glorious past and to the claim that they are descended from the house of the Prophet and that we are not worthy of their daughters because we are not pure Arabs." As he said that, he gave a broad smile. He turned to Saladin and saw that he was deep in thought, having recalled what al-Hikari had said—that if an Arab lineage was essential, he would make one up for him. This was quite apart from his expectation that the caliphate would eventually be his or his children's as a result of such a marriage. So when his father turned to him, he resumed the conversation and said, "Aren't they right to be proud of that noble ancestry?"

"Why not?" replied Najmudin. "That is why I said that they guard it jealously. So how can you hope that a proposal from a Kurd would be accepted?" And he laughed.

Saladin decided to leave matters there and see what the following day might bring. As he started to get up from the couch, he said, "When the caliph's reply comes, we will look at it!" As he rose, the dagger was still lying on the couch. 'Imadin hurried over to him and took it, saying: "Will my lord allow me to take this dagger?"

"Don't you have a dagger?" asked Saladin.

"I do, but"—and he said this with great emphasis—"I want to plunge *this* one into the breast of the tyrant that threatened us with it!"

"Are you still determined to kill him?" asked Saladin, dressing himself.

"I swore by my lord's life that I would kill him if there was no other way to protect my master," replied 'Imadin, "so I hope that you will not try to dissuade me. I beg my master, the emir Najmudin, that he will grant me his blessings and good wishes since I have sworn that the sun will not rise tomorrow before I have left Cairo!"

Najmudin gave 'Imadin a surprised look and smiled at him affectionately. "I am touched to see such valor and jealousy for Yusuf's sake—indeed, for the sake of all Muslims, for this despicable Isma'ili has frightened the whole world of Islam by his crimes and intrigues. If you can kill him, you will be a great emir and a mighty leader, superior to all in this state except for my son, Yusuf."

'Imadin greatly valued this clear promise of a notable reward, which could only strengthen his resolve. At the same time, he was embarrassed and remained silent as Najmudin continued, "But do you know which way to follow and the dangers you will face to accomplish your mission?"

"If I do not at this time," replied 'Imadin. "There is nothing to stop me finding out!"

"Then you should stay here for a few days to prepare yourself," said Najmudin.

"But I swore to leave this palace tonight," replied 'Imadin. "I have been trying to ensure that no one knows where I am heading or what my objective is!"

Saladin had finished dressing and said, "May you be blessed!" Then he turned to his father, who was looking at 'Imadin. "May God grant you success in your mission," he said. "Be brave and confident. And know that if you succeed in your purpose, you will have done a deed that no one else could have done and achieved what no one else could have!"

'Imadin kissed Najmudin's hand then Saladin's, saying, "I ask your permission to make my preparations today. You may not see me before my departure, for I have resolved to leave the country secretly."

"Do as you see fit!" replied Najmudin.

Chapter 25

The Letter

'Imadin left to make the necessary preparations for his journey. His mission, and the great dangers that accompanied it, had begun to appear to him more clearly, but he was determined to see it through, especially after hearing the promise of reward. He spent most of the day in the Pearl Guesthouse preparing for his journey, until he had readied everything he needed and the sun had begun to set. He was alone in his room thinking about his mission when someone knocked on his door. He jumped up, because no one usually knocked on his door at this late hour. He opened the door and saw a Sicilian slave boy, whose clothes and appearance suggested he was one of the caliph's palace servants. He thought it strange, but the boy came in and said, "Am I in the presence of 'Imadin, the knight?"

"Yes, what do you want?" asked 'Imadin.

The boy put his hand into his pocket while indicating to 'Imadin that he should close the door for fear that someone might see him. He took out a bundle, which he passed to him. No sooner had 'Imadin begun to open it than he started shaking all over, for it contained the lock of golden hair that he had returned to Sittalmulk. The surprise was evident on his face, but he steeled himself and began to look at the letter. It was a short note with no signature. Closing the door, he read the note as he paced the room.

To the brave hero 'Imadin...

You should know, sir, that you have saved a noble soul from shame and murder. This soul needs to see you to reward you for what you have done. This has prompted me to send you the token contained in this letter so that you may be certain of the sincerity of my words.

Come to us quickly, for we need you. You were at our service before without our needing to summon you. The bearer of this letter will show you the way…

When he finished reading the letter, he thought he must be dreaming. For a moment he wondered what he should do, as if in a trance. Should he respond to the writer's call when he was on the point of traveling? She had not apologized for appealing to him for help, and when he saw the hair, he felt a compulsion to respond. He recalled how he had been persuaded to take the lock of hair from Damascus to Cairo, where he had given it to its owner to preserve her honor although he did not know her. How, then, could he not go to her when she summoned him?

Meanwhile, the young man was standing there waiting for a reply. He took a step toward 'Imadin, who recovered his composure, turned to the young man, and asked, "What else have you brought me, apart from the letter?"

"That's all I have," he replied. "But I have been ordered to show you the way if you would like."

"How could that be necessary?" asked 'Imadin. "Is there anyone who doesn't know the way to the caliph's palace?"

The young man smiled, lowered his voice, and said, "It's not that the way to the palace is unknown, but the person who wrote this letter is in the women's palace. There is no way for a man to enter, especially since Bahadin Qaraqosh was put in charge of it. It's now more difficult to reach than the nest of a mountain eagle."

"How can one enter it, then?" asked 'Imadin.

"If you are determined to go, I will show you a path that will take you inside the women's palace without anyone noticing you," he replied.

"You must mean disguising myself in a slave girl's dress!" he ventured in astonishment.

"No, that would be of no use! No one can pass through the gate unless the gatekeeper knows his full name."

"How are we to go in the palace, then? Tell me!" asked 'Imadin.

"I know a secret path through underground tunnels between this guesthouse and the caliph's palace that only a few people know," he replied.

"Underground tunnels?" he asked.

"Yes, sir," replied the young man. "When the Fatimid caliphs built their palaces, they wanted their women to have a way of going out to their parks and gardens and to the observatories looking over the banks of the canal. So they constructed underground tunnels, to which there was access from inside the palace and along which the women could walk unveiled until they emerged into the parks. One of these tunnels leads from there to this guesthouse. It is used more than the others because the caliphs liked to stay here on different occasions. Three of them actually died in this guesthouse and were carried back to the palace through the tunnels. They were al-Amir, al-Hafiz, and al-Fa'iz. After that, when people other than the caliphs started to use this guesthouse, the tunnels were neglected. They have been completely forgotten for several years, but I know them, and if you would like me to, I can take you there."

Chapter 26

The Tunnels

'Imadin became very conflicted. He found the existence of these tunnels very odd, and he thought long and hard whether he should respond to the appeal or apologize on the basis that he was about to travel. He looked at the sun through the window in the room and saw that it was about to set. He had to leave Cairo that night, as he had sworn he would, so he called the slave and asked, "How long do we need to reach the palace?"

"Only a few minutes," he replied.

"I will respond to the appeal, then come back quickly and leave," he thought to himself, then turned to the slave and said, "Let's go!"

"Let's wait until sunset, so that we can go under cover of darkness; then no one in the palace will notice us," he replied.

'Imadin thought he might face considerable dangers, but he was too proud to show any fear or uneasiness now that he was committed to killing the Isma'ili leader. "Wait for me outside the guesthouse, then," he said, "and I will meet you there after sunset."

"Very good," replied the young servant. "I will wait for you under the sycamore tree beside the canal. When I see you coming, I will bring you the cloak in which you must wrap yourself on the way to the palace, so that you can enter the harem incognito."

So saying, he departed, leaving 'Imadin in a state of extreme agitation. Left to himself, 'Imadin reread the letter, recalling the first time he had seen the person to whom the lock of hair belonged and what he had heard about her in relation to Saladin. He thought that he might be able to render his master a service by persuading her to accept his master's proposal. When he contemplated that, jealousy stirred in his heart, but he resolved to ignore that feeling in the interest of his master.

When night had fallen, he went out, wearing his lightest clothes and taking his weapons with him. As he drew near to the sycamore tree, he saw a shadow like that of a woman coming toward him. Soon he recognized the slave boy, who had wrapped himself in something that appeared like a shawl. He gave 'Imadin another shawl to wrap around him, and the young servant led him into an orchard. All they could see were the shadows of trees, which stretched out between them and the horizon. They walked on for a time without speaking. Then the young servant turned to 'Imadin and took him by the hand. He led him down into a ditch, where he put his hand into some dry grass, which he thrust aside to reveal a door with a chain on it. Helped by 'Imadin, he took hold of it, and together they opened the door. 'Imadin felt a moist, musty breeze, which he realized must be coming from the tunnel. "Follow me, sir!" said the young servant. "Follow my footsteps!"

He followed him, sensing that he was walking on ground paved with stones. But it was pitch black and the musty smell was becoming more intense the further they walked along the tunnel. 'Imadin began to be afraid he had made a mistake in trusting the young servant. "Are you sure about this path?" he asked.

"Yes," the young servant replied. "That's the way I came to you earlier today."

He was reassured, but said nothing as he walked on, groping for the walls. Then he heard the sound of footsteps above the tunnel. "We are now under the small palace," said the young servant. "After a little while we will pass under the square, after which there is only the caliph's palace, then the women's palace."

When the young servant sensed that they were under the women's palace, he gestured to 'Imadin to stop, which he did. The young servant went forward and lifted up the tunnel gate, and 'Imadin saw a light. After a while he returned and took Imadin by the hand, telling him to make his way out of the tunnel; he climbed several steps and found himself in a room with a lamp in it. He looked at himself and his companion in the light and saw dust and cobwebs on them both. He shook his cloak and looked at the young servant, gesturing with his hand as to what he should do. He was told to take off his cloak as they entered a room furnished in extravagant style. He realized that he was in the caliph's palace. The young servant told him to wait there, then left, leaving him seated with his heart thumping in anticipation of what he might see that night. He remembered coming to this palace not so long ago and how he had seen Sittalmulk. He waited such a long time that he was becoming apprehensive, when the young servant returned with the maid Yaquta. As soon as his eyes fell on her, he recalled that he had seen her before.

Yaquta rushed toward him and greeted him, gesturing to the young servant to leave. When Yaquta was alone with 'Imadin, she said, "We have worn you out, sir, by bringing you here tonight."

"No matter," replied 'Imadin. "I just hope that I have not been summoned because of a serious matter."

She sighed and said, "No, thank God, it's nothing to worry about. Don't you remember seeing me, 'Imadin?"

"Yes, I remember it well," he replied.

"I will never forget your arrival on that critical day," said Yaquta, "nor the generosity and high-mindedness that you showed in saving my lady, Sittalmulk, from the danger of death. She never stops recalling that courageous and virtuous behavior of yours, and she has often expressed the wish to see you, to reward you for what you did, but you have never come back."

"I did not do what I did to reap any reward," replied 'Imadin hastily. "Thanks to my lord, Saladin, I have no need of reward."

"Of course," replied Yaquta. "But rewards are not always given out of need but rather to show the gratitude of the donor toward the recipient. Anyway, that is none of my business; it is a matter between you and her. When the two of you meet, my presence will be superfluous. Isn't that so?"

As she said that, she chuckled. Her eyes and her tone of voice conveyed much that could not be expressed in words, and 'Imadin read a meaning into what he heard that stirred his heart. He could not believe it, for he knew the great distance that separated him from Sittalmulk, who was the caliph's sister, and the "Lady of the Realm"[33] in Egypt. Pretending not to understand what she meant, he asked, "And how is my lady, Sittalmulk? I trust that she is well and in good health!"

"Didn't you receive her letter?" asked Yaquta.

"Of course," replied 'Imadin. "What else would have brought me now?"

"And the lock of hair?" inquired Yaquta.

He stretched out his hand and took it from his pocket. "Here it is!" he said.

"Don't you want to give it back to her as you did last time?" she asked.

"Yes," replied 'Imadin. "I came in response to your invitation because you said that Sittalmulk was calling for me. Does she have an important reason for calling for me?"

"It was her desire to reward you that prompted her," replied Yaquta. "And she told me to give you this necklace." With that, she took out a pearl necklace that 'Imadin had never seen before. He was dumbfounded. She handed him the necklace. He took it but instead of looking at it, he gave it back to her, saying, "Thanks to my lady, but I have no need for this because I did not do what I did in the hope of any reward."

Finding this rejection too much to bear, she replied, "I have been instructed to give you this present, and if you will not accept it, I will summon my mistress to present it to you herself. But please treat her gently, 'Imadin!"

This comment reinforced his earlier reading of what her words really conveyed. So he said nothing, but it heightened his perplexity about his place in this whole confusing situation.

---

33 The literal translation of Sittalmulk is Lady of the Realm. *Editor's note*

Chapter 27

The Meeting

Yaquta left the room, leaving the necklace on the carpet. 'Imadin found himself alone and confused, not knowing what to think or say. Then Yaquta came back with Sittalmulk behind her. She had put on a veil so that only her eyes and a part of her forehead were visible. She had a languid look that made her look very different to 'Imadin than when he last saw her. He stood up for her politely, without speaking. She came forward to him calmly and said, "Sit down, 'Imadin. You have done me a great service preserving my life and honor, so there is no need for you to stand up! Sit down! We have put you to a lot of trouble by summoning you tonight and inconveniencing you, so you have done us a double service!" So saying, she sat down and gestured to him to sit, which he did. Yaquta remained standing and picked up the necklace from the carpet. Handing it over to her mistress, she said, "I gave him this necklace according to your instructions, but he would not accept it!" She took it and asked 'Imadin, "Will you refuse a small gift that I have given you for saving my life?" She stretched out her arm with the necklace in the palm of her hand, expecting him to take it. When he hesitated, Yaquta intervened, "What did I advise you, 'Imadin? Did I not tell you to be gentle with my mistress?"

He looked embarrassed and took the necklace, saying, "I will accept it as a gift but not as a reward." As he did so, his fingertips brushed against the palm of her hand, and it was enough for him to feel a tremor going through her cold hand. As for Sittalmulk, she felt an electrifying tingle pass through her whole body, and her face beamed with pleasure. Yaquta, meanwhile, sat there, saying in a teasing voice, "See, he has accepted it from you when he would not accept it from me…"

'Imadin did not let her finish her sentence, "Because you wanted me to accept it as a reward for a service. But naturally I would not accept it as such. Any service I did was not done for any material gain. And…"

It was Yaquta's turn to interrupt him. "With the hope of what, then? It seems that you had met before that day and…" She stopped midway through her sentence and burst out laughing.

He thought it odd that this maid should hint at some mutual love between them, when he was aware of nothing of the kind. He knew that he found her attractive and liked her but had never dreamt that his feelings were reciprocated. For that reason, he had hardly thought about her, believing that she was not attracted to him and could never belong to him. But when Yaquta strongly hinted otherwise, he was taken aback, his heart skipped a beat, and he let his emotions come to the fore as he began to experience feelings of hope. But he quickly came back to earth as his thoughts were stifled by what he remembered hearing that day about Saladin and his proposal. He blamed himself for being in a situation where he could obstruct the designs of his master—to whom he had pledged his life. He had even begun to think that discussing his relationship with Sittalmulk was tantamount to treachery. And so he decided to avoid the subject at all cost. He feigned ignorance and said, "I did what I did that day out of chivalry. Who could see Sittalmulk surrounded by evil men wanting to harm her and not give his life for her?"

Sittalmulk turned toward him. Her veil was obstructing her, and she was afraid it would interfere with her words, so she pulled it aside and said, "There is no harm in showing you my face, for I owe its continued existence to your virtue and courage. You find it strange that anyone could see me in such danger and not sacrifice his life for me. You should not find it strange, 'Imadin, for there were dozens of people from my tribe and family in the palace, not one of whom came forward to do what you did. You seemed to have had an appointment with destiny… You gave me that lock of hair as a symbol of my virtue that you so valiantly protected. Should I be blamed if I look at you as an angel who came down from heaven to save me? But I do not know how you felt at that moment…"

Her praise was as clear an indication of her strong affection for him as there could be, but 'Imadin could not quite believe it and wanted to remain in a state of denial to avoid any conflicts with his master. "My feelings were that I was in the service of my master Saladin and that we had been ordered to stop throwing oil. Then my eye caught sight of a bottle of oil that had fallen into the living quarters of the palace, and I was certain that we had not thrown it ourselves. I was puzzled by where it had landed. I then saw a rogue, who appeared to have taken advantage of the fact that people in the palace were preoccupied in fending for themselves. He had slipped in like a ravenous wolf, with a band of men who wanted to seize you. I couldn't restrain myself from attacking them, though I did not know that they were after you or that you were Sittalmulk, the caliph's sister. When my eyes caught sight of you and I saw this golden hair, I immediately knew who you were. That lock of hair was in my pocket, so I gave it to you..."

When she heard Saladin's name, she balked, but she wanted to hear the story of the lock of hair, so she asked, "How did this lock of hair come to you?"

He hesitated for a long time before giving an answer—until he feared she might misinterpret his silence. Then he said, "I brought it from Sultan Nuradin's residence in Damascus. But why should we be concerned with that? You asked me how I felt at that moment, and I can tell you that I felt a zeal that drove me uncontrollably as I leaped to ward off those evil creatures, not knowing who they were or who they were attacking. It was not a kindness of mine to Sittalmulk, for I did not know that it was she who was exposed to harm. I just did what I did out of chivalry because it was the right thing to do."

Chapter 28

The Hint

As he was speaking, Sittalmulk looked intently at him, her eyes almost devouring him. When he mentioned chivalry, however, she spoke up assertively, "It was because of this chivalry that I felt as I did toward you and wanted to summon you to show my gratitude."

He was embarrassed to be so complimented, and he explained, "My lady, with all due respect, a man like me does not deserve such praise from the sister of the Commander of the Faithful, because we are mere servants, and it is our duty to do all we can to defend the inhabitants of this glorious palace!"

She interrupted him, saying, "Listen, 'Imadin. You are no servant. No. If you had performed such a chivalrous act for the sake of the caliph's sister, we would have said that you had done so to ingratiate yourself with the Commander of the Faithful. But you were impelled to do it because of your lofty principles, generosity, and chivalry, the likes of which we have seldom seen among the most prominent emirs or caliphs' sons that are known to us. Do not say that you are a slave, God forbid! Your noble actions qualify you to be an emir or a king. And you can soon become one if you so wish..."

Her eyes conveyed an unmistakable message that 'Imadin found impossible to ignore. He was pleased to hear her say he would be an emir, since on that very day he had already almost become one, thanks to the admiration and high esteem he sensed he enjoyed from Najmudin. He recalled the mission he was going to undertake and Najmudin's promise if it succeeded. Sittalmulk's words reinforced what Najmudin had said. He was elated as he repeated to himself what he had heard: "that he had all the qualities of the best of emirs and would soon become one!" Then, suddenly, he realized that a good part of the night had passed, and he began to fear the discussion could drag on for a long time. He had mixed feelings whenever he remembered what he learnt about Saladin's proposal to her brother. He thought that she must have summoned him for something related to this request, for he could not believe that he himself was the object of her affections and admiration. Wanting to confirm what must have appeared obvious, he said, "If I become someone of note, the credit for that will belong to my lady Sittalmulk, because she thought highly of her servant—so much so that his master Sultan Saladin promoted him yesterday to become one of his closest aides."

When she heard Saladin mentioned for the second time, she balked. She felt a tightness in her chest as she remembered what was happening to her because of him. Nor did she want her name linked to his at a time like this when all her attention was directed to 'Imadin. But she was pleased to learn that Saladin had promoted him and said, "There is nothing surprising about your being promoted. You are worthy of more than that. You are an emir and a gentleman, and you will attain a position that Saladin has not reached and will not reach—nor will other sultans and emirs. That is, if you want to..." Then her tongue faltered, and she lost control of herself; she lowered her eyes in a sign of modesty, and her face appeared covered in shame. She fell silent, realizing and regretting that she had said too much. She began to occupy herself by folding the end of the plait of hair that fell over her breast under her veil.

He, however, no longer had any doubt about what she meant. He was dumbfounded and felt as if he were transported by his emotions into another world. He felt a new compassion toward her after hearing her declaration of love for him and learning that she preferred him to Saladin. But he remembered that his master Saladin still wanted to marry her, notwithstanding her reservations. The last thing he wanted to do was to usurp his position, stand in his way, or encroach on his territory, when he owed him so much and was prepared to sacrifice his life for him. He could not prevent himself from getting up, wanting to take his leave, "My lady went too far in her lavish praise for her servant, for I am the creature of my lord the sultan. She needs to know that tonight I am going on a mission on his behalf for which I would not want to be delayed. If I stay here too long..."

She took his hand and sat him down. A sort of regal haughtiness had appeared on her face. In a commanding tone, she said, "No, you are no servant or creature of anyone. As I said before, you are an emir and a gentleman. No, no! You must not leave. I need you! When I asked for your help, do you not remember the impetuous generosity of spirit and sense of honor that impelled you to respond?"

As she held his hand, a tremor passed through his body, and he sat down despite himself. But fearing he would lose control of himself on hearing her words, he tried to get up. "It is this same chivalry," he said, "yes, this same chivalry that is impelling me to go now. I have committed myself to do something that makes it necessary for me to leave, and it concerns my lord Saladin. If my lady can see in me all these noble virtues, while I am Saladin's servant and protégé, how much more would she appreciate the sultan's own virtues as she came to know them."

She did not like this reply and let go of his hand, which she was still holding. She turned her face away, obviously angry. Yaquta, the maid, intervened forcefully, "What is wrong with you, 'Imadin? My lady speaks to you from the east, and you answer her from the west… Do you not understand what she means?"

"Yes, I understand, and I deeply appreciate the high esteem in which she holds me. She has overwhelmed me with her kindness and bounty. But I belong to Saladin, and I am proposing to travel in his service." Then he turned to Sittalmulk and asked, "Why are you upset with me, my lady? I only yearn for your approval."

She appreciated the way in which he rebuked her and turned toward him, a look of reproach in her eyes. But then she confronted him, "Why do you reply on behalf of Saladin when I ask for a reply on your own account? What has he to do with us? Leave him be in his sultanate and don't bring him into our discussion. Don't you understand?"

'Imadin felt totally at a loss. He began shaking as he realized that she did not even want to talk about Saladin. He thought he was losing his mind. Who could be in his shoes and not feel his heart overcome by passionate love? 'Imadin, however, was strong willed, and he respected Saladin greatly. That night, he could only think of the leader of the Isma'ilis and his impending journey—and of nobody and nothing else. He plucked up courage and got up calmly, saying, "I am trying to understand my lady as much as I can, but if I cannot do so fully, it is because I see myself as undeserving of her favors—and see Saladin as deserving them more. I implore you, my lady, not to be distraught. You do not know Saladin, and if you knew him, you would reject 'Imadin completely. Notwithstanding all this, I remain your humble servant, though…"

She interrupted him, moving toward him with a sad smile. The tears glistened in her eyes as she spoke. "Don't say that, but…just say that you will obey my every command."

"I will obey your every command," replied 'Imadin, "but only after I have returned from this journey. I have to travel, and I have sworn that by tomorrow morning I will have left the country. A good part of the night has passed, and I have yet to depart from my palace. Please let me go now!"

"Go now? Where to?" she asked, the surprise visible on her face.

"To the Pearl Guesthouse," replied 'Imadin. "From there I will immediately leave and begin my journey!"

"Your journey?" exclaimed Sittalmulk. "Goodness. Where to?"

"On a mission that concerns my lord the sultan," replied 'Imadin.

She fell silent, not knowing what to say. He was afraid that the conversation might turn in a direction he could not control. He had begun to feel that love was about to overcome his will, though he was determined to keep his promise to Saladin, especially after he had sworn an oath to that effect. "Allow me to go, my lady, and know that I am at your command," he said. "Had it not been for my prior commitment to this journey, I would not have contradicted you but fulfilled your every wish. But I will return safely, God willing. And then you will see that I will do everything I can to fulfill all your desires. And now, I commend you to God."

Chapter 29

The Surprise

As he said that, he stretched out his hand in farewell. But she did not stretch out her own hand, for she wanted to finish the conversation, or perhaps persuade him not to travel. Suddenly, she heard the sound of hurried footsteps outside the door. She looked at Yaquta and saw that she had turned pale. She made ready to get up, but scarcely had she stood when she saw the young servant who had brought 'Imadin come in, with surprise and fear written all over his face. "What is the matter with you?" she cried.

In a trembling voice, he replied, "Professor Bahadin is asking to see you!"

She recoiled on hearing mention of his name and asked, "How? Why? What does he want from us?"

"I stood by to listen for every movement, as ordered by my lady," replied the young servant. "I was looking over the palace from the balcony of the grand hall when I saw a shadowy figure coming toward the palace gate from the outside. I didn't recognize him for he was wrapped in a heavy cloak, as if he had come in disguise. I watched him until he reached the palace gate. He asked to see Professor Bahadin, who came to meet him, and they had a conversation that I didn't fully understand, but I noted that the visitor pressed him to search the interior of the palace. I became certain of that when I saw Professor Bahadin quickly go into the palace, while the other man returned from where he had come. Then I heard Professor Bahadin order one of the eunuchs to go to my lady, so I hurried to inform you."

They were all astonished, wondering what had happened. They remained in silence except for Sittalmulk, who said, "Curse that traitor! I don't know how he found out that 'Imadin had come here and gave us away to the professor."

"Do you think that Bahadin's visit has something to do with 'Imadin?" asked Yaquta.

"Obviously," replied Sittalmulk, "but he will return disappointed."

"Do not be afraid, my lady," said 'Imadin. "I will lay down my life for you. But what has happened?"

"Nothing has happened," replied Sittalmulk. "But I will let you go despite my wishes. That will please you, even though it makes me unhappy." Then she turned to the young servant and said, "Young servant, take 'Imadin back through this tunnel the same way that you brought him in!" Turning to 'Imadin, she added, "I hope you will keep your promise and remember me during your travels. This Bahadin prevented me from continuing our conversation, which we had only just begun. I will leave it to your intelligence and the feelings in your heart to understand all the things that were not said. I hope that my heart through my body language was better able to communicate the emotions I wanted to convey rather than any words. I was in complete distress before summoning you and was hoping that my despair would disappear as soon as you came. But now you are leaving just as this gentleman is arriving, and I have not been able to tell you everything that is in my heart. So all I will say to you, in short, is that I think of you all the time while I am a prisoner in this palace. I wish I could leave it with you this very instant!"

So saying, she burst into tears. Her words made a deep impression on 'Imadin. How could it have been otherwise? Here was a young servant in the prime of life with the noblest and most beautiful woman in Egypt declaring her love for him and inviting him to be by her side. His emotions raged, and he felt he was losing his sanity and forgetting his mission. But he was held back by his innate good character, strength of purpose, and respect for his master. So he stood firm and said nothing. With his demeanor and eyes, however, he unequivocally indicated to her that he would be at her command as soon as he returned. She wanted him to be even more explicit, but the maid intervened with a sigh, saying,

"That's enough, my lady, that's enough! Bahadin is asking to see you. He's insisting on it, and I can't hold him back any longer!" Then she went up to 'Imadin, took his hand, and pulled him out of the room to the tunnel entrance. The young servant was waiting for him, having already opened the gate. They both wrapped themselves in their cloaks and left, closing the gate behind them. Everything looked exactly the way it was before 'Imadin's arrival.

Sittalmulk walked through to the reception room and saw Bahadin waiting for her there. She expressed surprise that he had asked to see her that late at night.

"I have heard that a stranger came into the palace tonight," he said. "Where is he?"

"You are asking me a question that you should be better able to answer than I," she replied, "as you are the one who has the keys to the palace, and the paths and windows are closed to us. So if a stranger is able to come in, it is your responsibility..."

"No one entered through the palace gate," replied Bahadin.

"Then did he descend from heaven?" asked Sittalmulk sarcastically.

"Do not be upset, my lady," replied Bahadin. "I am merely putting the question out of concern for the honor of Sittalmulk, on the orders of the Commander of the Faithful."

In a mocking tone, she laughed scornfully and said, "You are very concerned about the orders of the Commander of the Faithful and his sister's honor! Who told you that men came to see us secretly?"

Bahadin was embarrassed by this reprimand and regretted that he had spoken too hastily. "I did not mean to suggest this was of your doing, my lady. I am merely repeating what I have heard. And I did not hear this from some ignorant or worthless man!"

She interrupted him. "Whoever told you that is a scheming liar," she said. "This is my palace, and you can look for whoever you want here." And with that, she stormed out of the hall to go to her room, with her maid hurrying after her. She was ecstatic at her ability to escape from such a shameful accusation so adroitly.

Chapter 30

The Power of Love

When Yaquta was alone with her mistress in her room, she bent over her and began caressing and kissing her. Sittalmulk said nothing, but her apprehensions had returned, and her spirits plummeted. Pulling herself away, she said, "Leave me now, Yaquta. Leave me now. I feel so miserable and frustrated. Oh dear, why so much misfortune? I had only just seen a possible way to happiness when all the doors were shut in my face and all my paths were blocked..." Then she burst into tears.

Yaquta tried to calm her and said, "Do not deny God's blessings. Are you not convinced that this honorable man loves you? Knowing this is the only thing that matters, and..."

Sittalmulk interrupted her, expressing doubts, "You say that he loves me? Did you understand from his words that he loves me? Did you not see how confused he was? Whenever I told him how I felt toward him, he changed the subject to his master Saladin... He only loves the sultan!"

As she said that, she wiped her eyes with her handkerchief. She was about to continue, but Yaquta forestalled her, "But that love is built on high-mindedness, generosity of spirit, and..."

"What use is it to me if he possesses all these qualities but doesn't love me?" asked Sittalmulk. "What is more, he is about to travel on a mission in his master's service and was not prepared to delay it even for one moment for my sake. I, on the other hand, have forsaken everything for him and exposed myself to the fury of my brother and the rest of my family for his sake. Does that show his love?"

"There is no doubt that he loves you," replied Yaquta. "I could see it in his eyes. But he is an honorable man, and if he makes a promise, he will carry it out. He swore that he would travel tonight, so he doesn't want to break his oath. I can assure you that if we had had more time together, you would have been elated with everything that you would have seen and heard from him. At the beginning of the conversation, he could not believe that you loved him nor could he have dreamt of such bliss. Just as he realized that this was no dream and his emotions began to take hold of him, he started to become responsive to your overtures. But then this eunuch arrived and cut short our conversation with him... but you can be sure that he will come back to you!"

Yaquta's analysis filled Sittalmulk with hope again—for a lover is full of doubts but also quick to believe and ready to hope. So when Yaquta told her he loved her and would come back to her, her face lit up and a smile appeared on her face. She looked closely at her, seeking reassurance that she really believed what she had said. "Really? Are you sure of what you are saying? Does he love me?" she asked. Then she stopped, as if returning to her senses, clasped her cheeks between her hands, and cried out, "Oh, dear, what has happened to me? Who am I? Aren't I Sittalmulk, the determined, intelligent daughter of the Commander of the Faithful, sister of the Commander of the Faithful, offspring of the radiant Fatima, daughter of the Prophet? What has come over me to make me lose all sense of balance and wisdom? My heart has become the captive of a young foreigner of no import, so that I hang on to his every word of love or affection, while my noble cousins are looking for some hint of appreciation and fondness. Oh, how cruel love is and how strong its power!"

Yaquta took these words to suggest she must be returning to her senses and escaping from the pangs of love. "Didn't I tell you, my lady?" she said. "You were happy and contented before..."

Sittalmulk quickly put the palm of her hand over Yaquta's mouth, to stop her talking. "Yet love is a consolation for everything," she said. "It is enough to have seen how I could be swayed by a word from 'Imadin. If he had said it, I would have thought of nothing else. But still, my hope to hear him say it made me forget the palaces, the caliphate, and any noble lineage. It made me forget everything. *That* is love, Yaquta!" she exclaimed. "There is nothing in the world that is more gratifying if it is mutual...God willing...isn't that so?"

Yaquta decided to humor her once more and said, "That is what I said to you, my lady. Trust in God, and be patient! Relief from suffering is at hand..."

Sittalmulk was happy to end the conversation with this promise and started to get ready for bed as Yaquta helped her.

As for 'Imadin, he entered the tunnel reluctantly—he did not want to go back to escape from Bahadin or anyone else, but rather to protect Sittalmulk's honor and proceed with his mission. He walked through the tunnel feeling his way, with the young servant walking in front of him, until they reached the other end at the Pearl Guesthouse and emerged. The young slave returned to the palace, while 'Imadin walked through the trees toward his room. He heard the muezzin giving the call to the dawn prayer and suddenly realized how late he was. He hurried to his room and ordered his horse to be made ready. He was about to leave before sunrise, according to his promise, when he heard Saladin calling him from his room. He hurried to see him sitting on his bed. He bowed down over his hand to kiss it, and Saladin asked him, "Are you setting out on your travels, 'Imadin?"

"Yes, my lord," he replied. "I am a little late, but I will have left Cairo before the sun rises, as I promised."

"I would have liked to have seen you earlier," replied Saladin, "to persuade you not to carry out your mission, for you are setting off on a journey that is not necessary. And we may need you here more than elsewhere."

"I am at your command, my lord," replied 'Imadin. "But I have made all my preparations for leaving, so wish me success. If I succeed, it will be through the blessing of my lord, and if I die, it will be for his sake." So saying, he stood and awaited orders.

"Go under God's protection," replied Saladin, "I do not need to tell you to be brave, for bravery is part of you, but I do want you to try and avoid mortal dangers, for you are precious to us. Go under God's protection..."

He kissed Saladin's hand again on his way out, mounted his horse, and left. A few minutes later, he had left Cairo as he was familiar with all the highways and byways. But when he was alone, his misgivings returned to him as he relived his astonishing and disturbing experiences of the night. As the sun rose, he imagined that it had all been a dream, for he found it incredible to have experienced such admiration and closeness from the leading lady of Egypt. But it was not long before he felt the necklace in his pocket, reassuring himself that all these events had really happened. So let us leave him to his thoughts and return to the people of Cairo.

Chapter 3 1

Al-Hikari and Bahadin

Bahadin had left Sittalmulk, astonished at what he had heard. But he fully expected to find someone in the palace, for Hasan had assured him that there had been a stranger there. He resumed his search all over the palace but couldn't find anyone, so he returned to his room near the palace gate, where he found Hasan waiting for him on tenterhooks. He had been expecting to see him come with 'Imadin in chains, but when he saw him alone, he shouted, "Where's the man?"

Bahadin paid attention to what Hasan wanted because of the influence he knew he enjoyed with the caliph, so he answered him calmly, "I didn't find anyone, Excellency!"

"Extraordinary. How could you not have found him?" replied Hasan. "I'm certain that he came into this palace. And you know him!"

"Who is he?" asked Bahadin.

"'Imadin, Sultan Saladin's guard."

"'Imadin...it doesn't make sense that he should come in here. The lad is one of our men and wouldn't dare come in. And how could he enter and leave the palace without my seeing him? I have been lying awake, being aware of the slightest movements of those who live here, and I hold the key in my hand. And what motive would he have for coming? Your information must be mistaken."

"I am certain, sir," replied Hasan. "'Imadin came into this palace. I don't know his motive. But I heard from one of the palace slaves that the young man knew people in this palace before Bahadin started to impose strict security measures. I heard that he came in on the day of the slave massacre..."

Bahadin thought this odd and said, "Tell me who informed you that he had entered the palace just now?"

"My servant, who knows everyone who comes in," replied Hasan.

"Summon him. Where is he?" replied Bahadin.

When the youth came in, Bahadin recalled that he had been one of the old slaves in the caliphs' palaces. "How is it that you are saying men are coming into this palace?" he asked. "How do you know?"

The slave turned to Hasan and said, "Shall I tell him what I know?"

"Yes, tell him everything!" replied Hasan.

He turned to Bahadin and said, "I know that he came in because I saw him going into the Great Hall."

"You saw him with your own eyes?" he said, raising his voice.

"Yes, sir," replied the slave. "He stayed there with Sittalmulk and her maid for some time."

"Why didn't you tell me?" asked Bahadin.

"I didn't dare, for fear of my lady," replied the slave. "I told my master Hasan so that he could inform you. He is a relative of the Commander of the Faithful, with considerable influence. And that is what he did!"

"This is impossible!" replied Bahadin. "It is impossible for anyone to come into this palace without my knowing. The palace has no other gate, unless someone were to come through the passageway that the caliph uses from the Golden Palace. But this has guards on it to prevent anyone passing. So how could this man have gotten in?"

"My master is new to this palace," replied the slave, "and does not know its ins and outs, or its hallways and tunnels, which include a tunnel linking it to the Pearl Guesthouse. Perhaps 'Imadin came through there."

When he heard the Pearl Guesthouse mentioned, he decided to postpone the investigation and closed the matter by saying, "In any event, there are no strangers in this palace now, and if there is one, he will not be able to escape, and he will receive his due punishment. For my lord the sultan has put me in charge of the palace and has stressed to me that I should protect those who live there. I am grateful to the noble Hasan for his vigilance."

Hasan interrupted him, "I am doing this out of concern for the noble ancestry that links me to the people in this palace. But never mind, the truth will be out!" Then he left, adding, "We have disturbed you tonight unnecessarily."

When Bahadin was alone, he started thinking again, reflecting on what the slave had said about there being hallways and tunnels. After mulling it over, he came to the conclusion that his suspicion was probably right, and he decided to raise the matter with Saladin. As the morning advanced, he rode over to the Pearl Guesthouse, but he decided to go to consult his friend al-Hikari before going in to see Saladin because al-Hikari had had more to do with Saladin lately. At the guesthouse, he inquired after the scholar 'Isa al-Hikari and was told that he was alone in his room. The guards stood up to greet Bahadin and wanted to convey the news of his arrival to Saladin, but he told them not to. Instead, he dismounted from his mule and made for al-Hikari's room in a corner of the orchard. When the scholar heard him coming, he came out and greeted him, for these two friends had worked very closely in the service of Saladin. They had made every effort to help him secure the office of vizier after the death of his uncle, and they spared no effort to protect his interests.

Al-Hikari greeted Bahadin warmly. "What happened?" he asked. "I haven't seen you for a long time. They gave you the job of guarding the women, but you are better suited to leading men!" Then he gestured to him to sit down on a cushion on the carpet.

Bahadin sat down. "Guarding women is far harder than leading an army, because it means guarding women *from* men. But what have you been up to? Have you thought of anything new to serve our great sultan? I cannot mention his name without my heart throbbing with joy!"

Al-Hikari interrupted him, speaking softly, "Especially when we recall that it was thanks to us that he is in his present position."

"Be careful—no one should hear you say that, my friend," Bahadin exclaimed anxiously. "But what are you doing now?"

Al-Hikari laughed and said, "I am busy with something on which I need your help. And if we succeed, we will have the right to be proud of the fine services we will have rendered to Sultan Saladin."

Bahadin craned his neck toward him and asked, "And what can you possibly be doing beyond what we have already done? He is sultan, with absolute authority, and has no ambition beyond that position."

"The sultan can aspire to the caliphate..." replied al-Hikari.

He turned his face away from him contemptuously and said, "There is no point in having an ambition that cannot be fulfilled."

"I have never known you be so hasty in your judgments," replied al-Hikari. "When you hear of the path I have devised, you will change your mind."

"And what might that path be?" asked Bahadin.

"The path of marriage," replied al-Hikari. "I have asked for the hand of Sittalmulk, the caliph's sister, on his behalf. If they marry, their son will acquire a right to the caliphate, and if he has all the authority of the state, it will be enough for him to become caliph, as the Seljuk Tughrul Bey wanted, and..."

Bahadin interrupted him, "I understand your plan, and it is an excellent one, but is the caliph really willing to give his sister in marriage to this Kurdish client?" He laughed and added doubtfully, "I don't think he will agree!"

"If he doesn't agree of his own free will, he can be made to agree," replied al-Hikari. "And he has promised us a reply soon."

"You just reminded me of what I came for, which all this talk of yours had made me forget," said Bahadin. "'Imadin, the sultan's servant, has committed an indiscretion. I don't know whether the sultan knows of it, or what the punishment might be, especially now that I have learned of his intention to wed the princess..."

Al-Hikari interrupted him, "Don't say 'the sultan's servant.' Say 'his friend and personal guard.'"

"When did he attain that position?" inquired Bahadin.

"His lordship Najmudin told me the day before yesterday," replied al-Hikari. "And he is an intelligent and upright man."

"You are right," replied Bahadin. "Najmudin is worthy of being this sultan's father. But where is 'Imadin? I would like to see him to congratulate him and ask him a question."

"He left the guesthouse this morning," said al-Hikari, "on a mission whose purpose no one really knows. But what do you want to ask him?"

Bahadin related to him the events of the previous day in detail. Al-Hikari expressed his doubts about the truth of what he heard, assuring him that 'Imadin had spent the whole night getting ready for his journey and had left the guesthouse at dawn. This confused Bahadin, who became even more mystified, especially after hearing talk of Saladin's proposal to marry the princess. At the same time, he wanted to tell Saladin all he had heard, so he sought al-Hikari's advice. "Leave him be for now," he replied. "Do not tell him, in case that shakes his determination to proceed with the engagement. I want the marriage to happen, because it will shape the future, God willing."

Chapter 32

A Historic Meeting

At this point, with Bahadin about to respond, al-Hikari's servant came in to announce that a messenger from the sultan was at the door.

He came in and when he saw Bahadin there, his face registered surprise. "Professor Bahadin is here?" he said. "I was on my way to see him as well."

"What brings you here?" asked al-Hikari.

"The sultan is requesting the presence of both of you in the hall right now," the servant replied. "And he has ordered me to summon the rest of his entourage. I had resolved to go to the big palace to summon my master in person, but he is here!"

"We are on our way," replied Bahadin. "But what might the reason be for this summons?"

"I do not know, Professor," the servant replied. "But I saw a messenger arrive this morning from Damascus with a letter that he gave to our lord, the sultan. Ever since he received it, he has been looking at it with a new, angry expression on his face. Then he consulted our lord Najmudin, and it appears that they have decided to hold a meeting to discuss something important."

Bahadin gestured to al-Hikari, as if to ask him what he knew of all this. Al-Hikari told the slave to leave and took Bahadin to one side to speak to him in confidence. "I learned about this letter this morning," he said. "The sultan summoned me to show it to me. I then did something for him that you will find very gratifying."

"What was that?" asked Bahadin.

"The letter was from Sultan Nuradin, ruler of Damascus, and it had a very harsh tone…"

"Why?" asked Bahadin.

"Don't you remember that our lord the sultan traveled to Syria this year during the month of Safar[34] to fight the Franks?" replied al-Hikari. "I accompanied him on this journey. After he had stormed the citadel of al-Shuwayk, he headed for Kerak[35] and surrounded it, besieging the Franks who were inside so effectively that they begged for mercy and offered to surrender if he would guarantee their security, which he granted them. They also asked for a reprieve of ten days, which Saladin granted. Sultan Nuradin was in Damascus, and when news reached him of Saladin's actions, he did not know what to do—you know how wary they are of each other and how ambitious Saladin is to secure power in Egypt for himself." He burst out laughing as he said this. But Bahadin interrupted him, "I don't think anyone other than yourself had as much ambition and hopes in this respect. And you were right…but finish what you were saying!"

"Weren't my ambitions justified?" asked al-Hikari. "But no matter. All this has nothing to do with us. When Nuradin heard what Saladin had done in Kerak and realized the Franks had been weakened, he resolved to leave Damascus, seizing the opportunity to fight the Franks, with Saladin pressing them from one side while he himself pressed them from the other, so that their kingdom would be destroyed once and for all. I saw some danger in that for our sultan. After humiliating and subduing the Franks, Nuradin might turn his attention to Saladin, his vizier. And since he naturally commanded more obedience among the people than his vizier, he would have no difficulty in thwarting Saladin's ambitions in Egypt once and for all. Better for Nuradin to carry on fighting the Franks without Saladin's involvement. He needed to take himself out of the way, so that God could bring the matter to a conclusion."

Bahadin interrupted him. "How ingenious!" he said. "And I suppose you put this view to the sultan."

34 Second month of the Islamic calendar—one of the twelve Hijri months. *Editor's Note*

35 Kerak is a city in present-day Jordan that is known for the famous crusader castle, Kerak. The castle is one of the three largest castles in the region, the other two being in Syria. *Editor's Note*

"Somebody did," replied al-Hikari, "and advised him to go back to Egypt on some fabricated excuse. Among other things, he was told, 'If Nuradin enters Frankish territory while they were encircled from both sides—by Nuradin on one side and you on the other—Nuradin would seize the Frankish kingdom. With the Franks out of the way, the possibility of your remaining in Egypt would become tennuous. Nuradin would then be able to have his way with you. He could leave you alone or not—and if he chose to come to Egypt, you would not be able to resist him. So it is in your interest to return to Egypt now."

"So Sultan Saladin returned to Egypt, as you know, and justified his return to Nuradin by claiming internal instability in Egypt. He had heard news of some problems connected with the 'Alawite community, who were determined to seize Egypt. He was afraid that if he stayed away, the 'Alawite would turn on those who had stayed in Egypt and expel them. His excuses were very long and convoluted. It seems that Nuradin did not believe them: he sent him a letter summoning him to come to Damascus at once. I met him this morning; he looked very upset, and he confided in me that he was furious. I tried to restrain him, but I do not think that he listened. So I think that his invitation must have something to do with that letter."

They had by now reached the meeting hall. The guards at the door drew back the curtain for them, and al-Hikari went in, followed by Bahadin. It was a large meeting, bringing together Saladin's inner circle as well as his family, including his father Najmudin, his maternal uncle,[36] and his nephew.[37]

Al-Hikari and Bahadin proffered their greetings, and Saladin responded, saying, "Welcome to the learned sage al-Hikari and to the heroic master, the controller of the palace, Bahadin." He made a gesture to them, and they sat down. Al-Hikari kept his eyes on Saladin. His anger was visible in his eyes, despite the impression he was trying to give of restraint, calmness, and peace of mind.

When everyone was seated, Saladin spoke, "Emirs, family, and friends... The Sultan Nuradin, master of Damascus, has disturbed our

---

36 Shihab al-Din al-Harimi. *Author's Note*

37 Taqi al-din. *Author's Note*

peace with his correspondence, demanding that we go to him without delay. You know how constrained our position is, surrounded by plots and intrigues in a country where everyone is an enemy, watching for the slightest slip or weakness in order to challenge us. When I explained all this as my reason for wanting to remain here, he wrote back threatening to attack us with his cavalry and on foot. You are my men and my family, and what is said to me is as good as if it were said to you. So I did not want to reply before consulting you. So what do you think?"

As Saladin spoke, those present were silent, as if awestruck. If you had delved into what went through their minds, you would have seen that they were all waiting for the others to speak, not wanting to put forward their own view first. Most of their eyes were turned toward Najmudin, Saladin's father, for they knew how prudent, shrewd, and high-minded he was, but he said nothing. Instead, he squatted silently on a high cushion with his head bowed, holding in his hands something that looked like a pen, which he fingered, not trying to hide his uneasiness from those who were looking at him.

Al-Hikari was sitting next to Bahadin. He had the feeling that he ought to speak and bolster Saladin's resolve to stand up to Nuradin. He turned to Bahadin to ask his advice, and Bahadin was about to offer his support, when suddenly Saladin's nephew stood up with the impetuosity of youth and said, "If my uncle the sultan has assembled us to consult us about whether we should support him against Nuradin, he knows that we followed him here to support him to the very end. If Nuradin comes to Egypt, we will ward him off with our swords."

Saladin's face registered pleasure and approval at such boldness. His smile had a great effect on those present, who started besting each other in supporting the young man's view. A great hubbub arose, but Najmudin remained silent. All eyes were fixed on him to see what he would say. Suddenly, he made a gesture with the pen in his hand, indicating that they should wait to hear his views. Everyone pricked up their ears, their eyes fixed on his lips. He gave Saladin's nephew a reproachful look and told him to sit down. Then he rebuked those who had agreed with him. He turned to Saladin and said, "Yusuf, I think that you are seeking something so ambitious that you are incapable of achieving it. I am your father, and here is your maternal uncle, and we love you more than any of the others you see in front of you. By God, if your uncle and I set eyes on the Sultan Nuradin, we would not hesitate to kill for him, and if he ordered us to strike your neck with the sword, we would do so."

"If we feel this way, how do you think the rest of us would react? All the emirs that you see before you would not dare to stay in their saddles if Nuradin confronted them face to face. This land is his; we belong to him and are his proxies here. If he gives an order, we hear and obey... So my view is that you should send him a letter saying, 'I have heard that you wish to enter this province, but what need is there for that? All you need to do is send one of your representatives here to put a collar around my neck and take me to you; there is no one here that will resist.' That is my opinion, my son..."

When they heard this, those present fell silent, mingling together and bemoaning the situation they found themselves in. As for Najmudin, as soon as he had finished speaking, he got up and left. Then the emirs all rose and dispersed, including 'Isa al-Hikari, who took Bahadin by the hand and led him out to a secluded place. "What is this?" asked Bahadin. "I have never known Najmudin to be so cowardly or weak-willed. Good God, I nearly stood up to oppose him!"

Al-Hikari laughed and said, "You are mistaken, Professor! There is no one here more strong-willed or braver, but he is also wise and intelligent. I could read his thoughts while he was silent, stealing glances at those present while they were speaking. He had noticed the fury in their speeches and was afraid to support what they said lest his strategy be undermined. If you want to confirm that, follow me, for I can see him going to Saladin's room alone."

Bahadin followed him until they were close to the room. Najmudin noticed them and asked them to enter. They did so and closed the door behind them. Saladin was about to berate his father for what he had heard him say, but Najmudin turned to al-Hikari and said, "You are a wise man and a wise administrator. Yusuf has told me how you made plans with Professor Bahadin to advance his interests. So I am not afraid to express my opinion in front of you." He turned to Saladin and said, "What reason did you have for doing this, Yusuf? Don't you realize that if Nuradin hears of our resolve to resist him and fight him, he will launch an attack on us, and we will not be able to beat him? But if he hears our assurance that we are at his service, he will leave us alone and worry about other things, while fate works its course." Turning to al-Hikari and Bahadin, he added, eyes blazing, "Good God, if Nuradin wanted a single cane of sugar from Egypt, I would fight him until I had either stopped him or else been killed!"

Saladin rose to kiss his father's hand and said, "You are right, father! What you have said is wise and the right course of action. That is what I shall do, by God's leave. How much we need your advice and guidance!"

Al-Hikari turned to Bahadin with an expression that seemed to say, "Didn't I tell you so?" while Bahadin bent over Najmudin's hand to kiss it, saying, "May God never deprive us of your wise counsel, my lord!" Before dispersing, they heard the call to prayer. They went to pray and then on to lunch.

Chapter 33

The Fox

Hasan had returned empty-handed, having failed both to apprehend 'Imadin or to rouse Sittalmulk to anger. He decided to inform the caliph of what he knew, in a way that would allow him to fulfill his objective. He held on until daybreak on Monday, one of the two days of each week on which the caliph held a public audience, the other one being Thursday. Hasan was therefore forced to wait for the meeting until the following day and spent the day hatching plots and devising stratagems. The following morning, he went early to the noble companion's house, greeted him, and inquired about the caliph. "He is sick," he was told. "In fact, his illness took such a turn for the worse yesterday that we were concerned about him..."

Hasan interrupted him, saying, "It seems that he suffered a setback when he heard the news about the women's palace."

The companion didn't understand what he meant and replied, "What happened?" before inviting him to enter.

He explained that he had made a mistake in being so open and that he wanted to be discreet in order to preserve the honor of the caliph's sister. "Nothing has happened," he said, swallowing hard, as he handed the mule's bridle to the groom and walked with the companion to the reception hall. But the companion would not be put off and asked, "How can nothing have happened, when you said that it *had* happened? Tell me, don't hide anything from me! I won't tell the caliph about it if you want me to keep it to myself!"

He sat down, pretending to make light of the whole matter. "This is not the time to be discussing what might upset the caliph," he said.

"What concerns me is that he should get better. What has happened to him? May God preserve him from any harm..."

"He has been indisposed since the fever struck him on the day of the meeting," replied the companion. "Yesterday morning, which was the day for his public audience, he did not appear, so I inquired about him and was told that he had spent the day in the women's palace. Then, in the afternoon, I discovered that the fever had attacked him again, more violently."

Hasan expressed his extreme concern and, with his eyes fixed on the carpet, asked, "He spent yesterday in the women's palace? And was struck by fever in the afternoon? Then my initial suspicion must have been correct!"

"And what was it?" inquired the companion. "Tell me, Hasan. I have never known you to hide anything from me! Tell me what happened in the women's palace!"

"I don't want this news to become common knowledge," replied Hasan, "to preserve the honor of the people in the palace. But I heard that a stranger entered the palace on the evening of the day before yesterday and spent most of the night there. When I heard about it, I hurried to the palace superintendent, Bahadin, and asked him to arrest the man. But he had fled through the tunnels. What do you think? Could it be fantasy?"

The companion was dumbstruck. He did not believe what he heard, for he knew that no one would dare to encroach on the honor of the caliph, and it was incomprehensible that anyone could have entered the palace when it was surrounded by guards. Then again, the caliph's sister was certainly not one to come under this sort of suspicion. His reluctance to believe the story was noticed by Hasan, who forestalled him, saying, "I can see that you are deep in thought, as if you don't believe what I am saying. You have the right to doubt me. But this lady, who claims that she doesn't want to marry to escape from me, is romantically attracted to a young foreigner, a Kurd, one of our enemies!"

"A Kurd? What do you mean?" asked the companion.

Hasan answered calmly, pretending almost to be pained, "And a Kurdish slave at that!"

The companion clapped his hands together and shouted, "What a scandal! What will become of the Commander of the Faithful if he hears this news? But…"

"And who will dare give him this news?" inquired Hasan. "He must not hear it. Or perhaps he has heard it and kept it under wraps, and that is why the fever has struck him! I am very sorry to have told you about it, but what was I to do? We will have to find some means of saving our honor from this disgrace!"

The companion was perturbed by what he had heard, which he now believed to be true. He was a good-natured soul; tears of anger filled his eyes—quite apart from his distress over the caliph's illness. He had been standing through the whole conversation, but now he sat down, exhausted. Hasan began to make a show of consoling him, preparing him mentally for a ploy to achieve his objective, and said, "It is right for us to cry today, so let us cry, my friend, let us cry!" Then he himself started to cry, so that the companion forgot his own grief and started to console Hasan, saying, "We have to be patient. Crying will do us no good. We have to devise a plan."

Hasan hurriedly wiped away his tears, wanting to appear serious and concerned. He turned to the companion and said, "Yes, we have to devise a plan, but the problem is more serious than you think, my friend."

"Could there be anything more serious than this?" the companion asked.

"The problem is serious enough in itself, as you know," replied Hasan. "But I am thinking of the future, trying to anticipate what fate may bring that we have not taken into account…"

The companion remained silent, deep in thought, and did not reply. But his chain of thought was broken by Hasan's next question, "Who is the Commander of the Faithful's doctor?"

"His doctor is Sheikh al-Sadid, the chief doctor," replied the companion. "He has confidence in him because of his vast knowledge and long experience."

"Sheikh al-Sadid?" asked Hasan. "Is he experienced in the art of medicine?"

"Of course!" replied the companion. "He held this position with the Fatimid caliphs, from the time of al-Amir—may God have mercy on him—when he was still young. His father was a doctor before him, and he later inherited the post. He has continued to treat the caliphs until today, though he is now an aged sheikh."

"And what has he to say about His Majesty's illness? Have you asked him?" inquired Hasan.

"I asked him, but he did not give me a clear answer," replied the companion.

"I am afraid of doctors' replies when they are not clear," said Hasan. "When they fear that their patients may be dying, they make their diagnoses ambiguous."

When he heard mention of death, the companion backed away, for he loved al-'Adid. "God forbid that Caliph al-'Adid should come to any harm!" he exclaimed.

"God forbid that any evil should emanate from my mouth or pass through my mind concerning our caliph," replied Hasan. "If anything has been fated for the Commander of the Faithful, then I ask God that he sacrifice my own life rather than inflict the slightest harm on our caliph. But an intelligent man thinks of everything before it happens, especially when it concerns the caliphate, for the caliph is a pivot around whom the affairs of state revolve, and men's lives depend on him. A calamity afflicting him is different from one afflicting anyone else. That is what I meant when I said that the problem is more serious than you think. Do you understand?"

The companion understood him to be asking what would be the state of the nation after al-'Adid died. "I understand, my son," he told him. "The matter is serious, but..."

Sly as a fox, Hasan quickly intervened. "We are all the prisoners of death, my friend," he said. "It may be that Caliph al-'Adid will live longer than any of us. I pray to God that he will hasten my own death while the caliph still lives."

As his eyes filled with tears, the companion was moved and said, "That is what we all hope for, and especially because our caliph—may God preserve him—is our only refuge. He has suffered during his caliphate from those Kurds as no one else has. I hate to think what we might have become were it not for his wisdom and resolve."

Hasan sat up straight, as if he had thought of something important, and said, "This is what has been going through my mind and has been on the tip of my tongue, though I could not bring myself to mention it: what will happen if our wish comes to pass and we die before him? If there were a man of resolve in al-'Adid's family to succeed him, then all would be well. But they are all children, as you know. And the burdens of this position cannot be borne except by someone of experience like yourself. How I wish you could influence this matter!"

The companion thought that this was excessive praise and started to deny he was deserving of any such thing. "I am a mere servant, a mere slave," he replied, "and do not deserve to have such a lofty role. Only someone like yourself, Hasan, could have such an ambition!"

Hasan began shaking his head in mock horror and said, "Me? Yes, I used to want this position, as you know, and you told me that the caliph was happy for me to be his successor. But I would be very hesitant to accept."

"You should not hesitate," replied the companion, "because your acceptance would save this dynasty."

He had now found a way to use the companion to witness that al-'Adid had promised him the succession. "Suppose that I was prepared to do so. Would people believe that al-'Adid had acknowledged me as his successor?"

"Yes, I could swear that that was true," replied the companion. "He had effectively accepted in accordance with the usual conditions we know of—even if he had postponed his decision temporarily, as I took up various other matters with him that distracted him from this question."

Hasan's heart jumped for joy when he heard this promise, and he resumed his deceptive tack. "I know that when someone like you testifies," he said, "his testimony is worthier than a binding treaty. But what has this got to do with us now? I hope that the need for your testimony will not come to pass, but that His Majesty the caliph will recover his health and that we will enjoy the sight of him, and kiss his hands, and pray behind him!"

"God willing, it shall be so!" replied the companion.

While they were talking, they heard the sound of hurried footsteps. A slave came in whom they recognized as one of the palace staff. They both jumped as the companion asked, "Why are you here?"

With a trembling voice, he replied, "My lord the caliph wants to see you now urgently!"

"How is he?" asked the companion.

"I don't know," replied the young servant. "But I saw Sheikh al-Sadid and a lot of other doctors with him."

The companion rose, saying, "It seems that his illness has deteriorated."

"You will have to go and see him now," said Hasan. "If I felt that I could be of use to him, I would accompany you. But I will try to calm down and go to the mosque to pray for his recovery." And so saying, he left the companion to ready himself to ride over to the caliph.

Chapter 34

Intrigue

Hasan returned home on his mule, retired alone to his room, and started to think of a way to secure his objectives. He was sure that the caliph's end was near. But he pondered how to smooth the path to succeed him, knowing that the testimony of the companion would not be sufficient and that Saladin would have the final word. If he gave his support to a candidate for the caliphate, that person would secure it. He sat in his room on a chair with the door locked and started to think how best to achieve his goal. After concentrating on the question for a full hour—without moving either his head or hands, but only his eyes and lips—he leaped up and clapped his hands. His servant appeared immediately and was told, "Saddle my mule!"

"It is still saddled, Excellency!" the young servant replied.

So he mounted his mule and set off for his friend 'Isa al-Hikari, who was in his usual room, looking at some books on *fiqh*.[38] When his servant announced the arrival of Hasan, he hurried to receive him cordially, for he had expected to be summoned to arrange some affairs for Saladin.

Hasan began by speaking of jurisprudence and history as if he were continuing the conversation they had had when they met in the library. "I see that you are still researching some books," he said. "Are you finding anything useful in them?"

"Of course," he replied. "Someone like you should not be asking such a question, sir!"

---

38 Religious doctrine or jurisprudence. *Editor's Note*

"You are right," replied Hasan. "But I'm not referring to the safeguarding of legal rights or legal doctrine. I mean practical usefulness that people can apply to their actions. Or are you, like me, only concerned with knowledge for its own sake?"

"I seek knowledge for its own sake," replied al-Hikari, "but the wise man may also derive practical lessons from such knowledge."

Hasan realized he was alluding to what al-Hikari had deduced from perusing the history of Tughrul Bey, giving him the idea of suggesting to Saladin that he should propose to marry the caliph's sister, as was recounted earlier. To achieve his goal, he resorted to praise and flattery. "You are wise and intelligent," he said, "and I know how devoted you are to the service of Sultan Saladin. Wasn't it you who advised him to propose to the caliph's sister? Don't deny it!"

Al-Hikari wanted to appear humble and not accept the credit for this, so he said, "I don't have that much influence, Hasan!"

"For all your refusal to accept the responsibility," replied Hasan, "I still believe that your word carries a lot of weight. But do you know why I have come to you at this time?"

"No," replied al-Hikari.

"I have come to talk to you about a most important matter. If you can realize its significance and act on it, you can perform a most valuable service for your master—although it will also be a service to yourself and your friend Hasan."

He leaned forward and said, "God bless all good initiatives. Now tell me what you want!"

"Do you realize that Caliph al-'Adid is on his death bed?" he asked.

"I know that he is gravely ill," replied al-Hikari. "Has his illness taken a turn for the worse?"

"He is as ill as anyone can be," replied Hasan. "If he dies, the caliphate will pass on to his legitimate successor. And you well know that the heir to the caliphate is a stubborn adolescent who does not recognize or appreciate the value of seasoned and wise men."

"What value do you mean?" al-Hikari asked.

"Listen," replied Hasan. "I will let you in on a secret that is important for you to know. Al-'Adid will die tonight or tomorrow. I know the merits of Sultan Saladin better than any of his family. I am not saying that I want him to take things over and take them out of our hands; and, in any case, even if I did say that to you, you would not believe me. But I know that resisting the dominant power is of no use. But if the caliphate passes on to the designated heir, whose immaturity is well known, it will lead to unrest. I know his ideas, and I know that he wants to stir up the Shi'a and incite them to resist the sultan and his forces. This will help neither side. I will not hide from you the fact that al-'Adid was determined to entrust the succession to me, and he did so through the noble companion. He was about to write a binding document but was prevented from doing so by illness. I am afraid that if he dies during his present illness, his supporters and his family will deny me the succession. But if you support me and entrust me with the succession, I will be ever grateful to you and reward you accordingly. I hope that you understand what I am driving at—I think that our old friendship is such that you can trust me and everything I am saying."

Al-Hikari listened intently to Hasan's words and turned them over in his mind. When Hasan paused at this point, he asked, "And then?"

"I mean that, if that view is presented to Sultan Saladin, he will be grateful to you, and you will be the winner in every respect. What I am proposing to you is of great importance. Saladin, you, and I will benefit from all this. So what do you say?"

Al-Hikari could see that what Hasan was saying made sense. He realized that to do what Hasan wanted would amount to treachery towards the caliph's family. But he looked at it from the point of view of the sultan's interests: if they helped this traitor to take over the caliphate, it would help them to achieve their objectives because it would make it easier for them to remove him later if they so desired. In addition, it would be easier for Saladin to wed Sittalmulk through him, so his plan would be complete. He gave Hasan a searching look and said, "You are embarking on an important action that will benefit you greatly."

"I don't deny that," replied Hasan. "But I am serving the interests of Sultan Saladin as well in all respects. If you do not listen to me, you will all suffer, because the hearts of the Egyptians are with their caliphs, as you well know. Show me your ability to bring this matter to fulfillment, and you can be sure you will enjoy a most favored position!"

"I will certainly do that for you," replied al-Hikari. "I will do everything in my power in this respect, and we will see what transpires."

Hasan started to get up, saying, "I am leaving. We will meet tomorrow. There is no need for me to warn you that everything we have said should remain in the utmost secrecy between us, unknown to anyone else."

"No, there is no need for you to tell me," replied al-Hikari.

Chapter 35

Hasan and Bahadin

Hasan rose, got on his mule, and went back, while al-Hikari remained standing for some time, turning over in his mind what he had heard. He could see the advantages of moving, so he set out to do so quickly. He went to see Saladin at the Pearl Guesthouse and found him sitting with his father on the balcony overlooking the canal. He asked to come in, and Najmudin invited him to sit down. He tried to do so calmly and project the image of a man in control of himself. But his inner excitement did not escape Saladin's notice, as his excitement could almost be seen in his eyes.

"What is the matter, 'Isa?" asked Saladin.

"My lord, I have come on important business," al-Hikari replied.

"Everything you bring with you is both important and beneficial," replied Saladin. "I will never forget what you have done for us. What do you have to say?"

He began to relate to him the conversation he had with Hasan from beginning to end. Saladin's interest was apparent in his eyes, increasing as the story unfolded. When he had finished speaking, Saladin's eyes lit up, and he looked at his father as if seeking his reaction. Najmudin had been listening closely to al-Hikari's words, weighing them and considering them carefully. When Saladin looked at him, he said, "It is an attractive idea, but it is a long way from fulfillment, for al-'Adid is still alive. If he dies, we will then consider the matter. God bless your resolve, 'Isa!" And he fell silent.

Al-Hikari understood that he was being asked to leave so that Saladin and his father could discuss the matter privately. So he excused himself and departed.

When Najmudin was alone with his son, he looked into his eyes, trying to elicit his thoughts, but Saladin merely asked, "What is my father's view of what he has just heard?"

"It is I who is asking you for your opinion," replied Najmudin.

"I see an opportunity that should not be lost," replied Saladin. "I do not deny that it is treachery on the part of Hasan, but it is in our interest. If we engineer his accession to the caliphate, our influence will increase as a result of our intervention, and he will become a tool in our hands."

Najmudin gave him an incredulous smile, appearing to dismiss what his son had said with a wave of his hand, "Yusuf, you are a man of decisive action and courage, but you still lack experience and guile. We gathered from this man's treacherous talk that if the caliph dies, the people will quarrel and fight among themselves. This is an opportunity to put an end to this caliphate at its root and severe all its branches. We should swear allegiance to neither party, but rather take possession of the palaces and imprison the male occupants with any claim to the caliphate until they perish. We have invoked the name of the 'Abbasid caliph in our mosques for some time. We need firmness and resolve, and that will bring the matter to the desired conclusion. Isn't that better than swearing allegiance to a new caliph and resurrecting all the troubles we had once again?"

Saladin had a high regard for his father's views and immediately saw how right they were. He was embarrassed not to have assessed the situation correctly and resolved to do as his father suggested. "God bless you, father!" he exclaimed. "You are so wise and prudent!"

"That is not enough," replied Najmudin. "We must prepare ourselves immediately and put the soldiers on alert to attack the palaces as soon as that ill-fated caliph takes his last breath. I beg you to conceal everything I am saying from all and sundry, until the time comes for action. And be careful not to do as you did yesterday and reveal your private thoughts in open assembly. Remember the proverb: 'Concealment helps to fulfill one's aims.'"

Saladin bowed his head in obedience and admiration and was about to kiss Najmudin's hand in acknowledgment of his wisdom and influence, but Najmudin pulled his hand away and said, "I hope that you will derive some benefit from what I say, my son. You will be a great sultan, so act with deliberation and prudence, and heed the advice of your father."

* * *

Hasan had taken his leave of al-Hikari, his heart filled with hope, having fulfilled his aim through a ploy. He headed straight for the caliph's palace, keeping an ear open for news of al-'Adid on the way. He learned that he was extremely ill and was certain he would die that night, so he set about thinking how to implement his plan. He convinced himself that he had already gained the caliphate, but it remained for him to win over Sittalmulk. He showed concern for the caliph's illness and inquired about the noble companion. He was told that he was in the caliph's room and was not permitted to leave. The doctors were also there, trying one medicine after another without success. Hasan contrived to approach Sheikh al-Sadid, the caliph's doctor, and inquire about the true condition of al-'Adid; he learnt that he was almost in his death throes. He cried in such an affected but convincing way that the doctor took pity on him and began to console him. Soon he left to go to the women's palace as the sun had begun to set. He asked to see Bahadin and was told that he had gone out to meet Sultan Saladin, so Hasan sat in the reception room at the palace gate waiting for him to return.

After a while, Bahadin returned, with signs of concern written all over his face. Hasan had expected that he would welcome him very warmly after having persuaded al-Hikari to promote his cause with Saladin. For he believed that the sultan must have discussed this matter with Bahadin. When he saw Bahadin approaching on horseback, he accosted him at the gate with a broad smile. But Bahadin took no notice of him and pretended not to see him. So Hasan addressed him directly, "Greetings, Professor. How was Saladin when you left him?"

Bahadin turned to him and cried out as if he had only just seen him, "Hasan, you are here?"

"I have been here waiting for you for an hour," replied Hasan. "How is His Majesty the caliph doing?"

"He is extremely ill, may God restore him to health!" replied Bahadin, as he sat down on a chair in the room—but without inviting Hasan to sit down as he normally would.

But Hasan took a seat anyway and began to express his sorrow at the state of al-'Adid, rubbing his palms together, pressing his eyes, and silently shaking his head. "Are you sure that he is in danger?" he asked.

"That is what I have just been told," replied Bahadin. "May God restore him to health. He was at peace with himself."

Hasan hastened to reply, expressing his concern as he said, "You are right, my friend! The caliph has the noblest character and the purest heart of anyone in the family, so..."

He cleared his throat and shook his head as if he were trying to withhold something that had just occurred to him, then turned to Bahadin and said, "With your perceptiveness, you must have noticed where his pureness of heart and easygoing nature has led us, Professor, even if you did not see all these developments in detail with your own eyes. But I certainly saw them myself. That is why matters are far more complex now than they appear to be and that you may realize. Our first need is to prevent evil before it occurs. I know how vigilant you are, staying awake late into the night thinking about these matters. I know there is little you do not know, so I apologize if you find me worried. But this is only because I value the reputation of my family—and it pains me when it is being called into question. I heard about that stranger entering the palace yesterday and leaving without our being able to apprehend him because some people in the palace helped him escape. I am not saying this to accuse anyone, because I believe that this was a consequence of confusion and ignorance rather than malevolent intentions. But if this is how Sittalmulk behaves when her brother is alive, then how on earth will things be when—may God forbid!—he is no longer?"

He cleared his throat and turned to face Bahadin squarely—as a mark of confidence and dependence on him. "There is something that I cannot hold back from you," he added, "although I have been keeping it a secret from almost everyone else—only your friend and mine, 'Isa al-Hikari, has any knowledge of it. That is, that the Caliph al-'Adid has acknowledged me as his successor to the caliphate, promising his sister to me, though she does not know it yet. Only the noble companion, my friend 'Isa, and Saladin himself know this. I had a long discussion with 'Isa about it this morning, but I do not know whether he told you about it."

Then he paused to gauge Bahadin's reaction. But the latter continued to listen, inscrutable as the sphinx, without any visible expression. Hasan continued, "If he has not told you of this already, he will doubtless do so shortly. For now I have only come to seek your help in preserving my honor and the honor of the caliph—may God restore him to health!—until the situation returns to normal and Saladin—may God preserve him!—assumes control. This is a matter that has been agreed between us. I ask you to protect this palace, as you are doing. However, I fear that our enemies may be able to enter it in secret, so I think that you should order the removal of the caliph's sister to another palace without tunnels. I think that the Pearl Guesthouse is the best palace for this purpose." So saying, he looked Bahadin in the eyes, waiting for his reaction.

Chapter 36

The Flight

Bahadin, however, appeared unconvinced and said, "I see no need for such action, Hasan, while the caliph is still alive."

"The wise man focuses on problems before they occur," replied Hasan. "It is of no use to recognize them only after they have happened. Listen, listen, isn't that the sound of women screaming in the palace? Al-'Adid must have died. Poor man..." And he started to strike his hands together in a sign of grief and burst into tears.

As soon as Bahadin heard the screaming, concern appeared all over his face. He stood up, murmured to Hasan that he should not leave but wait for him to return. As the din grew louder, Bahadin disappeared into the interior of the palace, and Hasan became certain that the caliph had died. He was eager to apprehend Sittalmulk and was sorry that Bahadin had disappeared, for reasons unknown to him. He sat in the room, deep in thought, on tenterhooks. Then he heard the crack of a whip and the neighing of horses, and he looked down from the window to see horsemen hurrying toward the palace. They seemed to be surrounding it from every direction, which surprised him. He then felt a hand taking hold of his shoulder and turned to find his personal servant, a slave whose job it was to spy on Sittalmulk in the palace, standing in front of him. He was trembling with apprehension etched on his face. "Jawhar, what is the matter?" he shouted at him.

"Come on, master," replied Jawhar, "You have to escape!"

"Where to?" asked Hasan. "No, I shall stay until I see this wretched woman and can apprehend her! Haven't you seen her?"

"Save yourself, master, save yourself!" replied Jawhar. "Things are not as you imagine them to be. Leave this room before the palace is surrounded. Leave!" So saying, he pulled him by his sleeve, taking advantage of people's preoccupation with the shouting and confusion, and took him away from the room. Panting with fear, he could not believe that he had left the palace. As Hasan followed him obediently, he asked, "Where are you taking me?"

"Come on, master, I'll tell you later. Just save yourself," replied the young servant, waving for him to follow him.

They continued walking until they were clear of the caliph's palaces and went into an ordinary house that would not arouse suspicion. It belonged to the slave, who hid there when necessary. When they had entered the house, the young servant bolted the door. He had turned pale, which Hasan found strange. On the basis of the conversation he had had with al-Hikari, he could not understand what led the young servant to behave the way he did.

When they sat down, Hasan asked, "Tell me now, why did you run away like that?"

"If I hadn't rescued you, you would be in prison by now," Jawhar replied.

Hasan scoffed and exclaimed, "In prison? Ha, ha, that's most unlikely! I don't blame you for being worried about me, though, because you don't know what happened to me this morning!"

"I know everything," replied Jawhar, "and I know that your plan has not succeeded. While you were waiting for the wretched Bahadin in the palace, he was with Saladin, having gone to see him on an urgent matter. He ordered him to surround the caliph's palaces with troops, so that as soon as the caliph died, he would arrest all the women, children, men, slaves, and anyone else inside the palaces."

Hasan heard this but did not believe it. "How do you know this?" he asked. "Who gave you this secret information, you fool? It's not impossible that Saladin would have ordered this eunuch to guard the palaces and everything in them, but he would have ordered that so that none of the other claimants could encroach on the caliphate besides himself. I don't blame you for your delusions because you don't know what I have been up to, which I will tell you some other time."

"I told you, sir, that I know everything," replied Jawhar. "I am not the fool you think I am. I am intelligent and concerned for the interest of my noble lord. I discovered that Saladin has ordered this eunuch of his to arrest all those in the palace and to seek you out in particular. If you do not believe me, go back to the palace and see what happens!"

Hasan could not believe his ears. He was shaking with anger but said nothing for a while. He started to finger his beard, as he reflected, amazed at what he had just heard. Meanwhile, the servant was silent and immobile. Then Hasan turned to him and asked, "Jawhar, are you certain of what you are saying?"

"I am absolutely certain," replied Jawhar. "If you don't believe me, go out in disguise, and you will see the troops searching for the noble Hasan, just as they are searching for the caliph's sons in the women's palace. And I cannot guarantee that they will not discover and arrest you, even if we disguise ourselves."

When Hasan became convinced of the truth of what his servant had told him, he realized he had failed, and his anger erupted. His chest heaved up and down seething like a cauldron; he overlooked his servant's presence and started to rage like a lion, then fume like a fox. Then he regained his self-control and, turning to his servant, said, "What have we to do with them? Let them be… I don't know why they should exact vengeance on me as well. I have put all my energy into serving them. Who will succeed al-'Adid on the caliph's throne, do you suppose?"

"It seems that no one will be installed in his place," replied Jawhar, "for they intend to arrest anyone of his lineage who is left. That is why I am afraid for you."

Hasan fell silent again, realizing he had failed on two counts. His hopes for the caliphate had vanished, and any relationship with Sittalmulk had become impossible—though he did not doubt that she would regret not being wed to him once Saladin had forced her to be his. He began to hatch a plan for exacting vengeance.

* * *

As for Sittalmulk, she had gone to bed the night before after 'Imadin had left her. But she could not sleep, tortured by the worries that were piling up on her. She got up early in the morning to inquire after her brother and was told that he was very sick but, because the doctors were with him, she was not allowed to see him. She waited patiently but was not given permission to see him until the afternoon. She found his condition to be better than she had expected and began consoling and comforting him. She remembered how she had stood up to him in the last two days on the matter of her engagement; she felt remorse for fear that his illness might have been precipitated by this incident. And she regretted that.

After a while, al-'Adid was told that the doctor and the companion had arrived; he told Sittalmulk to leave and reassured her that he was well. She went back to her room, anxious for her brother, for she still had misgivings about his condition. When Yaquta came and questioned her, she burst into tears despite herself, which made Yaquta think that the caliph had died; she gave out a great wail, which was heard by the rest of the servant girls, who did as she did and also wailed. These cries were heard while Hasan was with Bahadin and, as previously recounted, they thought that the caliph died, which was not the case.

Chapter 37

An Important Meeting

Bahadin had been summoned by Saladin that morning, immediately after his meeting with al-Hikari, during which he had promoted Hasan's plans for the caliphate and been made aware of the mood of the people. He had advised him to be on his guard and to station troops near the palaces. If he learned of al-'Adid's death, he should immediately order the troops to surround the palaces and inform him. None of the people inside should be allowed to leave under any pretext, and he should watch Hasan particularly carefully and arrest him. Bahadin now arrived, and Hasan was the first person he came across. So he asked him, in as natural a tone of voice as he could muster, to stay until he could assess how things would develop. When he heard the shrieking inside the palace and thought that the caliph must have died, he went out to issue his order to the horsemen—and also ordered Hasan to remain where he was until his return. But Hasan had left at the urging of his servant, Jawhar. Bahadin had the palace searched but could not find him anywhere. Distressed that his escape had resulted from his laxity, he planted spies to trace his whereabouts; then he decided it was time to tell Saladin of al-'Adid's death. But he learned that the caliph was still alive before doing so and was glad that he had not hurried to inform Saladin mistakenly of his death, for which he would surely have been reprimanded. Nevertheless, he left the troops around the palace to see how things would develop.

When it was almost sunset, a slave arrived and announced, "Our lord the sultan is coming with his entourage!" Bahadin hurried to meet him and saw him heading for the Golden Palace, where the caliph was staying. That surprised him, but he waited, not knowing why the sultan had come at that moment. Suddenly, his friend al-Hikari came forward to greet him. He asked him why the sultan had come, and al-Hikari replied, "Because al-'Adid has asked to see him!"

Bahadin thought that odd and raised his voice as he asked incredulously, "The caliph has asked to see our master, the sultan?"

"What is so strange about that?" replied al-Hikari.

"You know that better than I do! But we will know as soon as the meeting is finished." said Bahadin.

Bahadin ushered his friend al-Hikari in. As they sat down, they quietly began to discuss Saladin's qualities, Najmudin's cunning, and the like.

* * *

After a while, Sittalmulk realized that her crying and that of her maid's had fueled the rumor of the caliph's death. This was a bad omen, she thought, and so she shut herself away in her room in silence. She did not want to see anyone, for in her heart she was fearful for her brother's life, quite apart from her other troubles. Then as the sun set, she became even more depressed and anxious, as she thought of all the problems crowding in on her. Nightfall magnified her feelings, and she felt she urgently needed to see her brother. At that point her maid appeared and said, "His majesty, the Commander of the Faithful, is asking to see you!"

She was startled by this but also pleased as she quickly went to see him, having wrapped herself in a shawl and veil. As she followed her maid along the hallway, she heard a loud commotion coming from every side. The light was so dim she could not identify the faces, but she recognized some voices. Her maid told her she was hearing the voices of her brothers and the caliph's children.

She recoiled and stepped backwards. "What's the matter, my lady?" her maid asked.

"What has brought them here?" asked Sittalmulk. "What has happened? Is something wrong with my brother?"

"He sent for them, just as he did for you," replied Yaquta.

She walked with quivering knees, her heart racing, anticipating the worse in her brother's condition, for he would not summon his family unless his illness was exceptionally grave. When al-'Adid's sons learned that she had arrived, they made room for her. Daoud, the eldest—and annointed heir—came up to his aunt and kissed her hand. She returned his gesture, but with restraint, in order to encourage him to keep his own emotions under control. With trembling knees, she reached the door of her brother's room, listening carefully in the hope of hearing something that would reassure her. But instead she heard a weird noise that she could not recall having heard before. She wrapped her veil around her, and the guard let her in as he drew back the curtain from the door. The room had been lit with candles. She looked inside and saw her brother lying on the bed, his face looking very pale and extremely weak. When he saw her, a broad smile lighted his face as he greeted her, and tears swelled in his eyes. Sittalmulk threw herself on him and began to kiss him, without paying any attention to the other people present. "Don't worry, don't be afraid, brother. No ill will befall you!" she exclaimed.

He kissed her in turn but did not reply. She could feel tears streaming down her cheek, but she steeled herself and stood up, saying, "Don't be afraid, brother, you are in good health, praise be to God!" Then she turned around and saw the noble companion kneeling beside the caliph's bed, together with another man sitting on a cushion. As soon as she set eyes on him, her entire body shook, as she recalled having seen him through the windows at some official gatherings. It was Saladin. She seemed bewildered and was about to become agitated. But she exerted all her willpower to control herself and appear composed. She was in no doubt that Saladin had come to propose to her...

The other sons of the caliph had entered the room behind her. Al-'Adid motioned to them all to come forward, and one by one they kissed him. He was weeping, and his appearance was enough to break anyone's heart. None of those present could refrain from shedding some tears, even Saladin. Al-'Adid signaled to his sons to sit down around the room and motioned to Sittalmulk to sit down on the bed near him. So she sat down, carefully positioning herself so as not to show her face to Saladin.

Chapter 38

The Legacy

They all sat down, and silence reigned for a while. Then al-'Adid spoke in a weak, agitated voice, directing his words at Sittalmulk. "Sister, you know the standing you enjoy in my eyes... you are my sister, my friend, and my guide. How often have I consulted you, and how often have I relied on your guidance. But now the hour has come when I am conscious of the approach of death and of going to where I shall behold the face of God Almighty. And I want to assure myself of your situation and that of my sons after I am gone." He stopped speaking to rest, as everyone remained silent, then he said, "I have learned from experience that I cannot trust or rely on anyone among my family and staff in matters that concern you. You know my thinking regarding Sultan Yusuf Saladin." Saying so, he waved his hand toward him, "And I have often complained to you of his behavior. I am confessing this to you in my last hours on earth and my first hours in the world to come. I confess that I complained of his behavior. But now, I can find no one other than he whose word I can trust or who I am confident will do as he says. For I am surrounded by charlatans and flatterers who talk a lot but do not act. These people compete with each other to praise me, and steal my money, and use all kinds of stratagems and deception to attain high office. So I sent for the sultan, asking him to take the trouble to come here so I could entrust all of you to his good care." At this point, he raised his fingertips as a sign for them to let him pause and catch his breath. He fell silent, as he gasped for air.

No one spoke, but all held their breath as they choked back the tears that were in their eyes. No one looked at anyone else, so awestruck were they as they all contemplated the sight of the caliph and waited eagerly for what he would say next. Then al-'Adid spoke again, directing his words at Saladin this time, "My friend, this is my sister, Sittalmulk, for whom you sent a proposal of marriage. And these are my sons, the oldest of them being Daoud here. I am entrusting them to you for fear that some harm may befall them after I am gone. And I call God to witness that you will take them all in hand under your protection. Do you promise that you will do as I say?"

When Sittalmulk heard her brother mention the marriage proposal, she panicked—her heart became filled with fear and despair at the prospect of coming under Saladin's authority if her brother died, especially after he had given these instructions. Then she heard Saladin reply to her brother in these terms, "Commander of the Faithful, you will regain your health by God's leave. Your state is not so bad as to require a legacy. God willing, you will recover from this illness soon. But since you have mentioned the matter of a legacy, you should know, Your Majesty, that your vizier and servant hereby seated by your side will do what you have entrusted him with. Let Your Majesty—God exalt him!—have confidence in my promise. So long as I am alive, this family of yours will never come to any harm, and of that you have my promise before God."

Sittalmulk heard no mention of herself but was certain that her fate would be as she feared. This weighed heavily on her, quite apart from her fears for the caliph's life, and she began to weep uncontrollably again despite herself. She wanted to leave, to spare her brother, but he stretched out his hand and grasped hers to make her sit down. She felt his hand shaking, and her body quivered as she sat down and saw him looking at Saladin with his tear-filled eyes. He wanted to speak but found it impossible to do so. He pointed to his sister, and Saladin understood that he was entrusting her to him, so he hurriedly spoke, "You do not need to worry about Sittalmulk. She is your sister, and the best of sisters. But she is also my sister, as God is my witness…and that is enough!"

When Sittalmulk heard him refer to her as his sister, she breathed a sigh of immense relief. Despite her sadness and despair, she almost smiled, for she knew that Saladin would not have called her his sister unless he had abandoned the idea of marrying her, which was all she had wished for. And now that he had also guaranteed her protection, he would be obligated to shield her from Hasan's designs and hostility as well as that of others. Scarcely had she reassured herself on this account—which had distracted her from the critical condition of her brother—than he began coughing and shaking so much that he almost sat up in bed. It was a nervous attack that had struck him periodically over the last two days. The companion rose and hurried to summon the doctor, Sheikh al-Sadid, from another room. The doctor came in and asked those present to leave the room to allow him to treat the patient as he saw fit. Everyone dispersed, with Saladin leading the way like a lion and Sittalmulk watching him. From that moment on, she felt an admiring sort of love for him, for it was in her nature to admire brave and chivalrous men. This was what had attracted her to 'Imadin. She felt relaxed about Saladin and happy to see him…but then the companion suggested she should go to the women's palace and be with her family.

Chapter 39

Yaquta

As they were leaving, Sittalmulk received an affectionate glance from her brother. She felt reassured, having been distracted from her sorrow over his state of health. Her maid was in the hall, expecting to see her crying, especially because she learned that Saladin had been there. She prepared to console her, but she found her mistress looking cheerful, despite a few tears that still remained in her eyes, her swollen cheeks, and her visible fatigue. She took her hand and walked with her, realizing from her gait and body language that she was happy and at peace with herself. As soon as they reached her room in the palace, she quickly asked her, "How is his majesty, the Commander of the Faithful? I hope that he is in the best of health!"

Removing the veil from her head, Sittalmulk replied, "He is extremely weak. He has just had another serious attack. The doctor had to make us leave to treat him."

"God grant him health," replied the maid, and added, watching closely to see her reaction, "Who was with him while you were there?"

"The noble gentleman Saladin was there," she replied—then fell silent.

"Why are you so quiet?" asked the maid, "and how do you know that he is a gentleman? You seem to have refused him before because you didn't know him well, but now that you have seen him, it has become clear to you that he is worthy of your love." Teasingly, she added, as she helped her mistress remove the shawl from her shoulders, "But I wonder why he went to see the Commander of the Faithful today; perhaps to complete his proposal and make the engagement formal?"

"My brother sent for him," replied Sittalmulk as she looked in the mirror.

"The Commander of the Faithful sent for him? But why would he do such a thing?" asked Yaquta.

Remembering how her brother's life was in danger, she felt depressed and replied, "He sent for him to entrust us to him…"

Yaquta was astounded—not sure she understood. She asked, "Entrust you to him? Who do you mean?"

"I mean," replied Sittalmulk, "myself, my brothers, and my brother's sons. My brother—may God grant him health—believed he would not recover from this illness and confessed that he could not trust anyone among his men to take charge of us except for Saladin. So he sent for him and for all of us and entrusted us to him."

Yaquta continued to tease her mistress to distract her from her pain and said, "And Saladin no doubt agreed to the Commander of the Faithful's request, because he was obligated to do so on the basis of the relationship of marriage." Her eyes twinkled as they met Sittalmulk's eyes, to see what they might give away.

Sittalmulk smiled, the tears glistening in her eyes. "No, he said he was doing it out of brotherly affection, not because of any marriage relationship!"

Yaquta found this to be an odd formulation and asked, "From brotherly affection? What brotherly affection, my lady?"

"When my brother put me under Saladin's protection," replied Sittalmulk, "to emphasize that he would act according to his instructions, Saladin said, 'You do not need to worry about Sittalmulk. She is your sister, and the best of sisters. But she is also my sister, as God is my witness…and that is enough!'"

Hearing that, Yaquta could not restrain herself from pulling Sittalmulk to her breast and embracing her. "It is a terrible thing to have to bear the illness of our master, the Commander of the Faithful, but if the worst happens—God forbid—we will suffer much more. But amidst the deep shadows of this affliction, a ray of light has shone into my heart and dragged me out of the darkness of despair, because my greatest worry had been Saladin's request to marry you when your heart is attached to 'Imadin. I know Saladin's power, and I know that when he wants something, no one can stop him. But you just said that he had abandoned his proposal and undertaken to protect you as he would his sister. So be reassured, my lady, and do not be alarmed by troublemakers or slanderers."

Sittalmulk understood that she was referring to Hasan. Her eyes, and indeed her whole demeanor, indicated that she agreed wholeheartedly with Yaquta. But she suddenly once more became conscious of her brother's state of health and felt depressed. She clasped her hands together in a sign of agony and said, "Oh dear, my brother is desperately fighting for his life. What should I do? What will happen to us if he dies?" She swallowed hard and started to cry again, with Yaquta comforting her.

She spent most of that night in an agitated state and woke up in the morning to the voices of proclamations of death. The announcement of her brother's death came as no surprise, but its impact was nevertheless considerable. It was not long after that wailing could be heard in all the palaces: the ministers, men of state, scribes, and others came together, and the Golden Palace, as well as the other palaces, became crammed with people. The caliph's family wanted to hold a funeral ceremony worthy of a caliph, and the men of state wanted to swear allegiance to Daoud, the heir apparent, but Saladin's men had surrounded the palaces. Bahadin went to the noble companion and said, "The sultan wants you to make the funeral ceremony brief, for fear of disturbances. The dead man is dead; crying and wailing will not serve any purpose."

The people could only submit and obey, especially after learning how the caliph had summoned Saladin the previous day. Even though they did not know the details of what had transpired between them, the mere fact of his being summoned showed the high status he enjoyed in the eyes of the caliph. In any event, there is no arguing with power, and Saladin's troops had an iron grip on the city, so the people had no choice but to accept and submit to his authority.

Chapter 40

Bahadin

Sittalmulk heard that more stringent restrictions had been placed on people leaving the palace, and she could see troops surrounding it on every side, so she had to make do with staying and weeping in her room. She was lamenting the death of her brother, and her maid was crying with her.

While they were thus engaged, they heard the sound of footsteps at the palace gate. Sittalmulk became frightened, but her maid got up and said, "Don't be afraid, my lady—not after Saladin said that he would treat you like his sister!" She had only just reached the door of the room when she heard someone tapping gently. Relieved, she opened the door and saw Bahadin standing there, respectfully. "Is our lady Sittalmulk here?" he asked.

"Yes," replied Yaquta. "What do you want of her? She is grief stricken!"

"I want to console her and reassure her," replied Bahadin, "and ask her not to be concerned about any people she might see entering or leaving the palace. I also wish to ask her a question…"

"Come in, sir!" shouted Sittalmulk from inside. "What do you want?"

Bahadin went in and gave her a look of condolence and compassion. Sittalmulk turned to him and, swallowing hard, asked, "What is the matter this time? What do you want? The Commander of the Faithful has died, so you and your friends can relax!"

Bahadin knelt before her and said, "The death of the Commander of the Faithful has grieved me, my lady, but it is the will of God, and His decree cannot be undone. But now I have come to tell you that the sultan has ordered me to appropriate everything in these palaces, and especially the women who are in this palace—and there are a lot of them, as you know. The only exception I can make is for my lady, the Commander of the Faithful's sister, and any of the residents of the palace who are not of her family who wish to accompany her."

She interrupted him, saying, "And what will you do with my family? Where are they?"

"They are not in danger," replied Bahadin. "My late master—may God have mercy on him—charged the Sultan with looking after them, but he is determined to move them from this palace to another palace where they will be under his protection and where no harm can come to them. That especially applies to my lady, Sittalmulk. So who are the servants or companions that you will want to move out with you, and which furniture and vessels will you want to take?"

She said nothing and became dismayed by the prospect of leaving the palace, despite being reassured by the protection she would receive at the hands of Saladin. She could not help disliking the prospect intensely and asked, "You are chasing us from our palaces? And what will you do with the men, women, and children, who number in the thousands?"

"My lady, my lord Saladin will act in a way that does not encroach on the dignity of anyone. Maidservants who are married will leave with their husbands. Free women without husbands will be released. Slave girls will be given to his men. The caliph's family, both men and women, will be treated with great respect and kindness under his benovelent supervision. He will distribute gifts, clothes, and food to them so that no one lacks for anything, and they will live just as they were living in their palaces during the lifetime of the caliph—may God have mercy on him—and especially so for my lady, who will enjoy special attention and complete protection, together with her entourage."

She interrupted him, "And what will you do with the heir apparent, Daoud? Has he not sworn allegiance to the sultan?"

He swallowed hard and replied, "I do not think that swearing allegiance to him is required of anyone. Sultan Nuradin, our supreme leader, has ordered us to swear allegiance to the 'Abbasid Caliph al-

Mustadi' bi'llah, and there cannot be two caliphs on earth at the same time. As far as I am concerned, I can only regard the caliphate as a burden and a danger to the man who holds it; there is no benefit to be derived from it. I apologize to my lady for cutting the conversation short, but I have to attend to the orders of my lord, the sultan, and appropriate the contents of the palaces, as I told you. So tell me what you would like me to keep for you." As he said this, he rose and indicated that he wished to leave.

"I would like my maid here to accompany me," she replied. "She will tell you what furnishings and clothes I wish to take." She turned her face away, as Yaquta continued, "Leave this room and the one next to it without removing anything from them, and I will ready things we need to take. God bless you, Professor..."

After Bahadin departed, Yaquta, alone with her mistress, said to her, "Thank God, Saladin is going to keep his promise. I saw how carefully you asked your question and how surprised you were that they would not swear allegiance to Daoud. Thank God that they did not kill the rest of the caliph's family, as others have done in similar circumstances. Didn't Abu al-'Abbas al-Saffah order all the remaining Umayyads to be killed, so that there would be none left to claim the caliphate? If Saladin were to give a similar order, who would be able to oppose it? Or do you think that that conceited Hasan would oppose it? God curse him!"

When she heard mention of Hasan, she felt relieved at having escaped from his wiles under Saladin's protection. She got up to leave, saying with a sigh, "Ready what we need—only the most precious and lightest things." So Yaquta started to attend to it. This was the hardest day of all as one dynasty came to an end and another one was born.

Chapter 41

The End of the Dynasty

Bahadin seized all the women in the palaces and brought them before Saladin, who found that most of them were free women, so he let them go. He freed a good number of the slave girls and gave the others to a number of his own men so that the palaces were cleared of everyone who had been living in them. He and his men took a large number of ornaments and jewelry too numerous to list and describe. We will content ourselves with the account of the historian of the two dynasties[39] in enumerating what they seized:

> Saladin emptied al-'Adid's palaces and sealed all the gates, over which his soldiers had total control. There was nothing left to weigh or to count. He confiscated everything that was of value or potential use to himself or his family, those close to him, the retinue of emirs for which he was made responsible, leading mamluks, his servants, and his supporters: the most precious treasures, the rarest jewels, the most sumptuous clothes, the most beautiful dresses, the most unique necklaces, the rarest pearls, priceless rubies, topazes, and emeralds, jewels made of pure gold and others of grey amber, vases in sterling silver, platters of copper from China, various embossed leather goods, clothes embroidered with gold threads, shimmering embroidered satins—in short, everything that had any value. Necklaces, gold coins, engraved and sculpted molded objects, enameled jewels, without forgetting an innumerable variety of perfumes—everything was taken away and nothing was left. Saladin distributed all these treasures generously. He ordered that everything that was left should be sold: clothes, objects, old and new, used or not, expensive or affordable. Whatever could be carried away was transported and their sale

---

39 Shihaboudine Abu Shama al Muqaddisi, in his book *The Two Gardens*, dealing with Egypt under Saladin and Syria under Nuradin. *Author's Note*

required more than ten years all over the country, keeping busy an army of visitors, importers, and exporters of all types.

Saladin moved the caliph's family to the House of Barjawan, not far from his residence in the quarter named after him. He singled out Sittalmulk for particular honor, attention, and kindness.

Until that time, Egypt had been an independent caliphate. God's blessing had been invoked from the pulpits on the Shi'i caliph al-'Adid li-Din Allah. Toward the end of al-'Adid's illness, Saladin finally ordered that sermons be preached in the name of the 'Abbasid caliph, al-Mustadi' bi'llah, as Nuradin had demanded of him through his father Najmudin. He gave as his excuse for the delay his fear of social discord. But the reality is that he postponed it so that he could ask al-'Adid for his assistance against Nuradin, in the event that the latter should want to remove him from Egypt by force. In that event, he would have sided with al-'Adid and used him and the Egyptians to defeat the Syrian army. But when al-'Adid's grave illness became apparent and the end appeared to be aproaching rapidly, while at the same time his rivalry with Nuradin was growing, he decided to submit to Nuradin's demand and ordered that the sermon should again be given in the name of the 'Abbasids, thereby demonstrating his allegiance to Nuradin. All the religious *ulema*[40] accepted to begin a sermon in this way, except for a man of non-Arab extraction called al-Amir al-'Alim. On learning this, Saladin himself climbed on the pulpit and led the prayers invoking God's blessing on the 'Abbasid al-Mustadi; the people supported him, and no one showed any opposition. This was communicated in writing to the rest of Egypt, and it became the law of the land. All this happened towards the end of al-'Adid's illness, and he died without knowing it. So it was that one bright morning in the year 567 AH (1172 AD), Egypt woke and found itself under the sovereignty of the 'Abbasid caliph of Baghdad. The children of al-'Adid and other members of his family were prevented from marrying so that they would not produce offspring with a claim to the caliphate.

---

40 Religious scholar. *Editor's Note*

Chapter 42

Apprehensions

When Sittalmulk found herself in her new palace, the House of Barjawan, she thought it an admirable move. But when she heard news of the change of allegiance to the 'Abbasids, she was certain that the 'Alawite dynasty had passed, and this upset her greatly—in addition to her sorrow at the death of her brother. She spent days by herself in her palace room speaking to no one but Yaquta, who frequently came to console her. Whatever her other problems, it was her relationship with 'Imadin that preoccupied her most. She had parted from him on that terrible night in a state of great uncertainty. In her grief, she wanted to speak to Yaquta openly about him, in the hope that she might learn something that would give her some hope of meeting him again. But Yaquta would not do this, not out of any trepidation, but because she felt her mistress' preoccupation with her love for the young servant was futile and would lead nowhere. She wanted her to forget him and move on. She, therefore, did not think it wise to talk about him or even mention his name, thereby helping to calm and reassure her.

Sittalmulk had, however, sought Saladin's permission to take walks and relax in the gardens of the palace. Saladin had not allowed anyone else from the caliph's family to do so, but he was extremely solicitous of Sittalmulk and respected her wishes, as he had promised her brother he would do. That was among the greatest sources of consolation to her amidst her troubles. During the Syrian wars—at which time his own father had died in 568 AH (1173 AD)—Saladin did not have much time for her. During those periods he entrusted her to the care of Bahadin.

For some time, she heard nothing of 'Imadin. She did not know where he was living or what had happened to him, and she could find no way to inquire about him or search for him. She became depressed and began to despair. Gripped by pessimism, she could find no pleasure in diversions, nor relaxation in conversation. She began to eat less and stay awake at night and started to lose weight. Yaquta did all she could to console her, but when she saw how weak and depressed she was becoming, she did not know what to do to bring her back from the abyss she was sinking into. She had thought that 'Imadin's long absence would have made her forget him, and when she no longer heard her mention his name, she thought that she had indeed forgotten him. But she soon realized how wrong she was. One night, as she was sleeping in a room adjoining hers, she was awakened by Sittalmulk's voice calling, "Yaquta, Yaquta!"

She leapt from her bed to her mistress' bed. She saw her mistress sitting with her hair disheveled and a strange look on her face. She threw herself on her and shouted, "My lady, my dear lady, what is the matter? What can I do for you?"

"'Imadin, 'Imadin, where is he? I heard them calling him!" she replied.

"Where is he, my lady? He's not here," replied Yaquta. "You're having a dream. Don't you remember that he's left?"

She brushed her hair from her brow and looked around her. Her eyes betrayed an inner disturbance. "He's left?" she asked. "Oh, what a long journey it must be! I heard his name in a dream. I wish I could have slept more to hear it mentioned again, or perhaps his spirit might have appeared to me..." And she burst into tears.

Yaquta bent over her and began to console her, saying, "Why are you doing this to yourself, my lady? What is wrong with you? Where is your common sense and your wisdom?"

She pulled herself from her arms, saying, "Don't speak to me of wisdom and common sense! There's no room for them with love, Yaquta. Good God, what's happened to me? I am no longer afraid of saying what's in my heart. But I have kept it hidden for so long that it has almost destroyed me. Take things in hand and help me! Oh, 'Imadin!"

As she burst into tears again, Yaquta knelt down in front of her and said, "Calm down, my lady! You can rely on me! Why didn't you tell me all this before?"

"What's the point of talking?" replied Sittalmulk. "But now that I've said all this, tell me where 'Imadin is and how I can reach him. Don't you know where he is staying? Haven't you asked anyone about him? Tell me, please, I beseech you!"

"Yes," replied Yaquta, wiping her mistress' tears away with her handkerchief. "I asked about him and discovered from Professor Bahadin that he had left on a secret mission. If it is successful, he will become a great man, worthy of Sittalmulk. This is very important, my lady, for it would not be right for the caliph's sister or caliph's daughter to marry one of the common people, and..."

"Don't say 'caliph' or 'common people,'" she interrupted. "I am a prisoner in this palace, and he is free. My heart is also a prisoner, and I don't know whether his heart is, too..."

As she burst into tears again, Yaquta started drawing her to her breast and hugging her, wiping away her tears and kissing her. "Calm down, my lady!" she said. "Take it easy! Then we can decide what should be done."

"See what should be done?" exclaimed Sittalmulk. "He's been away such a long time, and I don't know what's happened to him!"

"Nothing's happened to him," replied Yaquta. "He is bound to come back successful and become an important man! And when Saladin learns of his fondness for you, he will advance him and promote him. It seems that you have forgotten this blessing...you have forgotten Saladin's concern for you and the way that he treats you as a brother treats his sister."

"No, I haven't forgotten that," replied Sittalmulk. "If it were not for him, I would have died of grief and sorrow. But what is it that made me hear the name of 'Imadin in my dream?"

"Perhaps it is a premonition that he will return soon," replied Yaquta. "Wait until tomorrow to see what happens." And with that, she suggested that Sittalmulk go back to sleep, which she did. Yaquta went back to her room, thinking about her mistress and regretting that she had failed to talk about 'Imadin to her mistress for so long. She believed that her mistress' hearing of 'Imadin's name was not fortuitous but an omen—and that something must be happening concerning him...

Her suspicions were confirmed the next morning, when Bahadin came to tell her that Sultan Saladin would be coming shortly to meet Sittalmulk. She was surprised by this unexpected visit but was hopeful about the meeting—for a desperate person will hope for relief from any new development. "This will be a good thing, for she is very depressed and anxious and will be pleased to see the sultan. I will go tell her that he is coming," she said.

Chapter 43

The Ploy

Sittalmulk was up and about ready to summon Yaquta. When she entered her room, she could see from her face that she was bearing good news. As her heart beat faster, she asked, "What is the matter?"

"Relief may be at hand," replied Yaquta with a smile. "Sultan Saladin is coming to see you."

"Did he ask to come of his own accord?" asked Sittalmulk, her cheeks blushing from surprise.

"Yes, my lady," replied Yaquta. "And perhaps he will bring you some news to cheer you up. Get up, and get dressed!"

Sittalmulk did so, and Yaquta helped her dress. She put on a simple dress, tidied her hair, covered her face, and went out to the reception hall. Her knees were quivering with emotion.

After a little while, she heard the sound of footsteps in the palace and saw that Bahadin had come in. "Our master the sultan is on his way!" he announced.

Sittalmulk prepared herself to meet him. Then Saladin entered. He greeted her courteously, and she was about to stand up, but he smiled and gestured to her to be seated. "My sister, I have not visited you for some time because of my absence from Egypt," he said. "How are you? I hope that you are well!"

She was delighted to hear him address her as his sister and relaxed as she said, "Praise be to God. So long as I enjoy the favor of Sultan Saladin, I shall be well!"

Saladin sat down on a cushion in front of her and told Bahadin to sit as well, while Yaquta remained standing. "I hope that you are finding every comfort in this palace," he said, addressing Sittalmulk.

"Yes," she replied. "Thanks to the sultan, I am lacking for nothing by way of comfort, for Professor Bahadin is sparing no effort in that regard. And it is sufficient to make me happy that Sultan Saladin should call me his sister."

"If you are happy with this relationship," replied Saladin, laughing, "there is no longer any reason to cover your face with a veil."

"Yes, you are right!" she replied, pulling the veil from her face.

She said nothing more out of modesty, but Saladin could see that her face was pale and that she had lost weight. "You don't seem to be your normal self, Sittalmulk!" he said. "Are you suffering from something?"

When she did not answer, he turned to Yaquta. "She is not in any pain," she replied, "she is just a little under the weather."

"Don't worry, my sister!" said Saladin. "I hope I have not disturbed you by visiting you. I just wanted to reassure myself about you and to inquire about something that I would not want any other person to know about. I think that you know more about that matter than anyone else."

Eager to know what he was referring to, she stared into his face to try to decipher what he had in mind. "Your wish is my command, my lord!" she said.

He looked to his left and then to his right as if to make certain no one else was there, then said, "You know that your brother—may God have mercy on him—entrusted you and the rest of your family to me, and I think that I am doing all that is necessary to fulfill his command."

Sittalmulk nodded, indicating her agreement with her eyes.

"I also think that I have not failed to take all necessary measures to improve the state of this country from every point of view. I have put an end to many of the injustices of the previous dynasty, which were committed by those around your late brother. I thought that this would unite the people in accepting my authority."

"I think that they are united," replied Sittalmulk. "Our lord the sultan has spared no effort to reduce the tax burden and establish justice."

"When the state passed into my hands." continued Saladin, "I could have killed all the emirs and viziers who had served the previous dynasty. But I didn't do so, believing they would be indebted to us for such treatment."

She was astonished at his words, figuring he was leading onto something she could not discern. She raised her eyebrows as if to seek clarification. "But I suspected that some emirs and nobles would conspire against us..." he continued.

She raised her eyes and asked, "Conspire against the sultan?"

"Yes," replied Saladin. "If they had simply conspired among themselves, they would not have been so dangerous. But they used our enemies against us. They contacted our enemies, the Franks, on the Syrian coast and in Sicily, and urged them to declare war on us so that they could rise against us, and we would thus lose control of our country."

As he spoke, his anger was obvious from his tone of voice. Sittalmulk sat up and said in disbelief, "Conspire with the Franks against their sultan? What treachery!" After a moment's silence, she added, "Are you certain of this information, my lord?"

"I am absolutely certain of what I am saying," replied Saladin. "The information came from a man whom I trust as much as I trust myself. God curse them! Preparing for the caliphate to pass from the 'Ubaydi dynasty[41] to the 'Abbasids, both of whom are Muslim, is bad enough, but what if it were to pass to the Franks, who are our deadly enemies— in terms of religion and of territory? Instead of working together to protect our country from them, would we show them our weak spots and spur them on to conquer our country? Have you ever seen anyone more treacherous and irresponsible than these people? Wouldn't it be right to kill people who try to do such deeds?" He was trying to temper his rage in front of Sittalmulk, but he had raised his voice, and his eyes blazed as he rubbed his beard to maintain his composure.

---

41 The 'Ubaydi state–also called the Fatimid state–was founded in Tunis in 297 AH (910 AD) and moved to Egypt in 362 AH (973 AD), where it was firmly established, and its power spread to a large part of the Muslim world, such as Syria and the Arabian Peninsula. Its rule began with al-Mu'izz li Din-Allah Mu'adh ibn al-Mansoor al-'Ubaydi. *Editor's Note*

Sittalmulk was angry, too, but felt a sort of embarrassment at the fact that the people who had hatched this conspiracy were her brother's people. "Yes, it's a terrible treachery," she said. "But I find it difficult to believe that intelligent people could do something like this. Presumably those involved are ignorant commoners."

"They are some of the most distinguished emirs and notables," replied Saladin, "and they include a man who maintains that he is descended from the 'Ubaydis, your relatives. But we failed to arrest him with your other people in the palace. We thought that he had simply run away and disappeared, but he is now among the most prominent people inciting treason. I think that you know him. If he hadn't been involved in this affair, I would not have bothered you by giving you the details of the treason. But I wanted to call on your help in examining his case, should you know anything about him. For he was the closest of anyone to your brother—may God have mercy on him—and he even aspired to be his heir."

Sittalmulk realized that he meant Hasan. She turned pale with anger and said, "Yes, I know him. I think you mean that lying nobleman, who claims to be related to us but is not one of us. Don't you mean Hasan?"

"Yes, that's who I mean," replied Saladin. "He is one of the biggest hypocrites and traitors because he approached us while the late, lamented al-'Adid was on his death bed, and begged us to transfer the succession to him, claiming he would assist us in everything we wanted. But we rejected his overtures, so he turned to hatching plots and setting traps. He was joined by a group of renegades, all of whom will be punished." Lowering his voice to give greater effect to his ensuing request, he added, "I am simply asking you to tell us what you know about Hasan's whereabouts."

She said nothing, hoping that what Saladin had said was true. That way Hasan would come to a dire end, and she would escape from him. Wanting to confirm the information she was given, she replied, "Yes, I know all about that man's faults, bad character, and ambitions. I will try to find out where he is. But I hope that my lord is confident of the truth of his information. And if he would like to give me further details, it will help me in my inquiries."

"I received this information from several sources," replied Saladin, "and I had my doubts about it, until I received it in the form of a letter from a man whose sincerity I do not doubt and who had written the letter in his own hand. It reached me secretly at dawn yesterday with a delegation sent by the Franks who support those traitors, on the pretext that they were sending me a gift from one of their kings. In fact, they were merely using this as a pretext to meet those conspirators and help them complete their betrayal. This is the letter. If you can read it, it will spare me the trouble of giving you any more explanations." And with that, he slipped his hand into his pocket, took a letter out of an envelope, and handed it to Bahadin to read.

Chapter 44

The Text of the Letter

Bahadin unscrolled the parchment and began to read:

I am writing this letter to my lord the sultan from the depths of prison in Jerusalem. I do not have time to describe in detail the reasons for my imprisonment, which would take a very long time, but I have been anxious to write this letter to convey to my lord some important information that I have learned from a trusted source. I fear there may be undesirable consequences if it does not reach you quickly. After I left Egypt I learned of the death of al-'Adid and of the transfer of authority to my lord the sultan. While in prison, I heard that some men belonging to al-'Adid's dynasty, the 'Ubaydis, were secretly meeting in al-Fustat, and conspiring to wrest power from his hands. They contacted the Franks in this region, conspiring with them to attack Egypt with a large army from here and from Sicily, saying that the Egyptian people would rise against you and stand with them against your army.

Those conspirators were headed by an 'Alawite called Hasan, who spurred on those disaffected with the old regime to side with him and seek the support of the Franks. The Franks responded positively and began to prepare for the attack, but the conspirators also assembled a group in the guise of a delegation to carry a gift from the king of the Franks to Sultan Saladin. What they really wanted, however, was to meet the group of conspirators and seal the deal. But through a friend of mine, God allowed me to find out about these plans and to send this message with the bearer of this letter. He will infiltrate the delegation, appearing to be one of its servants or one of its guides on the road, and so I have entrusted this letter to him. If it reaches you, give the bearer a hundred dinars and honor him. I myself will remain here and will stay until I am able to leave to undertake my life's mission in the service of my lord the sultan. By God's leave, I will succeed. Either I will return to you victorious, or I will die in the course of it in the service of my lord, because my life and the lives of all his men are at his disposal and at his service.

As Sittalmulk was listening to what was in the letter, her heart was telling her that it was connected with 'Imadin. When she heard mention in the last paragraph of the author's mission, her heart skipped a beat as she thought that the letter might be from 'Imadin himself, especially since it said that he had left Egypt before the death of her brother. The surprise was visible all over her face, and her heart beat faster. When Bahadin finished reading the letter, she could not help exclaiming, "Will the sultan allow me to know who wrote this letter?"

"We have to keep his name secret," replied Saladin. "But in view of the concern and sincerity evident in your tone of voice, I do not see any problem in telling you. He is a young servant with exceptional courage, enthusiasm, and loyalty. We had marked him out for an important task that no one but he would dare carry out, but I do not think that you know him."

As he was speaking, Saladin's eyes met Bahadin's. They seemed to suggest he should refrain from disclosing his name. He could not tell why this message was being conveyed to him. But after having promised to disclose the name, he had no choice but to do so. He looked at Sittalmulk and saw that she was craning her neck forward, her eyes fixed on his lips, as if wanting to milk the words from his mouth. "The writer of this letter is called 'Imadin," he said.

He had scarcely uttered his name when Sittalmulk cried out, "'Imadin? Ah, 'Imadin!" Then she suddenly fainted and fell to the floor. The sultan sprang up, shell-shocked. Yaquta hurried to fetch water, which she started to sprinkle on her mistress while rubbing her hands. Bahadin went up to Saladin and said, "I told your lordship not to mention this name!"

"Why is she so concerned about him?" asked Saladin. "Do you know why?"

Whispering in his ear, he replied, "I knew something about him before he left, but 'Isa al-Hikari prevented me from telling your lordship at the time, for fear that it might influence your attempt to seek the hand of this lady."

As he fell silent, Saladin replied, "But what is her relationship with him? It seems that she is in love with him!"

He gestured to him to follow him to another room while Yaquta finished attending to her mistress's needs. When they were alone, he told him the story of 'Imadin coming to the palace at night through the tunnel, and how Hasan had given him away, how they had been unable to arrest him, etc.

Saladin stood there, thinking back to what had happened in the meeting. He was pleased to learn of this secret relationship, for he liked 'Imadin and wanted to show respect to Sittalmulk. He was thankful that his proposal to marry her had gone nowhere. "I am glad to have found that out," he said to Bahadin. "We must try to bring these two lovers together. Thank God that Hasan's efforts did not meet with success."

"We can exploit her feelings to further our own interests," replied Bahadin, "encouraging her to help us discover the secrets of this conspiracy. She is one of the best placed people for that. And if she serves us faithfully in this regard, we will help her achieve her heart's desire."

Saladin laughed and said, "God bless you, Bahadin. You never think of doing a favor for anyone, unless it rebounds to your own benefit! Well done!"

"All that concerns me is to serve my lord, may God preserve him!" replied Bahadin.

Saladin then turned to the door and inquired about Sittalmulk. He was told that she had come to, so he went in and saw her sitting shyly on a pillow, not saying a word. Her face looked tired, and her eyes were pale. He went toward her and said, "I heard about and am pleased to know of your relationship with our beloved 'Imadin. You should know that I will do all I can to shorten his absence as much as possible and to ensure that your fondest desires will come to be. I have entrusted my friend Bahadin with the task of making sure that everything turns out well, and I commend you to God!"

She stood to bid him farewell, obviously embarrassed. She could not find words with which to express her gratitude, but her eyes conveyed her unequivocal thankfulness. At the same time, she was too worried about 'Imadin's fate and the fear of losing him that she felt compelled to speak up. With a trembling voice, she said, "But he is in the depths of prison, my lord!"

"With God's help, he will come out," replied Saladin. "And if he remains in prison, we will conquer Jerusalem to free him. And to add glory to the House of Islam! Have no fear!"

With that, he strode off like a lion, while she followed him with her eyes, more than ever admiring his strength of purpose and his greatness of spirit. She could see that his assumption of power at the end of her brother's dynasty had been a natural and inevitable consequence of the lack of resolve, corrupt ideas, and trivial disputes that afflicted her brother's reign during the final period of the Fatimid dynasty.

After Saladin left, Bahadin approached her and said, "I will return shortly, after you have had a rest. Keep calm!" And he burst out laughing.

Chapter 45

Jawhar

Sittalmulk and Yaquta were left on their own. "Thank God!" exclaimed Yaquta, her face radiant. "My suspicions were right, and we got what we wanted."

Sittalmulk sighed and said, "What have we got? From the text of that letter I have learned that 'Imadin has been imprisoned by the Franks and is determined to carry out a mission that seems extremely dangerous. And if he doesn't succeed, he will not come back..." she added, swallowing hard.

"My lady," replied Yaquta, "isn't it enough that we have learned he is still alive? And that Saladin will help him complete his mission quickly and succesfully? And take revenge on that traitor? Let us have something to eat and put our trust in God!"

Relieved, she got up and consented to eat. As she did so, they spoke about the conspiracy and Hasan. After the meal, Bahadin came in without further ceremony, and said, "Princess Sittalmulk, I am delighted to see how pleased Sultan Saladin is with you and congratulate you on the results of your meeting. He has entrusted you to me. We need to discover the whereabouts of this conspiracy. Do you know anything about it?"

She thought for a while then said, "How could I, when I do not know a single street in this city? I have spent my life shut up in the palace!"

Yaquta interrupted to say, "If I find out where it is..."

"Where is it?" asked Bahadin.

"I don't know," replied Yaquta. "But I hope to get some information about its location. Do you know the slave Jawhar?"

"I know him," replied Bahadin. "Wasn't he one of the palace slaves?"

"Yes," replied Yaquta. "And he is a spy of this traitor. He used to pass him information about us and our secrets."

"What's the point of knowing him if such is his character and he is a traitor to us?" asked Bahadin.

"A traitor is not faithful to anyone," replied Yaquta. "Yesterday he was on the side of Hasan against us, but today he can be on our side against him…"

"Where is he?" asked Bahadin.

"He is in this palace," replied Yaquta. "One of the slaves told me that he bore a grudge against Hasan because he had treated him badly. His feelings toward him had changed, and he no longer had any reason to remain there after my lady had left under the protection of our lord the sultan. So he fled and came over to us. Shall I summon him?"

Yaquta ordered one of the slaves to summon him, and when she returned, her mistress saw her eyes sparkling with happiness. "God bless you, Yaquta," she said. "You are wonderful!"

"The traitor will reap the seeds that he sowed!" said Yaquta.

When Jawhar arrived, his eyes were shifting rapidly from left to right, almost dancing in his face, so agitated was he—like a hypocrite who is not at peace with himself. Bahadin gave him a withering glance and said, "Jawhar, we have heard that Hasan deceived you for a while and persuaded you to stop obeying our mistress. But I am pleased that you have returned to your senses and realized that faithful service to Princess Sittalmulk and Sultan Saladin is the only way to serve your interests."

Jawhar bent down to kiss Bahadin's hand, with an expression of repentance and devotion. "God knows that I was deceived," he said. "That man certainly misled me. He made me believe that he spoke for the deceased caliph and that he could do as he pleased. Then I discovered his evil intentions. I had been brought up in the service of my lord, so it was not right for me to betray him. When I was certain of Hasan's disloyalty,

I left him, for I hate treachery, especially toward someone who has been good to me. In fact, I am my lord's creature and his servant…"

"God bless you," replied Bahadin, pretending to believe him. "You can be sure that I think well of you, and I will reward you generously. I don't want to delve into the past. All I ask of you is only one thing, which will be easy and will allow you to avenge yourself on that traitor. Will you obey me?"

Jawhar could not believe that he had gained his forgiveness and trust after his past crimes and said, "I am at your command, sir!"

"I am asking you to tell me where Hasan and his companions meet," said Bahadin. "Do you know where that is?"

"That is easy, sir," replied Jawhar. "Yes, I do know, and I know the people that meet with him, may God confound them! I had decided to tell you before you asked me, for it is my duty to do so. But embarrassment over my past behavior prevented me."

He patted him on the back and laughed. "God forgive you!" he exclaimed. "Is the place far from here?"

"It's in Fustat, sir!" said Jawhar.

"Now I am convinced of your trustworthiness," replied Bahadin, "because I already knew that it was there. From this moment on I will have faith in you… And you already know that my trust is the same as my lord Saladin's trust, so be aware that the person who enjoys this trust can only benefit greatly. I am setting right a previous wrong, Jawhar! My lady Sittalmulk has commended you to me and told me how faithful you were in her service before that traitor incited you to this betrayal. But what is past is past. Now come with me!" So saying, he turned, and Jawhar followed. He wanted to strike while the iron was hot before an unforeseen event might make this fickle youth change his mind. Also, he was intent on not letting him out of his sight before achieving his goal.

Suddenly, however, Bahadin remembered something that he had forgotten to say to Sittalmulk, so he went back to her. "My lady," he said, "you must confide in me should any thoughts concerning this matter come to your mind. Do not forget I knew about 'Imadin coming to your palace. Thank God that he got away safely!"

She took advantage of his favorable disposition toward her and his invitation to be close to him to probe into how much more he knew. "Bahadin, we are now in the same camp. You saw how pleased the sultan was with me. But I beseech you please tell me more about 'Imadin's circumstances."

"I know nothing more about his circumstances than is in the letter I have just read to you," he replied.

"I mean, what are the dangers he is encountering there?" asked Sittalmulk. "And when do you think he will return?"

"I don't know when he will return," he replied. "As for any dangers, he will know how to face them, for I am certain of his courage and intelligence. But we have to have faith in God. In any case, keep calm!" And with these words, he departed.

Jawhar followed him, pleased at the opportunity he had been given of receiving a reward. The consequences of killing or of destroying houses were of no concern to him. Traitors like him lack a moral compass, called conscience. They look at actions only from the point of view of the advantages to them and care about nothing else. They are incapable of any disinterested action. To them, the world has only two sides: the first must be maintained at all costs because it is advantageous to them, and the other one they consider nonexistent. As far as they are concerned, it can be wiped off the face of the earth and the people that inhabit it can be massacred. They delight in the suffering of other people, even if, as a result, they do not reap any benefit for themselves. But if they do, so much the better! God save us from such people, though thank goodness they are only few and far between—for if there had been more of them, they would have destroyed the world a long time ago.

Chapter 46

Fustat[42]

Bahadin went off with Jawhar the Abyssinian slave, attending him. He was intelligent, but he had no conscience, as we have already seen. As they were walking, Bahadin turned to him and asked, "Jawhar, what is to be done now?"

"It is up to you, master," he replied.

"I am relying on you to reach our destination," said Bahadin. "I want to see these people meeting and hear what they are saying. Will that be possible tonight?"

"Yes, master," replied Jawhar. "We will go after sunset, if you would like."

"Where to?" asked Bahadin.

"To Fustat," replied Jawhar. "They meet there in a house I know. No one but me knows the way. It is a ruined house that no one can get to except through dark, narrow alleys, and one needs to disguise oneself."

---

42 Fustat was the first capital of Egypt under Arab rule. It was built by the Arab general 'Amr ibn al-'As immediately after the Arab conquest of Egypt in 20 AH (641 AD) and featured the Mosque of 'Amr, the first mosque built in Egypt and in all of Africa. The city reached its peak in the twelfth century, with a population of approximately 200,000. It was the center of administrative power in Egypt until it was ordered burned in 563 AH (1168 AD) by its own vizier, Shawar, to keep its wealth out of the hands of the invading Crusaders. The remains of the city were eventually absorbed by nearby Cairo, which had been built to the north of Fustat in 358 AH (969 AD) when the Fatimids conquered the region and created a new city as a royal enclosure for the caliph. The area then fell into disrepair for hundreds of years and was used as a garbage dump. Today, Fustat is part of Old Cairo, with few buildings remaining from its days as the administrative capital. *Editor's Note*

"What do you think we should do?" asked Bahadin.

"I think, sir, that you should disguise yourself and wear a Christian doctor's clothes, and I will be your servant, carrying your sack of medicines and leading your mule."

"That is easy," replied Bahadin.

After a while, they reached Bahadin's house and went inside. Bahadin ordered that no one else should be admitted, even the Sultan Saladin himself. He ordered Jawhar to get whatever was necessary for the disguise and asked him about the meeting place and its location in Fustat. "Near the mosque of 'Amr," he replied, and he described the place in detail. He left him to make the necessary preparations and started to assemble a squadron of soldiers who would precede him and wait in an inn near the meeting place. Then he devised a plan for surrounding the house as soon as he gave them the order to do so.

Everything was ready before sunset. Bahadin had dressed up as a Christian doctor, with a girdle around his waist and a turban on his head. The mule had been readied for him; Jawhar walked with him, and no one who saw them could doubt that they were anybody other than a doctor and his servant.

They left Cairo at sunset and quickly completed the distance to Fustat. Bahadin surveyed Fustat from a hill, noting the effects of the fire, which were still visible. Most of the buildings had been razed on the orders of the vizier Shawar in 564 AH (1169 AD). He had been worried that the Crusaders might reach the city and occupy it, so he ordered the inhabitants to leave and move to Cairo. Then he set it alight and ordered it to be looted. As a result, the population was reduced to poverty, their possessions lost. The fire continued to burn for fifty-four days, so that the roads became indistinguishable and pedestrians could no longer recognize one alley from another. If it had not been for Jawhar and his excellent knowledge of the streets, it would have been impossible for Bahadin to find the place he was looking for. But the Abyssinian led the mule forward, making his way through the ruins as if he were walking through his own home. His most conspicuous landmark was the minaret of the mosque of 'Amr, which stood out from all the others in Fustat.

Darkness fell just before they passed the mosque of 'Amr, and everything turned pitch black. There were few pedestrians in the streets. Anyone looking at Fustat would see it was very different from Cairo. For Cairo is richer, more beautiful and cultured, has more antiquities, and covers a greater area. The emirs lived in Cairo because it was reserved for men of state, while the craftsmen and merchants lived in Fustat, together with a good many of the lower classes, as well as sailors because of its proximity to the Nile. The fire had increased the contrast between the two cities.

When Bahadin was in the middle of the city and saw that he was alone with Jawhar, it occurred to him that the Abyssinian might try to betray him, for he was a traitor who could not be trusted. So he turned to him and asked, "Where are we, Jawhar? It seems that we are a long way from the place you mentioned even though we have passed the mosque of 'Amr."

"You can be sure that I am taking you to the place I promised, master," replied Jawhar. "We have indeed passed that house right now, as you probably noticed, but I am taking you to an adjoining house from which you can look down on the house where the conspirators are meeting. Its entrance is in another street. From there you will not only be able to see the people meeting but also hear what they are saying to each other."

"Good," said Bahadin. "But slow down a bit!" As he said that, he looked carefully at his surroundings and realized that he was near the inn where he had ordered his soldiers to wait. "Tell me, Jawhar," he said, "where is the house where they are meeting? Point to it from here!"

He pointed to it with his finger and asked, "Can you see the light hanging from that pole?"

"Yes," replied Bahadin.

"You can see a ruined house behind it," said Jawhar. "They are meeting inside there."

Bahadin turned his mule toward the inn, and the leader of the troops met him by the door. Bahadin ordered him to station his soldiers around the house on every side in such a way that no one would notice them since none of the men would be positioned on the road itself. "When you see a lamp moving in a circle over one of these roofs," he ordered, "then attack the house from every side and seize everyone in it." Going back to his mule, Jawhar led it until they had entered the narrow road he was looking for. Bahadin was still riding his mule as they came to a door. Jawhar knocked on it, and someone opened the window. The head of an old man stretched out, with forelocks hanging over his cheeks. "Who's knocking?" he asked.

Jawhar stepped forward and said, "Doctor Samaan... Open up!"

"What does the doctor want from us?" asked the old man. "We haven't got anyone sick here!"

"He hasn't come to treat anyone," replied Jawhar. "He wants to spend the night here. He lives in Cairo and came to take a trip on the Nile, but he found that the ship he wanted to sail on had departed. He needs to spend the night in Fustat so he can go to the riverbank in the early morning and sail on another one. Open up, man!"

"Why hasn't he gone to the inn?" asked the old man. "It's near enough from here!"

"He doesn't want to spend the night in the inn," replied Jawhar. "He is not used to sleeping in inns. I've brought him here as a service to you. It seems that you don't recognize me, Master Hayyim," he added, whispering in his ear.

The man looked at him closely and said, "Yes, I recognize you now, Jawhar. Sorry, I didn't realize who you were earlier!"

"Never mind!" whispered Jawhar. "I've brought you this doctor to spend the night here. He's wealthy as well as generous and won't mind how much you charge him. The best thing would be to let him have the whole house—you can ask him for a dinar for each room. If he tells you that he only needs one room, tell him that you are only willing to rent him the entire house."

Hayyim was happy with this suggestion. The whole house contained furnishings hardly worth two dinars, so after Jawhar had whispered his suggestion, he spoke up audibly and said, "We can't let a stranger spend the night with us here, but if the doctor would like us to rent him the entire house, we will do so."

"And how much will the rent be?" asked Jawhar.

"There are five rooms," replied the sheikh, "and the rent is five dinars."

Jahwar acted as if he was trying to swindle Bahadin by this request and bargained, "Five dinars is too much, Master Hayyim. Wouldn't four be enough?" And he signaled with his finger that he should accept.

"No," he replied. "If this is too much, the inn is close by."

Changing his tune, he indicated his acceptance and said, "Good. My master, the doctor, is a generous man. But where will you sleep?"

"I have only my old wife with me," replied the sheikh. "We will go and stay with our son-in-law, who lives near here."

Jawhar turned to Bahadin, took the dinars from him, and passed them to Master Hayyim, whispering to him, "These are the dinars, but you must give me back one of them before we leave tomorrow morning. Do you understand?"

"Yes," replied the old man. He had no intention of paying him anything. To the contrary, he had planned to ask for a sixth dinar the following morning, claiming that they had lost some furnishings or something of the kind.

Then he went inside and came back after a little while with the lamp in his hand, accompanied by his wife. "It seems that this guest must be very dear to you, for you to have turned me out of my house for him," she said.

"Why not?" asked her husband. He gestured to Bahadin to come in. He dismounted from his mule, and Jawhar led it under a bridge by the house and tied it to a ring that had been set there for this purpose. Bahadin retired in the house while Hayyim gave the lamp to Jawhar. He then left, entrusting them with the house.

Chapter 47

A Private Meeting

As Bahadin entered the house he took no notice of the foul smells rising from the hallways. They shut and bolted the door. Jawhar carried the lamp ahead of Bahadin, both on tiptoe so that they would not be heard. They had not walked far before they heard a commotion. "We are on the other side of the meeting place, with only a thin wall separating us," said Jawhar. "Slow down for a bit!"

Ever since leaving home alone with Jawhar, Bahadin had been on tenterhooks, keeping his hand on his dagger, ready to plunge it into Jawhar's chest if he sensed the slightest hint of treachery on his part. But he had not noticed anything untoward. When Jawhar told him to slow down, he stopped to look at him and saw him gesturing for him to climb a narrow staircase leading to a passage above the room. He went up with him, and from this passage they moved through a narrow door that led out to the roof proper with the open sky full of twinkling stars over their heads. Bahadin looked around and saw they were surrounded by roofs. "Let's leave the lamp on the roof and move around in darkness so that we are not noticed," said Jawhar in a quiet voice.

Bahadin agreed, and Jawhar walked on, with the sound of the commotion growing louder and more distinct, until they arrived at another wall. "This is a wall of another side of the meeting hall," he said.

In the upper section of the wall, Bahadin could see an opening that let light through. He stepped toward it, with Jawhar in front of him. "Look here!" said Jawhar.

He looked and saw a hall crammed full of people sitting on cushions lined up around the room on a carpet. There was plenty of noise. At the door stood a man with his back leaning against it, looking as though he was ready to prevent anyone from going in. Jawhar whispered in Bahadin's ear, "Can you see all right?"

"Yes," replied Bahadin. "But I don't recognize any of them except for Hasan. Who is that sitting beside him?"

"The person you can see on his right is 'Amara,[43] the Yemeni poet, and to his left is the judge al-'Uwayris. Then seated just after him is the chief propagandist, and on the other side 'Abd al-Samad, the secretary, and some other people. All of them are Shi'a, as you know. Look in the middle of the room—what do you see?"

"I can see a sword and a Koran," replied Bahadin. "I think they are using them to take their oath of allegiance."

"Yes," replied Jawhar.

Bahadin started to scrutinize those present so that he would be able to recognize them in the future if necessary. Suddenly he saw Hasan make a gesture asking those present to listen. "Emirs," he said, "I can give you the good news that our deeds have been crowned with success. A delegation of Franks arrived this morning bearing gifts for the Kurd. He was delighted with the present and failed to see what lay behind it. Letters also arrived from our friends on the coast of Syria, who are ready to move at the first signal. So you can rejoice, for we have achieved our objective."

'Amara, the famous Yemeni poet, interrupted him, while looking at judge al-'Uwayris and the chief propagandist, both of whom occupied important positions in the state. "Our noble Lord Hasan is worthy of the oath we have sworn to him as caliph," he said, "because of his noble lineage, and because His Majesty, the late lamented caliph, appointed him as his successor, as reported by the noble companion. So we must obey him faithfully, to restore this state to its former glory after its corruption by non-Arabs; those surrounding the previous caliph were allowed to interfere in its affairs and give him very poor advice. It was they who advised him to seek the help of Nuradin, the ruler of Syria. This is how things fell into the hands of this Yusuf, the so-called Saladin. But when our plans come to fruition and we seize the reins of power, we shall

---

43 'Amara ibn Abu al-Hasan was his full name. *Author's Note*

avoid such errors in future. We will not entrust important positions to anyone unless they are Arab and we are confident of their loyalty and their devotion to 'Alawite doctrine. We are Arabs, and the Koran is Arab. We should never involve any non-Arabs in our affairs, as others have done."

"God bless you, 'Amara, our brother from Yemen," said 'Abd al-Samad, the secretary. "The time of weakness has passed, thank God. This caliph of ours," he said, pointing to Hasan, "combines cunning and decisiveness, and al-'Uwayris, this vizier of ours, has no rival in good judgment. And..."

He was interrupted by a man who had kept his silence for a full hour, as if he were deep in thought about something important, not taking any notice of what the others were saying. When he heard what 'Abd al-Samad said about the vizierate, however, he raised his head and said, "There is no agreement on the vizierate yet! And despite my respect for the honorable judge, I do not believe he has any claim to the vizierate, which belongs to the family of the viziers of al-Ruzayk. They held this office during the time of the previous caliphs, and they have a prior claim to it, so it is not right to transfer it to anyone else."

Meanwhile, another man had stood up and begun to whisper in the ear of Hasan, who nodded his head in agreement. "Slow down!" he said. "Let us not start quarreling about a post that is our right, and which was within our grasp yesterday!"

The advocate for the Banu[44] Ruzayk vizierate laughed and said, "You want to restore the vizierate to the Banu Shawar? Don't all these misfortunes spring from his period of office? Wasn't it he who burned this flourishing city through his mismanagement? The vizierate should belong to no one but al-Ruzayk. We are its original holders."

Hasan spoke gently with a smile on his face. "Control your anger, and return to your senses," he said. "We're not in a competition for posts right now; we are uniting to expel the enemy from our country. After we have done that, we can then agree on what should be done."

The advocate for the Banu Ruzayk vizierate replied, "Of course, Hasan does not wish to discuss posts now, because he has guaranteed

---

44 Banu, literally meaning "children of" is used to designate a tribe or an extended family. *Editor's Note*

himself the caliphate on the basis of his 'Ubaydi lineage. And no one has contested the accuracy of his lineage because the noble companion testified to its authenticity on the basis of what he had heard from the late caliph." And he laughed scornfully.

Chapter 48

The Attack

Bahadin had been listening intently to the conversation and following every movement, with Jawhar standing in front of him craning forward to see as much as he could. Satisfied with what he had heard and seen, Bahadin turned to Jawhar and made a gesture to him, "Where's the lamp? Give it to me..."

Jawhar went down to the passageway and brought the lamp. Bahadin took it and carried it to the roof, where he swung it around in a circle in the manner agreed to signal the troops to seize the house and all those in it. Then he went down, hid the lamp, and went back to observe people through the aperture at the top of the wall as they continued to argue and converse more and more vehemently and loudly. A few minutes later Bahadin's men stormed the hall and began to arrest those inside. None of them were able to resist—all they could do was yell and shout.

Bahadin directed his attention to Hasan in particular but could not find him among those who had been seized. He thought he must have been smuggled out of the hall. When he was certain that his men had successfully apprehended all the other conspirators, he told Jawhar to come down in order to return to Cairo. Jawhar held the lamp, with Bahadin following him. But as soon as he set foot in the passageway, he heard hurried footsteps coming from the house underneath him. Bahadin looked carefully in the dim light and saw a figure he did not recognize in a turban and cloak. "Come on, that's Hasan," whispered Jawhar. He quickly put out the lamp so as not to give away his location and hurried down to arrest Hasan. He thought that he must have come back following his prior agreement with the owner, one of his old accomplices, to spend the night there and then escape in the morning.

Jawhar then led Bahadin down to the ground floor, for he knew the entrances to the place. They pricked up their ears but could not hear any footsteps or voices. It was as if Hasan had been a mere passing shadow. Bahadin gestured to Jawhar to turn on the lamp to have a good look at his surroundings; he drew his dagger, ready to attack anyone who might appear in front of him. Jawhar had scarcely begun to light up the area when they heard the front door creak. They ran toward it and found the door open, with no one there. They lit the lamp and started to search everywhere for Hasan but could not find him. They were certain that he had escaped. "Jawhar, are you sure that it was Hasan that you just saw?" asked Bahadin.

"I think that it was most probably him," replied Jawhar, "but it could have been someone else. Come on, let's see if we can find him outside the house in the surrounding area. If we don't, he may be among the prisoners, or else he may have escaped, God curse him!"

They left, Bahadin got on his mule, and they started to look for him in the area around the house. But they could find no trace of him. Eventually they went back to Cairo, Bahadin fearing that Hasan had escaped—a fear that turned out to be fully justified.

The rest of the conspirators who had been arrested were condemned to death by crucifixion, with 'Amara the Yemeni at their head. He was crucified on 2 Ramadan[45] 569 AH (1174 AD). Saladin thus rid himself of those involved in this conspiracy, though he continued to worry about Hasan, the main cause of those intrigues...

As for Sittalmulk, she woke up the next morning and learned that the conspiracy had been defeated. She asked Yaquta to go and find out the details of what had happened. When she learned of the arrests, she was happy, but also concerned that Hasan, the cause of her troubles, had escaped. She knew that he would stop at nothing to achieve his aims— even if that meant taking illegal actions or reneging on his commitments. Looking at Yaquta, she said, "Saladin must be satisfied—he has achieved what he set out to do."

"I am very disturbed that that traitor has escaped," replied Yaquta. "But what can we do? His treachery is bound to backfire on him. God is

---

45 Ramadan is a holy month, the ninth of the Islamic calendar. *Editor's Note*

my witness! Besides, we no longer need to concern ourselves with him since we are under the protection of Saladin. And now I have come to talk to you about something different and take your thoughts away from all of this…"

Sittalmulk was so concerned about the fate of 'Imadin that she was taken aback. "What do you mean? Speak!"

Her reaction provoked Yaquta's laughter. "I am going to reprimand you on 'Imadin's behalf," she told her mistress. "You know that one of his messengers, who had recently seen and spoken to him, arrived. We found out from 'Imadin's letter that he was a prisoner, but you asked no further details about him from the messenger nor did you give him a letter to carry back to him."

"Oh, Yaquta," exclaimed Sittalmulk, "you are unsettling me with so many questions. Do you imagine that I hadn't thought of this? I would be very pleased to see 'Imadin's messenger; in fact, I have made up my mind to summon him. Where is he?"

"Bahadin has just told me that the messenger is asking to see you," replied Yaquta, "and that 'Imadin himself told him to do so…"

She blushed, overcome by joy, and could not help herself from saying in a loud voice, "'Imadin told him to see me! Thank God, he is thinking of me. He loves me, then!" Then she suddenly stopped, regretting her display of emotion and feeling embarrassed. She turned her face to a wall with a beautifully colored curtain on it and pretended to be examining it.

"Love! Oh God!" wondered Yaquta aloud, as if speaking to herself. "How is it that it can make Sittalmulk, the daughter of Fatimid caliphs and distinguished hostess and honored guest of sultans, get so carried away with happiness when a commoner merely asks about her?"

Sittalmulk interrupted her, "Please don't comment on 'Imadin. He towers above the caliphs and sultans in my eyes. You are right that love… Ah, I have started to mention love in front of you without being embarrassed. Love can make one do all sorts of things. But now, where is that messenger? Call him in!"

Chapter 49

The Beloved's Messenger

Yaquta went out, returning after a little while with a young man dressed in clothes like those the people of Jerusalem wear when traveling. Around his head was a turban like a woman's veil, and he wore short baggy trousers with a wide leather belt around his waist. He had fastened a small dagger into the front of his belt and wrapped his legs in a woven cloth that allowed him to walk quickly.

When he had come in, he stood politely at attention. Sittalmulk welcomed him, saying, "What is your name, young man?"

"My name is George," the young man replied.

"You are a Christian, then?" asked Sittalmulk.

"Yes, my lady," he replied.

"Where have you come from?"

"I have come from Jerusalem with a letter for Sultan Saladin," the youth replied. "I gave it to him yesterday. But the writer of the letter also entrusted me with a private matter concerning Sittalmulk."

"And what is that matter?" asked Sittalmulk. "You are now in the presence of Sittalmulk."

He bowed his head respectfully and asked, "And which one of you is she?"

Yaquta stepped forward, pointed at her mistress, and said, "This is my mistress, Sittalmulk. Tell us what you have to say, truthfully and completely."

"And how could I stand before her if I were not honest in my mission, especially as I am the bearer of a secret that no one is privy to but me?"

"You are right, young man," replied Yaquta. "God bless you!"

"His name is no longer 'Imadin," said the young man. "He is now called 'Abd al-Jabbar."

"A nice name," said Yaquta. "But how do you know him? And who entrusted you with this secret mission?"

"I got to know him under very special circumstances," replied the young man. "As soon as I made his acquaintance, I developed a liking for him and an admiration for his character—to such an extent that I began to think I would even give my life for him. He is a young person of unparalleled manliness, honesty, and bravery."

When Sittalmulk heard this praise, her face lit up, her heart beat faster, and she craned forward to hear the young man's story. Meanwhile, Yaquta prodded him on. "How strange," she said. "You seem almost to love him! Tell us how that happened. And what is the mission that has brought you here?"

"'Imadin was passing through Jerusalem on his way to the outskirts of Aleppo," the young man replied, "for what reason I do not know. But the Franks arrested him and imprisoned him. I was also imprisoned, so we got to know each other in jail. I immediately recognized in him the regal virtues that were part of his character. We developed a mutual affection; I liked him and found him sincere toward me. We exchanged many secrets, though he didn't tell me anything about Sittalmulk. Then I was released from prison, gained access to the Frankish ruler of Jerusalem, and made it my mission to save my friend from prison, though I have yet to succeed. But I always continued to visit him, trying to console him. Meanwhile, we had heard of what had happened here—the death of the caliph, may God have mercy on him, the change of circumstances, and that the caliph's family was living in full comfort in this palace under the protection of Saladin. I told him all that I knew, including the conspiracy that was known to all. The ruler of Jerusalem sent me here to guide the delegation that came bearing gifts to Saladin. When saying good-bye to my friend, he entrusted me with delivering a letter to Sultan

Saladin, then whispered under his breath that I should look for Princess Sittalmulk and reassure him about her condition. So here I am, standing in front of her..."

"And what did he tell you about his relationship with her?" asked Yaquta.

"He didn't give many details, because time was short," replied the young man. "But I understood from what he was saying that he had the greatest respect for Princess Sittalmulk. However, he thought that you might not believe me, so he gave me this jewel to prove the truth of my words." So saying, he took out a jewel from a pocket in his belt, which he gave to Yaquta. As soon as Sittalmulk saw it, she whispered, "This is one of the jewels from the necklace we gave him that night." Now certain that 'Imadin trusted this young man, she turned to him and said, "You spoke the truth. Now we are sure that you are his trusted messenger. How is he? When will he leave prison? And if he is released, will he come here?"

"He will be freed soon, God willing," replied the young man. "He is well, but if he is released, I do not think that he will come directly here, for he first has to complete a mission that I know nothing about. Except that he asked me to tell you that he would return after completing it."

This left her downcast and depressed, but raising her eyes, she said, "He is well, then. That is all that matters! And if we give you a memento, will you convey it to him?"

"Of course, my lady! My only wish is to be of assistance to him!" he said.

She gestured to Yaquta and ordered her to bring some precious jewels that she hoped would help 'Imadin, and then instructed her to write him a letter confirming her undying love and telling him she would wait for his return with the utmost patience.

She did all this and put the jewels and the letter in a bag, which she sewed up and gave to the messenger. She also gave him a purse containing fifty dinars. "This is for the expenses of the journey," she said. He took all this, thanking her, and left. Sittalmulk stayed behind chatting to Yaquta for some time about 'Imadin's qualities and the dangers he was facing, with Yaquta reassuring her and urging patience until his return.

Chapter 50

Sultan Nuradin

Hasan had escaped arrest that night because, with his great shrewdness and caution, he had taken preventive measures against all conceivable occurences. He had prepared an exit from the meeting hall to Hayyim's house so that if anyone tried to capture him he would be able to escape. He was not concerned about what would happen to his companions—his only concern was to be able to escape himself.

He spent several days hiding in that house before learning of the punishment meted out to his fellow conspirators—how they had been condemned to death by crucifixion. And he despaired of Egypt and the Egyptians. But his unbridled ambition continued to make him believe in the impossible. For when a man is really intent on obtaining something, however distant, his strong desire will make him see it as close at hand. So he turned his thoughts to something else—how to take revenge on Sittalmulk. While he had been biding his time to strike, he had realized that it was she who had sought the help of his servant Jawhar to expose them. This infuriated him. After considering the matter, he decided to sow discord between Sultan Nuradin, the ruler of Syria, and Saladin by conveying to the former secrets he knew relating to Saladin's desire to declare Egypt independent and the declaration Saladin had made against Nuradin. By so doing, he hoped he could persuade Nuradin to wage war on Saladin and expel him from Egypt by force. He started imagining that he himself would witness the conquest and would demand Sittalmulk as his share of the spoils. Minimizing every difficulty in the way of this plan, he thought it would be easy to achieve.

When he had convinced himself of the realism of his plans, he contrived to flee Egypt and head for Damascus. He traveled quickly, reached Damascus disguised in the clothes of an Egyptian merchant, and stayed in an inn near the citadel, which in those days was the residence of Sultan Nuradin. Damascus was proud of that great sultan and his family and happy with the uninterrupted victories he had achieved against the Franks in various parts of Syria. But Hasan had just settled in the inn when he heard people lamenting a decline in the sultan's health a few days earlier. People feared for his life because he had caught diphtheria. Hasan connived a way of getting himself into his audience chamber so that he could inform him about matters in Egypt.

He inquired about his personal physician and learned that it was al-Rahabi, one of the most skilled doctors of all, whom he already knew. He sought him and found him in his home, where the doctor gave him a warm reception. They had met in Egypt, and the doctor knew of his high standing with the caliph al-'Adid. In answer to Hasan's question about Sultan Nuradin's condition, he replied that he had caught diphtheria and that the disease had taken a toll on him because he had refused to be bled. Hassan expressed his regret then said, "Wouldn't it be a good idea for me to meet him? I might be able to persuade him to be bled, and I have something to say to him that might cheer him up—if I could only find a way to tell him about it."

The doctor thought this to be a good idea, for he knew how concerned Sultan Nuradin was about all the the happenings in Egypt— big and small. He thought that he would want to receive Hasan to get the latest news even though he was ill. So the doctor invited him to come back the following morning.

When Hasan returned in the morning, the doctor said, "Our master the sultan is better today. I mentioned your purpose in your wanting to meet him, and he expressed a desire to see you."

Hasan was pleased that he had accepted and rode with the doctor to the citadel. The sultan had been staying in a room there when the disease struck him, so he did not move from that room. The doctor went in first and asked permission for Hasan to enter, which the sultan granted. As Hasan entered, he greeted him with courtesy and respect. He had met the sultan on several occasions. Sultan Nuradin was a good-looking man with a robust constitution and a radiant face. He was tall, with a swarthy complexion, a broad forehead, a handsome face with a goatee, and charming eyes. But now Hasan could see that his condition was very different. The disease had robbed his eyes of their luster, and he looked very pale. When he saw Hasan come in, he smiled as usual, in a kindly and courteous manner.

Hasan bent over his hand as if wanting to kiss it, but Nuradin withdrew it and gestured to him to sit down. There was no furniture in the room because it was a reception hall; he just happened to find himself there when the disease struck him.

Hasan sat on a cushion and asked, "How is my lord today? I hope that he is well, because if he is well, the state will be well, and if he is healthy, Islam will be healthy. And I hope that I have not inconvenienced him by coming..."

"Praise be to God for everything!" replied Nuradin, his voice weakened by illness. "I am pleased that you have come, for I know that you have traveled from Egypt, where our beloved vizier al-Malik al-Nasir[46] is now. How was he when you left him?"

When he heard him call Saladin "our beloved," he demurred, but he also resolved to overcome what appeared to be an impediment to fulfilling his plan. "He is well, under the protection of your lordship Sultan al-Malik al-'Adil[47]," he replied.

"And how was Egypt when you left?" he continued.

"When I left, the people were eager to see our lord the sultan—may God exalt him—and wanting him to honor them with a visit to see his new territory."

Nuradin's face lit up. He was happy to hear this from an Egyptian emir who had been very close to the previous regime. "But we have heard that some of them have conspired to reject the new rulers. Is that true?"

"Yes, my lord," replied Hasan. "There was a conspiracy but not to reject the rule of Sultan Nuradin."

---

46 The literal Arabic translation of al-Malik al-Nasir is "The Victorious King", a name sometimes used to designate Sultan Saladin. *Editor's Note*

47 The literal Arabic translation of al-Malik al-'Adil is "The Just King", a name sometimes used to designate Sultan Nuradin. *Editor's Note*

"What was the conspiracy for, then?" inquired Nuradin, the surprise visible in his eyes. Forgetting his illness, he had started to finger the edge of his beard, as he looked intently into Hasan's eyes to see what he could fathom.

"The Egyptians are the most docile of people, but..." He swallowed hard and cleared his throat, giving the impression that he was holding back something that was difficult to divulge.

"What do you mean? But what?" asked Nuradin.

"I do not wish to upset my lord the sultan with matters that I do not think will please him," replied Hasan.

"Tell me, tell me!" said Nuradin, the anger apparent on his face. "There was a conspiracy to reject who?"

"There was a conspiracy to depose Saladin..."

"Doesn't obeying me mean obeying him?" asked Nuradin.

"Yes," replied Hasan. "That is how it should be, and if he had asked for our obedience in the name of Sultan Nuradin, he would have found no one to oppose him."

"How did he ask for it, then?" asked Nuradin.

"It seems that the messengers have been hiding the truth from the sultan," continued Hasan. "But if he will give me permission, I will speak..."

"Speak, yes, I give you permission!" replied Nuradin.

Hasan turned to the doctor, as if to consult him on how the emotional consequences of unpleasant revelations would affect the sultan's health. The doctor approached the sultan and said, "I can see anger in the face of our master the sultan, and he is ill. Couldn't this conversation be postponed to another time?"

"No," replied Nuradin. "I am well, praise be to God! Let him say whatever he wishes."

Hasan sat up straight and said, "Your vizier Saladin did not ask for the obedience of the Egyptians in your name, but in his own name. He declared that he was in charge, and not Sultan Nuradin, so we resisted him and conspired against him because we do not wish to acknowledge anyone except our lord Nuradin as sultan. I find it strange that you do not know this, for Saladin stated this openly in a public session, and his own father Najmudin reprimanded him and ordered him to restrain himself." These words were followed by a very long silence.

Chapter 51

Failure

Nuradin was extremely perceptive. He said nothing for a time as he reflected on what he had heard, manipulating his beard. He was not pleased to hear this denunciation from someone who was a natural enemy to both of them, especially after his confession that he had been one of the conspirators against Saladin. He realized that if his acceptance of Nuradin had been genuine, he would not have participated in such an act of disloyalty but would have conveyed the information about Saladin directly to him. Suspecting strongly he was lying, he asked, "And what do you think should happen now?"

"I think that your lordship Sultan al-Malik al-'Adil[48] should not take the ambitions of his vizier lightly. He had publicly declared the independence of Egypt even before Caliph al-'Adid had died, so can you imagine his attitude now? Your Lordship has no choice but to send an army to force him to submit to your authority. As for myself, I put my life at your disposal."

The sultan turned towards Hasan, his dark eyes so angry that sparks almost flew from them. "If you were sincere in the advice you are now giving us, you would have brought us this information much earlier," he said. "The fact that you have suppressed it until now does not give me any confidence in your motives or that of your fellow conspirators. You have conspired to depose Nuradin. In fact, you wanted to renounce allegiance to the 'Abbasid caliph because he is a Sunni; your sole purpose was to reclaim power for yourself." He said this lying down, shaking with anger and wanting to move to a sitting position. The doctor helped him, now regretting that he had allowed Hasan to come and see his patient.

---

48 The Just King—a designation sometimes applied to Nuradin. *op.cit. Editor's Note*

Hasan tried to defend himself against this accusation, "I didn't express my meaning clearly, your Lordship. The information I gave you was correct. What I told you was the truth. We support Sultan Nuradin, and..."

But Nuradin would not let him finish, "If you had been loyal, you would have obeyed my vizier and deputy Saladin rather than indulge in flattery and vacillation. What harm has Saladin done to you? Didn't you send your women's hair to us, seeking our help? And did we not dispatch his uncle, Shirkawih, who saved you? This is the Saladin who overcame dissent, revived the country, and canceled taxes. You should acknowledge his good deeds. But a people who have become so dishonored as to use their women's hair to plead for help cannot be expected to be loyal. I still remember how badly impressed our council members were when they saw the hair wrapped in handkerchiefs. The council had been convened to examine your caliph's demand, and among the young men present was one who asked me to give him a lock of the golden red hair. He was close to Saladin, so I gave him a lock to see his reaction. After he had looked at it carefully, he said, 'This beautiful lock of hair belongs to someone with no connection to these women, but is either the caliph's daughter or his sister. I will give it back to her.' So I let him have the lock of hair wrapped in its handkerchief, but I don't know whether he succeeded in returning it to the person to whom it belonged."

He continued, "How could you imagine that I would trust you to be faithful? Your purpose in coming to see me now is to sow enmity between me and my deputy. Let us suppose that he has indeed wanted to make Egypt independent. Well, let him do so! Allegiance to the caliph is indivisible, and it does not derive from you." At this point, he became visibly tired. He looked away, contemptuously, turned his back on Hasan, and went back to sleep, breathing heavily from exhaustion.

Hasan's blood froze in his veins. He felt utter failure, as if someone had poured a bucket of iced water over his head. He started shaking, for the information concerning the lock of hair had struck him like a thunderbolt. He knew that it was Sittalmulk's hair. The doctor asked him to leave immediately, for the sultan had had a relapse resulting from the anger that this encounter had caused him. Hasan was afraid that the sultan would have him arrested or worse. So he departed quickly and went into hiding in a place where no one would recognize him, waiting to see how things would turn out.

The following morning, criers went around the city announcing the death of Sultan Nuradin, who died on 11 Shawwal[49] 569 AH (or 1174 AD). Because of the recent improvement in his health, the view of the general public about the cause of his death was that someone he met had unleashed his fury to such an extent that it precipitated an attack that ended his life. Hasan's failure was complete. Overcome by despair, he decided to flee, for he could not see any way out of the predicament he had boxed himself in.

He left Damascus, so fuming with anger that his servant did not dare look him in the face. As he passed through al-Ghuta, he came to a spring of running water surrounded and shaded by all sorts of fruit trees—apples, quince, apricots, and others. Spring had set in, the flowers were in full bloom, and the birds were chirping. Nature was laughing and singing, but Hasan could see nothing but his abject failure before his eyes. He was prompted to stop by his mule, which had suddenly felt thirsty at the sound of the running water and headed for the water canal to drink. The sun was high in the sky, and Hasan found himself in the desert without anything to protect him. He decided to dismount and rest, asking his servant to take care of his mule. He wandered among the trees unnoticed by those guarding the orchard, who did not expect anyone to alight there at that time of day.

Hasan sat down, alone, by the trunk of an apricot tree with drooping branches and magnificent fruits that were the pride of the local populace. It was a type of reddish apricot that would ripen at the very beginning of spring, known as the Aleppan apricot. Syrians boasted it was superior to any other in the Levant; people came to al-Ghuta especially to see and taste it.

He was not conscious of any of this. But the blossoming of nature both reminded him of his past and threw into relief his present situation, and he became ever more depressed. He was deep in thought, paying no attention to the chirping of the birds as they flew playfully around each other. None of them seemed to be aware of or fear failure, for like other animals they demanded nothing from nature except the necessities of life,

---

49 The tenth month of the Islamic calendar. *Editor's Note*

which were in plentiful supply. Man, on the other hand, has demands that require toil and hard work—and in achieving them, he is prone to commit all sorts of questionable acts.

After sitting quietly for a while, he was brought to his senses by an insect crawling beside him in the grass. He became aware of the stunning beauty of the surrounding nature. The darkness he was sinking into now became apparent to him, and his life story flashed through his mind like an arrow. This merely made him even more depressed. It was clear to him that the reason for his misery was Sittalmulk's rejection of him—and he became ever more determined to exact vengeance on her. Taking advantage of his servant's absence, he began talking to himself. "Woe to you, you wretched woman," he said. "You prefer that young man to me? Wouldn't it have been better for me to be your husband and for us to have kept the caliphate? I could have killed Saladin, but I didn't because I wanted to reap the fruits of my exertions myself rather than let them be exploited by someone else. I knew that you had doubts about the truth of my lineage and that you did not believe that I was descended from the Banu 'Ubaydi[50] clan. You are right, I am not one of them, but nobility of lineage is an illusion. Men are known by their deeds, yet I claimed that heritage because people respect it, and I thought it would be a means of getting closer to you and the caliph. But when I was about to reach my goal, you put an end to all my efforts with your haughtiness and your relationship with that servant."

At this point, he recoiled and heard an apricot falling on the dry grass with a rustling sound. His thoughts turned in a different direction, and he remembered his youth. "Rashidin, the time has come for me to seek your help against this harlot—not to marry her, but to give her a taste of punishment. To let her see for herself the error of her ways, so that she repents, even though repentance will do her no good." Suddenly he seemed to have hit on another course of action that would lead him to success. His heart was at rest, and these thoughts lifted the black cloud off his mind. He felt thirsty, so he turned around but could see no one. He clapped his hands, called his servant, and told him to order the gardener to prepare him some food and bring him fruits. They ate as Hasan went back to planning his new course of action. Let us leave him there and follow 'Imadin's adventures after his departure from Egypt.

---

50 *Op cit.* See earlier footnotes on 'Ubaydi state and meaning of Banu. *Editor's Note*

Chapter 52

In Prison

We learnt that 'Imadin had suffered badly on his journey. The Franks arrested him near Jerusalem because they believed that he was a spy, then threw him in prison for a time, during which he got to know George. George was not a Christian as he claimed, but was a senior Isma'ili guerilla whose real name was 'Abd al-Rahim. Rashidin had sent him to kill the Frank, ruler of Jerusalem. So he took the name George as a disguise and contrived to make them arrest and imprison him. While in jail, he would get to know the junior palace officials and learn the palace secrets, enabling him to fulfill his mission. It was the usual practice of the guerillas when carrying out an order from their master Rashidin, that if one of them was commissioned to kill a ruler, he would first infiltrate himself among the junior servants. Often, he would put himself in charge of that ruler's horses to make it easier to get close to his target. When he mounted or dismounted, he would then take advantage of a moment of inattention to thrust his dagger into him.

While 'Abd al-Rahim, or George, was in prison, he got to know 'Imadin, whom he liked, and a close relationship developed between them. 'Abd al-Rahim told him the truth about himself, how he was a Muslim and was using prison as a means of achieving his goal of assassinating the ruler of Jerusalem on the orders of the Supreme Sheikh Rashidin. He wanted 'Imadin to share his enthusiasm for the Isma'ili guerillas with their noble purposes and powerful influence and his veneration for their charismatic leader Rashidin. He hoped that in time he would persuade 'Imadin to join the Isma'ilis. For his part, 'Imadin commended the reason that had landed him in that prison, for it had enabled them to become acquainted and made his mission easier. He showed that he appreciated

'Abd al-Rahim's ideas and promised him that he would join the Isma'ilis after his release. Secretly, he intended to make that organization a means of carrying out the mission for which he had come—to kill Rashidin. He made every effort to win 'Abd al-Rahim's trust, changing his name to 'Abd al-Jabbar as 'Abd al-Rahim had asked him to do.

The days in prison seemed long. There was nothing to do, and the inmates became bored. They were forced to spend their time chatting or playing games. 'Abd al-Rahim spent most of his time talking about Rashidin's supernatural powers and his personality—how he knew the secret world and could predict the future, solve the most intractable mysteries, talk to stones, and perform miracles. He did that not for worldly gain but only for a higher purpose—to promote Islam. As proof of that, he cited the mission he had come on to assassinate the ruler of Jerusalem. Whenever he mentioned Rashidin, his emotions were roused, and he became fired with zeal. He idolized him, elaborating on his virtues. With time and constant repetition, his words began to have their effect on 'Imadin, who began to regard Rashidin as a powerful force that could be used against the Franks, if he were able to gain his confidence. He was troubled by all he had heard about his supernatural powers, the miracles he could perform, and the descriptions of paradise that awaited his disciples. He yearned to find out for himself the truth about all this.

Their friendship grew closer. Then 'Abd al-Rahim's days in prison came to an end with his release. The palace officials liked him and recognized that some of his qualities could be useful to them—for he was a Christian who knew the language and the customs of the country. They cultivated him, while he exerted every effort to secure their acquiescence and achieve his objective. When negotiations between the 'Ubaydi party and the Franks in Cairo ended with the sending of a delegation to Egypt, they chose him to be a guide. He bid 'Imadin goodbye and told him his secret, as recounted earlier. He made a huge effort to support him in a friendly way, out of a desire to recruit him to the Isma'ili cause, for he saw in him unusual bravery and intelligence, and they were in need of such men.

After he returned from his mission, he intervened on behalf of 'Imadin's release from jail. He also informed him of how his letter to Saladin led to the arrest of the conspirators and their crucifixion, except for Hasan, who had escaped. He also gave him a letter from Saladin that thanked him for courage and loyalty, confirmed his affection, and included some money for him...

Then he told him of his meeting with Sittalmulk and passed him the letter written by Yaquta and the jewels that Sittalmulk sent him. 'Imadin took the jewels and gave some of them to 'Abd al-Rahim, who became even more attached to him. There is nothing like generosity to endear a person to people, however flawed that person may be. Hence the popular saying, "There is no fault that generosity cannot cover up." So much more, then, when the person concerned has few faults or is even faultless. If the rich knew how much generosity could make people overlook their faults, they would never be stingy. And just as generosity can cover up faults, so stinginess highlights faults that people may not possess.

'Imadin hurried to read Yaquta's letter. This is what it said:

Greetings, 'Imadin. Your friend came to me and told me that you were in good health. We were obviously unhappy to hear of your suffering in prison but were reassured by your friend's affection, and his evident virtue and heroic nature that we could clearly discern. We are now staying in the guesthouse under the protection of Saladin. He is a gallant man, who has been very generous to us. I am pleased to tell you that he considers our lady Sittalmulk as a sister. He treats her like a sister in every respect. You were mentioned once in front of him, and he sang your praises. What he wants for you is a happy future. Sittalmulk was most unhappy that you were in prison, but your friend George told us that you will soon be released safe and sound—though it is hard for us to accept that you will not come to us for some time. Complete your mission quickly and in the meantime continue to send us your news. Farewell!

As soon as he finished reading the letter, a new feeling took hold of him that he had never felt before. Up until then, his thoughts about Sittalmulk reflected the conflicts within him. On the one hand, he knew that Saladin had wanted her as a bride for himself. On the other, he had seen how strongly attached she was to him—so much so that she had conveyed in no uncertain terms and almost told him openly how desperately in love she was with him. He had been bewildered and had avoided dealing with the situation by traveling and immersing himself in all kinds of dangerous adventures while waiting to see what fate would bring. But when he realized from Yaquta's letter that Saladin did not want to marry Sittalmulk and when he remembered how kind she had been, he felt for the first time, and despite the letter's brevity, that she belonged to him alone. All at once, the fires of love blazed in his heart, as if all the suppressed love pangs that had not fully manifested themselves in the past had all surged in a single instant and now overcame him. Whichever way he turned, Sittalmulk's image was before his eyes, as he recalled the last time he saw her on the night she stood to say goodbye, urging him to leave quickly through the tunnels.

Chapter 53

The Journey

'Imadin recalled the lock of red hair, and how as a young man of no consequence he had dared to ask Nuradin for it; how Nuradin allowed him to take it; and then how he had successfully met its owner, who had been in great danger; and how he had saved her and given her back the lock. All this flashed through his mind in a mere second—it had come to pass that fate had given him this blessing. And if he were able to fulfill his mission, he would reach the pinnacle of happiness. From that moment on, he became ecstatic. There is no happiness without love. Men have differed in their views on how to define happiness, some seeing it in wealth, others in fame, and yet others in good health. But lovers know that happiness lies in the mutual love of two people, who hope and fear, meet and separate, but always enjoy the delight of coming together to share the past or plan the future. It does not matter whether they enjoy wealth or poverty, fame or anonymity, for they are happy under all circumstances.

After reading the letter, 'Imadin felt like he had never felt before. He desperately wanted to return quickly to Cairo. Meanwhile, 'Abd al-Rahim was watching his friend's reactions, fearing that the letter might contain something that would make him change his plans. He wanted to bring him into the Isma'ili fold. 'Imadin came to from his reverie and realized his friend was sitting beside him. "Thank you, my friend, for this valuable service!" he said. "May God reward you!"

"It was my duty to do so," replied 'Abd al-Rahim. "And I cannot claim any particular merit for doing so. If you had the opportunity to perform a similar service for me, would you hesitate?"

'Imadin felt a sense of gratitude and replied, "I would give my life for you!" No sooner had he said that, however, than something inside him made him realize that this was something he was not prepared to do. From that moment on, he felt that his soul did not belong to him, but that he wanted to live to return to his beloved and be united with her.

'Abd al-Rahim, however, was delighted to hear what he had heard. "You will meet someone who is more worthy of such a sacrifice than I am," he said. "Supreme Sheikh Rashidin, our imam and leader, is someone we would all give our lives for. You will feel this pleasure when you become one of us. Are you still resolved to join us? Or has this letter changed your mind?" And he laughed, inquisitively.

"Nothing has changed my mind," replied 'Imadin. "But how can I do that? Where should I go? By which route? I hope that you will help and guide me!"

'Abd al-Rahim was happy to hear this and said, "I am at your command. I will give you a letter of recommendation for Sheikh Dabbous, the supreme sheikh's deputy, who resides with him in the Misyaf fortress at Mount Summaq in the district of Aleppo. Then I will join you myself. You can leave today. Do you know the roads?"

"I know them well, for I was brought up in this area," replied 'Imadin.

'Abd al-Rahim wrote a letter of recommendation to Sheikh Dabbous, the deputy sheikh of the mountain. 'Imadin took it and bid him farewell. He mounted his horse and headed for the mountains of Summaq, a mountain range in the Aleppo district containing several towns and villages, with farms and orchards, as well as fortresses, all belonging to the Isma'ilis. There is little fresh water there, except for a few springs in specific locations. But despite that, there are all sorts of fruit trees and various crops, including cotton and sesame.

The mountains of Summaq are famous for harboring the Isma'ili Assassins' fortresses, of which there are many, the best known being Misyaf, Kahf, al-Khawabi, 'Aliqa, Marqab, and al-Rusafa, to mention only the most important. Our concern here is with Misyaf, where the Isma'ili leader Rashidin Sinan resided. It was about a twelve-hour ride on horseback, west of Hama.[51]

---

51 City located in present-day Syria. *Editor's Note*

Chapter 54

The Fortress of Misyaf

During the pinnacle of Isma'ili glory, the fortress of Misyaf was famous for being the residence of the supreme sheikh, leader and imam of this sect. It is situated on Mount Misyaf a high mountain surrounded on the east and west by vast swamps. Its highest summit faces north, on which is an impregnable fortress where the leader of the Isma'ilis resides.

It is virtually impregnable primarily because it stands on a high rock whose sides are quasi-vertical pillars, almost impossible to climb. It looks over marshes that surround it in every direction. Peasants who live in the valley beneath cultivate wheat and barley. At a distance from the mountain is the village of Misyaf, where the village folk live.

The fortress itself is surrounded by a thick wall with only one gate, over which is set a stone arch. After entering, one walks along a hallway, all of which is vaulted, leading to the top of the fortress with rooms behind and above it—all built of solid stone. Along the wall is a series of towers, in which the garrison protecting the fortress lives. Any attackers can be pelted with arrows or stones while they are still a long way from the gate. So it would be impossible to conquer the fortress without losing hundreds or thousands of men.

'Imadin left Jerusalem on horseback. A number of roads connect Jerusalem to Mount Summaq, but he preferred to travel through Damascus, where he had spent his childhood, for he was eager to see the city and its orchards again. After a few days, he arrived there in disguise—two days before Hasan. He walked around the city and visited the citadel, recognizing many people he knew. Sultan Nuradin happened to be returning from the racetrack on his horse, in a grandiose procession surrounded by his emirs and nobles. He was pleased to see him, but he continued to make every effort to pass unnoticed in disguise. He knew the tensions that existed between Saladin and Nuradin and would have liked this state of affairs to end, but he also hoped his master Saladin would prevail.

He spent most of the day in Damascus, eating local foods and fruits and enjoying the sights. As he left, he passed through al-Ghuta; indeed, he may even have passed the same spot that Hasan was to pass through two days later! At all events, he spent that night in a village on the outskirts of Damascus and set out the following day in the direction of the mountains of Summaq, spending the second night in an inn. He spent most of the following day on the road; he could have reached Misyaf that afternoon, but he preferred to arrive there the following morning, so he spent the night in a village and rode on in the morning. Two hours later he could see Mount Misyaf, with the fortress on the top almost touching the clouds. He found its impregnable position quite extraordinary, remarking to himself that it was more secure than an eagle in the sky. He dismounted there, and a peasant sheikh came up to him, thinking that he must be an Isma'ili leader and offering to be of service to him. The peasants were used to the displays of force and cruelty by members of the sect. They often witnessed fights to the death between them and attacking soldiers from Syria, Egypt, or the surrounding mountains, but they were always able to repulse and defeat the intruders. Also, there were stories of the miracles of Supreme Sheikh Rashidin that circulated, calling him "the sheikh of the mountain," after the title of the founder[52] of the sect. Because of their unlimited belief in his miraculous powers, everything unusual or frightening that happened was attributed to him, even natural phenomena like rain or thunder and lightning. He had become an object of fear to his enemies but of reassurance to his disciples.

'Imadin's intention when he arrived was to meet Sheikh Dabbous and give him the letter of recommendation from 'Abd al-Rahim. When the peasant sheikh appeared, 'Imadin inquired about the whereabouts of Rashidin. The man balked and stared at 'Imadin, then said, "It seems you are a stranger in these parts, sir!"

"Yes!" replied 'Imadin.

---

52 Al-Hasan ibn al-Sabah. *Author's Note*

"What brings you here, then?" asked the man. "What do you want from the sheikh of the mountain?"

"I am carrying a letter for his deputy, Sheikh Dabbous," 'Imadin replied.

"Dabbous... All right, I thought you were seeking Supreme Sheikh Rashidin himself. Nobody can hope to see him, even his friends and supporters. He doesn't meet anyone except under extraordinary circumstances."

"And you...who are you, my friend?" asked 'Imadin. "Could you be one of his men?"

The man interrupted him. "I wish I were," he said. "But someone like me cannot hope for such an honor. We are fortunate to be accepted by him because we provide him with the wheat that we grow, or the livestock that we graze for him and his men—as a result of which we are left alone..."

"Now I want to meet Sheikh Dabbous," said 'Imadin. "Will that be easy?"

"I don't know," replied the man. "Give me the letter if you like, and I will make sure he gets it. Then I'll bring you the reply."

He took the letter and raced off toward the mountain, leaving 'Imadin to await his return. He took hold of his horse's bridle and turned his eyes on the swamps that surrounded him and on the lofty mountain that stood in their midst. Above him was the fortress of Misyaf, surrounded by the wall and its towers. He could not make out any road leading to it. People must reach it on the wings of eagles or in balloons, he thought. That frightened him, as he imagined the danger that would confront anyone wanting to harm Rashidin, but it increased his desire to find out the truth about this man. Either he would do away with him or he would effect a reconciliation between him and Saladin.

Chapter 55

Sheikh Dabbous

An hour passed before the peasant sheikh returned, with a bare-headed, barefoot, and bare-chested young man, dressed as a messenger with short trousers. He looked like an elf. When he reached 'Imadin, he greeted him and asked him what he wanted. "I want to meet Sheikh Dabbous," he replied.

He stretched out his hand with the letter of recommendation and said, "This is your letter. What is your name?"

"'Abd al-Jabbar," replied 'Imadin.

"And you want to meet Sheikh Dabbous?" asked the young man.

"Yes," replied 'Imadin.

"Follow me," he said.

He followed him on foot, pulling his horse along. The young man walked in front of him, turning around to stare at him, which 'Imadin found strange. Many a man in his situation would have felt afraid, but he was a brave man who knew no fear.

After a little while they reached the base of the mountain, where the young man told 'Imadin to leave his horse and follow him. 'Imadin hesitated for a moment, but the young man said firmly, "You must leave your horse here. Otherwise, go back where you came from!"

So he obeyed and followed him along twisting paths, some of them cut into the rocks; others had steps of rock difficult to climb. The man leaped in front of him like a panther, not worried about wearing himself out, while 'Imadin did likewise, so as not to appear feeble. He was a man with a lot of pride. After climbing the twisting paths for an hour, they reached the strongly fortified castle gate. The young man stopped and told 'Imadin to wait. He advanced to the gate and tapped it with a measured knock. The gate screeched loudly as it was opened. He went in and shut the gate behind him. 'Imadin remained standing there, looking at the massive building, though he could see only the thick wall with towers on the top. Through the gaps in the towers and the narrow windows, he could see people who seemed to be soldiers coming and going.

After a little while, the messenger returned. His tone was now gentler, as he waved 'Imadin in. He entered through the gate under the thick arch and walked down a long twisting tunnel with a vaulted roof and a rough stone floor. On either side of it stood guards with spears and swords, like motionless statues. The sight frightened him, but he summoned his courage and resolved to be patient.

After walking through the tunnel for a while, he came to an opening that led to a square surrounded by closed doors. The messenger told him to follow him, until he came to a particular door on which he knocked. While the door was being opened, the messenger approached 'Imadin and handed him the letter of recommendation, then stepped back and indicated to him that he should enter. He stepped forward and found himself in a room with armed guards at the door. With the tips of their spears, they motioned for him to enter, which he did. When he stopped and looked around, he found himself in a spacious, carpeted room, the walls of which were covered with different types of weapons. Various types of torture instruments—chains and handcuffs—were strewn on all sides, and around the walls were seats made of carved stone, covered with bear and lion skins. He could see no one in the room except for Sheikh Dabbous, who was sitting in the middle of the room on the edge of a couch, wearing a cloak that enveloped him completely, with a large green turban on his head. 'Imadin greeted him and asked, "Sheikh Dabbous?"

The sheikh nodded and signaled for him to come forward and give him the letter. He broke the seal of the letter and read it. When he finished, he gestured to 'Imadin to sit down and said, "Our son 'Abd al-Rahim commends you to us. Sit down, 'Abd al-Jabbar, please." So he sat on the edge of the seat, waiting to see what would happen next. "'Abd al-Rahim says that you are asking for the privilege of approaching our supreme sheikh and imam Rashidin and becoming one of us," said Dabbous.

"Yes, my lord," replied 'Imadin. "Will this be possible for me?"

"Yes, 'Abd al-Jabbar," replied Sheikh Dabbous, "under certain conditions. You should know that first and foremost you should enlist only if your heart is pure and you are willing to submit completely and knowingly. Will you do that?"

"Yes," replied 'Imadin.

"Beware of deceiving yourself," replied Sheikh Dabbous. "I cannot know the secrets of your heart, but nothing is hidden from our imam the supreme sheikh. He knows every heart, for when he looks into your eyes, he knows that heart's secrets. If you have any doubt about your commitment or reservations about your willingness to submit, then you must leave here and not expose yourself to danger. I am giving you this advice because of the praise for your bravery and integrity that I have read in the letter of recommendation. If you are given the good fortune to join the organization and to take the oath of allegiance, then you will have guaranteed yourself the utmost happiness in both this world and the next. I will leave you for a full day in which you can weigh everything I have said and take counsel with your conscience. Then give me your decision."

The supreme sheikh's words made a big impression on 'Imadin, and he started to hesitate. He had begun to believe that what he had heard about the sheikh of the mountain and his ability to see the secrets of men's hearts was true. But he steeled himself and remained firm in his resolve. "I have resolved to do as I told you," he said. "But I will be patient for another day, as you have commanded, then give you my answer."

Sheikh Dabbous nodded approvingly and said, "Then remove your weapons, and give me any money or tools that you have. This is what we usually do in these circumstances. You do not need to worry about them, for these things will remain with me in your name."

This request weighed heavily on 'Imadin, for he was carrying jewels, and it was hard for him to leave his dagger and remain unarmed. So he stood there, speechless for some time.

"My son," said Sheikh Dabbous. "You must know that anyone wanting to come to terms with our leader the supreme sheikh must submit to every order without hesitation. I have given you the option of entering, in accordance with 'Abd al-Rahim's recommendation, because he enjoys a high reputation in our eyes. But if I see you straying from your resolve, we will return your things to you."

'Imadin did not know what to say and could see no alternative to obeying, so he stretched out his hand, took his dagger from his belt, and handed it to him. Then he took out the money and jewelry he was carrying and passed it all to Sheikh Dabbous. He was unsure what would happen to everything he gave the sheikh, but he calmed down a little when he saw Sheikh Dabbous's smile as he wrapped all his things in a handkerchief, hid them away in a hole beneath the seat, then gestured to him to move to another room to rest. A guard led him to that room, where he was left alone. He began to reflect on what he had heard. The danger that he had put himself in now became clear to him, and he was not sure what to do. Should he abandon his mission, after having promised Saladin that he would complete it? Or should he expose himself to danger by enlisting in the sect? He remembered what his friend 'Abd al-Rahim had told him about Rashidin's miraculous nature, as well as what was commonly said about his dignity and power. He began to waver, because abandoning his mission would not only detract from his esteem in Saladin's eyes and in the eyes of his beloved but above all in his own self-worth, for he could not allow himself to exhibit cowardice. On the other hand, joining would expose him to death or force him to work against Saladin's interests.

He reflected on all this as he paced about the room, which was unfurnished except for an old carpet and a mat. He looked out of a small window and saw the swamps, hills, plains, and valleys that stretched far beyond Mount Misyaf on all sides. He was so deep in thought that he forgot for a moment where he was. Then, hearing the sound of footsteps behind him, he turned around to find a man who looked like a servant who had brought him food and then left. 'Imadin thanked him before going back to his contemplations. He was so disturbed and preoccupied that he had no appetite for eating. As he looked through the window of the room, his attention was drawn to an edifice in the internal courtyard that he had not noticed before because it had been hidden by very high walls. He thought that it must be a small fort where the Isma'ilis took refuge in times of disturbance.

Chapter 56

The Miracle

He returned to his apprehensions, which were becoming more and more serious, until he became impatient with himself for being so indecisive. He felt hungry, as he had had no food yet. So he turned to the fruit and the little bread and meat that had been brought to him. He reached out to take the bread, but something instinctively impelled him to withdraw it. He began to feel suspicious and thought, "This food might be poisoned!" Then he recalled his friend 'Abd al-Rahim and his recommendation to Dabbous. His suspicions eased somewhat, and he allayed his hunger by eating only the fruit, which would be more difficult to poison.

While he was eating, he heard a commotion in the courtyard. He got up, looked out of the door, and saw a group of people from the castle— soldiers and guards—laughing and whispering to each other. Their joy was visible on their faces. He feared that this might be connected with his presence there, or that he might perhaps be in danger. When he listened more carefully, he could hear that they were speaking different languages, for the Isma'ilis were a mixture of different nations—Arabs, Persians, Turks, Kurds, and Circassians, all of whom spoke their own language, though Arabic predominated.

As he listened more carefully, he heard them talking about Sultan Nuradin. They seemed to be talking about his death, but he thought that this could not be and paid no attention to it, for he had left the sultan two days ago in good health and had seen him returning from the racetrack on his horse at the head of his troops, appearing to be as strong as a lion. He thought that they must be propagating false rumors among themselves. While he was thinking about all this, a messenger came from Sheikh Dabbous to summon him. He quickly followed him to Dabbous' chamber; he was sitting in the middle of the room. In front of him was a group of emirs, dressed identically, with turbans on their heads similar to Dabbous' own turban. He thought they must be his men, as they were all laughing merrily.

'Imadin stood in front of them. "Have you come from Jerusalem?" asked Dabbous.

"Yes," he replied.

"And did you come via Damascus?" asked Dabbous.

"Yes," he answered.

"And how was the Atabeg sultan, Nuradin? Did you see him?" continued Dabbous.

"Yes," replied 'Imadin. "I saw him returning on horseback from the racetrack around noon."

"And what day was that?" asked Dabbous.

'Imadin bowed his head as he made a calculation, then said, "Just over two days ago."

"He died this morning," replied Dabbous. "May God have mercy on him!"

He balked on hearing this, the surprise evident on his face. "He died? Are you sure of that?" he asked. "I don't think your information can be right. How can you already know that his death occured this morning when it takes more than two days to journey between here and Damascus?"

Dabbous laughed contemptuously, and those seated around him turned to each other and laughed as well. "You can't be blamed, my son, for not knowing the source of this information," said Dabbous. "It did not come to us by messenger; it was a revelation vouchsafed to our leader the imam and supreme sheikh—may God give us the benefits of his blessings and miracles for a long time. He did the same thing the day that the Caliph al-'Adid died in Cairo. We learned of it on the day of his death, even though Egypt is further away than Damascus. Similarly with the news of the conspiracy in which 'Amara and his companions were executed." He looked at those sitting around him as if to seek confirmation, and they bowed their heads, clearly indicating their agreement.

'Imadin was amazed but continued to suspect that there might be some deception involved, and that Nuradin had not died. "If his death is confirmed by a formal proclamation arriving from Damascus, as is normal practice, then this will confirm that this supreme sheikh has supernatural powers!" he thought to himself.

Sheikh Dabbous noticed his astonishment and hesitation. "Don't be surprised at what you are hearing, my son!" he said. "If you are blessed and enabled to embark on our path, you will see things even more amazing than this. Our leader the supreme sheikh speaks to rocks, and they answer him. Even the dead answer him at once if he speaks to them." Then he turned to the others and said, "I can give you some more information. Our leader the supreme sheikh— may God protect him and give him long life—informed me of the cause of the sultan's death. He said that he had died of diphtheria." Then he turned to 'Imadin and said, "We can let you wait for the proclamation to arrive tomorrow, if you like!"

'Imadin was totally mystified by what he had heard. He felt that he was on the point of believing in Rashidin's miracles, but he was still hesitant, waiting for the proclamation to arrive.

"Go to your room until you reach a decision," said Dabbous. "I invited you because I knew that you had come from Damascus and might perhaps have known about the events leading up to Nuradin's death. And also so that you might know that your friend 'Abd al-Rahim had recommended you very highly to us. May God extend his blessings to you and to him, for he also is a candidate for advancement. And all who strive will reap their share of the blessings according to their merit. These are words that you will not understand now, but you will in the future. Please…" And he gestured with his hand for him to leave.

'Imadin went back to his room in a daze. He did not know how to interpret the strange, astonishing things that he was witnessing. He resolved that if the truth of the prophecy of the death of Nuradin was confirmed, he would seek to join the group without further hesitation. He wished his friend 'Abd al-Rahim had been there to explain to him clearly some of the baffling things he found so incomprehensible.

Chapter 57

'Abd al-Rahim

'Imadin spent that night like a madman lost in the desert, subject to terrible nightmares that gave him no respite. He woke up in the morning to a knock on the door, which scared him. He sat up at once, to see his friend 'Abd al-Rahim standing in front of him. The sight of him reassured him considerably, and he calmed down somewhat and became more composed. It was like meeting his father or brother; he was so pleased to see him that he embraced him very warmly, almost crying with emotion, so moved was he.

'Abd al-Rahim embraced him with a smile, tapping his shoulder affectionately as he said, "From your eagerness to meet me, it seems that you must have been quite distraught."

"Not distraught," replied 'Imadin, "but conflicted about things for which I can find no explanation without your help. I feel as though you are a father or brother. I need to pour all my troubles on you and seek your advice."

'Abd al-Rahim gave him a reassuring smile, and 'Imadin gestured to him, saying, "Sit down. Where have you come from?"

"I have come from Sheikh Dabbous," he replied, "who has told me how much he admires your intelligence and bravery, and how he has treated you kindly and given you time to think about your situation."

"Yes," replied 'Imadin. "But this is precisely what I want to talk to you about. I am puzzled by something that I cannot explain."

"What is that?" asked 'Abd al-Rahim.

"Yesterday at midday, Sheikh Dabbous told me that Sultan Nuradin, the ruler of Damascus, had died that morning. Two days earlier, I had seen him with my own eyes, riding on his horse, hale and hearty, his face glowing with health after spending the day racing with his noblemen."

"This is all correct," replied 'Abd al-Rahim. "Yes, he came back from the racecourse in perfect health, but he had only just reached the citadel when he felt a pain in his throat, and on examination it appeared to be diphtheria."

'Imadin said nothing, but the shock was evident in his eyes. He could not imagine that Nuradin was struck down with diphtheria after he had seen him on horseback. "The illness must have struck him hard," he said, "and not left him much time to live. But if we suppose that that was what really happened, and that Nuradin had died that morning, how could the news have reached here before noon?"

'Abd al-Rahim laughed and said, "'Abd al-Jabbar, this is one of our leader the supreme sheikh's miracles, may God give us the benefits of his blessings. Didn't I tell you something about this when we were in Jerusalem? He has often passed on news to us as soon as it has happened, even though we were several days' journey from its source. But this is not the most remarkable of his miracles, as you will see. Do you think that his powers and great influence are without foundation? How would thousands of people, including wise and intelligent men, be subservient to him, if they did not see anything in him that was not exceptional and justified this? Do you know that his followers today number more than sixty thousand of the elite, including brave leaders and heroes, each one of whom gladly submits to him and would sacrifice himself in his service? Do you think that this could happen by chance, without his deserving it?"

"So you are advising me to stick to my resolution," said 'Imadin.

"That is my advice to you," replied 'Abd al-Rahim.

"They took my money and weapons from me," said 'Imadin.

"You need not worry about them," replied 'Abd al-Rahim. "If you change your mind, I guarantee to have them returned to you. But I do not think that you will change your mind, especially after you have seen the supreme sheikh himself, heard his words, and experienced his miracles.

There are many of them, but..." He stopped speaking, as though he had something to say about which he was hesitant.

"I sense that you are uncertain in the advice you are giving me," said 'Imadin.

"God forbid, my brother!" replied 'Abd al-Rahim. "You know that our mutual affection and friendship has no motive other than to bring our hearts closer together. And since this society of ours brings together the pick of the brave and heroic, I thought that you would be worthy of joining it. You will be grateful for my advice! However, I have been hesitant to tell you something that would relieve your anxiety, but which I am forbidden from telling you."

He fell silent, and 'Imadin spoke, "If you can tell me something to relieve my anxiety, I will think you even more virtuous. And no one will know of it, I promise you that!"

He lowered his voice and said, "When you declare your wish to join, they will test you in ways that only the brave and resolute can endure. You are indeed so. But I want to reassure you again that what may seem to you dangerous or impossible in those tests is of no consequence. Its sole purpose is to test the bravery of the applicant. So whatever is asked of you, do it and do not be afraid. I cannot reveal to you any more than that!"

"Test my bravery?" asked 'Imadin. "Let them test it, I have no fear. You know that. But I want to know something else. Will you tell me the truth?"

"Tell me what you want to know," replied 'Abd al-Rahim. "I may be able to answer your question."

"The only thing that I know about this sect," replied 'Imadin, "is that its leader Rashidin is a wise man who can perform miracles, and that his followers obey him blindly and will give their lives in his service. But I do not know what reward those followers can aspire to. And are they all at the same level, or are there different levels? I have seen some who seem like servants or soldiers, while others are like emirs. This Dabbous appears to be a king. What is the structure of this sect, or dynasty? It seems to be a unique structure..."

"You are right," replied 'Abd al-Rahim. "Its structure is unusual, even unique. But no harm will be done if I briefly explain to you this structure. This group, which has terrified the world through its organization and the bravery of its young men, is made up of two classes—the freedom fighters and the enlightened ones—above whom are the leaders and those in possession of the true secrets of the sect. Those who join the Isma'ili sect will join first as freedom fighters. Then, if they deserve promotion, they will become enlightened ones. To this day, I am still a freedom fighter."

'Abd al-Jabbar interrupted him to say, "And if I were to join tomorrow, I would be a freedom fighter like you?"

"Yes," replied 'Abd al-Rahim. "But I have just become a candidate for taking the oath to become an enlightened one soon, because the mission that took me to Jerusalem was the last test on the path of promotion. I have come here to be inititated in the secrets of the class of the enlightened."

"How have you come to deserve this promotion?" asked 'Imadin.

"I have earned it by faithful service in the interest of the community and by my total adoption of the path of obedience. Every freedom fighter has to do that before he can become an enlightened one. As for you, I am confident you will be promoted soon, for you deserve it, in view of your courage and lofty principles. There are not many like you among those who want to become members of our community."

'Imadin was silent for a while, as he mulled over his situation and the true nature of his mission and especially Sittalmulk. Ever since he had read Yaquta's letter, Sittalmulk had never left his mind—even though he was reassured because of her being under the protection of Saladin. All reasons for him to want to return quickly to Egypt. 'Abd al-Rahim noticed his preoccupation and said, "There is no need to hesitate. Your joining is assured. Don't worry about it! But I would prefer you to postpone it until the official announcement arrives from Damascus of the death of Sultan Nuradin and you are convinced of the miracles of our imam Rashidin before you enter his service."

'Imadin was embarrassed to hear this, though he himself had been thinking along those lines, but was afraid to say so lest he betray a lack of conviction. So he replied quickly, "I believe what I have heard, even though it appears strange to me."

"It is not strange," replied 'Abd al-Rahim. "And you will witness even stranger things than that. But for now, relax and keep calm. You will not come to any harm if you decide not to join. Our leader the supreme sheikh does not accept everyone who asks to join. If you want to check the truth of what I am saying, come with me and I will have you meet a group of those applicants." So saying, he rose, and 'Imadin followed him.

He walked along a narrow track that led through the mountain to a courtyard, from which a clamor could be heard well before they reached it. They stopped in their tracks, and 'Imadin listened carefully. He could hear shouting and quarreling in several languages and different dialects. He was led on until he could observe, from behind a wall, an area crowded with groups of men, some sitting and gossiping, while others stood arguing. Most of them had a rough demeanor, with features and clothes that betrayed their uncouth nature. "Look here, my brother," said 'Abd al-Rahim. "These are the people who want to join. You can see from their features how rough and unsophisticated they are and how quarrelsome and bloodthirsty they appear. This community of ours has become famous for its assassinations. Anyone experiencing hardships who has no qualms about killing innocents comes to us. But our aims are higher than that—so I believe, even though I have not yet discovered what those aims are. These people number in the dozens, as you can see, and they have been here for days, with Sheikh Dabbous paying them no attention. In fact, I think that he will accept the applications of only a few of them. But he has already noticed that you are far superior to any of them, and so I hope that you will be quickly promoted to the ranks of the enlightened."

While they were talking, they saw one of the Kurds stand up, holding a skull into which he had poured some wine. He staggered along pompously then drank the wine, with a look of contempt for his fellows, to whom he was showing off his bravery and uncouthness. One of the Turks became angry and mocked him, striking the skull with the back of his hand so that he dropped it, and the wine spilled onto the ground. The others laughed and giggled, pleased with what the Turk had done, but the Kurd could not stand this affront. So he drew his dagger and stabbed the Turk, killing him. Some of the others were on the point of attacking him to exact vengeance, but 'Abd al-Rahim shouted threateningly and stopped them; then he told one of the guards to detain the killer until his case could be referred to the supreme sheikh.

Chapter 58

Rashidin

What he had seen and heard of the behavior of potential recruits only increased 'Imadin's bewilderment. He went back to his room very moved by all this, while 'Abd al-Rahim returned to his business. The following day when he returned, the official announcement had arrived from the ruler of Damascus announcing the death of Nuradin from diphtheria exactly at the time that the supreme sheikh of the mountain had declared. Sheikh Dabbous read the announcement within earshot of the Isma'ilis, and this only confirmed 'Imadin's resolve to join them. This was necessary to complete the mission he had promised Saladin to undertake—namely, to be able to kill Rashidin. It was possible that Sittalmulk already knew of his determination to do so. The standing of the man and his supernatural powers had made his mission more difficult, but he was determined to proceed with it. At some point he had some hesitation in joining the community only because he thought the execution of his mission might perhaps be easier from the outside. But the more he thought about it, the more he concluded he could see no alternative to joining in order to get closer to the supreme sheikh and imam, and fulfill his plan to assassinate him.

The following day, 'Imadin awoke. He had an appointment to see the supreme sheikh to join the community of freedom fighters. The more he thought about it, the faster his heart raced. After a short time, his friend 'Abd al-Rahim came in and gave him an encouraging smile to calm him down. "Should I go to the supreme sheikh now or to Sheikh Dabbous?" asked 'Imadin.

"You must go to the supreme sheikh through Sheikh Dabbous," replied 'Abd al-Rahim. "Are you ready?"

"Yes," replied 'Imadin, careful not to show his nervousness.

"Let's go to Sheikh Dabbous, then," replied 'Abd al-Rahim.

They walked until they came into his presence, and 'Abd al-Rahim told him of their purpose. "'Abd al-Jabbar," said Sheikh Dabbous, "are you determined to join us?"

"Yes, sir," replied 'Imadin emphatically.

He ordered him to take off the clothes he was wearing and to put on a white flowing robe resembling a large and long shirt, which he handed him. He put it on, and it covered him to his ankles. Then he told him to take off his turban and to let down his hair, which was quite long, so that it fell over his shoulders. 'Abd al-Rahim told him to go up to Sheikh Dabbous and kiss his hand, which he did. Then he gestured to him to follow him. They walked along paths and tunnels, surrounded by guards with spears, until they reached a gallery leading to a large door. The door was covered by a curtain, on either side of which stood two guards with large heads who looked more like *jinn*[53] than men. As 'Abd al-Rahim approached them, he gestured to them to let him enter for they were deaf. They did so because they knew him, but they made 'Abd al-Jabbar wait outside. He stayed there, downcast, caught between resolve and regret, when suddenly his friend returned and said, "The supreme sheikh is busy with the trial of the Kurdish murderer, but he has given permission for us to enter."

He walked back, with 'Imadin behind, until they entered a dark hall with a large seat in the middle, on which was sitting the supreme sheikh. On either side of him sat men from his entourage. All had covered their faces except for Rashidin. 'Imadin took a little while for his eyes to get used to the darkness and make out the faces. Then he saw the Kurd standing with his hands bound, while in the middle of the hall lay the victim's corpse, smeared in blood. 'Abd al-Rahim told 'Imadin to stand out of the way, and as he did so, he began to look at Rashidin closely. He was wearing a black cloak, which covered him completely except for his face. With its wrinkles and white beard, his face indeed looked like that of an old man, though his eyes looked like lanterns from which sparks

---

53 Demons or magic spirits in Islamic folklore, which can take on various human and animal forms and make mischievous use of supernatural powers. *Editor's Note*

were almost flying. It was not long before Rashidin shouted at the Kurd, "You wretch, how did you dare to kill someone here in our own realm?"

"I didn't kill him, sire," the man shouted. "They're accusing me unjustly!"

"You lie as well?" asked Rashidin. "Do you think that we can be fooled like that? Don't you know that we can look into men's hearts and know their secrets?"

The man denied it again, saying, "They are accusing me wrongly, sire. If you want me to bring witnesses or swear to my innocence, I will do so!"

"There's no need for witnesses or an oath; I'll ask the victim, and he can tell me the facts," replied Rashidin.

When he said that, 'Imadin recoiled. He looked up and saw that Rashidin was standing, straight as a statue. Then he took a step toward the dead man and shouted at him, pointing at him as if to threaten him, "Didn't this Kurd kill you? Tell me!"

All those present fell silent, and their hearts beat faster in anticipation of what was to come. Then they heard the dead man say in a weak voice, "Yes, it was he that killed me!"

"And what did he kill you with?" he asked.

"With his dagger," he replied.

When 'Imadin heard this, his whole body trembled—quite naturally, for he had heard a dead man speak, and he was certain that the murder he witnessed had really happened. Rashidin returned to his seat and ordered some of his men to take the Kurd to jail and bury the victim, which they did. All those present were stunned, not least 'Imadin.

After a while, Rashidin dismissed those standing in the council, leaving behind only a few of his close followers, all of whom were wearing masks. He made a sign to 'Abd al-Rahim to bring 'Abd al-Jabbar forward. 'Abd al-Rahim took him by the hand until he stood before him. His knees were trembling, for he was awestruck by Rashidin.

Rashidin addressed 'Imadin. "'Abd al-Jabbar," he said, "I hope that you will trust us and not do what this Kurd has done. You are also a

Kurd, but I can read honesty in your face. Are you seeking to join our men?"

"Yes, sire," replied 'Imadin.

"Do you know what a momentous act you are undertaking?"

"Yes, sire."

"Don't deceive yourself," said Rashidin. "If you are hesitant or afraid, then go back to where you came from. We are only looking for people who are brave and trustworthy. Are you aware of the danger that surrounds you?"

"Yes, sire," replied 'Imadin.

"And what prompted you to want to join us?" asked Rashidin, clearing his throat.

"I should be honored to serve our leader the supreme sheikh," he replied.

"Where have you come from?" asked Rashidin.

"From Jerusalem," he answered. His whole body was shaking, for he was afraid that he might be asked about his true motives and that Rashidin's powers would expose him—in which case he would be in danger of death. But he composed himself and stood firm.

"I know that you have just come from Jerusalem," continued Rashidin, "but I would like you to tell me where you came from before you went to Jerusalem."

He said nothing, tongue-tied, wondering whether or not he should tell him the truth. He was afraid that Rashidin's miraculous powers of perception would reveal his true motive in coming. But Rashidin did not have the patience to wait for an answer and said, "You seem to be afraid. Don't be afraid, my son! You are a brave young man, not like those weak and ignorant people! I will not force you to say anything. I will ask one of the hairs on your head, and it will tell me!" Then he ordered 'Abd al-Rahim to bring him a hair from 'Imadin's head. Rashidin took it between his thumb and index finger then he started to address the hair, saying, "Tell me, hair of 'Abd al-Jabbar, where was your owner at that time? And who is he?"

"He was with Yusuf Saladin," the hair replied, "and he is one of his confidants."

When 'Imadin heard that, he trembled so much that he almost fell to the floor. He was at a loss for words, unable to reply, afraid that Rashidin would continue cross-examining him and learn the true purpose of his coming there. Two minutes passed that seemed longer than a year. Then he saw Rashidin sigh on hearing Saladin's name and throw the hair from his hand, saying, "Yusuf Saladin? May God prolong his life!"

'Imadin thought this strange and his hopes revived, but he remained silent.

"And how was Saladin when you left him?" inquired Rashidin. "Was he well and in good spirits?'

"Yes, sire," replied 'Imadin.

"Thank God for that," replied Rashidin. 'Imadin noticed a change in his expression that he could not explain. He was still afraid of being exposed, but then he heard Rashidin address him again, "I thank God for Saladin's health. Now, are you determined to join our men?"

"Yes, sire," replied 'Imadin.

"Do you know what is demanded from you?" Rashidin asked.

"No," responded 'Imadin, "but I will obey our leader and imam in anything he wishes."

Rashidin gave a smile, which did nothing to alter the gloomy appearance of his face. "I like your answer, 'Abd al-Jabbar," he said. "And if it is your destiny to join our men, both this world and the world to come will be yours. But this is not an easy matter." So saying, he stood up and ordered him to follow him.

As he did so, 'Imadin stole a glance at 'Abd al-Rahim, looking for any feedback—even if only a gesture—and saw him giving him encouraging and reassuring signs. Eventually, Rashidin reached a part of the vast, vacant hall, where he stopped and, gesturing to a hole in front of him, said to 'Imadin, "Look over here!"

'Imadin looked and found himself on the edge of a bottomless pit. "If you are sincere in what you say, throw yourself into this pit," ordered Rashidin.

He looked again and had no doubt that if he obeyed, he would inevitably die. He stealthily turned to 'Abd al-Rahim, who was encouraging him, motioning with his eyes that he should step forward. He was confident of his friend's trustworthiness but was still afraid that this might be some trap—that Rashidin had discovered the true nature of his mission and wanted to avenge himself in this way. But he recalled 'Abd al-Rahim's forewarning, and in any event was unaccustomed to fear or hesitation; spurred on by 'Abd al-Rahim's advice and his own bravery, his foot moved forward to leap into the opening of the pit. Suddenly he caught sight of a beam of wood that appeared from nowhere and blocked his access to the pit, while at the same time he found himself standing by a trapdoor that opened up another hole. He could not believe that he was still alive…

Rashidin took him by the hand and said, "Now I am convinced of your sincerity. If you had not believed me, you would have been killed, for the mouth of the pit would have moved to where you were standing originally." Then he ordered him to move toward the hall and said, "You have proved deserving of the blessing that you seek. From this moment, you are one of my virtuous sons."

Rashidin returned to his seat and ordered a servant to bring him a cup. He did so, and Rashidin took it and poured into it a liquid from a container beside him, saying, "This is the water of life and the way to paradise if you are truthful, but a deadly poison if you lie. So, if you are loyal and true to your promise to obey, then drink!"

'Imadin took the cup, hesitating for a moment as he looked at his friend 'Abd al-Rahim, who was encouraging him to drink, which he did. Then the supreme sheikh signaled to him to sit down. As he did so, after a little while he felt he was gradually losing consciousness. And he fainted.

Chapter 59

The Paradise of the Assassins

Do not ask about his surprise when he recovered consciousness and opened his eyes. He found himself in a garden that was just like paradise is described, with flowing streams, intertwining trees, and birds singing as they flew and hopped from branch to branch and drank from the clear streams. As soon as he awoke from his sleep, a breeze wafted over his face, and a hand touched his brow. He looked and saw that it was the hand of a nymph or *houri*[54] as beautiful as the full moon, wrapped in a transparent cloak that covered her body but did not hide her nudity. In her right hand was a wide fan of ostrich feathers with which she cooled him, while she placed her left hand on his brow as if to wipe away any sweat. At first, he thought he was in a dream and was afraid that if he stood up he would be deprived of those wonderful sights. So he waited a while, but the *houri* spoke to him in a sweet voice, saying, "Get up, my beloved! How long will you sleep?"

He got up and realized that he was wearing a robe like the robes worn by emirs; he had never seen a finer one even on Saladin. On his head was a turban embroidered with gold and silver. He was sitting on one of the most beautiful carpets, decorated with designs woven with threads of gold. He spent some time gripped with astonishment, looking sometimes at himself or in front of him at the enchanting *houri* and at other times at the trees and flowers that his eyes delighted on, hearing the gurgle of water, the chirping of birds, and smelling fragrant perfumes with a scent that he had never imagined, let alone ever smelled.

---

54 In Islamic belief, a beautiful young maiden who attends Muslim men in paradise. *Editor's Note*

While he was observing all this in a euphoric state, the *houri* approached him; she had removed her veil from her head and let her golden hair fall to her shoulders as she looked intently at 'Imadin with eyes that expressed her love laced with pangs of unfulfilled desire. He stood immobile as if in a hypnotic trance as he gazed at her, trying to withstand her charms. But she stretched out her hand in greeting, and as he gave her his own hand, he thought himself in a dream. Holding the tips of his fingers, she asked, "What is the matter, 'Abd al-Jabbar? Do you still think you are in a dream? Have you forgotten that you drank the water of life from the hand of our leader the supreme sheikh? You are in paradise now—a paradise that none will enter except those who are worthy of it!"

He remembered the cup from which he had drunk at the hands of Rashidin and began to believe in the truth of that man's claim—that he had really been transported to paradise with its rivers, its trees, and its birds, and that this nymph was one of the *houris* of paradise. Then he remembered Sittalmulk and recoiled. "How can this beautiful maiden be trying to win my heart, when it does not belong to me?" he said to himself. He pulled away from her, and she in turn withdrew with a reproachful look, moving away before vanishing from his sight.

He left her and walked over ground covered in green grass like an embroidered carpet, from which wafted stimulating smells. In the distance, his eyes could see a canal, flowing with pure, sparkling water. On either bank stood fruit trees, through the branches of which the sunlight fell onto the streaming water, taking on all the colors of the rainbow. He moved towards the canal and stood on its bank, looking at how the rays falling on the pebbles at the bottom were refracted and took on different colors. While he was there, a *houri* appeared from the trees on the opposite bank and walked toward him, smiling at him. He was relieved that a canal separated them, believing she could not reach him. He expected her to speak to him while standing on the opposite bank, but suddenly she left the bank and was walking toward him on the surface of the water.

His astonishment became even greater when she reached him, her bare feet carrying her over the surface of the flowing water without her feet plunging into the water or getting wet or disturbing its flow. He was certain that he was in a heavenly place, not on this earth, and that these *houris* were angels. As the *houri* reached him, the wind ruffled her hair and teased the edges of her dress. She came close to him as if to greet him. But he tried to fight his craving for her by recalling Sittalmulk and her love for him. He was eager to get away, but suddenly noticed that the *houri's* face resembled his beloved's face; startled, he looked more closely and began to think that it must be Sittalmulk herself who had come to paradise through one of Rashidin's miracles. He stood still until the *houri* reached him and stretched out her hand, and he in turn stretched out his to take her hand. He was watching her face closely, but the nearer she got to him, the less she resembled Sittalmulk. Nonetheless, he thought her attractive and was keen to talk to her about all that he was seeing and experiencing. As she got closer to him, a scent of perfume wafted from her dress. Then she put her hand on his shoulder, and his whole body trembled uncontrollably. "Who are you, and where am I?" he asked.

"Don't you know where you are?" she replied. "You are in the paradise of our leader the supreme sheikh of the mountain."

"And is this where all his followers reside?" he asked.

"Yes," replied the *houri*. "But only those who have performed well in the test of obedience remain here."

She took his hand and walked on, signaling to him to follow her over the canal. He hesitated for a moment, but she led him by the hand, saying, "Don't be afraid! Come on!" As he did, he felt he was walking on something solid that separated his feet from the water, giving him the impression that the water beneath his feet had turned solid. He reached the other bank and walked on with the *houri*, still doubting that what he was seeing was real. When he heard her words, he asked, "Am I destined to remain here?"

"You are a novice and have yet to prove yourself," she replied. "You have come to see what our leader has prepared for his followers and disciples if they carry out his orders. You may be one of those who are worthy of it."

He realized then that he was only there for a limited time and that he would soon be leaving this paradise. As he walked, his eyes darted between the trees and the herbs, watching the birds flying around the *houri*. There were cranes, beautifully colored peacocks, nightingales, and goldfinches, singing and chirping to one another. The *houri* would call them, and they would come and perch on her shoulder or her hand, dart between her hands, and fly off when she ordered them to, as though they understood what she was saying.

Then 'Imadin heard a roar, which he recognized as the roar of a lion, for he had heard it many times. He was startled and asked, "Isn't that the roar of a lion?"

"Yes," she replied. "Are you afraid of it? Lions don't harm people living here." She walked off until she reached the lion's den under a tree. The lion was lying there with its eyes gleaming, immobile in its place. The *houri* walked up to it, stretched her hand to its head, and ruffled its hair, just as you would ruffle a cat's hair. The lion stood motionless, which again 'Imadin thought very strange.

As he started to walk about again, his eyes fell on a number of cottages situated on one side of the garden, covered by branches and flowers. He asked her about them, and she replied, "These are the houses of those who are worthy of staying here, enjoying the pleasures of paradise without anyone disturbing them."

After walking on for a little longer, the *houri* stopped him near a wall and said, "Look here!"

He looked through a window in the wall at a barren valley that looked like a desert without a drop of water or the shadow of a tree. When he saw the snakes and wild animals prowling there among human skulls, he recoiled in horror and said, "I think that this must be Hell!"

"Yes," she replied, "it is! You now know the fate of those who disobey the imam!"

He wanted to leave, and the *houri* led him back, speaking gently to him as she plucked fruits to offer him. He was confounded and did not know what to make of all this. Suddenly, he heard a sound that made his whole body shake and the blood freeze in his veins: it was the voice of Sittalmulk, who was asking him for help. He started to turn left and right, thinking that she must be near him. Meanwhile, the *houri* was looking at him in astonishment. "What's up with you?" she asked. "What has made you stop?"

"Can't you hear anything?" asked 'Imadin.

"No, what can you hear?" she replied.

He said nothing but listened even more intently. But he could no longer hear anything. He thought it must have been a daydream, imagining what he heard only because he had been thinking too much about Sittalmulk. Her spirit had come to visit him, or perhaps it was her voice that came to greet him. But this explanation did not convince him, for the voice he heard was a cry for help. Was she in trouble? If she were, he should certainly try to help her!

He felt comfortable with the *houri* who had been with him for a while and had taken a lot of trouble to please him and win over his heart. He was a young man in the prime of life. He thought it most likely that he was in paradise, or somewhere akin it, transported there by a miracle of Rashidin. He had been on the point of forgetting Sittalmulk, and when he heard her voice, he believed it was the voice of his conscience, enjoining him to be steadfast in his love for Sittalmulk and not let anyone divert him from his beloved. This depressed him and made him want to escape from that paradise.

While he was deep in thought, he heard the sound of footsteps that were not those of his companion. He turned and saw a young man whose radiant face was reminiscent of a shining full moon. He was wearing a girdle of silk, part of which was protruding like an apron. His hair flowed in golden locks, and he was wearing a sky-blue colored robe. As he approached 'Imadin, he bowed respectfully and asked, in a gentle voice, "Would my master like to take some lunch?"

He turned to his companion as if to ask her for an explanation. "Please take some food, master!" she said with a smile. "It is time for lunch!"

He had forgotten about food, but when it was mentioned, he felt hungry. He walked on along a level path that seemed to have been covered with saffron, lined on both sides with a hedge of beautiful flowers, and leading to an impressive gate that one would find in a splendid palace. Aromas of delicious food wafted from it, such as he had only smelled in the palaces of the Fatimids at festival times. As they approached the gate, it was immediately opened, and two youths came forward to greet the newcomer, walking in front of him through several gates until they reached the dining hall. He himself was turning from one side to the other, appreciating the decorated curtains on the walls of the hallway. They depicted gardens, palaces, places of sacrifice and luxury—all fit to dazzle the eyes and captivate the heart. The dining hall itself, however, mesmerized him completely, as he froze in his tracks: the four walls were all covered in mirrors for their entire length from floor to ceiling, and anyone who entered would see his image reflected *ad infinitum* in all directions—a sight all the more stunning because it was most unusual in those days...

The *houri* walked on and motioned to 'Imadin to sit down, which he did, on a seat covered in decorated brocade. In front of him was a table covered with a pink silk cloth. Only a few moments elapsed before a succession of plates appeared, with all sorts of meats and fruits. The *houri* sat down beside 'Imadin, speaking softly to him, feeding him mouthful after mouthful, and honoring him to excess. In front of them stood servants ready to fulfill her orders, so that Sittalmulk's image began to fade from 'Imadin's mind—so bewitched by the beauty and kindness of the *houri* was he, as he was affected by the cups of fine wine that had begun to flow. He could think of nothing but the present, and in his mind, he began to really believe he was in paradise...

When the *houri* saw him relaxed and contented, she started to move away. He, on the other hand, was becoming more amorous, prodded by the alcohol that had loosened his inhibitions. He started to sidle toward her and wanted to flirt with her and press her against him, but she would not let him. When she was assured that he was becoming infatuated with her, she said, "Don't go too far! You are here only as a trial for a limited period, and satisfying your desires is not that easy. To do so, you will need to show your loyalty and obedience to the supreme imam..."

This rejection hit him hard, but it only served to increase his infatuation with her. He said, "A moment ago you were coming closer, and I was moving away. Were you trying to inflame my passion for you?"

"No," she replied, "but you will have to fulfill a task that will qualify you to stay permanently in this paradise. You can then do as you please. I will be at your command, and if you speak to the birds, they will answer you and your every wish will be fulfilled. You will see what paradise is truly like—now all you see is but a small sample of the pleasures of that paradise. Maybe you will do what is needed to deserve them. If truth be told, I am enchanted by your handsomeness and valor and feel something for you that I have never felt for anyone else. However, I cannot do anything that goes against our leader's pleasure, and I cannot hide anything from him, for he knows the secrets of the inner heart. But to reaffirm the ties of love between us, I will rub your hair with my own special perfume." So saying, she took a vial from her clothes and opened it. From it, there wafted a scent like no other that he had smelled in his life. When she took some of the perfume and rubbed his hands and hair with it, he felt ecstatic and fulfilled. "Keep this scent to remind you of me until we meet forever, God willing!" she said, looking at 'Imadin tenderly with sparkling eyes that also betrayed sadness. All this greatly affected him, and he felt even more in awe of the powers of this extraordinary imam. But he said nothing.

After he finished eating and drinking, 'Imadin was ready to sleep. He lay down on a bed of silk stuffed with ostrich feathers with the *houri* beside him, teasing him again as she turned away from him. A few minutes later he was fast asleep.

Chapter 60

An Amazing Secret

He awoke the following day to find himself in the dark hall where Rashidin had received him, still wearing the same white robe with his disheveled hair over his shoulders—just as he had been the day before. He looked around him in all directions, examining his robe. His first thoughts were that he must be dreaming. But he soon smelled the perfume on his hands and hair, which dispelled any doubt that what had happened was real. He soon came to and saw Rashidin sitting where he had left him, with his friend 'Abd al-Rahim beside him. He rejoiced at his presence—so much so that he pressed him to his chest. "The perfume of paradise is wafting from your hair," said 'Abd al-Rahim. "Congratulations, and may you be permitted to partake of eternal paradise! Rise, and kneel at the feet of our imam, kiss his knees, and pray that he may have a long life!"

He rose and threw himself at the feet of the supreme sheikh, truly believing in his miraculous powers. But the supreme sheikh pushed him away and offered him his hand, which he kissed. "You are now one of my freedom fighters," he said, "and I think you will soon reach the ranks of the enlightened. Stand up and go to your room; I have told Sheikh Dabbous to look after you well. But before you leave, I should like to give you a personal pledge." As he said that, he rose and made 'Imadin rise with him. As Rashidin looked at him, 'Imadin became conscious of the power emanating from his eyes, which was almost more than he could bear.

The supreme sheikh squeezed hard on 'Imadin's hands for several minutes then shouted at him, "Open your mouth!" When he had done so, he spat into it and said, "Be an obedient warrior!" Then he left, after telling 'Abd al-Rahim to take him to his room.

They walked back without speaking. 'Imadin was in a state of shock, like someone bewitched who had been hypnotized. When they reached Sheikh Dabbous, 'Imadin changed his clothes, and Dabbous congratulated him on securing the confidence of the supreme sheikh. Then he gave him back his dagger, his money, and his jewels, as he had become one of them.

No sooner had 'Imadin returned from the Isma'ilis' paradise, however, than his own concerns returned as he recalled Saladin and Sittalmulk. He became eager to ask 'Abd al-Rahim a question that had occurred to him the previous day when Rashidin had said, "May God grant Saladin a long life!"—something he could not explain, for he knew that he had tried on several occasions to have him assassinated.

'Abd al-Rahim, however, was spending the night away, for that night had been earmarked for his promotion to the ranks of the enlightened. So 'Abd al-Jabbar spent the night on tenterhooks, overwhelmed by his dark thoughts, full of contradictions and anomalies. But whenever he caught a whiff of perfume from his hair, he remembered the *houri* and the happiness that he had found with her.

He slept fitfully that night. When day broke, his friend 'Abd al-Rahim returned with happiness radiating from his eyes. 'Abd al-Jabbar got up, kissed him, and said, "You have now attained a higher rank than mine, and I cannot call you 'brother' any longer!"

'Abd al-Rahim burst out laughing and said, "Our friendship is much stronger than that. We were strangers, but we became fond of each other, and now we are brothers with a common purpose. It will not be long before you rise to my rank—something I hope and confidently expect will happen soon."

The promotion, however, was not what was on his mind. What concerned him was to find out what Rashidin really thought about Saladin. If he discovered that he was still intending to have him assassinated, then he would strive to fulfill his original mission. But if he was convinced of his sincerity in praying for him to have a long life, he would take a different view. "I don't expect to be promoted as soon as you think," he replied. "It's enough that you should be a friend of mine. But I would not wish to burden our friendship with an ambition I have that requires your help. I only ask that you explain something that I heard the supreme sheikh say yesterday, and which I found particularly surprising. I did not believe it, and perhaps you have had the same feeling, too."

"I believe you are referring to his statement asking God to grant Saladin a long life," replied 'Abd al-Rahim.

"Yes," confirmed 'Imadin. "That is what I mean. What do you think? Didn't you find his words strange? Did he really mean what he said? I know that he has sent his men to assassinate Saladin more than once. How could he do that and at the same time ask God to grant him a long life? That's what I would like explained."

'Abd al-Rahim looked at 'Imadin and smiled. He was on the point of answering but stopped himself. When 'Imadin saw his hesitation, he said, "If you know the truth, please tell me, for it worries me very much—you are perhaps one of the people best acquainted with my relationship with the sultan."

'Abd al-Rahim sat up straight, looking concerned, and said, "'Imadin, my friend. I was already aware of the supreme sheikh's words that you quoted, and until last night I was as mystified about them as you are. But then I learned something fortuitously—not as a secret entrusted to me like the other secrets of this community. So neither duty nor fear need prevent me from answering your question."

'Imadin leaned forward and asked, "Tell me, by God, does the supreme sheikh really want my lord Saladin to live a long life?"

"Yes, he wants that with all his heart," replied 'Abd al-Rahim. "He asks for it day and night!"

"Extraordinary!" replied 'Imadin. "How can he send someone to assassinate him then pray for him to have a long life?"

"Perhaps you are thinking of what happened to Saladin just before you left Egypt," replied 'Abd al-Rahim, "when he woke up one morning to find a dagger over his head and a threatening letter beside it."

"Yes, that is exactly what I had in mind," replied 'Imadin.

"That shows that the supreme sheikh wants a long life for Saladin. Otherwise, he would have ordered the freedom fighter who was able to plant the dagger in the pillow by his head to plant it in his chest instead.

There would have been nothing to stop him. But he was content to threaten him, while at the same time wishing him a long life."

'Imadin thought this very strange indeed and inquired, "But I don't understand the motive for that wish. Our supreme sheikh—may God preserve him—is famous for assassinating caliphs and sultans. There is not one of them that does not fear him, even Saladin himself. So how could he want them to stay alive?"

"No, no!" 'Abd al-Rahim interrupted. "His wish for a long life applies only to Saladin—not any of the others."

"Why?" asked 'Imadin. "Please explain this to me!"

"The reason, my brother," replied 'Abd al-Rahim, "is that our supreme sheikh—may God preserve him—received a revelation telling him he is destined to die in the same year as Saladin. If one of them dies, he will inevitably be followed by the other in the same year. That is why he is as anxious to preserve Saladin's life as he is about preserving his own. Do you doubt the truth of this revelation? I have seen enough of the supreme sheikh's miracles, even though I have seen only a few of them."

'Imadin bowed his head and began to ponder what he had heard. After all he had seen for himself, he believed Rashidin's prophecy that the two men would indeed die in the same year. So it was in the interest of Saladin that Rashidin should live longer. All of a sudden his concern shifted from killing Rashidin to preserving his life. Considering his original mission ended, he now wanted to leave the citadel and hurry back to Saladin to give him the good news and see his beloved Sittalmulk. For a moment, the scent of the perfume and the memory of his experiences in that paradise made him think otherwise, but reality soon proved stronger than fantasy, and he became determined to leave. However, the only way to achieve that would be for Rashidin to send him on a mission to assassinate a caliph or emir. He turned to his friend 'Abd al-Rahim, his gratitude evident on his face, and said, "I shall never forget your friendship, 'Abd al-Rahim. I feel the sincerity of your friendship as something I can almost touch. That is why I have had such great trust in you. But there is something that I cannot withold from you, so will you allow me to exploit this trust?"

"Speak as you wish," replied 'Abd al-Rahim.

"I do not need to explain the reasons that compel me to leave the citadel quickly," said 'Imadin, "for you know how attached I am to Egypt. So I hope that you will help me to do so."

"You will only be able to leave if they arrange for you to undertake a mission to assasinate an important person," replied 'Abd al-Rahim.

"So be it. I will do whatever they order," said 'Imadin.

"Give me a day or two to find an opportunity to arrange it," replied 'Abd al-Rahim.

"I will wait to see what you can do, may God bless you," replied 'Imadin.

"Now let me go," said 'Abd al-Rahim, "for I have duties to carry out in connection with my new position. I will return to you with whatever success I may be able to achieve."

"Thank you, my brother," replied 'Imadin. And with that, 'Abd al-Rahim rose and left.

Chapter 61

Doubts and Apprehensions

When 'Imadin was alone, he started to think again about all the worrisome, fascinating, and frightening things that he had experienced, which only increased his apprehensions. As he reflected on the rumors he had heard about the Isma'ili leader's duplicity, his belief in this man and his supernatural powers began to fade. But he could not find a rational explanation for the miracles he had seen. How could he know of events in faraway places before there was time for the news to travel to him? How could he address a dead man and receive an answer? How could he speak to a hair and be told a secret? And what about this paradise, with all the delights that it contained and the *houris* who walked on water without disturbing its flow or getting wet, who talked to birds that obeyed them and played with lions without being harmed—when he thought about all these things, he could see no alternative to believing in Supreme Sheikh Rashidin's miraculous powers.

He tired of such thoughts and decided to take a walk around the citadel of Misyaf. There was no longer anything to stop him from doing so, for he had become one of its residents. As he did so, he started to go up on the walls and towers of the citadel and saw that the ground surrounding it was barren of any vegetation, except for the distant plains between the mountains. Recalling the trees and rivers that he had seen the previous day in paradise, he was determined to find out what this paradise really consisted of and where it was located. So he climbed the highest point of the citadel in the hope of discovering this heavenly garden. He had no success, but as his gaze wandered over the plain where he had stayed on the day of his arrival, his eyes fell on some riders. They were too far off for him to see their faces, but as they approached, he could see that there were several masked horsemen accompanied by a group of men on foot who looked like servants. He took no notice of them but continued thinking about his nightmarish situation, seeking a way of leaving quickly the citadel of Misyaf. He had thought of fleeing, but found that that would be impossible for him to do without exposing himself to extreme danger. He had spared himself that by seeking the help of his friend 'Abd al-Rahim—who, he had no doubt, would spare no effort to do everything he could to help him leave safely.

He looked for the riders again and saw that they were now so close to the mountain that they were hidden from view by the foothills. He thought that they probably came from the mountain area or were stationed nearby. He felt hungry, so he moved over to where the freedom fighters gathered and mingled with them as he ate his food with them, even though none came close to him in terms of generosity of spirit or refinement. Feeling ever more eager to leave, he continued waiting on tenterhooks for 'Abd al-Rahim to return.

That day and the next passed without him seeing 'Abd al-Rahim. He thought long and hard but could find no reason why it took 'Abd al-Rahim so long to come back. He became even more concerned and anxious when he noticed that Sheikh Dabbous had also been away from his room for those two days. He was told that he had urgent business with the supreme sheikh, investigating some important developments that had occurred since the arrival of some people the day before. He remembered the riders he had seen a day earlier and was determined to find out who they really were. But no one could tell him the facts because that information was only known to a small number of the enlightened. So he decided to wait for the return of his friend 'Abd al-Rahim. When he did not come, he asked a colleague about him and was told that he was with a select group of new recruits busy with the supreme sheikh.

He was ever more eager to discover the truth, but he could see no alternative to waiting. Half of the fourth day elapsed, and he had still not seen him. He felt uneasy with nothing to do. He had made up his mind to look for him when suddenly he saw him coming toward him. He greeted him like a thirsty man being given water. 'Abd al-Rahim bent down and kissed him and apologized for having taken so long. "Forgive me, my brother," he said, "I had some business that I had not reckoned with, and whenever I made up my mind to come back, something new arose."

"I forgot my anxiety and nervousness as soon as I saw you," replied 'Imadin. "I feel that I am a burden on you. Never mind, you can remove that burden by devising a mission that will take me out of the citadel. Have you succeeded at all?"

"I was able to meet only half your request," he replied, with a teasing laugh.

"What do you mean?" asked 'Imadin.

"You asked to be ordered to leave this citadel to kill an emir, and I have indeed obtained an order for you to kill an emir, but without leaving the citadel."

'Imadin thought this very odd. Thinking that he was joking, he said, "Tell me the truth, by God! Didn't you have any more success than that?"

"I am telling you the truth," 'Abd al-Rahim replied. "The supreme sheikh has issued an order for you to kill an emir who is staying in this citadel."

He saw from 'Abd al-Rahim's eyes that he was serious, and he felt depressed because his real wish was to leave, not to kill or murder. "Explain, my brother," he replied. "This piece of good news has upset me. You know that I was asking to leave rather than to assassinate anyone."

"I know that," replied 'Abd al-Rahim, "but what can I do when the supreme sheikh has issued his order? It shows enormous trust in you, because the task to be entrusted to you is a difficult one. And it will be a reason to promote you quickly, which you know the supreme sheikh is very keen to do."

'Imadin said nothing, but reflected on what he had heard. He could see no way out. "Am I to take your words as an official instruction?" he asked.

"No," replied 'Abd al-Rahim. "The supreme sheikh and imam will summon you himself, inspire you with the spirit of determination and steadfastness, and give you such orders as he wills. I am merely speaking to you as a friend in secret to relieve your anxiety."

'Imadin interrupted him, "Forgive me, my brother, if I tell you that you have made me even more anxious with this piece of news."

"You will be fully relieved of your anxiety after you receive your orders," responded 'Abd al-Rahim, smiling without wanting to say any more.

"I don't understand what you mean," replied 'Imadin. "Couldn't you relieve some of my anxiety, if only with a hint? I know the virtue of keeping a secret, but I am not asking you to reveal a sacred secret that you have been entrusted with. Please relieve my anxiety a little! Tell me, who is the emir or noble man living here that I am to be commissioned to kill? I don't know the important people in the citadel!"

"He is not one of our leaders," replied 'Abd al-Rahim. "He is a visitor who arrived here two days ago."

'Imadin thought of the riders he had seen approaching on the plain and asked, "I saw a group of riders coming from the mountain several days ago. Could he be one of them?"

"Yes," replied 'Abd al-Rahim. "He came in a group of riders." He lowered his voice and added, "You should be aware that what I am telling you is highly secret."

"I know that," replied 'Imadin. "But I find it strange that an enemy should arrive and put his life at the mercy of his opponent when he knows that he has the power to kill him."

"He is not an enemy of the supreme sheikh, but one of his closest friends and confidants," replied 'Abd al-Rahim. "They parted when they were young, before the office of supreme sheikh passed to our imam Rashidin. You may know that our leader, before becoming imam, lived in a place called 'Aqr al-Sadan and served the leader of the Isma'ilis at Alamut in Daylam.[55] It was at his hand that he acquired his erudition and knowledge of religion. He also became famous for his piety, and people flocked to him. He would sit on a rock, looking imposing, as immobile as the rock itself. He charmed people with his eloquence, so that his

---

55 Daylam was a province of Persia, now part of Gulan, Iran. It was the place of origin of the Buyid dynasty. The Buyid Empire, also known as the Buyids (or Buyahids, or Buyyids) were a Shi'a Persian dynasty that founded a confederation that controlled most of modern-day Iran and Iraq in the tenth and eleventh centuries. *Editor's Note*

disciples and companions multiplied. At that time the Isma'ili supreme sheikh was a man called Abu Muhammad. Fearing for his position, Abu Muhammad sent someone to assassinate him, so he hid in a cave near Aleppo and remained in hiding until Abu Muhammad fell from power— at which point, he succeeded him and moved here. That, in essence, is the story of our imam's life. Today's guest is one of his dearest friends, a person who fought for his victory and accompanied him to the cave before going his own way. He has now returned, for what purpose I do not know, and has been given a warm reception by our imam, who has met alone with him more than once. I do not know what has taken place between them, but the common belief among our men is that our imam was very happy to see him and that he is one of his closest friends. Nonetheless, he sent for me secretly yesterday, told me that he had appraised your valor, and asked me if you were ready for an important mission. I assured him that you were and that you were eager to be entrusted with a mission. But I did not reckon that he would make it inside the citadel. He demonstrated the greatest confidence in me as he revealed that he wanted to free himself from his old friend at your hands. And it should be evident to you that this mission represents great trust in you, for you have been among the ranks of the assassins for only a few days."

As 'Abd al-Rahim was speaking, 'Imad in listened carefully, reflecting on the tyrant's cunning and how he had determined to assassinate an old friend because he thought his continued existence would be a stumbling block in his path. His faith in him waned further because he knew of no moral or religious principle emanating from no less than an imam that would allow the betrayal of one's friends. His ideas about him began to change, and he started to fear for himself as he could be in a potentially dangerous situation. For the supreme sheikh could suspect that he might want to harm him and order him assassinated. He preferred to keep this thought to himself, however. "Indeed, it does show great confidence in both of us," he said casually, not daring to bring up any of his fears. "But are you certain that the man in question was one of the supreme sheikh's friends?"

"I am completely certain of it," replied 'Abd al-Rahim. "I have no doubt at all. I know many facts that support this that I cannot share with you now, but which you will find out yourself in due course. You might think of criticizing our leader's behavior at this time because he has decided to kill a friend, but you will praise his actions later. But now…"

'Imadin interrupted him. "He may be right to do this to defend his authority," he said, "and I can forgive him for that. But I have started to fear for my own life, as well as yours."

Those words were spoken frankly straight from his heart, despite the danger they might expose him to. But his frankness pleased 'Abd al-Rahim, who smiled and said, "I do not blame you for having these doubts, for I have had them, too. There are things that have become apparent since I joined the ranks of the enlightened that I will perhaps have a chance to explain to you later. At this point, what is needed is for you to learn about the mission that is to be entrusted to you so that you can accept it without any hesitation. You will then see that I am giving you good advice. The supreme sheikh's messenger will be coming soon to summon you to him, but I myself have to go. We will meet later." And with these words, he left.

Chapter 62

Sheikh Suleiman

'Imadin was still in an agitated state, as he thought again about what he had heard concerning Rashidin. He was now overcome by doubts about his power to perform miracles, though he still respected his power. While he was deep in thought contemplating all this, the supreme sheikh's servant appeared. He was deaf and dumb—an attribute of all the supreme sheikh's servants, calculated to make sure they would be unable to hear and understand anything being said between him and his men. These servants received their orders by signs. They took 'Imadin to Rashidin, who was alone in a small room, lightly dressed and wearing a small turban. Rashidin rose and started to walk up and down, limping slightly, with his hands behind his back.

'Imadin stood respectfully as Rashidin gestured to the servant to leave, and 'Imadin found himself alone with Rashidin. Rashidin smiled at him and said "Look into my eyes!" 'Imadin did so and saw that they were twinkling—indeed, the sparks were almost flying from them.

"What do you see in them?" asked Rashidin.

"I can see nothing in them, sire, except light and intelligence," he replied, thinking this an odd question.

"I can see many things in *your* eyes," said Rashidin. "I can read in them the secrets of your heart."

"There is nothing strange about that," replied 'Imadin, afraid that Rashidin might be able to detect the doubts that he had begun to feel about him. "We always knew this."

"I was pleased to have satisfied myself of your sincerity and obedience," said Rashidin, "and for that reason I have seen fit to reward you quickly. This can only be done through your carrying out a mission, and in my desire for speed, I have made it close to the citadel. Do you understand?"

"I am at your command, sire," replied 'Imadin.

Rashidin continued, "In this secluded house, within the walls of this citadel, there is an important emir who must leave this world without clamor or complaint, and this is to happen by your hand. What do you think?"

He prostrated himself to show his obedience and said, "Can the servant have a view in the presence of his master? He will do whatever he is commanded to do."

Rashidin pressed 'Imadin's fingertips between his palms and ordered him to look into his eyes, then said, "'Abd al-Jabbar, I want you to kill the wretched Sheikh Suleiman. That is what I want!"

When 'Imadin heard that, he was unable to stop himself from letting out a frightened sound, and a tremor passed through his body; he closed his eyes despite himself, as if a spark of electricity had flashed in front of him. "Well done, 'Abd al-Jabbar," continued Rashidin, "you will do as I wish, and you will receive a reward for your faithfulness. From this moment, you will act as a servant to Suleiman, or Sheikh Suleiman as they call him, supplying his every need. Change your clothes, put on the garb of a servant, and make every effort to please him until, unbeknownst to anyone, he gives you an opportunity to kill him. I should prefer that to be outside the citadel. Then you will become one of the class of the enlightened." Bringing his lips close to his ear, he whispered, "The man has with him a woman of extraordinary beauty, who will be your prize together with his furnishings and the rest of his possessions. You can rely on your friend, our son 'Abd al-Rahim, for some details. But that is enough; now go to my deputy Sheikh Dabbous, who will help you complete the necessary preparations."

So saying, he let go of 'Imadin's fingers. 'Imadin took his leave, trembling with emotion, and began to try to figure out who this Suleiman might be. In any case, it did not matter to him that his wife should be beautiful, for he would never be happy with anyone other than Sittalmulk.

As instructed, he immediately went to Sheikh Dabbous, even though he did not need any further explanations, being already clear about what was demanded of him.

"Come in and shut the door, 'Abd al-Jabbar," said Dabbous as he entered. Sheikh Dabbous rose and gave him servants' clothes, adjusting his hairstyle and dress so that his appearance changed so much that he became unrecognizable. Then he handed him a letter, saying, "You will take this letter to that house and be a servant to the person living there, as our imam, the supreme sheikh, ordered you. Do you understand?"

He signaled his obedience then left just as a servant would. Before leaving, he looked at himself in the mirror and saw he could not be recognized. In his hand he had Sheikh Dabbous' note to Suleiman, but he was hesitant about going. "How can I kill this man?" he said to himself, "when we have no feud between us?" Then he recalled 'Abd al-Rahim's saying that he would eventually find comfort in killing him; he was confused and no longer knew what to think.

He soon reached the house where he was told to go but found the door closed. He started to inquire about Sheikh Suleiman in the surrounding area near the house but could glean no information. He sat on a rock beside the house waiting for him to appear, thinking that he might have gone off on an errand and would soon be back. Feeling more and more misgivings, he handled the dagger that he had hidden in his clothes, thinking of how to create an opportunity to do as he was instructed, though he remained hesitant about the killing.

Suddenly, he saw a man approaching in the distance, wearing a large green turban under which he had let his hair hang down to his shoulders. He was wearing a long cloak with a long rosary hanging from his chest and was carrying another rosary in his hand, muttering as he counted the beads, as if he were praying. He seemed to have withdrawn from the world to the realm of prayer. He thought that this must be Sheikh Suleiman. As he approached, he observed his movements until he was close to him. Then he went forward to him, kissing his hands and handing him Sheikh Dabbous' note. Suleiman took it, opened it, and read it without acknowledging 'Imadin or even looking at him. When he had finished, he eyed him and said, "Our brother Sheikh Dabbous says that the supreme sheikh has sent you to be my servant."

"Yes, master," replied 'Imadin. "And will I have this honor and good fortune?"

"I have no need for a servant because I like to be alone for prayer and contemplation and invoking Almighty God," replied Suleiman. "And our food comes to us from the communal kitchen, so why should I need servants?"

As 'Imadin listened to him, he looked carefully at his face. He thought that he had seen that face and heard that voice before. When Suleiman finished speaking, 'Imadin responded, "I was ordered by the supreme sheikh to stand by my master's door and to serve him in his every need. If he wants to be left alone with his prayers or otherwise occupied, then I will not disturb him. But I will obey any orders he gives me and bring him food or anything else he desires."

"Very well," replied Suleiman. "What is your name?"

"'Abd al-Jabbar," he replied.

"Excellent. Sit down here!" said Suleiman. "I will thank the supreme sheikh for his kindness. At any rate, I have no need of you at night, so you can leave at sunset." As he went to the door and took hold of the key to open it, 'Imadin watched his movements, trying very hard to remember where he had seen this man before. Could it have been in Damascus, Jerusalem, or Cairo? But he could think of no one he knew with this name.

Sheikh Suleiman went into the house, while 'Imadin remained seated on a rock. He was preoccupied with the man, but he could not recall where he had seen him and thought that he must be imagining that he had come across him before. So he turned his thoughts back to how to leave the citadel to return to Egypt to see Saladin as well as his beloved Sittalmulk.

The sun was about to set, so he went to bring Sheikh Suleiman his supper. They had prepared it for him in shallow bowls, which he carried on his head. When he reached the door, he knocked and waited a long time before Suleiman opened it and took the food from him, handing him a dinar. "It is sunset, 'Abd al-Jabbar," he said, "so go your own way now."

He took the dinar with a display of contrived gratitude and left, wondering why this man seemed so concerned for his house—a concern so great that he would not even allow his servant to enter it. As he walked back, he met 'Abd al-Rahim, who greeted him and asked him what had happened. 'Imadin told him and commented on his astonishment at Sheikh Suleiman's behavior. 'Abd al-Rahim laughed and said, "So he didn't let you in? Never mind. Can't you remember if you already know him?"

"At first, I thought I had seen his face, or at least heard his voice, but then I thought it must be my imagination," said 'Imadin.

"You may be imagining it, but the truth will soon become clear to you!" replied 'Abd al-Rahim, rubbing his beard as he chuckled softly to himself. "But why would he tell you to leave now, when he may need you during the night?"

"I don't know," replied 'Imadin. "I guess he is hiding from me things he does not want me to see. But I think you know something about him that you haven't told me!"

"I know many things about him that I cannot reveal to you, as you know," replied 'Abd al-Rahim, "but I can tell you that he has political ambitions, and it is these that will lead to his death. I think that he may have wanted to share power with our supreme sheikh or asked him for things that he could not accept. He has known him since they were both young. Our supreme sheikh was afraid that if he upset him, he would spread rumors about him that would damage his reputation, which is why he wanted to get rid of him. This is what I have observed so far, but you are far more likely than I to discover the truth!"

"This is my first day with him," said 'Imadin, "and he dismissed me at sunset. But I will go back to him tomorrow morning."

"Even if he dismisses you," replied 'Abd al-Rahim, "you must still remain close to his house. He may need something from you, or he may give you a suitable opportunity to carry out your mission."

Chapter 63

On the Road

As they walked on, darkness fell, and the shadows began to thicken. "Where are we going now?" asked 'Imadin.

"Wherever you like," replied 'Abd al-Rahim.

"I should like to talk to you about something important," said 'Imadin.

"Come to my room," replied 'Abd al-Rahim. "It is quite near to here." His room had a dim lamp, which a servant lit. "I would prefer that we be alone," said 'Imadin.

'Abd al-Rahim dismissed his servant and invited his friend to sit near him. 'Imadin did so with a sigh. "What's the matter, my friend?" asked 'Abd al-Rahim. "Why are you sighing?"

"I am sighing, brother, because I feel trapped in a cage from which I can see no escape. I have obeyed you in everything, as you know. And I cannot deny the sincerity and wisdom of your advice in every instance. But you also know that I cannot stay here for long, that I have people in Egypt who are awaiting my return…and…"

As he fell silent, 'Abd al-Rahim realized what he meant and asked, "Do you want to leave this citadel?"

"Yes," replied 'Imadin. "That is what I fervently desire. And I hope you can help me do that."

"I promised I would do what you wanted, so I will devise a way for us all to leave."

'Imadin was delighted at his response and asked, "Are you also determined to leave?"

"Yes," replied 'Abd al-Rahim. "And we may be able to leave together."

"That would be best," said 'Imadin. "Now I feel more at ease, even though I am not sure why you should want to leave, after being accepted into the Isma'ili inner circle and being privy to their secrets."

'Abd al-Rahim crossed his lips with his fingers and said, "We will talk about that on another occasion. So far as your own departure is concerned, I will arrange it after you complete your mission. Come and see me; you will find me here most of the time—and all you need do is to carry out the mission you agreed to."

"Good," replied 'Imadin, "I will do as I said." Then, pointing to his waist, he said, "This is the dagger that I will plunge into the heart of the sheikh, though he is guiltless as far as I am concerned. Supreme Sheikh Rashidin also told me," he added, "that the man has a wife who will be my prize. Is she with him in this house? The supreme sheikh told me you could provide me with more details. Do you know?"

'Abd al-Rahim replied, "My view is that you should kill this guest at the first opportunity. The woman that the supreme sheikh mentioned is not here. She is in a house outside the citadel at the edge of the village nearby, with the rest of his family and servants."

"Our supreme sheikh told me that he would prefer that I kill him outside the citadel," said 'Imadin. "Will he be going there?"

"He has given him permission to leave whenever he likes, so he goes there nearly every night," replied 'Abd al-Rahim. "The best thing would be for you to stalk him and kill him outside the house. After that, his wife and all his other things will become your lawful possessions."

"Allow me to consult you about something else," said 'Imadin. "What would you think if I were to carry out my mission outside the citadel and not come back but continue my journey back to Egypt from there?"

"A good idea," replied 'Abd al-Rahim. "Then I would quickly follow you."

"How will you know when I complete my mission?" asked 'Imadin.

"When you reach the end of the plain," replied 'Abd al-Rahim, "light a double torch. As soon as I see the torch, I will go out to meet you, and we will leave together."

'Imadin was delighted by this reply and was on the point of leaving, but 'Abd al-Rahim grabbed him, pulled him toward him, and said, "Be careful not to be tempted to flee without killing Sheikh Suleiman when you are outside the citadel. You have to kill him, even if you cannot escape. Follow my advice this time, too!"

"All right, I will do as you say," said 'Imadin. "But can I leave through the gate of the citadel without permission?"

"If you are pressed for time before I can get permission for you, just give the gatekeeper the exit password, and he will open the gate for you."

"And what is that password?" asked 'Imadin.

"Say 'al-Hasan ibn al-Sabah[56] in Alamut,' and he will let you out," replied 'Abd al-Rahim.

"God bless you!" replied 'Imadin. "Now I feel relieved. I will remember this favor among your many other favors!" As he said that, he started walking toward Sheikh Suleiman's house. It had become pitch dark, and as he approached the house he saw the sheikh emerging with a lantern in his hand.

He approached him, pretending to have caught sight of him by chance, greeted him, and bent over his hand to kiss it. "How is it that you are carrying a lantern in your hand, when I am your servant?" he asked. "Our leader the supreme sheikh ordered me to serve you!" As he said that, he took the lantern from his hand and walked in front of him until he reached the gate. He gave the password to the gatekeeper, who opened it for him. The sheikh wanted to take the lantern back from him, but he refused to give it to him, saying that it was no trouble for him. "If our leader the supreme sheikh finds out that I have not been serving you properly," he added, "he will be angry and reprimand me!"

Suleiman gave in, and 'Imadin continued to walk in front of him. No one stopped him, for he had given the password to the gatekeeper. The path was mostly downhill. When they reached the bottom, the

56 Name of the founder of the sect of the Assassins. *Op.cit. Author's Note*

sheikh stopped and said, "Give me the lantern, God bless you! I am near my house now!"

"I will walk with you to the door of your house," replied 'Imadin.

"There is no need to inconvenience yourself," the sheikh replied, pointing to a dim light, the only one to be seen on the plain. "This is my house!"

"No, I will walk with you as my master instructed," replied 'Imadin.

The sheikh stopped and put his hand out to try to take the lantern from him, but 'Imadin refused to give it to him. "Give me the lamp, boy, and go away!" said the sheikh angrily.

"Is this the reward for someone who wants to serve you?" asked 'Imadin, and with those words he drew his dagger and thrust it into his heart. The sheikh covered his bleeding wound with his hand and screamed, "You wretch! Oh, why have you killed me? What have I done to *you*?" 'Imadin was about to plunge the dagger a second time, grabbing his clothes as the sheikh started shaking like a leaf. But the sheikh grabbed him with his hand and said, "One dagger thrust is enough to kill me... Put the second one in that woman's heart! The traitress! I forgive you for killing me because I deserve to die. But there is a woman, there... in this house...you can see...the light...a woman—she deserves to die more than I do. Go, by God, kill her, and take the money and jewels in my pocket as your reward!" So gasping, he collapsed.

'Imadin could not make any sense of what he had just heard. He bent over him to search his pockets. He found papers, money, and jewels, which he removed before leaving him to wallow in his own blood.

He walked on, wondering whether to go and take a look at the house or travel straight to Egypt, now that he had enough money. He thought it best to travel directly to Egypt—fearing that if he went to the house something might happen that would interefere with his trip, or Rashidin might send someone to summon him back to the citadel. He would actually have preferred to flee before killing the man and would have done so had 'Abd al-Rahim not insisted otherwise. He wasn't sure why he had obeyed him except that his instincts told him it was best to do so.

Chapter 64

The House

Having made up his mind to flee, he paused to think which road would lead him to Egypt. It had become pitch black, and he was unable to make out the road or determine the right direction. He recalled the dead man's strange last words and concluded from them that he wanted vengeance on a woman he was keen to see dead. He decided to go to the house to ask the way to Egypt. He wiped and sheathed his dagger, composed himself, and put out the lamp so that no one would see him. Then he walked toward the light. As he approached the house, he began to tiptoe, feeling his way, pricking his ears, and craning his neck forward. He took a few steps and was on the point of knocking on the door when he heard a man speaking to someone else in the house, asking him whether he had seen the sheikh's lamp.

"I saw a lamp like his in the distance a few moments ago," his friend replied.

"It was his lamp, but then it went out. What do you suppose happened to him?"

"Don't worry about him, he's a survivor!"

"Sounds like you envy his ability to survive, when he is one of the most wretched of God's creatures!"

"You are right, I have never seen anyone more wretched!"

The other man interrupted him, "No, there is someone more wretched—this poor woman that he never stops torturing and beating and..."

"You are right. The poor woman! My heart goes out to her. Sometimes I think I'd like so much to help her!"

"Why should we be concerned about her? We just have to look after our own interests. If he keeps his promise to us, we will be rich and happy, won't we? We'll become important emirs."

"Do you believe everything the sheikh tells us?" asked the other.

"If only a part of it is true, we should be satisfied. It seems you haven't understood the true nature of his mission with the supreme sheikh of the Isma'ilis."

"I do. How can I fail to?" replied the other.

"No, no, you haven't understood it fully. You need to be aware that this sheikh, our master, was a friend of Supreme Sheikh Rashidin Sinan before he became the Isma'ili leader. He helped him and cooperated with him in many operations, until Rashidin's leadership position became secure. Then our friend became jealous of him and wanted to best him, so he went to Cairo hoping to become caliph."

"Hoping to become caliph?" asked the other man, with an incredulous laugh.

"Yes, he hoped to become caliph. He called himself Hasan and laid claim to Fatimid ancestry, and people believed him. When al-'Adid, the Egyptian caliph, died, a group of Egyptians swore allegiance to him. But this conspiracy was exposed by Saladin, and his supporters were arrested, though he himself escaped and came to Syria. You know what happened after that: he commissioned some freedom fighters—who will kill anyone for a couple of dinars—to abduct this woman for him from her house, although she had rejected his overtures and could not bear to see him."

Someone else interrupted him and whispered, "You should be careful about criticizing the freedom fighters! We are in their territory. And you don't know who this woman is. This poor woman—you don't know how much she has suffered at his hands. God curse him! I don't think there is any way for her to escape unless he dies!"

The other man laughed and said, "He's a survivor; don't worry about him! If truth be told, he loves this woman and promises her all sorts of things to try to be worthy of her love. But she despises him, and this arouses his fury and makes him beat her."

Hearing all this, 'Imadin realized that he had killed Hasan. But he was not aware of his relationship with Sittalmulk. He only knew that he was one of Saladin's opponents and that he had escaped being crucified. His heart leaped with joy, for he would be bringing Saladin two important pieces of news: the first that his life was no longer in danger from Rashidin, the second that Hasan was no longer a threat to him. But he had heard in the conversation that he tormented his wife so much that the servants pitied her. He recalled that Hasan had enjoined him to kill her. But after becoming attached to Sittalmulk, 'Imadin had begun to have sympathy for any woman in her situation. He therefore felt he should save the poor woman from the injustice that she was being subjected to. So he went up to the door and knocked. The two men balked, and one of them called out, "Who's that? Perhaps it is our master, Sheikh Suleiman," he added to his friend. "Didn't I tell you that I saw his lamp?"

One of them opened the door, and the other brought out a light and held it close to 'Imadin's face. They looked at each other, but he didn't recall that he knew either of them. From their dress, as well as their dialect, he realized that they came from Damascus. They were both middle-aged. One of them approached and asked 'Imadin what he wanted.

"Sheikh Suleiman has sent me on a mission," he replied, "I am carrying this lamp to demonstrate the mission is genuine, even though it went out along the way."

"Good, but what do you want?"

"He ordered me to bring him his wife on her mule," he replied. "He is waiting for her at the citadel gate."

The two men looked at each other in astonishment as if to say, "But why should the man send for his wife to be brought to the citadel on a mule? What would he want with her there?"

"And does he only want his wife?" asked one of them.

"He wants her, with all her possessions and clothes she can carry," he replied.

"We must give her the message," he replied. The man went in with the light in his hand. Groans and sighs could be heard, and a weak voice saying, "Woe to you from God, you traitor! Are you not afraid of being punished on the Day of Judgment? Death, where are you? When will my hour come, so that I may escape from this miserable life? Oh, why are they conspiring against me like this?"

When 'Imadin heard that voice, he felt goose bumps all over his body, for it sounded just like Sittalmulk's voice. He was tempted to go and see that woman, but he stayed where he was to hear what transpired between her and the servant. "My master, the sheikh, is summoning my lady to go and see him in the citadel," he was saying to her.

"To where?" she screamed. "And who is this master of yours? Why are you bothering me with these questions? Stop persecuting me! Let me sleep and forget my agony!"

"Don't be angry, my lady!" he replied. "My master has sent a special messenger, one of Supreme Sheikh Rashidin's servants, to take you to him, together with such of your clothes and other possessions that you can carry..."

"No! No!" she screamed again. "I am not going anywhere—you'll have to tie me and carry me on a plank to take me. Spare me from him, God curse him! Woe to him from God and the Day of Judgment! He has brought me to a country where no one knows or pities me. Oh, woe is me!"

'Imadin started to tremble. He was upset because the voice was so much like Sittalmulk's voice. Had he known of Hasan's designs, he would not have doubted that it was her. But he thought it impossible for her to be here because she was under Saladin's protection. He was striving to help a wronged woman to honor his beloved because she belonged to the same sex—and what made him angrier and more determined was that her voice sounded so much like Sittalmulk's. Then he heard the man talking to her, "My lady, what do you want us to do now? We have to take you to him as he instructed—this is his messenger standing at the door! Is it possible to ignore his instructions? Better for you to go willingly!"

When she heard these threats, she let out a loud shriek that made 'Imadin's hair stand on end. "Are you threatening to take me away by force?" she roared. "Is this wretch wanting to have me carried off by robbers, as he did before?" Then she lowered her voice and choked back her tears, saying, "But God sent me a brave angel on that occasion who rescued me from the clutches of death and saved my honor and my life!" Then she sighed and said, "Oh, where are you, 'Imadin?"

'Imadin sprang forward like a ferocious lion as soon as he heard his name, for it was now clear that the wronged woman was indeed his beloved Sittalmulk. "Here I am, at your service, my lady!" he replied at the top of his voice.

No sooner did she hear his voice than he was standing in front of her. He had pushed the servants away and walked toward her, saying, "My lady, Sittalmulk! Is that really you here who is being subjected to this ordeal?"

She gave him a feeble look, as if she had been struck down by lightening. Her eyes froze, her tongue was tied, and she could no longer speak. But she came to, emerging from her delirious state. In a choked and broken voice, she exclaimed, "'Imadin! 'Imadin! Oh, this can only be a dream. When I wake up, the nightmare that my life has become will continue!" Then she covered her face with her hands and started to sob uncontrollably.

'Imadin came up to her, his heart frozen to see her in such a state of weakness and despair. Had he not heard her call his name, he would not have recognized her. Holding her hand, he said, "This is no dream, my lady! I am 'Imadin. You are awake! Have no fear—I am here to fulfill all your desires!"

Chapter 65

The Truth

When she heard his voice, she opened her eyes, which were filled with tears. She looked at him and saw he was dressed like a servant, differently from his normal attire. But she recognized his voice. She gazed into his face but could see nothing because of her tears. Then, wiping her eyes with her sleeve, she recognized his eyes and exclaimed, "'Imadin! Are you 'Imadin? Who sent you to me? No, no, you cannot be 'Imadin. You are that traitor's servant, and you've come to take me to him! Tell me the truth, by God, are you 'Imadin?"

Then she sneered like a demented person as she repeated, incredulously, "Are you 'Imadin? Miracles do not repeat themselves! Yes, 'Imadin had come to save me in a similar difficult situation. I just hope he can come again!" Then she said nothing, as if she had returned to her senses. She wiped her eyes again and gave 'Imadin a searching look, as he knelt before her, his eyes staring into hers. His heart was torn apart. She quickly convinced herself that she was indeed seeing 'Imadin and screamed at the top of her voice, "'Imadin, 'Imadin!" Then she threw herself on him and fainted. He picked her up, and the servants rushed to bring water to revive her. He sprinkled it on her, wiping her face and her eyes with his handkerchief. He gave her a sip of water to drink, and as she revived, she looked again at 'Imadin, laughing with the delight of a child who had just got back his long-lost favorite toy.

Her childish laughter, however, made 'Imadin cry. It was hard for him to see the caliph's sister lose her regal status and come under the protection of Saladin only to be abducted against her will by that accursed Hasan. 'Imadin was very upset. But as soon as he recalled that he had killed him, he felt better and returned to comforting Sittalmulk. "You are right, my lady," he said, "I am your slave, 'Imadin!"

"You still say that you are my slave?" she exclaimed. " No! You are my lord and master and the apple of my eye! You have saved me twice from death and disgrace. You are my soul! You are my life! You, oh, oh…you…finally I can let my heart speak freely! But I have said far too much…" And she covered her eyes in embarrassment.

'Imadin noticed that the two servants were still there. He had observed their hatred of Hasan and their sympathy for Sittalmulk, so he said to the elder one, "Perhaps you find what you have witnessed tonight very strange. But I know about your revulsion toward this wicked man, and that your hearts are with this lady… Isn't that so?" As he said that, he put his hand into his pocket, which held Hasan's money, and gave them a pile of money without bothering to count it.

His generosity amazed them. "That is right," said one of them, "and it seems that you are not a servant as you claimed. No, you are an emir sent from heaven to save this lady. She broke both our hearts—indeed, we were about to rescue her from this tyrant."

"So you are pleased that she has been rescued?" he asked.

"And we are at your disposal for any service you may ask of us," they replied, "even killing that wretch!"

"There will be no need to kill him," he replied. "God has spared us his evil this evening. I have already given you some of the money that he had, and here is the rest." And he handed them another payment.

This surprised them even more. "You killed him?" asked one of them. "May God show him no mercy!"

As 'Imadin spoke to the two men, Sittalmulk gazed at him with love and admiration. She had turned pale, and her eyes were sunken and emaciated. But when she heard mention of Hasan being killed, she gripped 'Imadin's hand and pulled him toward her. "You killed him?" she asked.

"Yes," replied 'Imadin. "And I wish that I had got to know him before I killed him. I would have killed him many times over and told him while he was in his death throes that I had killed him to avenge his barbarity and uncouthness."

"But why did you kill him, and how?" asked Sittalmulk.

"I did it at the command of a man who seemed to know of my grudge against him and urged me to kill him," replied 'Imadin. "He said that I would praise the result of my deed, and he was right." Then he recalled Hasan's last words before he died and said, "God curse him! I never heard of a more wicked man. Do you know what he told me? That he deserved to die, handing me this money while saying, 'I am asking you to kill my wife who is at home, because she deserves death more than I do.' Think about that—saying that in the last moments of his life, about to enter the Hereafter... He wanted to take revenge on this angel, and he paid a price to have it done. What a monster!"

Then he turned to the two men and asked them, "Do you want to remain with us?"

"Yes," they replied. "We are at your service, as you will."

"Get ready to leave now, then," said 'Imadin. "Get the luggage ready, and we will travel together!"

The pair began to make their preparations, while 'Imadin sat in front of Sittalmulk and asked her how she had come to be here. She told him that the wretched man had plotted to have her abducted by freedom fighters, who disguised themselves as servants and observed her until she left the palace to go into the garden with her maid Yaquta. Hasan had managed to slip in a group of people who lay in wait. They attacked the pair of them. Yaquta put up a good defense, but they beat her until she fell unconscious to the ground. Then the wretches carried her off alone and took her away gagged and handcuffed. Meanwhile Hasan had gone to wait for Sittalmulk and the others on the outskirts of Cairo. He started treating her roughly to exact his revenge, for he had come to perceive her as the cause of his failure and misery. Then he took her to Syria, where he made use of these two eunuchs, showering them with money. "Finally he brought us all to this citadel," she concluded, "and left them with me in that house, before going to Rashidin to seek his help in assassinating Saladin—trying to get one of the freedom fighters to do so."

That is the gist of what Sittalmulk told 'Imadin as he sat in front of her listening intently. This was the happiest day of her life even though she was in a barren desert, feeling completely worn out. But love is the source of happiness, just as it is the source of misery; otherwise, life would be cold and barren, joyless and meaningless.

'Imadin told her of his mission for Saladin, of the suffering he had experienced, and of how it had ended in success with Saladin having nothing to fear from the freedom fighters. When she heard Saladin's name, her face lit up, and she said, "God bless Saladin. There are few men like him..."

He laughed and said, "Did I not tell you so on the last night we were together, when you were so angry at him?"

"I didn't know him then," she replied, "But I did praise his manliness and courage. You, though, were praising him for other things—things with regard to which my judgment on him remains as it always was... especially when I compare him with 'Imadin." She laughed, and as she spoke, her eyes fixated on him, almost gobbling him up.

Shortly afterward, the two servants appeared, having readied the animals and secured the luggage. They all mounted their mules. It was midnight, and the moon was coming out from behind the mountains of Samaq. 'Imadin remembered his agreement with 'Abd al-Rahim. As soon as he moved onto the plain, he ordered the men to light a double torch, which they did.

The caravan moved on, with Sittalmulk riding next to 'Imadin. They were inexhaustible in narrating to each other their adventures in the long interval since they had parted. This is not surprising—when lovers are separated for just an hour, they will have things to say to each other for days. They will find a special pleasure that only lovers can experience in sharing these stories. A lover cannot bear to hide anything from his beloved; he seems to regard discretion as a betrayal, as if their hearts demand disclosure of everything. In the same way that they reproach and chide each other, they also find pleasure in disclosing their love and in sharing every detail of the tales that reside in their hearts.

Chapter 66

The Journey to Egypt

As they rode away from the mountains of Summaq, they heard the sound of horses' hooves behind them. 'Imadin had been constantly listening out for them, anxious for the arrival of his friend 'Abd al-Rahim, eager to see him and learn about the things he had hinted at in the citadel.

When he heard the sound of horses' hooves, he slowed down to link with his friend 'Abd al-Rahim. Sittalmulk slowed down as well, but he told her to carry on, with the servants following her. He found his friend riding his horse to a gallop as though he were being pursued by people behind him. "'Abd al-Rahim?" he called out to him.

"'Imadin?" came the reply.

"What's up?" asked 'Imadin. "I see that you are hurrying. Are you in some trouble?"

"No," replied 'Abd al-Rahim, "but I fear for you!"

"Why should you fear for us?" asked 'Imadin. "We are safe."

"I was following you when you delivered the decisive blow to that wretch," replied 'Abd al-Rahim. "I followed you until I saw you enter his house. I waited for a long time without seeing your lamp. I feared that some harm might have befallen you. Then I saw the lamp and hurried to you; are you in any trouble?"

"We are well—praise be to God—and enjoying His blessings!" replied 'Imadin.

"Do you know now who the Sheikh Suleiman that you killed really is?" asked 'Abd al-Rahim.

"Yes," replied 'Imadin. "I know that he is no other than Hasan, who started the revolt in Cairo that led you to take that blessed letter to Egypt and bring back that precious reply. You were so insistent that I should kill him, but I could not understand why. Now it is clear that you helped to free me from that wicked man. This is a piece of good news to convey to my lord Saladin, and the credit belongs to you!"

"We will convey another piece of good news to him," said 'Abd al-Rahim. "His life is now secure from the Isma'ili menace."

"Of course," replied 'Imadin. "And I will convey to him and to you another piece of good news that in my view is even more important."

"And what is that?" asked 'Abd al-Rahim.

"You haven't inquired about the identity of my companions," said 'Imadin.

"I was going to ask you, but I reckoned that they must be the wife and servants of that wretch, and now of course she is your wife."

"Do you recall the letter that you brought with you from Cairo, and the lady with whom you spoke? You were effusive in your admiration for her kindness and strength of character."

"Sittalmulk, the caliph's sister?" he asked in astonishment.

"Yes, Sittalmulk," replied 'Imadin. "The traitor abducted her with the help of some freedom fighters and brought her here, where he started to abuse her. But I was able to save her."

"The lady riding the mule is Sittalmulk?" asked 'Abd al-Rahim, incredulously.

"Yes," replied 'Imadin. "Do you want to meet her?"

"Of course!" said 'Abd al-Rahim. "But let's wait a while until we stop at a place at dawn, for she needs to rest."

"Are you coming with us to Egypt?" asked 'Imadin.

"If you will put up with me," he replied.

Almost instantaneously, he objected, saying that it would be his good fortune. "How I should like you to be with me and for us to live together," he went on, "so that I can reward you and tell Sultan Saladin of your role in bringing this mission to such a good and happy ending.

This would be a fourth piece of good news to convey to him. But how is it that you left the band of Isma'ilis after becoming one of their leaders and gaining such influence over their weird leader? I will never forget the incredible things I have witnessed in these two days."

'Abd al-Rahim let out a deep sigh and said, "If I had not attained the rank of the enlightened, it would never have crossed my mind to leave the society. Did you not notice how I had changed after my promotion? If I had stayed a freedom fighter, I would have continued hankering for promotion and for access to the secrets of the sect. But after they were revealed to me, I realized that I had been deceived and regretted joining the sect."

"How surprising," replied 'Imadin. "But why didn't those who had been promoted to this rank before you also leave the society?"

"They remained to satisfy their desire for sensual pleasures and physical enjoyment," replied 'Abd al-Rahim. "Little did they care that they could only do so at the expense of young, brave freedom fighters like yourself. For myself, however, I do not like such a life of deception."

'Imadin bent his head and busied himself stroking the mane of his horse with his fingertips. He was astonished at his friend's maturity. Then he asked, "So you no longer believe in Supreme Sheikh Rashidin's miracles?"

"I'm not saying this. But since I was promoted, I discovered many things that led me to revise my judgment of them," replied 'Abd al-Rahim. "There are many phenomena in this world that appear amazing and inexplicable at first sight but that can quickly be interpreted once you look at them more closely and understand their causes."

"I would very much like to know the secret of the man's miracles that you witnessed," replied 'Imadin, "like how he can know the news of events just as they happen and before there is time for the news of these events to travel to him; or speaking to dead men or stones and hearing their replies—quite apart from the paradise I experienced, where the *houris* walk on water and converse with birds. All are quite incredible events and miracles!"

"You are right," replied 'Abd al-Rahim, "they are indeed incredible! I would have liked to reveal their secrets to you, but I swore a solemn oath to keep their secret, and you would not be pleased if I broke my oath. Even though I have left the society, I have lost neither my honor nor my conscience. I can tell you, however, that these miracles do not involve any extraordinary powers—only human ones that many of us have. They do not involve any divine revelation or supernatural power as we used to think. But now, we have come close to a place with a spring of water and an inn whose owner I know. I think we should dismount here to rest until you wish to resume our journey."

'Imadin hurried to Sittalmulk to tell her of his friend 'Abd al-Rahim's suggestion, and she agreed. Dawn had appeared, so they dismounted; then 'Imadin walked forward with 'Abd al-Rahim to Sittalmulk and introduced him to her, explaining to her the part he had played in the success of his mission. Sittalmulk was full of praise for the way in which he had mentored and advised her beloved.

Chapter 67

The Meeting

Let us leave them all to rest and return to Cairo which we left some time ago, after 'Amara and his fellow conspirators had been crucified, and 'Imadin's messenger 'Abd al-Rahim had left for Jerusalem with the letter and jewels. Sittalmulk was happy and reassured that she had not been forgotten by her beloved. Hasan had escaped to Damascus, but his anger after his failure to persuade Nuradin to attack Saladin had driven him to think of nothing but revenge on Sittalmulk by any means. So he hired some desperate freedom fighters to abduct her and went with them to Egypt. They took advantage of her visit with her maidservant to the orchards near Saladin's palace and abducted her as previously related, with Yaquta falling in a swoon. When she recovered hours later, she realized the bandits had escaped with her mistress. She told Bahadin, and he, in turn, informed Saladin. The news unleashed a violent fury in Saladin, who ordered his troops to rake the city in search for Sittalmulk. He also sent spies to try to find her. But all this was to no avail— there was no trace of her anywhere.

This angered him considerably. He was even angrier at the lack of news about 'Imadin and regretted letting him go. He had become aware of his true worth after seeing how loyal and determined he was in serving him and protecting his interests. He wanted him to come back and to celebrate his marriage to Sittalmulk, for their absence was making him unhappy. The wars with the Crusaders were preoccupying him. They were at their fiercest during that period as he had begun to prepare for the conquest of Jerusalem.

While he was so preoccupied, Bahadin came to tell him that 'Imadin's messenger had arrived bearing important news. As the messenger came in and stood politely, he asked him, "What is up? You only bring us good news!"

"This is through God's favor and the blessing of my lord the sultan," he replied. "I can tell my lord that his servant 'Imadin has returned safely from his successful mission. He would have liked to have brought this piece of good news himself, but he was caring for Sittalmulk, so I asked his permission to convey the news to you before his arrival."

"And is Sittalmulk with him?" asked Saladin.

"Yes, sir," he replied.

He turned to Bahadin, believing he would be just as surprised. "That is indeed extraordinary," said Bahadin. "Has he rescued her from danger once again? Isn't that a sign that they were made to be married?"

"There is no doubt about that," replied Saladin. "This is my dearest wish. Send someone to meet them with an escort worthy of their status!"

Bahadin prepared a welcoming procession, which met the new arrivals in the Khanqah near Cairo. It had a large number of horsemen surrounding a royal canopied palanquin[57] for Sittalmulk. As the procession drew near to Saladin's palace, they directed the palanquin towards Sittalmulk's palace. Yaquta had learned that she was coming and greeted her effusively, throwing herself in her arms, kissing her mistress, and crying with happiness as she thanked God for his blessing. She could see that her mistress was weak, and her face was pale. So she tried to lighten her spirits by telling her that 'Imadin would soon be her husband. "Don't you think this young man deserves my heart, Yaquta?" she asked. "He has saved me from death and disgrace once more!" Then she recounted the highlights of her story.

'Imadin himself had continued in the procession and dismounted before reaching Saladin's palace, completing his journey on foot. As he entered into Saladin's presence, he fell to his knees to kiss his hands. "I thank God that he has shown me the face of my lord the sultan safe and sound!" he exclaimed. Then the ministers and commanders came up to him to greet and honor him. None of them knew the purpose of his

---

57 A covered seat carried on poles held parallel to the ground on the shoulders of two or four people, used in former times to transport an important person. *Editor's Note*

mission, but they all knew the high esteem in which the sultan held him, and so they joined in welcoming him.

Saladin then asked everyone to leave, except for Bahadin and 'Imadin. He inquired about the results of 'Imadin's mission, who told him what had happened from beginning to end. He was greatly impressed by his bravery and the patience he had demonstrated in the face of the difficulties he had encountered, all of which he had overcome. But his greatest surprise was to hear of Hasan's murder and the rescue of Sittalmulk. At this point, the sultan smiled and said, "God bless you! This is true bravery! God have mercy on my father. He was a clear-sighted man and could see in you the virtues of a real leader. And he was right in his judgment, for you have done what no other of our men could have done. You are now one of our leading commanders and closest advisers!"

Then he turned to Bahadin and said, "Bahadin, this is the young man who fled from the Women's Palace in front of your eyes and of whom I had complained to you. Don't you think he is worthy of being Sittalmulk's husband, having saved us from Hasan, as you heard?"

"He is worthy of every consideration and honor," replied Bahadin. "It is enough that our Lord Najmudin could see such potential in him."

"It is time for him to recover from the hardships of his journey," said Saladin. "And I would like you to celebrate his marriage in a royal style fit for caliphs and the best of commanders!"

'Imadin bent over to kiss Saladin's hands, and Saladin kissed him on his head. Then 'Imadin said, "I should like to ask my lord's permission to tell him a little about my friend 'Abd al-Rahim. You have heard how much he sacrificed in our service, and he will be a great help to us in the wars against the Franks, because he knows Jerusalem street by street, and..."

Saladin did not wait for him to finish his sentence and said, "He is worthy to be a member of our inner circle. Bahadin here knows his worth and values him highly. But now I would like to see Sittalmulk and congratulate her on her safe return."

Bahadin hurried over to the Women's Palace to inform Sittalmulk of the sultan's impending visit, and she readied herself to receive him. On arrival, he greeted her with these words, "You are right to have preferred

'Imadin to me, for he has saved you from death twice and spared us from our worst enemies. He is worthy of you, and we shall see to it that he is wed to you." She felt embarassement mingled with equal doses of surprise and delight.

She bowed her head meekly, saying nothing for a while, then lifted her gaze and said, "I have only given preference to 'Imadin because of the virtues that appeal to Sultan Saladin. It is because of these virtues that he was elevated above ordinary people and became one of the sultan's closest and most loyal companions. And neither he nor I prefer anyone to the sultan. We live under his protection and in his shadow."

Her reply delighted him. "You were indeed under my protection," he said, "but now you are under the protection of your heroic knight, 'Imadin. You should be proud of him, just as he should be proud of you. May you both be happy for the rest of your lives!"

So saying, he departed, leaving Sittalmulk with her heart overflowing with joy and having forgotten all her trials and misfortunes. And so the whole of Egypt celebrated over several weeks the wedding of Sittalmulk and 'Imadin in truly regal style.

The End

Saladin and the Assassins

Study Guide⁵⁸

1. Who was Jurji Zaidan?

Jurji Zaidan was a famous Arab writer who was born and grew up in Lebanon and lived in Egypt. He was born in 1861 in Beirut, where, as a teenager, he helped his father run a small restaurant. When he was nineteen years old, Zaidan enrolled in the medical school at what was then the Syrian Protestant College, now the American University in Beirut. However, after taking part in a student strike, he decided to leave the university. He soon left his native Lebanon and moved to Cairo, Egypt. Once settled there, Zaidan began a long career as a writer and journalist. In 1892, he established a magazine called *Al-Hilal* (The Crescent Moon), which is being published to this day. He wrote twenty-two novels, all of which were published in serialized form in that magazine. *Saladin and the Assassins* is one of them. In addition to the novels, he also published books and wrote articles in his magazine on a large number of topics: the history of Islamic civilization, the history and development of languages, as well as on political, social, educational, and ethical issues. He thus played a very important role in making readers of Arabic more aware of the important events in their history and in developing a sense of national identity. He died in 1914.

2. What is a historical novel?

A historical novel is a kind of fiction that makes use of important events from history and people who took part in them, in order to provide readers with a vivid portrayal of previous eras in the life of their national

---

58 The preparation of this Study Guide relied on material provided by Roger Allen (in particular the answers to questions 1 to 3) as well on Sir Hamilton Gibb's, *The Life of Saladin* and *The Achievement of Saladin* (listed under Other Resources below). Paul M. Cobb made some comments especially on the section concerning the Assassins. None is responsible for any remaining errors.

community. Among prominent writers of historical novels are Sir Walter Scott (d. 1832) who, among other novels, wrote *Ivanhoe* (set in twelfth-century England) and *Rob Roy* (set in Scotland just before the Jacobite rising in the eighteenth century). He made Saladin one of the heroes of another novel, *The Talisman* (1825), that Hamilton Gibb used to recommend to his students as "a work of art from which they could learn much about Islamic history." Muslim historiography has immortalized Saladin as a paragon of princely virtue. He has also held enduring fascination for Western writers, including modern novelists. Other noted historical novelists include the Russian author Leo Tolstoy (d. 1910) whose colossal novel *War and Peace* describes Russian society before and during Napoleon's invasion in 1812, and the American writer James Fenimore Cooper (d. 1851) whose *The Last of the Mohicans* portrays the role of Native Americans during the 1757 war in the North American colonies. This type of novel often provides the reader with a sense of what it was like to live in the historical period and region in question. It also brings the events to life by revealing through conversations how the people involved in those events interact with each other and share their views and emotions. In Zaidan's case, the novels include a love story that is the backdrop against which ordinary people are depicted responding to the important events going on around them. In *Saladin and the Assassins*, the two lovers are actually important participants in the events leading up to Saladin's assumption of power in Egypt.

3. What is the early history of the Arabic novel?

Like most new kinds of literature that appeared in the Arabic-speaking world during the nineteenth and into the twentieth century, the novel's development involved a combination of imported examples translated into Arabic from Western literature and revived and adapted examples of types of narrative from the pre-modern heritage. Among the first European works to be translated into Arabic was Alexandre Dumas's famous novel, *The Count of Monte Cristo*, which served as a model and precedent for the appearance of a number of serialized works, including, for example, those of Salim al-Bustani published in his family's journal, *Al-Jinan*. Alongside these translations of European works and the imitations they inspired, there were other narratives that revived earlier types and styles of Arabic story-writing, such as Ahmad Faris al-Shidyaq's

Al-Saq 'Ala al-Saq (One Leg Over Another, 1855) and Muhammad al-Muwaylihi's *Hadith 'Isa ibn Hisham* ('Isa ibn Hisham's Tale, 1907). The novels that Zaidan wrote and published were a very important part of the developmental process through which the novel was accepted into Middle Eastern culture as a form of narrative that could express the hopes and aspirations of people in quest of national identity. In the first three decades of the twentieth century, these different strands were gradually fused together into a form of narrative writing that was to see its acceptance into Arabic culture crowned by the work of Naguib Mahfouz, the great Egyptian novelist and winner of the Nobel Prize in 1988.

4. What historical period does *Saladin and the Assassins* cover?

When Egypt fell under Fatimid control in 358 AH (969 AD), the political situation changed and it became a completely independent state, referring no matter to any outside authority and acknowledging no sovereignty other than that of the Fatimid caliph residing in Cairo. This was the first time that Egypt had become a fully independent sovereign state since the coming of Islam. There were eleven Fatimid caliphs, who ruled Egypt in succession for just over two hundred years, 358-567 AH (969-1172 AD), and Caliph al-'Adid li-Din Allah ibn Yusuf was the last one. Around the beginning of the twelfth century, the Fatimid caliphs weakened considerably and became puppets in the hands of the army and powerful viziers or ministers. Upon al-'Adid's death, his vizier Saladin won the title of sultan by recognizing the 'Abbasid caliph of Baghdad. Saladin restored the official status of Sunni Islam and the formal authority of the 'Abbasid caliphate in Egypt, thereby bringing to an end the Shi'ite Fatimid dynasty. The events in this novel end shortly after Saladin becomes sultan of Egypt and precede Saladin's later exploits in uniting much of the Islamic world and his battles with the Franks and the conquest of Jerusalem (see answer to question 5). But his ability to become the ruler of an independent Egypt laid the groundwork for his later exploits.

5. Who was Saladin?

Born in Tikrit, Iraq, Saladin, as he is known in the West (more properly Salah al-Din Al-Ayyubi), was a Kurd. At age fourteen, he joined other members of his family (the Ayyubids) in the service of the Syrian ruler Nur al-Din. Between 1164 and 1169 AD, he distinguished himself in three expeditions, sent by Nur al-Din to aid the decadent Fatimid rulers of Egypt against the attacks of Christian crusaders based in Palestine.

During the First Crusade (1096-1099 AD)—a military campaign by Western European Christians to recapture Jerusalem from the Muslims—Egypt faced a possible invasion. Although the Crusaders captured Jerusalem from a small Fatimid garrison in 1099, they did not invade Egypt. The Fatimids formed diplomatic and commercial ties with the newly established Crusader state known as the Latin Kingdom of Jerusalem, with other Crusader states along the Mediterranean coast of the Middle East, and with the various kingdoms and principalities of Christian Europe. Fatimid power declined in the twelfth century, and in 1171 AD Saladin overthrew the dynasty.

After Nur al-Din's death in 1174 AD, Saladin expanded his power in Syria and northern Mesopotamia, mainly at the expense of his Muslim rivals. Numerous Muslim armies in various cities of Syria and Iraq allied under Saladin's command, ready to move against the Crusaders. Soon afterward, he united Egypt with Syria. He also launched sporadic invasions of the Kingdom of Jerusalem. These achieved little until, in 1187 AD, Saladin led an army across the Jordan and, by commencing a siege of the town of Tiberias, lured Guy de Lusignan on to a waterless march toward military disaster at the Battle of Hattin. In the wake of his victory, Saladin was able to reconquer Jerusalem and the greater part of the Crusader Kingdom. In 1189 AD, the nations of western Europe launched the Third Crusade to win back the holy city.

Despite Saladin's relentless military and diplomatic efforts, a Christian land and naval blockade forced the surrender of the Palestinian stronghold of Acre in 1191, but the Crusaders failed to follow up this victory in their quest for Jerusalem. In 1192 AD, Saladin concluded an armistice agreement with King Richard I of England that allowed the Crusaders to reconstitute their kingdom along the Palestinian-Syrian coast but left Jerusalem in Muslim hands. On March 4, 1193 AD, Saladin died in Damascus after a brief illness.

Saladin's descendants, the Ayyubids, ruled Egypt, as well as parts of Syria and Yemen, until 1250 AD. Ayyubid relations with the Crusader states varied; some rulers encouraged European Christians to settle in Palestine and even leased Jerusalem to the Crusaders for a short time. However, Egypt's Nile Delta suffered Crusader attacks from 1218 to 1221 and from 1249 to 1250. The latter invasion, during the Third Crusade, led to the overthrow of the Ayyubid dynasty by the mamluks, who regarded the Ayyubid rulers as weak and corrupt. The mamluks were slaves from Central Asia and Caucasia whom the Ayyubids had used as soldiers.

6. Who were the Assassins?

Assassin is a word derived from the Arabic word *Hashshashin* (alternately spelled as *Hashashin* or *Hashashiyyin*) Between 1090 and 1272 AD, an Islamic movement known as the Assassins embraced notions of self-sacrifice and suicidal martyrdom, still evident in some Islamic terrorist groups today. They were small and relatively powerless communities without any armies of their own who resorted to targeted murder to promote their agendas.[59] Those that were slain during their campaigns were guaranteed they would ascend to a glorious heaven should they perish during the task. They used these tactics in their struggle against the Christian Crusaders who had invaded what is today part of Syria.

The Assassins were also known as the Isma'ilis (or Batinis) and were a group of Shi'is with a connection to the Fatimid dynasty at its inception that few people were aware of at that time. The Isma'ili creed and that of the Fatimid dynasty were similar. The Fatimid dynasty promoted this ideology, especially the caliph al-Hakim bi-Amr Allah. This group was first established in Persia in Mount Alamut near to Qazvin, a Persian city located to the northwest of present day Teheran, about a century before the events of this novel took place. Subsequently, during the time of the events of this novel, the group's main base moved to Syria in Mount al-Summaq in the province of Aleppo, where they had strongholds and fortresses and propagandists in the region. Their missionary zeal spread through Syria after the Franks had conquered it. The Franks formed alliances with the Isma'ilis and sought their help against the Muslims in many places, sometimes openly, sometimes covertly. The Frankish

---

59 This is the accepted reason today for their resort to assassinations. Earlier, their embrace of assassinations was ascribed to a sacramental need. See the two books by Farhad Daftary listed at the end of the study guide.

king who controlled parts of Syria gave them permission to reside in the mountains of al-Summaq not far from the summit of al-Nusayriyya, and they established their central headquarters in the castle of Misyaf near the present-day Syrian city of Hama. They were able to exterminate a group of kings and commanders in Egypt and Syria, among them al-Malik al-Afdal, the leader of the army in Egypt, because they claimed he had usurped the authority of the Fatimid caliph al Amr. They also killed many Franks on various pretexts, among them Raymond, the master of Tripoli.

7. How was Saladin viewed by European historians? What were his goals, and did he achieve them?

In *The Decline and Fall of the Roman Empire*, **Edward Gibbon** presented Saladin as a Muslim saint: "Both in faith and practice he was a rigid Moslem: he deplored that the defense of religion had not allowed him to accomplish the pilgrimage of Mecca, but at the stated hours, five times each day, the sultan devoutly prayed with his brethren: the involuntary omission of fasting was scrupulously repaid; and his perusal of the Koran, on horseback between the approaching armies, may be quoted as a proof, however ostentatious, of piety and courage."

Sir Hamilton Gibb provided this assessment of Saladin's place in history in his essay "The Achievement of Saladin": "The just ruler Saladin was preeminently a leader who kept the *umma* on the right path, reformed its institutions and rescued it from demoralization. Whereas Saladin's precursor, Nur al-Din, had operated from within the structure of politics of his age, Saladin rose above that structure. He faced down opposition from Shi'is, extremist Sufis and cynics, as well as, of course, Christian Crusaders. But not even Saladin was able to lead his people back to the conditions that prevailed in the heyday of the 'Abbasid Caliphate of the eighth and ninth centuries when Muslims were more united, more confident and more adventurous in their intellectual investigations. Saladin's prosecution of the *jihad* and his defeat of the Crusaders, though celebrated by medieval and modern historians, was only part of his grander project: he wanted to end the Muslim political weakness and division that made the Crusades possible in the first place, and then to spearhead a more general moral rearmament that would restore Muslims spiritually and politically to the position they achieved under the 'Abbasids in Baghdad.

This he did not succeed in doing. So, Saladin was indeed a hero but he was also a failure. Things were to fall apart under his quarrelling Ayyubid kinsmen, and in the thirteenth century there were further Crusades."

He described Saladin's personal traits in these terms: "Neither warrior nor governor by training or inclination, it was he who inspired and gathered round himself all the elements and forces making for the unity of Islam against the invaders. And this he did, not so much by the example of his personal courage and resolution—which were undeniable—as by his unselfishness, his humility and generosity, his moral vindication of Islam against both its enemies and its professed adherents. He was no simpleton, but for all that an utterly simple and transparently honest man. He baffled his enemies, internal and external, because they expected to find him animated by the same motives as they were, and playing the political game as they played it. Guileless himself, he never expected and seldom understood guile in others—a weakness of which his own family and others took advantage, but only (as a general rule) to come up at the end against his single-minded devotion, which nobody and nothing could bend, to the service of his ideals." It is an idealistic portrait but one that Gibb believed.

8. Who are the principle characters of *Saladin and the Assassins,* and what role did they play in the novel's story?

Al-'Adid (Caliph al-'Adid li-Din Allah ibn Yusuf). There were eleven Fatimid caliphs, who ruled Egypt in succession for just over two hundred years 358-567 AH (969-1172 AD). Al-'Adid is the last of the Fatimid caliphs, bringing to an end a Shi'ite dynasty. When Egypt fell under Fatimid control in 358 AH (969 AD), the political situation changed, and it became a completely independent state, referring no matter to any outside authority and acknowledging no sovereignty other than that of the Fatimid caliph residing in Cairo. This was the first time that Egypt had become a fully independent sovereign state since the coming of Islam. The events of the novel begin during the last years of his reign and after his death in 567 AH (1172 AD).

Nuradin (Sultan Nur al-Din) the Seljuk commander, ruler of Syria. Toward the end of the Fatimid period, the position of the Shi'a had weakened in Persia and Iraq, and this deteriorating situation was reflected in Egypt, where Sultan Nur al-Din, the Seljuk commander who ruled

Syria, had become the effective authority. Among Nuradin's commanders were a group of courageous Kurds, including Najm al-Din al-Ayyubi (Najmudin), Saladin's father, and his brother Asad al-Din Shirkawih (Asadin), Saladin's uncle. In 556 AH (1161 AD), the caliphate in Egypt had passed to al-'Adid li-Din Allah ibn Yusuf, who was weak-willed. His ministers competed with each other for influence and gained control of the state, and over time they destroyed the country, while the caliph became impotent. Among the rivals for power was a vizier called Shawar, who had lost influence. So he asked Nuradin for assistance against his rival for the ministry. Nuradin took that opportunity to seize control of Egypt. He sent him Asadin Shirkawih with an army of mamluks, who restored the ministry to Shawar.

Saladin (Sultan Yusuf Saladin or Salah al-Din al-Ayyubi). Saladin was an ambitious man whose aim was to rule Egypt as an independent state. The Crusader wars had erupted during this period, and Nuradin and his deputy in Egypt, Shirkawih, had begun to intervene more in Egypt's affairs, together with Shirkawih's nephew Yusuf ibn Najmudin, who is none other than Saladin. Shirkawih died in Egypt in 564 AH (1161 AD) and was succeeded by Saladin in the office of deputy, with the title of vizier. Saladin used this position to become the ruler of an independent Egypt. How he did so is the subject of this novel.

Najmudin (Najm al-Din al-Ayyubi) is Saladin's father and wise counselor, who visits him from Syria, relaying Nuradin's wishes, and advises him to humor him and abide by those wishes rather confront him.

Sittalmulk (Princess Sitt al-Mulk or "Lady of the Realm")—sister of the caliph al-'Adid. Hasan sought to wed her to further his designs to succeed al-'Adid, and Saladin was reluctantly persuaded that a union with her would further his ambition to become the sole ruler of Egypt. But he was ambivalent about this and so sounded out al-'Adid informally and indirectly about asking the hand of his sister. Al-'Adid was receptive— Saladin had helped him consolidate his power in the past and this would be a way to neutralize the designs of Hasan on his sister and ultimately the caliphate. But Sittalmulk was a strong-willed person who knew her mind. She detested and vehemently rejected her brother's advice and Hasan's overtures and did not want to wed Saladin either—her heart had been stolen by 'Imadin ('Imad al-Din)—a commoner, one of Saladin's inner circle, who had saved her life and her honor when his master Saladin first came to Egypt.

Yaquta—the princess's loyal maid and close confidante with whom the princess shares all her secrets and who is privy to her most personal emotions. She tries to convince her mistress to accept Saladin as her husband in line with the wishes of her brother and indirectly dissuade her mistress from her love for 'Imadin. But when she realizes this is a lost cause, she becomes the conduit between her mistress and 'Imadin—arranging to bring him surreptitiously to see her mistress the night before his departure and later for the communications between her mistress and 'Imadin during his travels.

'Imadin ('Imad al-Din)—a commoner, one of Saladin's inner circle. His loyalty to Saladin, courage, chivalry, and integrity were second to none. After saving Sittalmulk's life and honor, he volunteers to go to Syria on a dangerous mission to avenge the Assassins' threats on his master's life. He is conflicted about his emotions toward Sittlamulk and does not quite know how to respond to her declarations of love. He is attracted to her but is also aware of his master's plan to ask her to marry him and does not want to come between the princess and his master. When Saladin takes Sittalmulk under his protection following al-'Adid's death and declares her to be "like his sister," this conflict is resolved. But Hasan has had her kidnapped and is determined to have his way with her notwithstanding her rejection of him. How this contest for her heart is resolved constitutes a central plot of this novel.

Hasan (Abu al-Hasan)—a conspirator with few scruples aspiring to the caliphate seeks to get rid of Saladin by every means. He claims Fatimid ancestry and is trusted by the people. After al-'Adid's death, a group of Egyptians swore loyalty to Hasan; when Saladin discovered this, his supporters were arrested, but Hasan himself escaped. He then tried to convince Sultan Nuradin of his vizier's desire to make Egypt independent in order to sow the seeds of discord between them. When this scheme failed, he tried to persuade the supreme sheikh of the Assassins to kill Saladin. He also wanted to marry the caliph's sister to enhance his claim to the caliphate. But when she rejects his overtures, he arranges to have her abducted to Syria, where he fled. Meanwhile, 'Imadin was on a mission on Saladin's behalf. In a surprise twist, 'Imadin had the good

fortune to be her deliverer from the suffering that she endured while she was imprisoned.

Rashidin (Rashid al-Din Sinan)—supreme sheikh, imam, and leader of the Isma'ilis, also known as the Assassins. He was originally from Basra and had served the leader of the Isma'ilis in Alamut in Persia, where he studied science and philosophy. Then he moved to Syria and took up residence near Hama in the mountains of Misyaf. He was lame and was able to win over the common people by a great show of piety and religiosity, but he was one of the most evil leaders of this sect. Rashidin had had a relationship with Hasan before he became the leader of the Isma'ilis, which Hasan sought to exploit to thwart Saladin's ambitions in view of the sect's support of the Fatimids.

OTHER RESOURCES

Farhat Daftary, *The Assassins Legends*, St Martin's Press, 1994.

Farhat Daftary, *A Short History of the Isma'ilis*, Edinburgh University Press, 1998.

Anne Marie Eddé, *Saladin,* translated from the French by Jane Marie Todd, Harvard University Press, 2011.

Sir Hamilton Gibb, *The Life of Saladin*, Oxford University Press, 2006, with a Foreword by Robert Irwin.

Sir Hamilton Gibb, "The Achievement of Saladin," in *Bulletin of the John Rylands Library*, 35, 1952.

Malcolm C. Lyons and D.E.P. Jackson, *Saladin: The Politics of War*, Cambridge University Press, 1982.

Hannes Mohring, *Saladin: The Sultan and His Times, 1138-1193*. Translated into English by David S. Bachrach with an Introduction by Paul M.Cobb, John Hopkins University Press, 2008.

Philipp, Thomas, *Gurji Zaidan. His Life and Thought*. Wiesbaden, Germany: Steiner Verlag, 1979.

Zaidan, Jurji, *The Autobiography of Jurji Zaidan,* edited and translated by Thomas Philip, Washington, DC: Three Continents Press, 1990.

Thomas Philipp, *Jurji Zaidan's Secular Analysis of History and Language as Foundations of Arab Nationalism* (Forthcoming).

www.ingramcontent.com/pod-product-compliance
Lightning Source LLC
Chambersburg PA
CBHW030404030726
47497CB00002B/472